CW01020892

SAPLINGS

Persephone Book Nº16
Published by Persephone Books Ltd 2000

First published in 1945 by Collins

© The Estate of Noel Streatfeild 1945

Afterword © Dr Jeremy Holmes 2000

Reprinted 2002, 2005, 2008, 2011 and 2021

Endpapers taken from 'Aircraft', a screen printed
linen and rayon fabric by Marion Dorn for the Old Bleach Linen
Company 1938, reproduced by courtesy of the Trustees of the
Victoria and Albert Museum

Typeset in ITC Baskerville by Keystroke,
Wolverhampton

Printed and bound in Germany
by GGP Media GmbH, Pössneck

ISBN 978 1 903155 059

Persephone Books Ltd
8 Edgar Buildings
Bath BA1 2EE
01225 425050

www.persephonebooks.co.uk

SAPLINGS

by

NOEL STREATFEILD

with a new afterword by

DR JEREMY HOLMES

PERSEPHONE BOOKS
BATH

FOR MY MOTHER

SAPLINGS

I

As the outgoing tide uncovered the little stretch of sand amongst the pebbles, the children took possession of it, marking it as their own with their spades, pails, shrimping nets and their mother's camp stool.

It was early and the beach was almost deserted. There were a few bathers of the sort that swim for exercise, but the majority of the bathing machines and tents were empty. The sea was grey-blue, spangled with gold dancing specks. Far out the raft bobbed.

The cool air, the fresh smell of the sea, the knowledge that it was another lovely day and there were no lessons and few restrictions, filled the children with that sort of happiness that starts in the solar plexus and rises to the throat, and then, before it can reach the top of the head, has to be given an outlet; anything will do, violent action, shouting or just silliness.

Laurel, at eleven, was conscious of being happy. She was almost afraid of it. 'I'll never be as happy again.' 'When I'm quite old, as old as thirty, I'll come back to this bit of Eastbourne. I'll come on the same day in June and remember me now.' Then, because of the tight, bursting feeling of pleasure, she turned two cartwheels and attempted to stand on her hands.

Tony's happiness was mixed with thoughts of his father. It

had been simply gorgeous having this holiday. It was marvellous Nick Pulton having infantile paralysis and parents who flapped, having their boys sent home. He had known for certain he would be sent home, knowing Mum, it was a certainty she'd flap. Queer, this month in Eastbourne. One day they were in London, and the next they were here. It had been marvellous, for even after he was out of quarantine, just hanging around waiting for Laurel and Kim to finish lessons hadn't been much catch. Besides, what a holiday! Like a birthday every day; there was nothing they asked Miss Glover for they didn't have, and it was like old Foxglove to keep saying 'yes'. But now Dad had come, that put the cap on it. He'd show Dad how fast he could reach the raft. It was just like Dad to want, on his very first day, to do something sensible like prawning at Birling Gap. Whoopee! What a day it was going to be! Tony seized Kim round the neck and threw him on the sand and rolled on top of him.

Kim was singing to a tune of his own, 'The sea, the sea, the lovely sea.' His happiness was given a sharp edge by fright. The day was going to be scrumptious. Dad and Mum were here, and there was going to be a picnic and prawning; but first there'd be the bathe and Dad would make him swim to the raft. He had asked the Foxglove every day to let him and he had pretended to be fed up when he wasn't allowed to, but actually he had only asked because he knew she'd say 'no'. It had been all right at breakfast, because when he had told Dad he wanted to swim to the raft Mum had made a face. He liked that, it was nice when everybody looked at you. Still, could he swim to the raft? He could swim but it was an awful long way, simply miles. What a super day! What would it be like to drown? Then Tony knocked him down and happiness swamped him.

Tuesday sat down and filled her bucket with sand. She hummed, a contented tuneless sound. She had asked Nan every day when Dad and Mum would come, and Nan had said 'soon, dear'. Tuesday did not know that for a fortnight she had felt insecure because she was in one place and her father and mother in another, nor why today she was happy. Because she was only four and people underrated her intelligence and spoke in front of her, she was the one of the children who was aware that Nan and Miss Glover and the servants at home were afraid of something. Because they were afraid Tuesday was afraid. She wanted everybody where she could see them. If Laurel or Tony or Kim were out of sight she was in a ferment. 'Where's Laurel, Nan?' 'Where's Kim?' At night she woke up and listened to Nan's snores and sometimes she cried. Nan said it was the change of air and she needed one of her powders. Tuesday had swallowed a whole box of her powders during the fortnight she had been at Eastbourne. Today she hummed; a tiny stretch of sand shared with the others, Mum and Dad on the parade, Miss Glover in the hotel sewing, and soon Nan would come with her bag bulging with the bottles of milk and the buns. In ecstasy Tuesday seized her spade and smashed the sand pie she had just turned out of her pail.

Tony and Kim, exhausted, stopped punching each other and lay side by side panting. Tony rolled on to his elbows and looked at the raft.

'It isn't as far when you're in the sea, and I'll be there as well as Dad.'

Kim raised his voice.

'Nobody won't have to help me. I could swim twice as far as that.'

Laurel as well as Tony was listening but neither answered. To be afraid of things was natural and so was pretending you were not. They had tried curing fright that way themselves.

Laurel threw herself on to her hands. She spoke while she was upside down.

'I do hope Mum won't want us to look all posh at lunch.'

Tony tried to catch a sandfly as it popped out of the sand.

'I should think she would. Everybody will speak to her in the lounge and we'll have to keep saying how d'you do.'

Tuesday glanced up from her sand pie.

'And look up and smile when we're spoke to.'

'Which we all do, goodness knows,' Laurel pointed out.

'If we didn't we jolly well ought to,' said Kim. 'I was first told that when I was so little I was in a pram.'

Laurel sat down to rest. She hugged her knees and pictured them round the hotel table. She was conscious people stared. It was because they were so fair and Kim like a picture. Just being looked at did not matter in itself, because if they were all being ordinary it did not last long. It was when Kim showed off it was so awful, because then it was more than staring. It was when Mum was there, she thought Kim showing off funny. Grown-up people being so stupid about Kim was puzzling. Even Dad really didn't understand. He snubbed him and then he showed off more. It came of looking like he did and people pawing him at first, and then not exactly pushing him away but not liking him as much. He was all right really, she and Tony hardly had to sit on him at all.

As if Kim felt her mind was on him he turned to her.

'I think Mum will want us all blue. You and Tuesday in those blue frocks and Tony and me in our blue shirts.'

Tony made a grab at another sandfly.

'If you suggest that, and I'll find out if you do, you'll prawn in Coventry this afternoon.'

Kim made a proud face.

'I wouldn't care, I'd talk to Mum and Dad.'

Tony's voice was relentless.

'Mum won't be prawning, she'll be sitting on the beach and that means nearly all the time Dad'll have to sit with her, so if you do talk to them you'll not be able to prawn.'

For Kim the beauty of the morning was gone, he wanted to hurt everybody. The others were being beastly as usual.

Laurel, watching him, leant forward and patted his knee.

'But nothing awful has happened yet, Kim. All you have to do is just not to talk about clothes to Mum.' The world had seemed so black that Kim could not believe that the way back to gaiety was as easy as Laurel made out. She grasped just what he was thinking. She spoke slowly. 'That's absolutely all you've got to do. Not talk about clothes to Mum.'

Tuesday, raising her head from her bucket, saw Nannie coming down the beach. She scrambled to her feet and went to meet her.

Nannie was what she called 'on the spread'. The grey coat and skirt which she wore out of doors no matter how hot the day, had been let out in every seam, as lighter and rather shiny strips showed, but further space would be needed and a new coat and skirt was planned. Nannie's face was reminiscent of a grazing cow's. It had a placidity which seemed unshakable, and eyes large, grave, and unclouded by thought.

'How's Nan's pet?' she said to Tuesday, and threw her eye over the other three. Nannie had a lot in common with sea captains. She stood, as it were, on a bridge and looked down and around, and was able at once to detect if all was not normal. Now, as she plodded down a bank of shingle in her flat, wide black shoes, one hand holding a leather bag of milk and buns, and the other her own bag with her needlework, she was registering rather than thinking. 'Something's upset Kim but it's passing off. I'll send them up to put on their bathing things; never does children any good to get sitting about.'

The children had changed into their bathing things when Alex and Lena found them.

'I say, Dad, you've been simply ages,' Tony complained. 'You can almost walk to the raft.'

Laurel looked anxiously at her mother.

'There isn't any shade but it isn't really hot, we put your stool here because it's nice on the sand.'

The sight of his father made Kim's inside feel as if it were turning over. He strutted up and down shouting.

'Yes, we can almost walk to the raft, and I wanted to swim miles and miles.'

Tuesday got to her feet but she said nothing. This was perfection, everybody together.

Alex grinned at his children.

'Do you know what your mother and I thought when we looked down on you from the parade? That you could easily be mistaken for four shrimps; you're almost exactly the same colour as the sand.' He glanced at the raft, which now looked like a jam pot surrounded by wasps. 'Not much of a swim for you, Tony, old man, but about right for Kim.'

Kim strutted and wagged his head from side to side.

'I can swim miles and miles.'

'Well, you're not going to, darling,' said his mother. 'You're only a little boy of seven.'

Kim stopped strutting and came hopefully to his mother. Laurel knew what would happen. Kim would manage to look tired and Mum would say he was not to bathe, and Dad would make him just the same. Then Mum would mind Dad doing something she did not like, and Dad would have to be extra nice to her all day and perhaps not be able to prawn at all. Her thoughts ran round like mice behind wainscoting, but she could not think of the sensible thing to say. It was Nannie who, without apparently thinking at all, found exactly the phrase needed.

'The children ought to bathe now, sir.' She turned to Lena. 'I reckoned to have them out of the sea by eleven-thirty 'm, otherwise the buns and milk will sit in the way of their lunch, seeing we're having it early.'

Tony went to the bathing tent while his father changed. He ran his fingers up and down one of the supporting poles.

7

'I thought, as Kim's swimming to the raft the first time, I'd swim one side of him.'

'He can swim all right. What he needs is confidence, if we make a song and dance about it he'll feel he's managed something that can't be done every day.'

Tony fingered the supporting pole as if in it he could find the way to say what was on his mind.

'I think he's in a bit of a funk really.'

'Of course he is. So were you and so was I the first time. It's just old Kim's got a comic way of showing it. You and I are more alike; you couldn't get your first swim over quick enough when you knew you'd got to do it, neither could I when I started. Old Kim would put it off if he could.'

Tony stopped fingering the supporting pole. How grand Dad was! He knew lots of things you never thought he knew, and he talked sense, as if you weren't a child.

'I say, Dad, one day while you're here could we have a boat and fish?'

'Shouldn't wonder, but I may have to go up to London a good many days.'

'Oh, I say, Dad, this is your holiday, and you absolutely promised . . .'

Alex took Tony by the shoulders and turned him to face him.

'As a matter of fact I'm going to have a word with you later today, but in the meantime you're to keep that I may have to go up and down under your hat.'

'But, Dad . . .'

'Can't help myself. I've got some new gadgets to make. Means all sorts of shifting about.'

'What sort of things?'

'It's all a bit hush.'

Tony stared up at his father feeling excited and important.

'In case we fight Germany?'

'That's it. But mind you, not a word about war or my going to London in front of your mother. Come on now, and if you should be swimming to the raft the same time as myself and Kim I shan't notice.'

All hope was dead. Kim watched Laurel shoot through the water and in panic saw her reach the raft, looking, in his eyes, as she poised to dive, no bigger than a doll.

'Come on, old man,' said Alex taking his hand. 'We can walk almost half-way.'

Kim hesitated. His mother, who would have helped, was out of earshot of pleading, but she was watching. He waited until he was well above his knees in water, then he snatched his hand from his father's and pretended to slip and hurt himself. He uttered loud cries:

'Oh, Dad! Oh, my foot! My foot!'

Lena got off her camp stool.

'Alex, bring him to me.'

Nannie did not raise her head from her sewing. She judged by the tone of Kim's voice.

'It's all right 'm. Such play acting!'

Tony, who had been hovering on the rocks, splashed towards Kim. Alex took charge. He picked Kim up and pushed him into deep water, then let him go. Spluttering, certain he was about to drown, Kim swam.

They sat on the raft.

'Pretty good,' said Laurel. 'He swims all right, doesn't he, Dad?'

Alex nodded. He disliked that trait in Kim which had made him pretend to slip. He and the children had for the moment the raft to themselves; he did not want to moralise but he had to say something.

'You've got quite good style, Kim, but it was a pity you made an ass of yourself at the start. No harm in feeling in a bit of a funk, but pretending you've hurt yourself to hide you're funky is a fool of a way to go on.'

Because Kim was bound to argue Tony and Laurel both started to speak. Tony got his words out first.

'But you oughtn't to say you're in a funk, ought you?'

'Miss Glover says that it's bad manners to talk about how you feel,' Laurel added. It was not accurate reporting of Miss Glover's words, but it would do to stave off a scene with Kim.

Alex weighed his words, trying not to sound ponderous.

'Not much point in making a song and dance about anything, but if you feel you've got to say something it's better to speak the truth. It takes a brave person to funk something and admit it, brave that is, of course, if they do it just the same, funk or not.'

Laurel stood up.

'Watch me, Dad, I'm going to do a back dive.'

Tony slid gently into the water.

'Come on, Kim, I'll give you a start while I count five and then I'll race you in.' Then, seeing hesitation on Kim's face, he seized his legs and pulled him off the raft. 'Come on, the tide's almost full out. Soon the raft will be on the beach.'

Alex kept his eye on Kim but stayed on the raft. The bit of sermonising he had just done reminded him of something when he had been about Tony's age. He had nicked some money he was given for a school charity to pay a fine for a hole he had made in one of the school windows. Somehow the fact he had not passed the subscription on, came out, and rather than confess to the window he had written home that he had spent the money on sweets. It was the end of term and back home the true story had been gouged out of him. The resulting pi-jaw had been shared by all the family. It was on speaking the whole truth, and making a clean breast of things. His father had finished up by saying: 'Apart from what's right and what's wrong, you'll be surprised to find what a difference a complete confession makes. It's like having had a tremendous walk home in wet clothes, and then letting the whole lot drop off.' Perhaps because of the metaphor chosen, a discomfort and a relief with which they were all familiar, he had never forgotten that lecture. He mentally shook his head at himself. He had not made much of a shot at what he had wanted to say. The kids clearly had hardly listened. He couldn't blame them. What ill-chosen words! Not even sense, if you worked them out. Disgusted with himself he dived off the far side of the raft and, for exercise, swam out seawards.

Laurel, back on the raft, attempted some more backward dives. Each month or two she tried to be first-class at something. She had discovered that if you were admittedly good at something, it seemed to allow you to be just ordinary about everything else. 'Ginnie dances beautifully.' 'Alison is a wonderful skater.' 'Have you heard Pauline play her violin lately? She's going to be first-class they say.' 'Betty has a wonderful style at tennis.' Oh, just once to know all the mothers and nurses and governesses were saying as she passed: 'That's Laurel, she's marvellous at . . .' Being good at something was like walking in a fog, it made you a shadow, nobody noticed your looks or your character or what you wore. Being in a funk of things, what Dad was jawing at Kim about, was queer. Dad meant a funk properly, not the sort of things she funked, like that awful eternity, or Kim being quicker at answering at lessons than she was, or minding being the plainest. Those weren't the sort of things Dad meant, but they were the things that made you go all damp and made your teeth chatter, and if that wasn't funk, what was?

Alex climbed back on to the raft.

'How's the world's champion diver getting on?' She half got up to show him, he pulled her back. 'I've watched. You're coming along well. Going to represent the nation at the Olympic Games?'

Laurel felt relaxed. How gorgeous Dad was! He didn't exactly laugh at you, but somehow he made everything seem to matter less. She leant against him.

'I'd like to be really good. Don't you like being good at electrical things?'

'I'm lucky, of course, my job's my hobby and I was lucky, too, to have an uncle's firm to step into.'

Laurel hugged her knees.

'But it's the other people knowing you're good. When you're with other people who do the same sort of things, their knowing you are super at it.'

'See what you mean, though you've got a very exaggerated view of your father's position. What you're trying to say is that in whatever field you choose, you want to be accepted as first-class.'

'As absolutely the best that could be.'

'Don't want much, do you? If I thought it mattered if you shone or not I'd tell you that you were going the wrong way about it. In the last couple of years you've had a try at championship standard at tennis, golf and now diving; there was that Florence Nightingale patch and you were going to be an actress. Oh yes, and a singer.'

She gave his arm a hug.

'Don't tease.'

'I'm not, it's true. What I'm going to get from all this energy is a daughter who's a good all-rounder. I shall like that.'

'Not at lessons I won't be. I'm a dreadful disappointment to Miss Glover.'

He laughed.

'It's terrible, isn't it? And I should have so liked a brilliant daughter.'

She knew he was teasing but she had to probe.

'But, Dad, wouldn't you like to be proud of me?'

It was in his mind to tell her how proud he was. How he loved her comic small face and her fair pig-tails, and her earnestness, and her elder sister ways which were such an endearing part of the family set-up; but he held back his thoughts. No good going in for a lot of chat, making her self-conscious.

'Come on in, you're shivering.'

On the beach Nannie was handing out the buns and milk. Kim, with his swim safely behind him, was entirely above himself. He had succeeded and he was not now prepared to let it become an ordinary morning. Everybody had been looking and thinking of him and it had got to go on being Kim's day. He talked too loud, he threw his bun about, he pretended to have sand in his eye.

There were by now other families round them. The mothers looked at Kim and smiled at Lena. The smiles said, 'What a lovely child!' Lena could see herself, fair and slim, little Tuesday lolling against her and exquisite Kim playing around, and she knew what a picture they must look, and the thought amused rather than pleased her. There was nothing she liked better than to be envied and admired, but this was not the picture she wanted exhibited. That picture was of her and Alex. Of course the children must be there too, but as charming decorations, not interfering with the original portrait of two people.

Alex and Laurel came splashing out of the sea. Lena noticed how happy Alex was with Laurel, and cared and was disgusted with herself because she cared. She held herself in check but she could hear the faint edge behind her voice.

'Oh, there you are! Run along and get off that wet bathing dress, Laurel. She's been in too long, Alex, she's shivering.'

Alex picked up the bathrobe he had left on the sand and put it on.

'Yes, scuttle along.' He sat down by Lena. 'I don't think she's really cold, it's grand in the water.'

The edge left her voice. She ran her comb through his

hair, she knew he hated that sort of thing but it put, from the onlookers' view-point, their family group into the right perspective.

Alex smoothed his wet hair with his hand to push away her comb, but at the same time, so as not to hurt her, he smiled up into her face.

'Where's Tony?'

Kim pranced over and sat by his father.

'He's gone to buy Mum a magazine. I bet I catch simply hundreds of prawns.'

Alex, because he did not always want to be squashing Kim, turned to Tuesday, who was leaning against her mother decorating her wooden spade with bands of seaweed. She looked the personification of contentment.

'What about Tuesday? Are you going to catch a lot of prawns?'

Lena shook her head.

'She's too small to drag over there. You'll spend a lovely afternoon on the beach with Nannie, won't you, pet?'

Tuesday raised her eyes to her father's. They were, he noticed, brimming with fright, but she said nothing.

Nannie spoke without looking up from her work.

'Tuesday's expecting to have her treat with the others, 'm. Her rest's fixed for before her lunch. Miss Glover's walking over and meeting us there.'

'Is she though?' said Alex. 'I wouldn't mind the walk myself.'

Tony, holding *The Tatler*, had joined the family in time to hear the last words.

'Could we walk, Dad?'

Lena held out her hand for the magazine.

'No, you can't because you've got a selfish Mummie who wants to have fun too.'

'But we shan't be very much behind you,' Tony protested. 'We could start earlier.'

Lena seemed absorbed in her magazine.

'I don't mind sitting on a beach watching you all prawn, but I'd like to dance this evening and I don't want a creaking, exhausted husband who says he's too tired.'

Tony lay down beside Nannie and took his bun out of her bag.

'When do you get too old to dance?'

Lena at thirty-three knew herself still lovely and could afford to laugh.

'Not ever, I hope.'

'You and Dad will look pretty comic bumping round when you're old and fat.'

Alex got up.

'A horrible picture, Tony, I assure you we'll give up long before then.'

Lena, without looking up from her magazine, felt Alex leave her side. He would have gone to the tent to put on his things. When they were first married, or even a few years ago, she would have gone with him. She would not have missed those seconds in the hot tent, the flash of passion that would have come from the closeness of his cool, naked body. But he had got so self-conscious, always worrying about what the children were thinking. She had faced that. He wanted to switch things. He wanted to be a family man, bless him. The children were darlings, but she was not a family woman, she was utterly wife, and, if it came to that, a mistress too, and she meant to go on being just those things. It didn't matter giving in to him occasionally, letting him be all father. When they were alone she would brush that away and have him where she wanted him.

Laurel, in her shorts and shirt, came down the beach wringing out her bathing dress. She had tired herself diving and felt disgruntled and prickly.

'Here's your milk, dear,' said Nannie. Laurel paid no attention to the proffered glass. Nannie glanced at her. 'Too long in the water,' she thought. She raised her voice slightly. 'You have to drink it as well you know, so you may as well get it down first as last.'

Laurel twisted her bathing dress.

'Oh, shut up! I don't want the silly old milk.'

Alex had come back. He took the mug from Nannie.

'Come on, my girl, throw it back.'

Laurel hated herself for being bad-tempered but did not know how to stop. She snatched the mug.

'Oh, all right. But it's idiotic, it's almost lunch time.'

If there was one thing Lena understood it was feeling edgy for no particular reason, especially she understood such a mood in her own sex. She got up and held out a hand to Laurel. 'Come on, darling. We'll put some eau-de-Cologne in my bath and I'll wash the salt off you. Then you'll put on a clean frock for lunch.'

'Oh goodness, not my blue!'

Lena laughed.

'Don't be angry, you shan't wear anything you don't want to.' She nodded at Alex. 'I'll meet you for a cocktail at half-past twelve.'

Lena bathed Laurel and dusted her with bath powder. She went to the child's room and fetched the blue dress. She was unutterably charming, Laurel was unable to withstand her. She flung her arms round her neck.

'You're the most absolutely gorgeous mother in the world.'

Tony met Laurel in the corridor. He had found his clean blue shirt on his bed and been ordered to put it on. He was furious.

'Dressed up monkeys just to eat lunch!'

Laurel, soothed and stroked not only back to good temper but to the radiant happiness of the early morning, danced towards the lift.

'Oh, I don't mind, we can get back into our beach things directly afterwards.'

Tony looked at her bitterly.

'Just like a girl! Dress-up – dress-up. You don't care how often you change or what a fool you look.'

Laurel reached the lift first.

'You can press the button. It's not that I like dressing up but it's such an absolutely perfect day now Dad and Mum have come, I can't let a silly old frock spoil it.'

Tony was busy peering for the lift.

'Well, one thing, Kim won't be able to show off with Dad there. I tell you what, I'll get the liftman to let me open the gates, and he just might let us work the lift.'

II

Ruth Glover was in her late twenties. The daughter of a parson who knew that after church teaching, his main parental duty was to see that his sons were well educated. He had four sons, and the two daughters who completed what he was fond of calling his quiver had been aided by what he described as the goodness of God, and less high-minded people called charity. The school the girls were sent to was for the daughters of poor clergy, and fees were settled by a means test. When the means test showed an exceptionally low state of finance there were no fees, and even clothes were provided. By the time the four sons had been sent to good preparatory schools, followed by Marlborough, there were no means left in the vicarage, so Ruth and her sister were dressed and educated free. 'Nobody,' the headmistress said, 'knows what any parent pays, nor does anybody care. We are just one happy family.' Ruth and her sister found this a grossly inaccurate statement. The sister, who was frail, staged an ill-health campaign and was removed after two terms to live at home, dimly educated by her father and, after school hours, by the mistress of the village school. Ruth remained. She was highly-strung and acutely sensitive and, to defend herself, drew away from her childhood, studying it with detachment, waiting patiently to be grown up. As a legacy of these bitter school years she possessed a profound understanding of children.

Ruth's grey eyes wandered round the table. She kept her eyes down, for she knew she was incapable of hiding the amusement which would flick across them. Such a pretty sight! Daddy and Mummy Wiltshire and the four fair blue shirted or frocked children. The solid good Nannie, and (she hoped) the suitable looking, suitably dressed governess. Lena was at her radiant best. She had been doing her 'perfect Mummie' act and was pleased with herself, and would glow on the children all through lunch. 'Not,' thought Ruth fairly, 'that it's an act while she's doing it. She means every word of it. The truth is, of course, she's all impulses. She knows so well herself what it's like to feel fratchy and to want coaxing and petting back to normal, that seeing Laurel in that state she had an impulse to snap her out of it.' Ruth glanced at Laurel, who was sitting next to her. The child was silent, with a secret look which Ruth knew meant she was hugging the perfect minutes, aware that she was happy and that it was a fragile condition, broken in a split second. 'Poor little thing!' thought Ruth. 'I wish she was less vulnerable.' She turned over a problem which was always at the back of her mind. Was Lena a good mother? There was no doubt that children were lucky who had parents, particularly a mother, whom they could show off. She had suffered too acutely from her own mother's occasional visits to her school, not to know what shame a dowdy, unpolished mother could bring. The children were too young to care yet but in a year or two Lena's well-groomed appearance and her flair for saying and doing the right thing would be highly valued, though probably casually taken for granted. Security mattered more than anything else to children, and in Lena they had the security of a mother who was always in the picture. The Wiltshire children would never offer secret prayers, 'Oh, God, don't let Mother wear that evening blouse like it is. It could be made to look better; do let her have it altered before she comes for the half-term concert.' 'Oh, God, don't let Mother tell stories about us in a loud voice, especially don't let her tell stories about our not knowing how babies come; I know she thinks it funny but everybody else just wonders why she hasn't brought us up properly.'

On other counts Lena was not so good. She never even pretended the children came first. But did that matter? Was that not out-balanced by the perfect love always before the children's eyes? Ruth, helping herself to peas, knew one of her more noticeably amused flicks was crossing her eyes. Was it perfect love the children saw? Certainly Lena loved Alex, but perfect love in her philosophy was an ill-balanced affair, almost all body, the merest whiff of soul.

As an employer Lena could scarcely be bettered; she stated what she wanted, and then withdrew. Nothing, Ruth believed, was worse for children from a character training point of view, than to have a second authority to run to. Lena liked her children prettily dressed, good-mannered and well tended, but when she was about she liked those who saw to these things to be as inconspicuous as possible. This lunch was turning out well from that point of view. Because the children were still thrilled by the arrival of their parents, it chanced they had not spoken to their governess, but if they did all the answer they would get would be a monosyllable. Yes, on points Lena worked out well. Her lack of maternal instinct fitted the family scheme, and yet nobody could be, when she felt like it, a more tender mother. Ruth placed tenderness, petting and cuddling, even when it was spasmodic, high amongst a child's necessities. And how well Lena's way of mind suited Alex. Did Lena know how firmly Alex held the reins of his children's lives? Probably not, for he was far too shrewd to allow her to get jealous of her children. All his talks with herself and with Nannie were at carefully chosen times, when Lena was either out or too engrossed in something else to mind if he was in the nursery or schoolroom. It was one of those odd wordless arrangements. Ruth had never been told that she must discuss all she did for the children, and almost all she thought about them, with Alex, but that was what he expected and he expected something of the same sort from Nannie. Ruth had often wondered how Alex had arranged the engaging of Nannie for Laurel. The Nannie for the first baby would be engaged by the wife's mother, if the wife didn't do it. But Nannie was Alex's choice. Lena would have liked, and had probably tried to get, a young Norland or the equivalent, looking smart in her uniform, and she would have seen that the nursery maid looked smart too. Yet Alex had felt, probably just because Lena was as she was, that his child must have somebody a little old-fashioned, solid, placid, and imperturbable, so he had acquired Nannie, who had engaged her own nursery maids and very much ruled her nurseries ever since. And what a success she was! She gave, unknowingly, a feeling of permanence to all in the house. Nobody could imagine the Wiltshires without Nannie. To the children, even as they grew away from her, she was unutterably important. She was always there, always the same, and seemed in her unchangeableness a shield to hold away the fears of growing up.

Ruth looked across at Nannie and wondered what she would say if she told her the thoughts she had about her. Nothing probably, for nobody could discourage foolish chat more ably than Nannie. Or she might produce one of her convictions, which seemed to flow through her, uninterrupted by thought. 'Children like things just so, even the untidiest gets upset if his things aren't in the place he expects.'

'If it's a decent day tomorrow,' said Alex to Lena, 'shall we go to church in one of the downland villages?'

The waiter brought strawberry ice-cream. Lena, with pleasure, watched the exchange of glances between the children. They were not allowed to mention food at the table, but their expressions were sweet, especially Kim's. If Kim kept even half his looks what a riot with the girls he was going to be. Sunday church was one of Alex's things. He was quite ridiculous about it but he made such a point of it that she went en famille nearly every Sunday. She thought it a fearful bore and she let Alex know that she did, and his fear that she might stop attending was a little weapon in reserve. She was a hoarder of weapons.

'I should have thought we needn't go to church on a holiday,' said Tony. 'I have to go twice every Sunday at school.'

'Fat lot of term you've had, my boy,' Laurel pointed out.

Kim looked up at his mother.

'Tuesday and me will say our prayers on the beach with Nannie.'

'Tuesday and you, if you don't go to church in the

morning, will go to the children's service in the afternoon,' said Nannie. She turned to Alex. 'All together in the morning would be nice, sir, and take the little ones out before the sermon.'

Laurel touched Ruth's arm to get her attention. 'Nannie's magazine had an article on life at Sandringham. I knew she'd work it out on us.'

Nannie, as Ruth hoped, answered.

'And a nicer example you couldn't wish.'

'Couldn't we all go out before the sermon as it's a holiday?' Laurel suggested. 'I just hate sermons, I get pins and needles all over trying to look interested.'

She was sitting on Alex's left. He gave one of her pig-tails an affectionate pull.

'My poor daughter, what a tragic picture!'

'It's true though,' Laurel persisted. 'And it makes me simply hate going to church, which I wouldn't except for sermons.'

Tony, seated on Alex's other side, raised a puzzled face to his father's.

'Does it make you like going to church being made to go all the time you're a child?'

Alex, enjoying his lunch, was unwilling for serious conversation, especially, in front of Lena, this particular conversation, but he always gave the children straight answers to direct questions.

'No. In fact it might put you off. But you'll be a nuisance to yourself when you grow up if you've not learnt self-discipline.'

Tony scowled, as he was apt to do when he was out of his depth.

'What's that?'

'Sitting still when you've pins and needles is an example. It goes much further than that, of course, but it's one of the things.'

Ruth took a swift look at Lena. Was she listening? What was she thinking? She was disciplined in her own way presumably, otherwise how had she acquired her unshakable poise? But of the self-discipline Alex believed in she probably hadn't an inkling. For all her perfection you couldn't help feeling that Lena was more blown together than built on a foundation.

Kim, bored with talk of discipline, had gone off on a trail of his own.

'The sea, when I saw it from the raft, was blue like bluebells when they are new.'

Lena had Kim next to her. He really was a most ornamental child, both in looks and in the way he said things. She saw that with charmed smiles the next table was listening. She led Kim on.

'Or like the butterflies on the downs.'

Kim thought of chalk-blue butterflies. He raised his eyes to the ceiling. He looked like a Hollywood choir boy rounding off a film in which the hero or heroine's soul in the last reel flies heavenwards.

Nannie, Ruth, Laurel and Tony knew he was not at that moment showing off but considering chalk-blue butterflies in relation to the sea. Alex, disgustedly aware of the next table, opened his mouth. He, Laurel and Tony spoke at once.

'Eat your ice, Kim. You look like a half-wit mooning at the ceiling.'

'The sea looked blue all right,' said Tony, 'but it was pretty filthy really. That horse did number two in it.'

Laurel stammered because she had nothing to say and was afraid of looking a fool.

'Blue butterflies and bluebells are the same colour anyway.'

Nannie was squashing Tuesday's ice in the belief it would take the chill off it.

'Number two's not a thing you mention at table, as well you know, Tony.'

'When it's a horse you can. It's manure then.'

Kim saw an opening to clown.

'Or a monkey's, or a bear's, or a hippopotamus's, only then it's such a lot I should think. . . .'

Lena laid a hand on Kim and shook her head at Tony. These were not the well-brought-up children she expected to exhibit.

'I shall give a prize to whoever catches the most prawns this afternoon.'

There was excitement. What prize? Laurel wanted it to be a new bathing cap with special ear bits, like the man who dived off the pier wore. Tony thought a fountain pen. Kim wanted pounds and pounds of chocolates which could be eaten whenever you liked. Tuesday, all her wants supplied by those she loved being at the table, could make no suggestion, but when given hints by the other children accepted that a balloon would be nice.

'What'll you give Dad if he wins?' Tony asked.

Lena smiled at Alex.

'Whatever he wants.'

Ruth glued her eyes to her plate. She hoped the corners of her lips weren't twitching. What a woman! Did her thoughts ever leave beds?

'I'll have a hundred cigarettes,' said Alex.

Lena was still too pleased with herself for the pleasure she had given Laurel, and too conscious of the charming effect created by the family party to let Alex's being tiresome disturb her. He was, of course, being deliberately annoying. All that self-conscious nonsense about the children growing up and what they would think. Quite time enough to worry about that when they were old enough to know there was anything to think about. All the same, she never allowed Alex to get away with anything, that was the beginning of the end. If he was once permitted not to answer smile for smile, and covert look for covert look, he would be one shade nearer that dreary he wanted to be, the perfect father, the family man. She leant forward and blew him a kiss, and smiled intimately as though at an exchanged thought.

Ruth, though her eyes appeared to be on her plate, registered and admired this performance. It was queer how she had learnt to read Lena. When she had first come to the family she had seen nothing but Lena's poised, lovely exterior, which had made her clumsy and tongue-tied and convinced that she herself looked as though she had slept in her clothes.

Tony regretfully laid down his spoon.

'That nurse I had when I was in quarantine told me that there were illnesses you could have where eating ices was ordered by the doctor.'

Laurel gasped at so enchanting a picture.

'Just imagine lying in bed and every sort of ice-cream coming, and people wanting you to eat them!'

'Greedy little pig!' Alex spoke so firmly that the children glanced up to see if he was cross. He gave them reassuring grins, but he changed the subject. 'Hope we can hire those metal fronted nets, those are the fellows for catching the prawns.'

Ruth was glad for the over-sensitive Laurel that Alex had shown he was teasing. Not that the relationship between Laurel and her father could be out of gear for long, but the child was so happy it was a pity to upset her even momentarily. Alex had probably known he had spoken sharply and regretted it. He was still annoyed about that nurse. If there was a way to ruffle his even temper it was coddling the children and making them health-conscious. For once Ruth had been on Lena's side. Lena used ill-health as if it were a feminine charm and, if given a chance, she fussed about the children, for none of which, as a rule, Ruth had any use; but when she got hysterical about Tony, Ruth could sympathise. There was not, of course, any purpose in letting her imagination run riot as it had, jumping from the one case of infantile paralysis at Tony's school to, first Tony in an iron lung and then in his coffin, but she had sympathised over having him home and had been thankful to know he was under the roof. She could not quite see how so fond a father as Alex could have endured the anxiety of leaving him at school; and if he was home, segregated in the spare-room, somebody had to look after him, and that nice sensible young nurse had been perfect for the job. She had her wits about her and her well-trained eyes would have detected the first sign of anything wrong, but as Tony remained his usual radiant self, she had been as pleased as he was to visit the Zoo and other outdoor amusements. Of course the truth was it was Kim that Alex was afraid for. A hundred hospital nurses attending on him day and night could not make Tony a malade imaginaire, but Kim had so much of his mother in him, he relished and used delicacy almost in the way she did, and it upset his father to see it. All the same, having got Tony home it was Alex who decided on this holiday. How queer that was. Of course the news was bad but it was unlike him to let Tony miss school. Somebody must have said something about the future which had made him think off his usual lines. She was so accustomed to his behaving and thinking exactly as she expected that she was still surprised to find herself at Eastbourne. It was so unlike him to allow the quiet pattern of nursery and schoolroom life to be disturbed. 'You are going to Eastbourne for a month and my wife and I will come for the last fortnight. I want the children to have so good a time that they'll never forget it. I know you won't spoil them, but for this one month I want them within reason to have all they want.'

Nannie was watching to see Tuesday did not scrape her plate. Tony, Laurel and Alex were still happily engrossed with the subject of prawning. Lena and Kim felt as if the sun were behind a cloud. The moments were passing and being wasted. Lena opened her bag and took out her glass. Was Alex not looking at her because her face was out of order?

29

Kim gazed soulfully at the waiter who had come to clear and bring cheese.

'Have you ever met the Holy Ghost?'

Laurel paused half-way through a sentence, crimson with mortification. This was Kim at his very worst, saying things for effect and pretending it was just a little boy not knowing he was saying anything odd.

Tony was exasperated. What made Kim such a blithering idiot? He'd give him a good punch afterwards.

Ruth raised her head. Poor little beast, there he went again and Alex would snub him. Not that this time there was much else to do; the people at the next table were repeating Kim's remark to each other; the waiter was grinning; but snubbing was the worst way to treat Kim, each snub buried itself under his need for self-expression and would erupt in further showings off.

Nannie undid Tuesday's feeder.

'Say your grace, dear, and we'll go up and get ready, and you too, Kim.'

Kim leant against his mother.

'Can't I wait for Mum?'

'No, you can't,' said Alex. 'She's going to have coffee. Go along and don't argue.'

Kim's eyes brimmed with tears. Lena put her arm round him and kissed him. It hurt her to see him unhappy but she was glad to get rid of the children.

'Run along, all of you. Dad and I will meet you outside in quarter of an hour.'

III

Tony and Alex turned over their combined catch. Tony picked up a shrimp.

'It's a pity not to keep them but they better go, they aren't prawns.'

Alex jerked his head at Laurel's tense, absorbed figure behind them.

'Not much good our chucking ours out, she's sure to have a lot.'

'And so'll Kim if he's caught any at all.'

'Seeing the tide's wrong we can't afford to be proud.' Alex looked up the beach to where Lena lay sun bathing. 'I wonder if Mum's getting bored.'

Tony stared with experienced eyes at the distant patch of pink which was Lena.

'She isn't in a fuss yet or she'd be sitting up.'

The sun burned warm on Alex's back. It was pleasant wading beside Tony. Likely enough, as Lena had changed into a sun-bathing rig-out and oiled herself, she would be all right for another half-hour. When she sun bathed she did it as a beauty treatment and gave herself to it, as to any type of beauty treatment, seriously. He swung the bag of prawns over his shoulder.

'All right then, let's see if we can catch some real big prawns.'

Tony did not move.

'Dad, even if the Germans are going to fight us must you go up to London?'

'Yes. Come on, push along beside me and I'll explain.' He marshalled his thoughts. 'You know the sort of stuff we make.'

'I know it's electrical but I thought it was lighting, mostly for things like exhibitions.'

'Not only exhibitions, just happens I tell you about those. If there should be a war we swap over at once to make other things.'

'What sort of things?'

'I can't tell you that, it's secret. I fixed this holiday because I'm very much afraid there will be a war, and if there is it may be some time before we could manage another holiday all together.'

'Don't people have holidays in wars?'

'If it comes I've got to send you all out of London. I fixed up to do the same thing when we thought it was coming that time last year when we went for our gas-masks.'

'Where shall we go?'

'You'll go to school, of course, so will Laurel. Your mother, Kim and Tuesday will go to the grandparents, and that's where you'll go in the holidays. But mind you, not a word to anyone. I'm taking you into my confidence.'

'Aren't you going to tell Laurel?'

'You mean because she's the eldest? There is that but it's a pretty good disturbance for her. You see, you know your school, and when the holidays start you'll just go to Grandfather and Gran instead of London, it won't change things for you all that much.'

'I should think it just would change things. I've got all my tools at home and my film projector and. . . .'

'If things look like going on for long I dare say we can get the things you all want sent up to the grandparents, there's plenty of room there.'

'And I shouldn't think it holidays at all if you're in London and I'm at Gran's and Grandfather's.'

'Oh, cheer up! I dare say I'll manage to get away to see you, but, you see, Laurel won't have only the holidays to think of but going to a boarding school as well.'

'What'll happen to Miss Glover?'

'She'll go with Mum to teach Kim, and I suppose Tuesday will soon be starting lessons.'

'Will Nannie go?'

'Of course.'

They stopped to examine their nets. Shaking out the greyish sand and sorting the mass of seaweed, starfish, pebbles and prawns left behind. Tony gave a gasp.

'Oh, my goodness, Dad, look at this one! Isn't he enormous! And this other one's better than the others we've caught.' Alex having admired the catch and held open the prawn bag to receive it, they pushed on. Tony churned the future over in his mind, unable to imagine life without his home. He felt that his father had not fully seen all the disadvantages. 'I shouldn't think Mum would like living with Gran and Grandfather.'

Alex said nothing for a moment because he wanted to snap out a lying contradiction. What a horrible flair children had for putting into the boldest words thoughts that you yourself were succeeding in smothering.

'I'm afraid she'll have to put up with it. As you know, Mum's-Mum's in California.'

'That's an awfully good thing. If we've got not to live at home it will be better with Gran and Grandfather. Just suppose we'd had to live with Mum's-Mum. I shouldn't think there could be anything worse happen to anybody.'

'You're an ungrateful little beast, she's a wonderful grandmother.'

'All those little dogs, and that paint on her face, and scent everywhere, and asking everybody if her hat suits her. And I simply hate the way she calls Mum "precious", as if it was her name.'

'Your mother's her only child.'

'Thank goodness I'm not an only one if being an only one makes people slop like that.'

'Thank goodness you're not an only one from every angle. I like a family.'

Tony was still considering his maternal grandmother.

'Dad, can I ask you something?'

'Of course.'

'It was a nice wedding and all that, but do people usually marry grandmothers?'

'It's quite often done. She isn't old as grandmothers go.'

Tony stopped to clear his net.

'Well, it's very queer, and I'm glad he wanted to live in America.'

Alex looked at his watch.

'Perhaps we'd better push the other way, then we'll join up with Laurel.'

Tony turned.

'You said you liked a family. Would you like there to be lots and lots of us? Ten or something like that?'

'I'm quite pleased with what I've got. Two boys and two girls is fine. Being an only boy has made me keen to have a better divided family.'

Tony jumped at the opening to get his father on to talking of his childhood. That his father had been a little boy, and even Gran had been a little girl, that in those old days they had the same sort of things happening to them which happened to him today, gave him a wonderful feeling of permanence. He liked, without knowing it, to believe in things going on as they had always done.

'Weren't the aunts nice to you?'

'Aunt Dot was always clever, and she was a good deal older. She used to help me with my home work when I was at a day school.' He smiled. 'And she wanted to coach me in the holidays.'

'I bet you wouldn't let her.'

'No. You know about your Aunt Lindsey, I've always told you how we fought.'

'How she banged your head on a door.'

'The tough stuff wasn't all on her side.'

'I like Uncle John best of the uncles.'

'He spoils you children. He and your Aunt Lindsey ought to have had some of their own.'

'I expect they haven't time to look after any. Aunt Lindsey couldn't write her books if she had children, could she?'

'No, I dare say the books would have suffered.'

'But it was you and Aunt Sylvia who were the same ages.

Dad's-Nan said when you were little, people thought you were twins. You wore a sailor suit with long trousers and she wore a sailor collar on a frock.'

'Your Aunt Sylvia's a darling.'

'If only she hadn't married Uncle Andrew. I'm so glad you aren't a clergyman.'

'He's a very good man, you know.'

Tony stopped to examine his net.

'I don't like people just because they're good, do you, Dad?'

Alex thought of his impractical, rather helpless brother-in-law clutching at his belief in God as if it were a rope dangling from heaven. Good, he undoubtedly was, but hanging on to his rope his feet barely brushed the ground. Many were the occasions when Alex had straightened the affairs of his brother-in-law, and always he had come away wondering whether true saintliness was not best shown by living as a good citizen of this world. He changed the subject.

'You like Aunt Selina.'

'But I simply hate the cousins.'

Alex laughed.

'I'm certain they return the compliment. Intolerant little beasts the lot of you.'

'I like that, Dad, you must own they're the most disgusting show-offs. Laurel and I go all over gooseflesh waiting and waiting, knowing Fiona's going to dance and Bertie play the piano.'

'Let's be fair, they're a brilliant couple. We've nothing like that to show.'

'But you wouldn't like Laurel to be like Fiona or me like Bertie.'

Alex ran his hand through Tony's hair and stood it on end.

'You've no idea what I would like. Perhaps I'd like to see you with long hair like Bertie's.' He lowered his voice because they were within hailing distance of Laurel. 'Now mind, not a word to a soul about what I've told you, especially Mum. She's not to know I've spoken to you. Naturally it's upsetting for her to have her home broken up. She knows it may happen and she's being splendid about it, but it's not a thing we talk about. Understand?'

Tony was filled with pride. It was grand having Dad telling things to just him. There was nobody like Dad. He wanted to do something to show how he felt. He stepped back and butted his father with his head.

'I would have laughed if I'd knocked you over.'

Alex raised his voice.

'Come and protect your poor father, Laurel. This brother of yours is turning into a goat.'

IV

Lena, lying on her back gazing at the sky through her dark glasses, felt at peace. She was sheltered from the wind and had put on her bathing dress in order to give her skin a chance to take on its first film of tan. She loved the sun. Warmth from the sun made her relax, which few things did, and content flow through her. She was still glowing from the memory of the morning. Darling Laurel, it was so easy to please her. It would have been so simple by other handling to spoil her day. If only everybody would realise that with a little effort bad moods could be soothed away. The trouble was, of course, that most people were so insensitive, they didn't know what a mood was. The children should always know that she understood, and didn't think being on edge was naughtiness. That sort of understanding was what mothers ought to give.

Ruth came down the beach and sat down by Nannie and Tuesday. Drowsily Lena heard their conversation. They spoke in low voices so as not to disturb her. She liked that, it was sympathetic and added to her feeling of wellbeing.

'Tired I should think, aren't you?'

'No, it was lovely. I'm just in time to help you lay tea. How's the prawning been getting on?'

'Tony and his father have kept stopping and putting things in those bags. Kim got cross because he didn't catch anything, so I gave him some crumbs from the cake tin to throw on the water, I said that would bring them into his net.'

'What are you going to say when he comes back without any?'

'He'll have a shrimp or two I shouldn't wonder. He was too impatient, his net wasn't in before it was out. Now I've told him the crumbs won't act unless he counts twenty-five slowly before he picks his net up.'

'I wonder how Laurel's done.'

'She's not caring properly. Miss Live-in-the-clouds this afternoon.'

Ruth rolled over on to her elbows.

'Oh Tuesday, what dear little moulds!'

Nannie's voice was full of approval.

'They were in a box of little things Gran sent for Christmas, weren't they, pet?'

Tuesday explained her work.

'That sort with green seaweed are sugar cake, and that sort with brown seaweed have chocolate on them.'

Nannie felt making cakes of sand was a most suitable occupation.

'Gran always seems to send us just what we want, doesn't she, pet?'

Lena moved slightly. What a fuss everybody made of Alex's mother. She couldn't do the simplest thing without a chorus of praise. She was quite nice, considering she had led a dull domestic life. It was unkind really the way everybody kept building her up into something she wasn't. It put people off her. You didn't get a chance to like people who were held up to you as examples.

Ruth had turned to watch the prawners.

'It would be nice if the children could have their prawns for tea.'

Nannie considered the difficulties.

'We haven't anything to cook them in. Besides, to crisp they ought to have a red hot poker put in the water.'

Lena saw a picnic fire in her mind's eye. Of course the children would love their prawns for tea. It was nonsense to say it couldn't be managed. Somebody could borrow a saucepan, and somebody could make a fire.

'We're going to have a fire.' She considered the labour problem. Finding wood would be tiresome, besides, if a saucepan had to be borrowed she was the one to do it, charm got that kind of thing. She saw herself smiling on a cottage doorstep, then she added Tuesday to the picture. She stretched out a hand for her frock and buttoned it on. 'You two collect wood and get a lovely fire going and Tuesday and I will fetch a saucepan of water.'

It was natural to Lena to intend that when she gave time to any of her children that time was made memorable. She had been brought up that way. Her mother had always been her ideal of all that was feminine and delicious. It had not hurt her as a child to be petted and exhibited one moment and to be shut away in her schoolroom or nursery the next. It had been understood that people as lovely as Mummie had to be shared. She had not got one unlovely memory of her parents when she had been a child, they never scolded, they were never out of temper before her, they left all of what her mother collectively described as 'the drearies' of upbringing to nurses and governesses. Mummie and Daddy were all charm, fun and happiness.

It was no distance to the coastguard's cottage from which they borrowed a saucepan filled with hot water, but Lena made every foot enthralling. She and Tuesday were butter-flies. She had Tuesday shouting with excitement, darting from flower to flower.

'Look, Mum, I'm sitting on a harebell.' 'Look, Mum, this butterfly is liking this little yellow flower.'

Back on the beach a fire of driftwood was blazing and Ruth, who had been a Guide at her school, had a makeshift stove built so that the draught kept the fire going. Even so the fire needed watching and it was getting late, there was tea to lay, both Ruth and Nannie were busy. Nannie spoke firmly to Tuesday.

'Sit down, dear, and make some more sand cakes.'

'But I'm a butterfly and butterflies can go simply anywhere. You watch this butterfly jump in the tea basket.'

Nannie's voice was not raised.

'Don't be silly, dear. There's a time for everything. You get back to your sand cakes or we'll have tears before bedtime.'

Tuesday turned to Lena. She had invented this gorgeous game, she wouldn't want a butterfly to go back to making sand cakes. But Lena had seen that the boring business of unpacking the tea basket was going on, she threw the group round the fire off as if they were a frock she had worn in the morning and had changed out of for the afternoon. She strolled down the beach towards the rest of her family.

Ruth, unwrapping packets of bread and butter, patted a piece of sand by her side. Whatever was offered was a poor substitute for Lena's game, but she hated to see Tuesday brought quite so suddenly back to the everyday.

'You lay the tea for us, and if we've time we'll get some flowers to make the table cloth look pretty.'

V

The children's voices rose and fell, now all four together, then Tuesday's careful small notes, Laurel's eager tone breaking in, topped by Kim, his words ripping over each other, or Tony's rounder rather serious voice. It was the perfect picnic. What could be more glorious when you climbed up the beach with your catch than to find water boiling for the cooking! What a superb rounding off of the afternoon's work it had been when Kim had caught the little lobster. The actual chasing of the lobster had been a family affair, but it was Kim's net that had roused the lobster and, therefore of course, Kim's lobster. They were all beside themselves. Surely nobody else had ever gone out to prawn and caught a lobster. Lobsters were things caught in nets far out. It was a miracle. Every angle of the whole affair was recounted. It was a song, a saga for evermore. 'That day we caught the lobster.'

'I do wish,' said Kim, 'we had crackers. It's the one thing missing to make this the most perfect picnic that ever was.'

Laurel's tone was reproving.

'Crackers, my boy, belong to birthdays and Christmas. We'll have crackers next in August on your birthday.'

Kim looked at his father.

'Where are we going this August?'

The remark fell like a breath of wind on the surface of a pond. The ruffle of the first thought spreading through the minds of the adults in ring after ring of anxious wondering.

Even Nannie was disturbed. This holiday was very nice, but give her the rooms she knew, those two fine nurseries overlooking Regent's Park, the boys' bedroom at the back, and the little dressing-room for Laurel on the floor below. Of course it was all right at old Mrs. Wiltshire's. The nurseries had been kept very nicely for the grandchildren, and the old lady wasn't one to want ways interfered with; but what was all right for a holiday wasn't all right for keeps.

Ruth resented fear. You did not become adult with a life which was your own to handle, to have your vision clouded by fear. The mention of war made her feel she must toss up her chin and throw back her shoulders. All right, there is going to be a war, with gas, bombs and all the rest of it. Everything that could be done must be done to spare children from the worst of it, but adults should face it in their imaginations to the ghastly end, and then, no matter what came, they were armed. But nobody was doing that, at least the Wiltshires weren't. Alex was in a way. This holiday was the proof of it but not in a good whole-hoggish way. All right, war is coming, and when it comes we will do the following things. We will prepare everything in advance so that the children feel there's some order and arrangement in it all.

Lena deliberately did not look at Alex. He must answer Kim. She didn't want that silly argument re-opened. Go with the children to his mother indeed! The children mustn't be separated from both their parents. How funny and dense he could be! He couldn't really think she'd live apart from him.

Alex grinned at Kim. Behind his grin was a wish to turn him over his knee and spank him for the way in which his six word query had driven straight to the middle of the subject that they were struggling to avoid. He had not got an answer for he had not any idea where they would be. If war hadn't broken out he might pack them off somewhere, probably just with Nannie and Ruth. On the other hand, if it had started, they would, of course, be with their grandmother and he didn't want to make a statement because one of the children would be sure to say, 'Are you and Mum coming with us?' Lena would never start an argument in front of the children, but he didn't want to talk about the subject again, for he had managed to blunt her flat refusal by, 'Oh well, it hasn't happened yet. No need to make a decision today.' It was a wretched shelving of the problem, but you had to shelve things when you dealt with Lena.

'I'm not sure,' he answered Kim. 'Where would you like to go?'

'Abroad,' said Kim. 'I liked that time we spent with Mum's-Mum at that Cannes.'

'You couldn't have really, Kim,' Laurel protested. 'She made a fuss all the time because she hadn't the Pekineses because of not being able to bring them back to England.'

Tony's tone was heartfelt.

'Thank goodness we can't go there again, it was dress up, dress up all the time and I never understood a word anybody said.'   .

'Shows how bad your French is!' Alex pointed out. Laurel leant forward.

'You know, I wouldn't mind stopping at home.'

There were protests from Tony and Kim.

'In August!'

'Nobody ever stays in London in August.'

Laurel stuck to her idea.

'I wouldn't mind a bit. Other people in the Crescent would be away and we could look through their windows without being rude, and there's a lot of summer things I want to do that we've never done except on Saturdays, because we're always away in August.'

Tony reached for some more bread and butter.

'What sort of things?'

'I've wanted for simply ages to go to the docks on that river boat. Then there's things at home. I want to move all my nicest books out of the schoolroom and put them in my bedroom. I've been meaning to and meaning to but I've never had time.'

'Poor overworked girl!' said Alex.

'It's true. With lessons at home and dancing, gym and special French to go to, and the concerts and going to look at pictures, I don't get much time over, that's why I wouldn't mind a whole summer holiday at home, and anyway I'd always rather be at home than anywhere else on earth.'

'What about this diving?' Alex asked. 'Have you thought of that in your sweeping statement?'

Tony buried his prawn shells.

'I know what Laurel means. Everywhere else is nice to come to but London's different. I suppose it's because it's where we live.' He turned to Laurel. 'Of course, if the whole house and all of us could fly to somewhere like this beach, that would be different.'

'I'd still rather it was where it is,' said Laurel. 'I like Regent's Park and hearing the Zoo noises in the night. I think just where we live is the loveliest place to be.' She swung round to her father. 'That's why I'm so awfully glad that you said you liked daughters to be at home and not sent away to boarding schools.'

'I said it was old-fashioned of me.'

Laurel was next to Lena. She patted her mother's knee.

'You wouldn't let me go. You don't even want Tony to be at a boarding school, do you?'

Alex gave Lena no time to answer.

'I said we might send you to one sometime, you know.'

Laurel's eyes twinkled at him while she quoted him.

'Perhaps when you're fourteen we may send you to a school for a year or two to teach you to mix. But I'm not fourteen for two years and eleven months, so we needn't worry about that yet.'

'If our house could fly,' said Kim, 'I'd fly it to a different place every month, sometimes I'd be here and sometimes with Mum's-Mum in California.'

There was the beginning of an absorbing family game here. 'You choose where we go first, Laurel, you're the eldest, only for this game you can't keep the house where it is.'

VI

Nannie was putting Kim to bed. Tuesday was already asleep. Laurel and Tony were with their parents in their private sitting-room. Tony was sorting a packet of foreign stamps. Laurel was on a stool by her mother's chair. She had a cape round her shoulders and Lena was brushing and combing her hair. Alex was reading out loud *David Copperfield*. Both the children and Alex were absorbed by the story. Lena's mind was on Laurel's hair. It was pretty hair. Wasn't it rather a pity to keep it in plaits? She hadn't much beauty, poor darling, it seemed a shame not to make the most of what she had. On the other hand it made a party occasion when she wore it loose.

A girl couldn't start too early making the best of herself, and when you got the gauche type, like Laurel, the best way to train them was to make them feel they looked lovely at a party. It would be rather fun to try how Laurel would look in leaf-green, awfully plain, nothing but the colour against her fairness. Moved by the picture, Lena stroked the hair in her hands. Laurel, though most of her mind was with David trudging to Dover, turned and rubbed her cheek against Lena's knees.

There was a knock on the door and the waiter came in to lay the table for the children's supper. Alex finished the chapter and closed the book.

'There, that'll have to be all for tonight. Your mother and I must go and dress.' The children protested. 'Nobody could need all that time to dress.' 'Just one more chapter.' Alex laughed and put an arm round Lena. 'I'll be lucky if I get Mum down before midnight as it is.'

Lena leant slightly against Alex, happy to feel his arm. She blew the children a kiss.

'We'll be along to tuck you up.'

Laurel and Tony sat on the window seat.

'We're having supper alone,' said Tony. 'The Foxglove's gone out.'

Laurel swung the blind cord to and fro.

'Do you know what I think? We ought to make lists of all the things we most want to do now Dad and Mum are here. All the time I've kept thinking I'll save that until they come and now I'm afraid I've forgotten some of them.'

'They couldn't have been things you wanted to do very badly if you've forgotten what they were.'

'It was not real things like going to the Circus or for a picnic, just things I wanted them to see, that place where all those harebells are on the downs is one.'

Tony went to the writing table and got a sheet of notepaper.

'Let's write down two important things for each day and then we can add the little things in brackets.'

'We ought to add in what the little ones want.'

Tony drew a rough line down the middle of the paper. On one side he wrote 'morning' and on the other 'afternoon'.

'Kim wouldn't agree to anything we suggested, but he'll like what we plan all right if he doesn't feel left out. Tuesday's too little for real things.'

'There's that Circus, we'll all like that, and most awfully I want to go to that fête that we saw the advertisement of.'

'What on earth for! I call that a ghastly waste of an afternoon.'

'There's dancing by some girls, I want to see how good they are, and there'll be hoop-la, you'll like that, besides Mum'll like it, it will be a dress-up occasion.'

'I tell you what, let's put that down the day Dad takes me out in a boat to fish. You won't come because of being sick, and Mum won't because it bores her.'

'I hate missing an afternoon of Dad.'

'You'll hate it worse if you're sick. That year in Cornwall when we caught mackerel you went on being half the next day.'

Laurel shuddered reminiscently.

'Let's hope Kim doesn't want to come and then Mum and

I can have a lovely time.' She sighed. 'This holiday is being so super it makes me all the time on the edge of being sad.'

Tony never answered that sort of talk. He supposed Laurel had to say things like that because she was a girl. He knew, of course, exactly what she meant but such feelings were not for talking about. He turned his mind to his day's fishing. It would not be just an affair of an afternoon. There would be the hiring of the boat. He and Dad would do that the day before. There would be fishing lines to arrange about, and bait. It was going to be a gorgeous day. He spoke ecstatically.

'I should think Dad and I would get up awfully early and go right down the other end of the town to buy our bait.'

VII

'Do you think we ought to tell Laurel about her school? You heard what she said at tea.'

Lena hated talking when she was dancing. They had circled half the room before she answered.

'Not while we're here. It would be a shame to spoil her holiday.'

Alex chewed over this.

'I suppose really our kids aren't as dependent on us as we think. I mean, after they've got used to things they'll settle down anywhere.'

'It's only a temporary thing after all, and they've got us.' She looked up into his face. 'Old fusser, aren't you?'

'It's stupid how one forgets. When I was a kid, did news

come to me gradually or did I have a shock? I suppose, being a boy, I'd always known I was going away to school.'

Lena smiled.

'This is a heavenly tune, and I won't let you spoil it by worrying about something that may never happen, or if it does happen, quite likely won't upset Laurel at all. She's like me, you know, in some ways. She has to be sure she's loved; other things may look important but they aren't.'

Alex tried to keep to the subject of the children.

'Bless her heart, she can be sure of that.'

Lena spoke in a whisper.

'Girls like I was, or like Laurel, store up love just waiting to be women to pour it out on some man.' She looked at her watch. 'It's nearly midnight. Shall we go up and just peep at the children. And then bed?'

VIII

They could only look at Tuesday from the balcony, for though Nannie was snoring she would be unutterably shocked if she knew Alex had been in her room while she was in bed.

The boys had beds side by side. Kim asleep was so beautiful that Lena hugged Alex's arm.

'He ought to be painted like that, the darling.'

Her whisper, or perhaps the door opening, had stirred Tony. He half-opened his eyes. 'Dad,' he murmured happily. 'Dad,' and went to sleep again.

Laurel lay on her side, her face towards the open window. She looked, in the mixture of street lighting and moonlight, frail and defenceless. Lena gently lifted a wisp of hair away from her eyes. Alex stooped and brushed her head with his lips.

Out in the corridor Lena felt a sensation of escape. The children were enchanting but Alex was her life. She put her hand in his.

'Shall we stop being heavy parents and have a little fun?'

IX

Colonel Wiltshire sniffed the morning. He had *The Times* under his arm, and his four dogs running round him. Sims, his head-gardener, seeing him, subconsciously noted that it must be close on nine. The Colonel had finished breakfast, had taken *The Times* with him to the lavatory and was now, as was his custom no matter what the weather, having a feel of the day.

The Colonel looked across his lawn to his rose-beds. Wonderful show still. He saw that Sims had stakes and string, that would be to tie up the early autumn plants. Below where the lawn sloped out of sight the roof of his summer-house caught his eye. The thatch was almost hidden by honeysuckle. He turned back into his hall. As he passed it he unconsciously tapped the barometer. The official tapping and setting of the barometer took place at three minutes to eight on his way in to breakfast. The other taps, which took place every time he passed, were a habit arising from pleasure in his possessions. In the same way, though he had no idea of it, each time he passed them he ran his hand over the heads of the elephants holding a gong which he had brought back from India, stroked the side of the grandfather clock, and patted the Dutch chest.

Elsa Wiltshire was still sitting at the breakfast table reading her letters. She never read them until after breakfast, a legacy from her training which had taught her that to read letters at table was bad manners and a novel in the morning immoral.

'We'll have to cut that honeysuckle back this year, Elsa.'

'Nonsense, you and Sims can chop what you like about, that you plant, but any cutting that's done to my things I'll do myself.' She spoke mechanically, she was merely standing by an established custom. 'I think you'd better read Alex's letter.'

'What's the trouble?'

'Lena, she's finally refused to come here.'

'She'll have to if they start bombing London.'

'I should think that quite possibly she's brave.'

'It isn't a case of brave, my dear. If any of what they're expecting happens any woman who's not got to stay will be a nuisance. Government will probably order them out.'

'Anyway, to start with, the children are coming without her. I consider it wrong and I shall say so. If there's a risk she should be with her children, no point in their being orphans.'

The Colonel fell back on an oft-repeated statement.

'I've always liked the little thing.'

'I know you have. She's not my type but she loves Alex and up to a point she's a good mother, and I hope I've always made her feel that I welcome any girl my boy chooses. Alex is doubtful what train he'll get them on, he'll ring up when they've started.'

'That Miss Plant is coming up again this morning.'

Elsa got up. She went across to the window and looked out.

'I must keep a room for Lena. Nannie will need the nurseries, of course, then there's Miss Glover. Tony can share Laurel's room with Kim until his term begins, but I shall need a room for Laurel until her term starts.'

'Laurel can have my dressing-room.'

'I don't know how the servants are going to take it.'

'Can't be the only ones to stand out.'

'Miss Plant's so vague about what's coming. She thinks it'll be expectant mothers, that's so awkward with a house full of children.'

'We must manage, my dear.'

Elsa left the window.

'But quite likely it won't be expectant mothers. Great Pattenham expected two thousand unaccompanied children and they got three thousand mothers and babies. It's not that I want to shirk our share, but I can't bear every room to be occupied. I shall hate to think I can't put up the girls if they want to come. It seems unfair on Dot, Sylvia and Selina that we can't have their children because we've got Alex's.'

'Alex is the only one living in London. Anyhow, it's a plain duty, my dear.'

Elsa gave him an amused look.

'I could see nothing but my duty if I had none of the arranging to do. You try telling Cook that she's not only going to cook for perhaps a dozen extra people, but that some of them will be eating and living in the servants' sitting-room.'

'You'll manage, my dear. You always do.'

Elsa collected her letters.

'I will, but this is not a question for me, it's a question for the servants. If they won't cope I can't. It's a mercy they're sending Laurel away to school, it's easier with the nursery age. I rather wish they could have sent her and Tony to an hotel or something with Miss Glover until their terms start. However, we must just do the best we can.'

X

Alex had dragged himself away from his work to spend their last evening at home with the children. Already home, as the children had always known it, had become submerged. Their belongings were packed. The hall was full of trunks and suitcases. The household who were not packing were stitching at black-out curtains. There were beds in the cellar.

Kim and Tuesday were in bed. Laurel and Tony wandered up and down the house as if they only partially belonged. A couple of fidgety ghosts. They fell on their father with delirious hugs. Alex looked round the hall.

'Everything done?'

Tony nodded.

'Even labelled. Laurel and I did that.' He pointed to the hall table. 'And we've put labels on all the gas-mask boxes.'

'Where's Mum?'

'Out,' said Laurel. 'She went to get the things to keep in the cellar like it says in the A.R.P. book. She said you'd be late so she'd go to the Savoy to say good-bye to the Van Meakens. They're going back to America.'

Alex put an arm round each of them.

'Then we'll go and sit in my study.'

The black-out curtains were finished in the study. The organdie curtains had been removed and the black ones hung in their places. Alex and the children stared at them.

'Not pretty,' said Alex, 'but I suppose we'll get used to it.'

Laurel smelt the curtains.

'Come and smell, Dad. I think it's paraffin but Tony says it's bathing-suits-put-away-for-the-winter smell.'

Alex sat in an armchair.

'I can smell them from here, thank you.'

Laurel sat on one arm of his chair, Tony on the other. Tony leaned against his father.

'Dad, if the Germans don't bomb us can we come home at Christmas?'

'I'm afraid there's not a doubt they will, old man.'

Laurel giggled.

'Tony and I have been reading the A.R.P. book. I'd like to see our cellar if they use gas. Of course you'll all have gas-masks on but even then, considering cook and all the other maids will be there, I should think you'd feel a bit public doing everything in one room.'

Alex put an arm round her.

'Conditions will be slightly primitive.'

Tony hung on to his point. The excitement of the move and the general fuss had exhilarated him all day, but underneath was a wretchedness that, now bedtime was near, was rising to the surface. He could not explain how he felt so he hung his need for expression on to a recognisable grievance.

'I'll simply have to come here because of all my trains.'

Alex remembered in his childhood trying futilely to put off a long stay with relatives during some epidemic on the ground that his rabbits would die, that absolutely nobody would feed them if he didn't. He knew even as he answered that a solution of the train situation was not what Tony was asking.

'It was hardly worth adding to your luggage taking them up now that your holiday's almost over, but I think you can fix up with Gran to clear a space somewhere.'

Tony believed this to be true and grew angry as his legitimate ground for being miserable was chipped away.

'Who's going to pack all the lines and everything? Nobody can do it except me.'

Alex laid a hand on his knee.

'I'll see to it, old son. I promise every bit of packing shall be done by me, and I'll bring it all up to you myself.'

Laurel had alternated between tears and a kind of hectic pseudo-gaiety ever since the move to Gran's and Grandfather's was certain and her school-uniform purchased. She was scared. At eleven she understood what was going on around her. She had watched the hasty evacuation of other children. She had heard scraps of conversation. 'They're ready for thirty thousand casualties a night.' 'Those trenches in the Green Park are built from what they learnt in Spain, they found you get sickness and diarrhœa from fright.' 'They say they have bombs that kill everybody within twenty miles.' Strung, as always, to live at extremes, she alternated between abject terror that this departure was good-bye to both parents, and when she shied from that, took refuge in the compensating picture of herself dashing about under bomb fire rescuing wounded, finishing with a flourish by her mother saying in a voice as proud as when people admired Kim, 'Yes, we're going to keep her with us. She's more useful here than in a school.' She believed in the worst and knew herself to be imagining the best. As a shield she made loud fun of all war precautions. Behind her immediate dreads there lurked the dread of school. That would come to the top nearer the beginning of term. It didn't matter being the plain one at home, people were used to it. If only she had managed to be super at something, then she could have gone into the Abbey School carrying her ability like a screen. No one would say, 'Who's that plain girl?' Everyone would say, 'That's Laurel Wiltshire who dives,' or dances, or nurses, or whatever it was, 'better than anybody else,' and never think of her as a person at all.

Alex hardly knew what he wanted of this evening. If only he had the words he might have found something useful to say, but he was hating everything too much. This home, which Lena's gift for home-making had moulded into such a perfect place for the children, to be broken up. There were plenty of people to say the war wouldn't last long. That Germany had gone hungry to make guns and wouldn't have her heart in the business. That only a proportion of the people were behind Adolf Hitler. He had been frequently to Germany on business of recent years and had no illusions. He had not, of course, said so to Lena but across his board table he had prophesied a long hard war full of horrors as yet unimagined.

It seemed unsatisfactory, believing these things, to have nothing memorable to say to your children whom you would possibly not see again, but there it was. His mind could only run to palliatives.

'I expect Grandfather and Gran are planning no end of a good time for you all. I've asked Gran to see that you two get all the riding you can before term starts.'

Tony discovered something else on which to hang his wretchedness. He drummed his heels on the chair.

'I expect I won't have anything in my box for school. Mum and Cook packed it last time and they won't be there.'

'Rubbish, old man, it wouldn't surprise me if at this very moment Gran and her Cook were talking about your tuck box.'

'Even if they are it won't be the same as here. Mum and I went to Fortnum's before last term and chose things.'

Tony's voice had wobbled. Alex knew that whether he felt like it or not he must find something to say that would help.

'I know it's tough for you two, but getting on with it all without a fuss is the bit of service everybody can give. We don't want a war. The way we, as a family, feel now is how we feel as a nation. You two want life exactly as it is.'

'Without us going to school,' Tony put in.

Alex gave the child's knees an affectionate pat.

'War or no war you'd go to school. But you want the house and all of us and everything in it just as it was, we'll say, a week or two ago.'

Laurel had a lump in her throat, she spoke with difficulty.

'It was simply perfect.'

Alex tightened the arm round her shoulders.

'And that's being said in hundreds and thousands of homes. I'm not going to point out that other people's break-ups are worse. You know for yourselves that you going to your grandparents is a different cup of tea to young Tom and Mary Smith evacuated with labels round their necks to strangers. I've explained to you before about Poland and national honour, I'm not bothering with that now. Instead, I want you to see yourselves as part of the nation. Everybody's on the move and practically nobody wants to be. Sailors are joining ships. Soldiers their regiments. For a year now people have trained for wardens and so on and they're standing by to go on duty. And children are being sent away from danger. What's making all this possible without much excitement? Because nearly everybody, including the children, are doing what they have to do without fuss. People of other countries find us a bit difficult to understand just because we hate fuss, but in a time like this you can see for yourselves how useful it is. Tomorrow when you go off there'll be no more fuss than when you went to Eastbourne in June. You may want to say or do a bit more but you won't because by keeping quiet you'll be helping things along.'

The lump in Laurel's throat disappeared. She saw herself standing quietly in the hall, probably holding Kim's hand, while Dad and everybody got the luggage on to the car. She liked the words 'part of the nation'. She could see herself being so splendid tomorrow that when the train went out Dad and Mum said to each other they didn't know what they would have done if she hadn't been there.

Tony felt as if he were bursting. His love for his father, completely wordless, seemed to have swollen in his inside. Dad was grand. No flapping about but making things clear.

Alex hoped what he had said had struck the right note, any way it was enough and better not be meddled with. He took out his note case.

'And now we come to the burning question. How much pocket money do evacuated offspring want?'

XI

Alex heard Lena's key in the front door. He went out to meet her. She looked lovely but tired. The door was open and Greville, the chauffeur, was carrying in armloads of parcels and piling them on the hall table. Lena spoke with an edge of excitement to her voice.

'Food. Everybody says that things will get scarce at once, so I've got three months' supply.'

Alex looked at the ever-growing heap.

'Looks more like a year.'

'Some of it's candles and things of that sort. People say that one of the first things that will happen when the bombing starts is that the lights will all fail.'

Alex looked at Greville's face. He too had a home but not the money to lay in stores for a siege. What did he think of all these preparations?

'Did your children get off today?'

Greville was stacking the parcels.

'Yes, sir. Wales it was thought.'

Alex touched the parcels.

'You'll know where to come if you run short.'

Greville grinned at him and Alex was warmed by the knowledge that Greville knew that all this ostentatious buying was not money but Lena's way of planning for her husband. That probably Greville, in a lesser way, was seeing the same thing at home. That every penny Mrs. Greville could lay hands on was going on what in Mrs. Greville's opinion would keep Greville in health. Greville added to this mental picture.

'I was glad that the kids were safely off, for, as I said to Mrs. Greville, if you had to store stuff for them as well as us I wouldn't get in at the door.' He turned to Lena. 'Under the stairs is what Mrs. Greville's heard's safe.'

Lena was rummaging amongst the parcels.

'People had told me that.'

Alex smiled at her tense, concentrated back view.

'People haven't half been telling you a lot.' He went with Greville to the door. 'The children's train leaves at 10.15. I thought we ought to leave here about 8.30.'

'Better make it eight, sir. You never saw anything like the station when the kids went off. It's not only the children, it's troops and all that.'

Alex closed the front door. He stood by Lena. He wanted an opening to tell her tactfully that the children had only a light control of their emotions and that casualness rather than extra affection was needed on this final goodnight round. He edged to his subject.

'I'll help move all that stuff when we've tucked up the children.'

Lena went on rummaging amongst her parcels.

'You can laugh as much as you like, but I'm not going to see you starve.' She found what she was searching for. 'Oh, here they are. Elva plums, the children love them. I thought two or three at bedtime as a treat would be nice.'

As he followed her up the stairs Alex felt humble. Here was he thinking that Lena would need his advice, and yet Lena, without being in the house or seeing the children's mood, had sensed just how they would feel and had picked on probably an excellent palliative.

They met Nannie at the top of the nursery stairs.

'Tuesday's awake. She's woke up crying and now she's brought up her tea.'

'Poor lamb,' said Lena. 'I suppose it's excitement, but she'll love staying with the grandparents.'

Nannie opened the night nursery door.

'Like animals, little children. Get in a tear when the boxes are brought down.'

Tuesday lay on her back looking very small and pale. She was gripping with unnatural ferocity her Teddy-bear. Her mouth was under the sheet. Her eyes, peering at her parents, had a puzzled, scared look.

Lena stroked her hair.

'I'm sorry you've been sick, pet.'

Alex tried to think of something to get the child to relax.

'Do you remember that puppy that Sims had last time you stayed at Gran's?'

Tuesday shook her head.

'Yes. A sort of fox-terrier. You wanted to bring him home.'

Tuesday's hold on her Teddy-bear lessened.

'Pincher.'

'What a good memory! Well, if you ask Nannie, I think she'll let Pincher go for walks with you.'

'Can he come on my bed?'

Nannie was in the doorway.

'That depends on what Mr. Sims and your Gran say, but if they've no objection I shan't have. Now kiss your Mum and Dad and then drink down this nice stuff Nannie's mixed for you and we'll all be Sir Garnet Wolsey in the morning.'

Tony was awake and sitting up in bed looking clean and unnaturally angelic. Kim was asleep. Lena opened the box of plums.

'You can have two, darling. I'll put one by Kim for the morning.'

Tony took his plums. He seemed suddenly unaware that this evening was any different from other evenings. He was so cool, almost off-hand, that Lena and Alex felt snubbed.

'Good-night, my darling,' Lena said giving him a kiss. Tony raised his face submissively.

'Kim won't know I ate two plums tonight so couldn't I have one for the morning too?'

Alex put a plum on the table by Tony's bed.

'You greedy little beast. Good-night, son.'

Once more Tony raised an obedient cheek.

'Good-night, Dad.'

Lena and Alex paused by Kim's bed, not so much to look at Kim as to give Tony a chance to say more. Tony spat out a stone.

'I shall put the stones on this envelope.'

'Good-night, darling,' Lena repeated.

Tony apparently did not hear her, he was busy with his second plum.

Laurel had been crying. Her cheeks had a stiff shiny look. Alex's heart was wrung. He wanted to sit down by her and tell her how gloomy the house would be without her. That of all his children she had more tentacles round his heart. That he detested packing her off to a boarding school. That every night he would look for her funny plain little face and brisk plaits and would mind afresh because they were not there. But he had never spoken to her like that and tonight, poor scrap, was not the night to start. One wrong word might start her crying again.

'Look what Mum's brought you.'

Laurel took the box and pretended that which plums were hers was a matter for careful choice.

'Where did you buy them, Mum?'

'Fortnum's.'

'What else did you buy there?'

'Just useful things, biscuits and sardines and things like that.'

'Where else did you go? You shopped all the afternoon.'

Alex thought of the early start. He gave one of her pigtails an affectionate pull.

'It's time you were asleep, old lady.'

Laurel gazed fixedly at the plums. Then hurriedly put one in her mouth and another one on the table beside her. Lena stooped to kiss her. Laurel, awkwardly, almost angrily, jerked her cheek up towards her mother's mouth. Always Laurel was demonstrative, it was natural to her to throw her arms round her parents' necks, but now she was markedly unresponsive. Alex guessed she was afraid to speak. He gave her a quick hug.

Nannie came in to the boys' room to draw the curtains. Tony was still chewing.

'How much is the railway fare from London to Gran's and Grandfather's?'

'Not so much for you because you're a half ticket.'

'But how much?'

'If I remember rightly, the full ticket's something like one pound four shillings return.'

'Is my school farther than Gran's and Grandfather's?'

'What a Mister Want to Know! It is a bit but not much.'

'Not more than a pound single ticket?'

'Not as much. Now go to sleep and forget about tickets.'

When the door closed behind her Tony felt under his pillow for his new and most cherished possession, a torch. He turned it on and got out of bed. On a shelf there were the things that were not going with them, and among these was a birthday present of Kim's, some fancy note-paper and envelopes. Tony took an envelope and carried it to the dressing table, where he had put the two pound notes his father had given him as pocket money, one of the notes he folded and placed it in the envelope. He turned his torch so that he could see to write and printed on the envelope, 'Fare home not to be used for anything else urgent important.' He got back into bed and put the envelope under his pillow.

He was just dropping asleep when the door opened. He sat up.

'Who's that?'

Laurel closed the door softly.

'It's me. I've brought you an Elva plum.'

'I've had two and I've got one for the morning.'

'Well, you can eat another, can't you?'

Tony took the plum.

'Why don't you eat it?'

'I did try and eat one but something's gone wrong with my swallow so I had to spit it out.'

'What an awful waste!'

Laurel drew back the curtains.

'Yes. I came to show you the searchlights. They're catching an aeroplane. I thought we'd see better up here.'

Tony was out of bed and on the window seat peering through the bars. Laurel knelt beside him. A plane was darting to and fro like a moth in a room full of lights. The searchlights, as if they were human, tried to catch it. The children gaped, both taking sides with the plane.

'He's got away all right.'

'They've got him again but I bet he gets away.'

Suddenly the entertainment was over. The searchlights vanished, the plane roared out of hearing. Laurel yawned and went back to her room. Tony got into his bed and, with his fingers touching his envelope, fell asleep.

XII

It was a relief when the train started. Breakfast at seven o'clock had been served for them all in the dining-room. Alex had determined to be down first. He was there calmly putting bacon and scrambled eggs on to plates when Tony came in, and just looked up and said 'good morning, old man'. Tony had come down crushed with wordless misery, hoping he would not cry, patting at intervals the envelope in his breast pocket. He did not exactly picture himself using the money but it was good to feel it; if he simply had to see Dad he had the way to do it. Alex's calm greeting made him feel better. Dad wasn't fussing, and he would if he thought their not coming home was going on for long.

Laurel had obviously been crying; that was over now and she had made a pact with God to prevent a recurrence. 'Oh God, if you help me not to cry, at least until I'm in bed to-night, I swear I'll listen to every word of every sermon I hear for the rest of my life.' Fortified with this support she made quite a jaunty entrance into the dining-room, then, as she sat down, began to wonder if all her vowing had been necessary, now that she was with Dad it seemed such a much more ordinary day.

Ruth, when she came in, was thankful and surprised to see both children eating a good breakfast. Alex was telling them a piece of news he had kept for this moment. Through the headmaster of Tony's school they had learnt of the school for Laurel. It was sufficiently near for the children to meet occasionally, and when he or their mother came to see them they could have both of them out at the same time. Tony, in the superiority of a partly completed first term, told Laurel that if she was coming to his school she'd got to posh up. Laurel retaliated. There was for a few minutes almost gaiety in the dining-room. It was then that Kim screamed.

The charlady was cleaning the stairs as Nannie brought Kim and Tuesday down for their breakfast. Kim, who was excited, stopped to speak.

'Did you know we were going to live with Gran and Grandfather?'

The charlady answered him, and then shook her head at Nannie, her eyes full of tears, and murmured:

'Poor little innocent!'

Kim was exalted. Tears for him! Head shakings for him! He had no idea what it was all about, he had heard there was going to be a war, though it meant nothing to him, but all his senses told him this was a prime moment to be the centre of the picture. He ran ahead of Nannie and threw himself across one of the boxes in the hall, screaming: 'I don't want to go away. I want to stay here with Mum and Dad.'

The result of this display was beyond anything Kim had ever known. The charlady knelt beside him calling him 'love' and saying it was a shame. The servants ran from the kitchen and patted and cooed and told him to be a brave little boy, and they too said it was a shame. Lena rushed down the stairs and held him in her arms, whispering, 'Hush, darling. Hush.' Alex leapt out of the dining-room muttering 'Oh, my God!' but when he reached Kim, anxious for the sake of the others and because Kim, crying or not, had to be got on to the train, he said placatingly: 'Shut up, old man. You come and see what there is for breakfast.'

In the dining-room Tony and Laurel looked at each other.

'Now he'll scream all the way to Paddington,' said Laurel.

Tony finished his scrambled egg.

'If nobody had listened or run he'd have stopped by now.'

Ruth went to the door with a dim idea of getting Alex back and giving Kim the tip that his screams were impressing nobody, but one glance at the scene showed her that this was far from true.

Nannie, as if nothing was happening, brought Tuesday to the table and tied on her feeder and put her breakfast in front of her. She spoke with a note of command that she seldom needed to use.

'And not one bit to be left, and then there's a stick of barley sugar to suck in the car.'

'Can't you stop Kim making that noise, Nannie?' Tony asked.

Nannie sipped her tea.

'Miss Glover and I have other things to do, dear, than be troubled with acting-up.'

Kim, having got his audience, held it. Unmoved by the scorn in Laurel's and Tony's eyes he allowed himself to be fed sitting on Lena's knee. When it was time to leave the house his howls were so appalling that Alex carried him into the car. But it was at the station that the morning blossomed in its full glory for him. There was so much noise, so many processions of singing labelled children, that Kim's senses warned him further screaming would not be effective. He had, moreover, long ago begun to believe in his own tears. He looked white and exhausted. Alex and Greville piled up the luggage and sat Kim on it. Kim at no time escaped stares, but pale, with tears on his cheeks, he was incredibly arresting. In no time the camera men, looking for evacuation pictures, had found him. Under various captions he wrung the hearts of half the nation the next morning. Kim, surrounded by kind men, felt better. He managed a watery smile. When the train came in he gave his best and, as it happened, his only useful performance. He screamed and struggled in Alex's arms.

'I don't want to go away. I want to stay with you, Dad.'

People gulped and made way and so it was that Nannie, with Tuesday on her knee, got one corner seat, with Tony in the corner facing her and Laurel next to him. Kim, still howling, was wedged between Nannie and Ruth. There was no opportunity for good-byes. With a quick wave Lena and Alex were gone.

Nannie had the ability to make any place, even the end of a crowded railway carriage, her own. She laid a newspaper on Tony's and Laurel's knees, and as if this was now her nursery table, spread out some brown bread and butter and bars of chocolate, a form of food she called 'Kings and Queens'.

'You take yours, Laurel, the eldest sets the example. Don't want any nonsense about not being hungry. Now you, Tony.' She took Tuesday's and folded the bread and butter for her. Kim, who was hungry, stretched out his hand. Nannie stopped him. 'One minute, Mr. Snatch, are you going to behave yourself or else, before the train starts, I'll ask Miss Glover to be so good as to step up to the Guard and ask if you can travel in the van along with the dogs? We've had enough noise all of us for one day.'

Kim looked round the carriage. It was packed, people standing, everybody too thankful to have wedged their way in at all to have time to think of crying children. He knew Laurel and Tony were angry with him, he glanced furtively at Ruth, but though she knew of the black mood which would engulf him as a result of the morning's excitement, she had not sufficient energy at the moment to struggle for him. He turned back to Nannie.

'I'll be quiet now.'

XIII

At the other end of the train Albert and Ernie Parker were travelling. They were part of a carriage full of noisy children being evacuated from South London. Albert and Ernie were noisy too, for being noisy was an antidote for fear. They had never been away from their parents for a night. It was their father who had said they must go. Their mother had been against it. She accepted that there might be bombs and gas, she did not know those dangers, but she did know the dangers which she had fought against since the boys were born. Picking up nasty ways from other children not brought up as carefully as she tried to bring up her own. Catching things in their hair from children whose mothers were not so regular in having a look with a comb as she was. Above all she dreaded home-sickness. She had heard of a child who had been taken to a hospital to have its tonsils out, and, because it was separated from its mother, had died there of a broken heart. Her husband had laughed when she had told him this story, but she could not get it out of her head. Like the majority of girls brought up as she had been she spoilt her children. In Albert and Ernie's case the spoiling was continuous, not varied by slaps and scoldings, as was usual in their neighbourhood. She believed beyond reasoning that everything should be sacrificed to give her kids what they wanted. Albert and Ernie had seen their mother cry as she packed their things. 'There,' she said with ferocity, 'nobody can say your things weren't nice.' 'If any one says you came with anything dirty you tell them to write to me. I'll tell them it's a lie.' 'Your Dad has signed to say you can go to the dentist and that, if they want to take you, but you stand up for yourselves. You tell them your Mum says to pull out your teeth, but no stoppings as you can't take the pain.' Albert and Ernie could not imagine a world that had not got Mum to run to, and Dad, in the background, to fight the family battles. They knew only their flat in an L.C.C. block and rooms at Margate, where they had stayed as a family for a week each summer. They had heard the expression 'bein' 'vacuated' bandied about for days. But what was it? What was this world into which this train was whirling them, which Mum expected to be full of women who would be rude about their posh new clothes and toothbrushes, and who would want to have all their teeth stopped? But neither Albert nor Ernie showed their fear. Their mother's spoiling had not been a shield from the tough world made up of the other children of their housing block and the surrounding streets. You had to hold your own there or be branded as a whiner and a tale-bearer. It was true Dad was around to knock down a neighbour or, if it came to that, a schoolmaster if they raised a hand to his kids; but there were lots of knocks it was better to take without telling Dad about them. No good being known as a sissy. Besides, though Dad might be prepared to have a hell of a row because someone had sloshed you, he could equally slosh you himself if he thought whoever had done the sloshing was right in thinking you needed sloshing, though not right in thinking they could do it to someone else's kid.

The train roared and clanged. The carriage full of children grew sillier and sillier and screamed their sillinesses above the noise of the train. Albert and Ernie screamed as loud as the rest. Noise and throwing things about, that was the stuff, that was the way to kill fear.

One of the children started to sing. Soon the whole carriage was howling, 'Daisy, Daisy, give me your answer do.'

XIV

The children reached their grandparents' front door to find another car was before them. In the hall a woman driver was delivering Albert and Ernie. Miss Plant, she told Elsa, had especially selected these two nice clean-looking children. In her mind's eye she could see Miss Plant in the station yard surrounded by several hundred more children. She could not wait so she gave Albert and Ernie a gentle push towards Elsa and hurried out of the front door, colliding with Ruth and Tony who were coming up the front steps.

Laurel had held all day to her father's words. Everybody was having to move. Nobody, except Kim, was making a fuss. She had tried to be an example of helpfulness on the journey, but there had been no opportunity. Nannie and Ruth had done everything that wanted doing, like passing round food, and books to read, and keeping Kim quiet. It had been a let down really. She had meant to be splendid, and not being allowed to be had rubbed her up the wrong way. She was not cross exactly, just that sort of miserable that wants to kick something. But now they had arrived. In the hall would be Gran and Grandfather, waiting as they always did when they came to stay. After kissing they would look at them to see how they had grown, and then Gran would tell them the lovely things she had planned that they should do. Grandfather would not say much but he would look pleased and smiling, and he would go off with the dogs and he liked it if you came too. But the most unchanged thing would be her bedroom. She loved it almost as much as her room at home. She had slept in it since she had been six. The first time she had slept alone was in that room and when Gran came in to say good-night she had asked if she would rather sleep in the nursery. But she had felt grand and said 'no' and could it be her own room for always. Gran had said yes, other people would sleep in it when she was not there but it should always be known as 'Laurel's room'. It was a beautiful room, she thought. Gran's was the only house she knew where there were wall papers. The one in her room, roses against silver-grey stripes, she considered perfect. She liked too the pictures. Landscapes painted in water-colour by forgotten friends, framed in gold with gold surrounds. There was something fascinating too about the heavy mahogany furniture. Laurel often lay in bed and worked out schemes by which it had been brought in. Her favourite put it in place before the ceiling or roof had been built. Sitting in the train, weighed down by flat greyish gloom, her room had been a shaft of light. However awful the day, presently she would be in her room, and her door would be shut, and then, if she wanted to, she could cry as much as she liked. Crying in your bedroom with your doors shut was not what Dad meant by 'fuss'.

Everything in the hall looked exactly as usual except that there were two little boys with labels round their necks standing beside Grandfather and Gran. Laurel gave her grandparents a cheerful smile, even seeing them made her feel better. It was then things began to go wrong. Gran, instead of hugging her, gave her a quick nod and spoke over her head to Nannie.

'The nurseries are ready.'

Nannie looked round the hall. There was no more surprise in her face than there is on a hen's who has been presented as nurselings with chicks which are none of hers. Nannie's reaction was identical with the hen's. Here were chicks and here was she, the where and why-fors could be left to wiser heads. In that second she added Albert and Ernie to her family.

'I've put Kim in the double spare room for the moment,' Elsa went on. 'Until he goes to school Tony can share it. You've the little single blue room as usual, Miss Glover.'

Grandfather felt too much attention was being paid to his grandchildren and insufficient to Albert and Ernie.

'And where are these young men sleeping?'

'Laurel's room.' Elsa turned back to Nannie. 'I've put a second bed in there. Laurel dear, you're in Grandfather's dressing-room, it's rather a makeshift, but you won't be here for long.'

Everything had been planned. The servants placated. Things had turned out far better than they might have done. It had been a great relief to see Albert and Ernie, who seemed quiet little boys. So much easier to have children than expectant mothers. Elsa would be seventy in two years time. She loved her grandchildren, but as visitors. She had brought up five children of her own and had no wish to reopen her nurseries and schoolrooms again as a permanent thing. She loved her home and the routine of her life and flinched from change and upset. She was fond of her servants and they were fond of her. She disliked the alteration in her relationship with them which had been forced on her. Her voice saying, 'I know you'll manage splendidly. You always do,' and the doubtful, 'We must do our best, 'm.' It was so false. Elderly servants used to looking after two elderly people, with only short visits from the grandchildren, could not be expected to be enthusiastic at the arrival of a governess, nurse and four children as permanent residents, and two more who would be with them all the school holidays. Elsa was courageous, nothing showed on her face but serenity and cheerfulness. She was not insensitive as a rule. It was extraordinary for her to give away Laurel's room as if it were a matter of no moment. The truth was that, busy organising, she did not consider the children's angle except to suppose they were, as usual, happy.

They always had enjoyed coming to stay and Laurel was old enough to realise what was going on and was sure to be splendid and helpful, dear child.

Ruth could remember embittered moments in her childhood when she had been forgotten and pushed on one side. 'Oh, we needn't count Ruth, she'll be packing, her term starts the next day.' She moved towards Laurel. Nannie, her foot on the stairs, turned.

'Perhaps you'd take the two little boys up and unpack for them, Miss Glover.' She looked enquiringly at Albert. 'What are your names, dears?'

Albert, from fright, had lost his voice. Tony looked first at his label and then at Ernie's.

'This is Albert Parker and this one is Ernest Parker.'

Nannie nodded.

'Albert and Ernest. Well, Miss Glover, if you'd see to them and then bring them up.' She glanced at Elsa. 'Where'll we be having our dinner, 'm?'

Elsa had not dared to hope that Nannie would immediately adopt Albert and Ernie. She was sure, knowing her, that she would help, but she might think having them to nursery meals going rather far. She had visualised that they would have at any rate their first meals in the servants' hall, which might be disastrous. She smiled gratefully at Nannie.

'In the nursery. Laurel and Tony will lunch in the dining-room.'

As she took hold of Albert and Ernie's hands Ruth tried to catch Laurel's eye, but Laurel was staring at the floor.

Tony and Kim raced up to their room. Tony had been

immensely cheered at the sight of Albert. Someone to play with! He would show him all the special things in the grounds after lunch. Because he felt better he butted Kim in the small of the back.

It was Laurel's first experience of bitterness. She had never known people could be cruel. Her bedroom given away! Poked into grandfather's dressing-room! Gran had not said it but what she had meant was anything will do for Laurel. It was agony. She sat on the edge of the little bed in the dressing-room rocking to and fro, her arms folded as if to protect her heart.

XV

The car was full, the luggage was strapped on the back. There were hugs and kisses and last minute tips. Nannie and Ruth sat in the corners with Tuesday and Kim between them. Laurel and Ernie had the little seats, Tony and Albert were in front with Williams, the chauffeur. The picnic lunch had been Ruth's idea. Laurel and Tony had not to be at the junction to meet the school train until three. A picnic lunch would be a nice send-off, and as well a relief to the household to have them out of the way for a day; but it had been a mistake. Laurel, who had looked wretched enough before, poor child, had become infinitely worse. It hurt Ruth to look at her. She was never pretty but since they had arrived she had gone about with a perpetual scowl and the corners of her mouth turned down. Ruth had tried to talk to her but Laurel, usually so affectionate and forthcoming, was in a black-dog mood and refused to come out of it. There were good moments, of course, when she laughed and was her usual self, but they were ephemeral; in a second some unskilfully worded remark, even a misunderstood glance, and her animation died and she sank back amongst her scowls. Her grandparents had noticed, of course, and had supposed the child was worried about being sent to school. At every meal her Grandmother told her stories of her aunts at school. 'Your Aunt Dot said . . .' 'Your naughty Aunt Lindsey!' 'I can see your Aunt Sylvia as if it were yesterday. . . .' 'Your Aunt Selina, funny little thing. . . .' Often the stories beguiled Laurel for the time being, but Ruth knew that, though she dreaded her school, it was not the bottom of her trouble.

Nannie kept an eye on the back of Tony and Albert. The two had become enormous friends but had an exciting effect on each other. 'I'll give you such a slosh' had become Tony's favourite expression, and unless prevented he carried out the threat. Nannie expected boys to be rough but objected when they were rough at the wrong times, and in a car was a wrong time. On the whole she approved of Albert and Ernie. They had what she called 'common voices', but that was only to be expected. They had not so much bad table manners, as different, but she was putting those right. In being good to those younger than themselves she had never in her long experience met their equals. Tuesday was unused to it. She was the only really nursery one left and was more or less ignored by the others. But not by Albert and Ernie. At their very first meal in the house Tuesday had asked for Pincher. Could Pincher come up? Could Pincher sleep on her bed? Nannie had been vague. 'I dare say, dear. We'll see, dear.' Albert had been so shocked that his voice, up till then a whisper, had come back. "Oo's Pincher?' Kim had told him. "Oo's Sims?' Albert had wanted, and indeed expected, to take Tuesday into the garden with him after lunch, but when she was not allowed to come he found Sims on his own. 'Give us a loan of Pincher.' Sims considered Albert. 'You'll be one of our 'vacuees.' 'Give us a loan of Pincher,' Albert had repeated and then had explained, 'It's for the little 'un.' He had brought Pincher up to the nursery and, mainly through his efforts, Pincher spent most of his days with Tuesday. It was the same about everything where Tuesday was concerned. Offered sweets, Albert, Ernie, or both, immediately asked if there were any for Tuesday, and at intervals all day they were up in arms before they were convinced that she was not in some way being neglected or slighted. Not that either of them cared especially for Tuesday, but she was the youngest, the little one and the whole of their upbringing had taught them to put the welfare and happiness of small children before everything. Apart from this chivalry to Tuesday, Albert and Ernie had the natural entrée to Nannie's heart. They were in her eyes thin and peaky and they were homesick. For some nights Nannie had sat with them until their sobs died down and they fell asleep. Then, as the first pangs of homesickness evaporated, she taught them not to be afraid of the silent corridor and the big house. She gave them a night light and left the door open so that the gleam from the passage light came in. It was Nannie who saw Elsa about the school situation.

"Tisn't right nor what any child would think fair to send

them to the village school while Tony and Kim are still having their holiday.'

'But it's the law,' Elsa objected. 'They're of school age and ought to go. I'll have Miss Plant after me.'

'Another fortnight running round will set them up for the winter. Ernie's still too pale for my liking and Albert's bowels are stubborn.'

Nannie, watching Tony's and Albert's backs to see there was not a scrimmage, felt placidly pleased. Tony had enjoyed his time with his grandparents, bless him. It was wonderful really for he was such a father's boy.

'I hope his father gets to see him for his birthday,' she said to Ruth.

Ruth pulled her mind from Laurel.

'November.' She smiled at Laurel. 'Both their father and their mother will have been down to see them before that.'

Albert and Tony were not fooling but having a quite serious conversation.

'We didn't ought to 'ave been sent,' Albert explained.

'If your father, who's a warden, says you can come back at Christmas I should jolly well think we could too. I shall write and tell Dad your father says it's safe.'

Williams had Albert next to him.

'Your father better leave you where you are. The war hasn't started, not properly. You can't tell what's coming.'

'But his father's a warden.' Tony's words fell over each other. 'He ought to know if anybody does.'

Albert felt in his pocket and produced a crumpled post card from his mother. He read it out loud.

'Your Dad says he should not wonder if there was not no bombs after all and you can be home Christmas. . . .'

Williams was unmoved.

'We'll see. Anyway you and young Ernie are looking a sight better since you came here. I shouldn't think you'd want to be in a hurry to go back.'

Albert did not answer Williams, his face was blank but behind it his being was in revolt. It was all right here, but it was not home. He wanted his Mum and the small flat, and the smell of the food cooking. The clatter of feet on the stone steps of 'The Buildings'. He wanted the black and white of London, the screaming noisy games in the sunlight, and the whisperings and half understood goings on in the shadows. He wanted cinemas, and the doors of stores standing wide so that wireless sets could shriek into the streets. He wanted excitement of living huddled against your neighbours. To hear the groans, to watch somebody running for the doctor. To see the blinds down in his home for a dead baby whom nobody knew. To have the right to be pushed forward to peer at the coffin. There was an edge and a smell to life at home. There were scenes and makings-up and danger round the corner. Here there was nothing, the meals were dull and there was a sameness about life. He and Tony had managed a bit of fun but Tony was going. He would have to stick it out a bit longer but they would be home for Christmas. Trust Mum for that.

They found a little wood in which to eat their lunch. It was not by design that Ruth was alone with Laurel. They had gone to the brook to wash. Laurel, in her green tunic and crested cardigan, looked unlike herself. She made Ruth's heart ache and gave her courage to say what in recent days she had not risked in case Laurel snubbed her, and the bloom was brushed from their friendship.

'Oh, Laurel, my pet, I am going to miss you.'

Laurel looked up from the water. There was a moment when it seemed that a snub was on her lips. Then she was up, her arms round Ruth's neck, sobbing.

'It was always my bedroom – even Tony never speaks to me, he's always playing with Albert and Ernie – Gran's glad I'm going to school, she doesn't pretend she isn't – everybody's glad I'm being sent away – Dad promised we'd have a lot of riding, we haven't ridden once – it's extra awful me going to school, I'm ugly and I'm not good at anything – '

Ruth surreptitiously looked at her watch. It would do the child good to say all that was in her mind, but she could not plant her in a railway carriage filled with strange girls with her face swollen from crying. She gave Laurel a kiss.

'Mop your face. I can't hand you over to your housemistress, or whoever it is, looking as if you'd got mumps.' She waited a moment while Laurel struggled for self-control. 'I'm sorry about the bedroom, but where else were Albert and Ernie to be put?'

'I know that and it makes it worse because there's no one to be angry with.'

Ruth laughed though she did not entirely agree. Elsa had been rushed but she had not shown tact in handling a child that she should have guessed was already upset.

'You know why you didn't ride.'

'Yes. I quite see what Grandfather means about us not doing things Albert and Ernie can't do. But the other part of me sees Tony and me having our holidays spoilt because of Albert and Ernie.'

'Tony's holidays haven't been spoilt, and you don't really mind his making friends with Albert, and you're not plain, and though I know you want to be champion class at something, you're a nice average all-rounder.'

'Not really. Everybody at dancing was better than me but three. Everybody at gym except the people who don't like gym. I'm nearly always beaten at games. I haven't ever won a swimming cup, and you've often said there were days when I seem to go backwards at lessons. And it's no good saying I'm not the plainest in the family, I can see my own face in my looking-glass.'

Ruth took out her comb and tidied Laurel's hair.

'It's a terrible picture. From the sound of it the Abbey School won't keep you.' She took the child's chin and turned her face towards her. 'You know you're talking nonsense.'

There was a moment's pause. Laurel gulped, her voice was a whisper.

'Nearly everybody is glad the holidays are over and I'm going to a boarding school.'

It was true. The house was overcrowded. They were all waiting for Laurel and Tony to leave to get in a routine. Albert and Ernie would go to school. She could get on with Kim's lessons. Kim was to move into his grandfather's dressing-room. One less bedroom and two less beds for the housemaid. Cook's burden would be eased. The dining-room menus could be thought out without considering favourite dishes or what children ought to eat. There would be no light supper meal at seven for Laurel. There had been, especially during the last few days, an attempt to devise treats, even now probably the grandparents were enjoying their after lunch coffee the better because they had only themselves and their pleasure and comfort to consider, and had not to be wondering what was making Laurel so awkward. Ruth would not insult Laurel by lying.

'There's something in what you say, but you put yourself in your Gran and Grandfather's places. Having people to stay and having people to live are two different things, they like their own ways and with Albert and Ernie we are rather a house full, but it will be all right when you come back at Christmas. We'll have shaken down and we'll be counting the days until you come back, just as we would if you were living at home.'

Laurel got up.

'Dust me. I mustn't arrive in a uniform all over grass.' She waited while Ruth gave her skirt a brush. Then she hugged her. 'Anyway you'll always be you, and I find that a great consolation.'

Ruth's heart ached. She gave Laurel an affectionate shake.

'Consolation indeed! I don't mind telling you I'm not glad your term's started. I shall miss you abominably.'

XVI

Lena, Alex, Laurel and Tony sat on a sofa in the hotel lounge. It was a raw day, not nice enough for a walk. Throughout the lounge other parents and children were huddled. The feeling of being overlooked by their fellow school-mates made the children self-conscious, they spoke in monosyllables or in forced unnatural voices. Alex and Lena started hares of conversation. Laurel and Tony sniffed at their scent and then let them go. Tony wanted to hear about his trains but not here, trains were home things. Laurel wanted to know about friends who had gone to classes with her in London, but not when other girls were about with flapping ears. It was only an hour and a half since they had been collected from their respective schools, and though they had barely swallowed their lunch the time was dragging so it felt like tea-time. Even their pride in Lena had died down. It had been grand seeing everybody look at her at lunch, but of course people had got used to her.

Alex could bear it no longer. He knew Lena would not come out but he had come to see how his children were getting along and he meant to do it.

'That roast beef is sitting a bit heavy. How about yours, Laurel? Shall we take a quick walk?' He saw Tony was about to jump up. 'Then I shall drag you out, old man. Half an hour's walk for each of you to give you an appetite for tea.'

Outside there was a blustering wind with a spit of rain in it, but Laurel's heart soared. Alex tucked her hand into his arm.

'Well. How d'you like it?'

Laurel rubbed her face against his sleeve.

'Actually, though I never thought I would, I rather do. There are such a lot of us and being all dressed alike I find very consoling.'

Alex looked at her green overcoat and beret with its badge and made a face.

'I liked you better in your own things. What's that head-mistress of yours like?'

Laurel was shocked at the casual way in which he spoke.

'Miss Brownlow. I don't know. Though, as a matter of fact, she startled me this morning by knowing who I was. I was waiting for you in the hall and she said, "Good-morning, Laurel." I nearly dropped dead I was so surprised.'

'I should hope she did know you, I've entrusted a valued daughter to her.'

'But there are more than two hundred of us and I'm new. She saw me my first day. She was pretty super.'

'What about?'

'She asked me why I was called Laurel when my name was Ann, so I explained about you liking plain names and us all being christened them, and Mum liking queer names, so us all being called by them. She said would I like to be called Ann at school.'

'Would you?'

'I don't think I'd ever answer to it and that would be simply awful. You have to be frightfully quick answering when your name's called or you get a bad mark for inattention, and ten bad marks in any week and you get an order mark. Order marks are given out after evening prayers on Sundays and Miss Brownlow calls the girls up who've got them. Imagine, with all the school looking! I should die of shame.'

'Have you had many bad marks?'

'Oh no, none and I hope I never will. If you answer quickly and learn what all the bells mean I don't think you ever need. Because you don't get them for not being bright. You're only supposed to do work that you can do. I'm just right. Not the oldest and not the youngest, just in the middle, and I'm about all right at my lessons. My form mistress said I'd been well grounded. I wrote and told the Foxglove. I bet she's bucked.'

'What about this champion business? What's the aim at the moment?'

Laurel hugged his arm.

'Don't tease. That's all finished. It's awful to be especially good at something in a school. People point you out. It's the other way round to being at home. At home if you were super at something it was a sort of cover; you were sort of marked, and at other things it didn't matter your being a mutt because people said it wasn't your subject. At school nobody notices you if you're just average and I think it's simply gorgeous. Why, hardly anybody in the school knows I've come to it.'

Alex wondered if this wish for anonymity was good. Then he looked at Laurel's contented face, and felt her hand squeeze his arm. It had one advantage, it was not altering the daughter he loved. Her wish not to be noticed meant that her quality was untouched, she continued to be herself, and the mass of similarly dressed, similarly acting girls round her relaxed her. She would probably in time dare to blossom because she was less vulnerable to bruising and hurt.

Lena had produced a solitaire board. Just two across a table arranging the marbles and things were easier. The interest of the game took away Tony's self-consciousness, he became less aware that other boys from his school were present. Lena took immense trouble. This coming down for the day was a bore. Schools seemed to be built near the most ghastly hotels where there was nothing whatsoever to do. She hoped they had not made a mistake in sending Laurel to the Abbey School; the parents seemed even tattier than the parents of the boys from Tony's school, if that was possible. Still, as they had made the effort the day must be built into a success. Alex was probably right to make a martyr of himself and take each of the children separately for a walk. It was simpler with one of them alone, you could do more to charm and please. Shocking the way school affected children. They became so monosyllabic and drab. And those ghastly clothes! Of course nobody could do much with Laurel, poor little thing, but what had they done to her good-looking Tony? They had cut his hair too short, and she hated the pale lemon tie, it was not a bit his colour. And he had a spot on his chin, he never had spots at home.

'Tony, put the last marble into its niche.'

'Mum, do you think we could come home at Christmas as there aren't any bombs or gas?'

Lena would not admit to anyone, even to herself, that she was unable to influence Alex, so she must appear to side with him.

'Not this holidays, darling. It's too early yet to be sure.'

'Albert and Ernie's father's a warden and he's quite likely letting them go back for Christmas. I should think if he does Dad ought to let us. After all, a warden must know.'

Lena thought everything to do with the war nonsense. It was obvious the Germans did not want to fight, and it would probably come to nothing and this fearful upset would all be

89

unnecessary. Alex absolutely living at his factory, only coming home to sleep. The children with their grandparents, probably being made prim and losing their charm. Everybody trying to get into a uniform and do something they were quite unsuited for. However, no good arguing with Alex. In fact it was dangerous, for it started the old idea that she should be with the children. She had taken her stand on that. She would visit the children whenever he did but not on her own. She missed them and hated the house without them, but where Alex was there she intended to be. Women had to make up their minds on which side of the fence they were coming down and stick to it.

'Not Christmas, I think, but perhaps Easter. Dad and I are coming to spend Christmas with you. Christmas is rather fun in the country.'

'I'd rather be at home.'

'I know, darling, we miss you terribly.'

Tony was playing. He moved several marbles before he spoke again.

'It seems to me no good having air-raid wardens if you can't believe them when they say there won't be bombs.'

'You tell Dad about the air-raid warden. Perhaps he doesn't know.'

'Will you come for my birthday?'

'I think so. Dad's trying to get away. We've booked a room here for the night.'

'I should think he jolly well ought to get off. It's my most important birthday so far, going into double figures.'

Lena smiled at his frowning face.

'Don't be angry with us, darling. It's not our fault there's a war.'

'I know but I think it's mean we can't go back to London if Albert and Ernie can.'

He was still harping on the same theme when Alex and Laurel came in from their walk. Lena gave him an affectionate push.

'Go and put on your coat and scold Dad instead of me.'

Laurel did not play solitaire but arranged the marbles in a pattern while she talked to Lena.

'What's Tony cross about?'

'The evacuees that Gran has are probably going back to London at Christmas. Tony thinks he should too.'

Laurel sighed.

'I wish we could. But you're coming to spend the holidays with us.'

'Part of them anyway. I've had invitations from the Aunts for you. Would you like to stay with Aunt Dot, Aunt Selina or Aunt Sylvia?'

Laurel grinned at Lena, supposing that she was being funny.

'My goodness no! Of course I've always liked staying with Gran and Grandfather, though they'll never seem a home, but with you coming it won't be so bad. But going anywhere else would be awful. When you go to a boarding school you do want a place in the holidays where you belong in which to rest your bones.'

Tony, head down to the wind, argued with Alex.

'Well, anyway, for a week. I don't want my tools and

projector and trains moved. I want them where they are. I shall look pretty silly having to stay in the country while Albert and Ernie go back to London. And if you don't mind my saying so, Dad, their father simply must know more about air-raids and gas than you do.'

Alex was tired. The turning over of his factories to the manufacture of war materials was exacting work. Lena was a problem. He was out of the house all of the day and often part of the night. She was too much alone, and though she did not complain he knew she was missing the children. Life was far from normal, there was very little entertaining and no theatres or cinemas open. Most difficult of all, many of her friends were coming back to London, laughing loudly because none of the horrors they had been told to expect had come upon them. They were not going to the length of reopening their whole houses but they were talking of having their children back for Christmas if things went on being quiet. Quite a lot of thinking people were being fooled, were saying Germany would not fight. Alex, with his business ramifications all over Europe, was puzzled by the lull but heart heavy with forebodings; and at the same time scared, and angry because he was scared, of peace overtures. Would a pacifist Prime Minister and a soft, peace-loving nation, backed by a more than willing France, patch things for another year or two? He had to hold himself in to answer Tony gently.

'You're not coming back, old man, whatever any one else is doing, and I want the subject dropped.'

Tony flushed.

'Do you mean we're never coming home?'

'Not until all danger of air attack's over.'

Tony knew that tone in his father's voice. Even on a half-term holiday when you could say almost anything you liked you could not ignore it. They were not going home. It was to be Gran's and Grandfather's. And Albert, who was the same age as he was, would be back in London.

Alex asked about the school rugger teams, and Tony answered politely. Both father and son were conscious that there was strain and hated it, but neither could break it down. Depressed they turned round and walked back to the hotel.

XVII

Kim was a changed child. The schoolroom was his and he had the undivided attention of Ruth. On Sundays he came down to the dining-room to lunch with his grandparents. There was a riding school in the neighbourhood and he rode most afternoons. The riding mistress, who, when not teaching children to ride, gave her life in adoring service to three Pekinese, was bowled over by Kim's good looks and lavished on him the same baby talking worship she gave to her dogs. He missed Laurel and Tony but gained from their absence and knew it. There was sometimes friction in the nursery, where Nannie, looking on Albert and Ernie as the least privileged of her chicks, saw to it that when there were favours going they were the first to receive them. Yet, though this seeming unfairness did sometimes at the time throw Kim into rages, fits of showing off or bleak depression, Albert contributed to his feeling of well-being, for, provided that Ernie, who was within a few months the same age as Kim got his rights, he was willing to give way to Kim as a 'little 'un'.

Ruth worried about Kim. Was he being spoilt? Was he going to be difficult in the holidays because term time was easy for him? It was quite impossible for her to be unduly strict with him, for he was the most engaging pupil, full of tremendous interest, bursting with intelligent and amusing questions; furious with himself if he did badly. What caused her real distress was that Kim gained from being away from his parents. He was on the jump when Alex was about, he felt inferior, and then swaggered and showed off. Lena's obvious worship was not good for him either. You could not miss the fact that because Kim was feeling easier, life for him was easier, and this meant he was better liked. Ruth dreaded Christmas for him. Poor little creature, he was sure to make an abominable nuisance of himself.

Nannie had settled down. It was easier for her with Laurel and Tony away. She accepted that they were schoolroom children, but naturally, having brought them up, she knew their insides better than any one else, and she had to what she called 'Keep an eye'. But they were not really under her wing any more, and sometimes when they were home she felt restive, and, had she been the hen she resembled, she would have clucked.

Tuesday had been a trouble. Nannie doubted if the water suited her. She had taken to biting her nails, and she sometimes screamed in her sleep. However, she was getting better. The house was not home but Nannie had managed to establish regular ways, everything done at its proper time. In her opinion there was nothing like regular ways, helped out in Tuesday's case by her powders, for putting a child to rights.

Albert and Ernie gave Nannie great satisfaction. She fought quite a fight with Albert over his bowels, for Albert was convinced that Nannie's interest was not nice. She had gained her way mainly owing to her faith, which nothing could shake, that nobody would obstruct her will in her nurseries. Ernie was a success. The country air, long nights, regular, well-chosen meals, had changed him from a peaky child into a solid, red-cheeked one.

Mr. and Mrs. Parker had been down to see how their children were getting on. Elsa had offered them a bed for the night. The visit had not made for anyone's happiness. Albert and Ernie became unsettled and were homesick for days afterwards. Mr. Parker approved so well of the entire household and the arrangements for his boys that he wanted them to stay, and tried to withdraw his promise that if things went on being quiet they might come home at Christmas. It took a fortnight's tears from Mrs. Parker to make him again change his mind, and though Mrs. Parker had no idea of it, he only did give in because of a conversation he had with the Colonel.

Colonel Wiltshire, with *The Times* under his arm and his four dogs running round him, had come out to get his feel of the day. Mr. Parker had come out to have a smoke and to be out of the way. They exchanged greetings and then the Colonel asked him if he would care to have a look round the garden. They were on their way back to the house when Mr. Parker, with difficulty, expressed his thanks.

'Been proper good to my kids.'

'Nice boys. Sorry you're taking them away. Ought to stop.'

'Too right they ought. What I says is, they wouldn't be giving us all this practise if nothing was expected. Course I'm only a part-timer but you wouldn't believe the time I 'ave to put in. Gas, that's what's comin'.'

'Why not leave them here?'

'The missus. Been lookin' very rough since they've been gone. Still, I'll 'ave another try but she's set they've got to be back for Christmas, and once they're back she won't let them go again until he drops things, and then it'll be too late, like as not.'

The Colonel whistled up his dogs.

'Remember this. If you have to have them back, you can send them here the moment trouble starts. I don't say there'll be beds, but we'll always manage something.'

Mr. Parker, worn down by his wife's tears, did remember. He saw the Colonel, with his straight military back and his honesty that nobody could doubt. If he said the boys could always come back then it was a certainty that they could. Mr. Parker still felt he was acting foolishly but he was sick of tears.

'All right, they can come, but one bomb and they'll be goin' back, so keep their things ready, see.'

XVIII

It was snowing. The yellowish black sky gave promise of more snow. Even in the warmed hall the children could see their breath, it hung like smoke on the air. Tony tapped the barometer. Laurel glanced over her shoulder.

'It won't move again yet. It's not more than an hour since Grandfather gave it its morning set.'

Tony left the barometer and wandered back to the french window.

'It would be the deepest snow we'll probably know in our whole lives, and us having to be in those awful tableaux.'

Kim bounced up and down.

'I don't think they're awful. I like them.'

'You would.' It was an inadequate retort. It was entirely due to Kim that they had to appear in the tableaux. A local woman, feeling passionately about the Finns, had planned tableaux and carols at Christmas to raise money to buy them comforts. 'Just the dear, familiar carols,' she had said, 'and a crib and some yards of blue veiling and you can make the most beautiful pictures.' It was after she had seen Kim that she grew ambitious. She had asked Elsa if she could borrow him and had been promised all four children. Tuesday and Tony were to be angels, and Laurel one of a group of kneeling peasant children, but Kim as Christ as a small boy was the high spot to which the tableaux led. Laurel and Tony, on hearing what was to happen to them, had accepted philosophically; the performances were towards the end of the holidays, and the end of the holidays, with the arrival of their parents and Christmas, so much nearer, had seemed æons away. But now there were two more days of rehearsals, and two days of performances, and they were happening on days when there was snow.

Tony kicked at the window frame.

'In our gum boots, wearing things tied over out heads, we

shouldn't get cold. We'd go out if Dad was here to say we might.'

The Colonel, who was crossing the hall, heard what Tony said. He paused, caressing the head of one of the carved elephants holding the gong.

'Who said you couldn't go out?'

Laurel came over to him and scratched the trunk of the other elephant.

'Nannie.'

'I thought Miss Glover had the arranging of the doings of you elder ones.'

Laurel nodded.

'She does but today's different. Nannie's cross because she has to take off Tuesday's combinations and Tony has to take off his vest to be angels, and when she's cross, which she hardly ever is, Gran and the Foxglove give in.'

'And what would your father do?'

Tony joined his Grandfather and Laurel.

'He'd fix it somehow.'

'It's not only Nannie,' Laurel explained. 'It's early lunch because of the rehearsal. Tony and I asked Gran if we need go to the rehearsal. There's only six days of the holidays left and there's another rehearsal tomorrow, and then two proper acting days. Most likely there won't be snow after today and it seems a wicked waste not to use it. Of course Kim's got to go to rehearsal but he likes them, don't you, Kim?'

Every second of the rehearsal was entrancing to Kim. He had so far behaved well, and was petted and admired and passed from knee to knee; however, if Laurel and Tony were going to feel ill-used he was not going to be out of it.

'I wanted to make the most enormous snowman in the world.'

Grandfather moved casually towards the stairs.

'I will speak to nurse.'

The children, wide-eyed, stared after him. Grandfather seeing Nannie! Grandfather, who always said, 'Ask your Grandmother' or 'Ask Miss Glover' or 'Ask your nurse' about everything! Grandfather never decided things, he wasn't that sort of person. He was much loved but he was unimportant somehow.

Just as deliberately as he had gone up the Colonel came down the stairs.

'Get your things on. We're going to the loft over the old stables. There's some sledges there your father and your aunts had when they were children.'

It was lovely shuffling across to the stables almost blinded by falling snow, but up in the loft it was cold and oiling the sledges hard work. Kim got bored. He tried to amuse himself and draw the interest of the other three by climbing about and attempting to swing from a beam. Laurel and Tony refused to pay attention to him. The Colonel bore with him for a bit, then suddenly he straightened up.

'Come and do your share, old fellow, or you go in.' Kim continued to jump at the rafter, the Colonel gave Tony a nod. 'See him across the yard, and mind he takes those boots off by the side door. Don't want a lot of snow in the house.'

Kim's day lay in ruins. The snow was no longer exciting, it was cold, and the flakes which before had seemed to stroke, now bit and slashed. Tears blinded his eyes and he stumbled. Tony gripped his elbow.

'It's all right. You didn't want to hang about cleaning sledges. You'll like it much better in the nursery by the fire.'

'He's mean and I hate him.'

'You'll be all right this afternoon. You're going to wear that white silk shirt thing and that halo.'

'I expect he'll stop me doing that too. Everyone stops me doing things I like.'

They were at the side door. Tony opened it and pushed Kim on to a chair.

'Rats. Give me your foot and I'll pull your boots off. You'll go all right. And all those ladies will make faces and pigeon noises and you'll like it.'

It was after Kim had left the loft that Laurel and Tony discovered their grandfather. It was queer, considering that they had always supposed they knew him, yet now it seemed it was a puppet that they thought they knew, moving and speaking like the real person, but having little of the substance of grandfather in its make-up. He was not always thinking of other things, or just walking away with his dogs to be by himself. He listened and noticed and, most surprising of all, thought differently from Gran.

'Nuisance this acting business,' he said, 'but the snow will lie for days, shouldn't wonder.'

Their grandmother had thought acting in the tableaux would be fun for them, and, as well, children should help in time of war. Tony reminded the Colonel of this.

'I suppose we ought to help the Finns.'

Grandfather was busy getting some rust away from a runner with emery paper. He looked up with a smile that was almost a wink.

'We've taken three tickets here at a guinea each. They could have had that anyway. Same goes for the rest of the tickets sold shouldn't wonder.'

Laurel gasped.

'Do you mean to say I kneel for all those hours and hours singing "Once in Royal David's City" and I'm not helping Finland?'

The Colonel scratched with his emery paper.

'Can't be sure, but half the time those sort of shows are held because a pack of women want to dress up. Muddled thinking, you know.'

Tony took his sledge to the window to see if it was clear of rust.

'How can you be muddled about the people in Finland? They do need clothes, and they've been ruthlessly attacked by the Russians, we learnt that at General Knowledge.'

'Can about anything. Mrs. Parker is about young Albert and Ernie, for instance.'

The fact that Albert and Ernie had gone home still rankled in Tony. He spoke fiercely.

'Why?'

'She didn't get them home because she thinks the danger's over but because she's lonely without them.'

Laurel stopped working and leant on her sledge.

'I think that's a very good reason. Mothers should miss their children. Ours does. Dad said she'd missed us so much she's getting thin.'

Grandfather accepted this with a nod.

'What I meant was that the reason isn't the one she thinks it is.'

Tony had found another speck of rust.

'You can't give always the right reason. It would often be very rude. Lots of times I've heard Mum ask Dad to think of some reason why she needn't go somewhere, and he did too. But it wasn't the real reason which was that Mum hates being bored.'

'But your mother knew the real reason and that's the thing that matters.'

'You mean,' Laurel said, 'that if when Lady Thomas was getting up the tableaux it was the fun of doing it and not Finland needing help that made her get them up, it's all right as long as she knew it?'

'That's it. Very important not to fool yourself. Used to tell your father that.'

Tony put his sledge on the floor.

'I bet he never does.'

Grandfather laid down his piece of emery paper.

'We'll get the dogs and take these sledges up to the near field. Not much good while it's snowing but we've half an hour before lunch.'

Neither Laurel nor Tony spoke of this conversation to the other, but it affected them both. With the tableaux and the snow there was so much to do that the end of the holidays seemed to arrive as if the days had been concertinaed. Yet Tony managed to talk now and again to his grandfather, and from these talks he came away feeling more at home in the house. It was not that Grandfather said anything startling or interfered in any way, but he gave the impression that he was to be relied on. In a way Tony classed him with the pound note which he always carried on him. Laurel, too, from that moment, talked more to her grandfather. In her case it was not so much seeing more of him as drawing him into conversations and expecting him to add to them and embellish them. It amused Elsa. 'You're making quite a chatterbox of your Grandfather.'

On the morning when she was to return to school Laurel was in the hall early, and met her grandfather about to set the barometer. He kissed her.

'Sorry you have to go today. I shall miss you.'

'Will you? I think that shows a very nice nature. It must be nicer really having the house to yourselves, isn't it?'

'Never did much. If your Aunt Dot wasn't here with Henry, Alice and Maria then your Aunt Sylvia came along with her family.'

'Bringing Uncle Andrew.'

'Sometimes.'

'And then you had morning prayers.'

'Yes.'

'And, of course, sometimes you had Aunt Selina with Bertie and Fiona.'

He chuckled.

'Your Aunt Selina was always determined to have swans and she had them.'

'Instead of ducks, you mean?'

'Yes.'

Laurel considered themselves.

'I'm certainly a duck, and so's Tony, and so's Tuesday but I think Kim's a swan.'

Grandfather put a hand on her shoulder and led her towards the dining-room.

'So, as you see, one way and another there was a lot of coming and going.'

'So you don't mind having us.'

'No.' He paused. 'You happy?'

She stared at him.

'How do you mean?'

'You weren't last holidays. Better now?'

Laurel considered her condition. They had been pretty good holidays. Dad and Mum had come for a week. She had her room back. There had been tobogganing and learning to skate. It was not home, but it was the next best thing.

'Except for missing Mum and Dad and, of course, our house, it's been super.'

He pressed the shoulder on which his hand lay.

'Good.'

XIX

Evacuation had almost doubled the number of boys at Tony's school. To grapple with this emergency new and younger boys had to share desks. For half the term Tony kept his desk to himself, then another new boy arrived and Tony was told to shift his belongings to make room for the newcomer. Tony would have taken this calmly if his desk had been the right choice, but there was a boy who had come to the school half a term later than he had but who still had his desk to himself. Tony explained this to his form master, taking it for granted that a slip had been made and would be adjusted. The form master was overworked and, though he was fond of Tony, not in the mood to be badgered about small matters.

'I dare say Andrews did come half a term later, but you weren't there for most of the term.'

Tony, in common with all the younger boys affected, considered that desk sharing had clearly defined rules, the most important of which was that you had to share according to when you first came to the school. Naturally there was luck in who was picked when there was a bunch who had all joined the school together, but beyond that it was a perfectly fair system. Tony knew he was next on the list after Andrews. He had been the only new boy in his term and so it must be he. He persisted, sure that his form master had made a mistake.

'But, sir, I joined first and that's what counts.'

The form master gave him a friendly push.

'Run along, Wiltshire, and get your stuff moved. You may have joined the school but you weren't here.'

Tony had not before met what he considered injustice. It made him fighting mad. The new boy, a harmless, homesick child called Perkins was waiting with his few belongings by Tony's desk. Tony, his words tumbling over each other, shouted at him.

'You're not sharing my desk. I'll throw everything on the floor if you try. You put your stuff in Andrews' desk where it belongs.'

From that moment a battle began. Andrews insisted that it was his luck he had not been picked, and he was not going to share. Tony threw Perkins' books on the floor each time when, much against his will, the unfortunate child was ordered to put them away. By ill-luck it was a garbled version of what was happening which reached the headmaster. In ordinary times he would have had a talk with Tony and sorted the affair out, but he was rushed and anxious, some of his staff had been called up and there were domestic troubles. He did not give Tony a chance to defend himself.

'I won't have bullying. I hear you've made a dead set at Perkins, a new boy far younger than yourself, throwing his books about and generally behaving like a cad.'

He gave Tony a good caning and told him that if there should be any more trouble he would have no desk and Perkins should have it to himself.

Tony was no letter writer but he felt he must see his father. Dad would understand and see the head and everything would be all right. Letters were written on Sunday afternoons. A joint letter in most cases to both parents. Tony did not feel he could explain what was wrong on paper so he wrote his usual dreary, 'It is only four weeks to Easter we played Cadman School at rugger this week and won. . . .' but he added, 'will you please come and see me Dad the first minute after you get this it is something speshull.'

Tony's letter never reached Alex who was up in the North organising the start of a new factory. Lena had remained in London and kept the children's letters for Alex to see, but by the time he returned there had been another letter from Tony and that was the one he read. The second letter was full of a boxing tournament and made no mention of the previous letter, except to say, 'Which Sunday are you coming?', a query that finished all Laurel's letters and most of Tony's. Alex was tired and worried. His factories were on most important work, he could not find exactly the man he wanted to run his new place in the North, he was quite prepared for a certain amount of travelling but he had to be in London for continual conferences; he saw that he was going to get very little leisure and decided it was better to break this to the children. In his letters to both Laurel and Tony he said, 'I shan't be able to get down to see you this term as I have important things which must come first, but I will manage at least one night during the holidays.' Laurel, though disappointed, was not upset. She was happy at school. It had been nice at Gran's and Grandfather's last holidays. She had her room back. It was hateful not seeing Dad and Mum but the war would not last long. All her form said so. To Tony, Alex's letter read as a kick. He had been hurt by what he had taken as his first reply because it had made no mention of his request, and had actually been written by Alex in the train; but now Dad had answered and a most hateful answer it was. Dad knew he would not say something was special unless it was special. If he had replied he was sorry about the special but the war had to come first, that would have been miserable but understandable, but not to answer him at all, just to ignore what he had said as if he had never written! That was too mean. Not to his best friends or anybody could Tony talk of his trouble. Dad was not to be criticised, so he endured his hurt by himself. He became as the cat that walked alone. He avoided his friends. He wanted the light out in the dormitory so that he could mutter without anybody noticing, 'It's mean. Everybody's hateful and mean.'

XX

Elsa and the Colonel were at breakfast. Elsa threw a letter across the table.

'We shall have to get Alex and Lena to fix an hotel or something for the children for the Easter holidays. Read that.'

The letter was from Dot. She was taking on a big job for W.V.S. as soon as the holidays were over. It was the last chance she had to bring the children to see their grandparents. Could they make room? The Colonel folded the letter and put it back in its envelope.

'Mistake to shift the children. Settling down.'

'I know, but a change will do them good.'

'Not Laurel or Tony. They want a home.'

'I dare say, but we ought to consider Dot too, it's lonely for her with Paul away. She ought not to take on a job, she has more than enough to do running her house and looking after the children.'

'Well, send away Nurse and Kim and Tuesday. That gives you two rooms.'

Elsa looked at him with grim amusement.

'How like a man! You make it all sound so simple.'

'You could fix it.'

Elsa was thinking ahead.

'Lena and Alex could find a nice quiet hotel somewhere which specialises in nursery parties, I could move. . . . Well, we'll see.'

The arrangements for Easter happened suddenly. Lena

heard of a most suitable hotel in Devon, and Elsa had an attack of bronchitis. Lena came down to see her and, finding her worried by her household, packed Ruth, Nannie, Kim and Tuesday off at a day's notice. Dot and her children were to be put off, and, if Elsa had not entirely recovered, Laurel and Tony would be sent to the Devon hotel with the rest of the family. Elsa made a good recovery. She thought seeing Dot and her children would cheer her up, and she set about arranging the house for Easter. She suspected that she was still lackadaisical and lazy-minded, so, to get herself up to the mark, refused the simple way of doing anything. It was too easy to leave Laurel's and Tony's things where they were, and not fair to Dot to push her girls up into the night nursery, they were all grandchildren and must not feel that one family was more favoured than another.

Dot, at forty-seven, saw a new world opening before her. She had meant to take up a career but somehow it had not happened and she had married. Paul Enden was a gunner and they had spent the first years of their marriage in India. The problems of India had absorbed Dot and she had really studied and tried to help, and when they returned to England she would have felt thwarted and lacking in interests only almost at once she started to produce Henry. Henry was followed in 1928 by Alice and in 1933 by Maria. When Maria was two, Paul was retired from the Army. Dot had been patient, and had struggled manfully to be tolerant and kind, but she had no patience with a fumbling makeshift existence. She never believed in first the hens, and then the bees, which were to provide the extra money needed to supplement their income. She thought she had succeeded in veiling her disbelief and that Paul had no idea that she looked upon his efforts just as she looked upon Maria's to build a house of toy bricks. She wondered why he had changed so much, had become so silent and inclined to be dull. When war was declared and after a few months' delay he was called back into the Army she had been shocked at his gaiety. 'You men! I believe you enjoy wars.'

Dot never did anything without purpose. It was perfectly true that she was taking on a war job, it was a fact that it was quite a while since the children had seen their grandparents, but the real reason why this visit was planned was that she needed approval for steps she intended to take. Paul was rather silly about the children, particularly about girls, and, judging by his letters, had got worse since his battery had gone to France. She knew everything that she was arranging was for the best and she did not want Paul to worry. Nothing would allay any worry he might feel more completely than a letter from the Colonel. Paul had a tremendous opinion of his father-in-law.

The Endens arrived a day earlier than Laurel and Tony. Elsa met them at the station. Driving to the house she told them of her arrangements.

'I hope you won't mind having Tony in your room, Henry. He's quite a good little boy. I've put Maria and you together in Laurel's room, Alice dear.'

Alice wore spectacles. They gave her an earnest look.

'I thought Laurel was coming.'

'Yes, dear, to-morrow. She doesn't really break up until a

day later, but she is being allowed to leave a day early so that the car can pick both her and Tony up at the junction.'

Alice had stayed with her Wiltshire cousins in London. She and Laurel were almost exactly the same age and near enough in size to share clothes. Alice's clothes were what her mother called 'sensible'. To her Laurel had a wardrobe suitable for a princess. When Lena had taken the two to a charity fête Laurel had sensed that Alice had not thought her best frock suitable and had suggested to Lena that one of her own was borrowed. Lena had been charming and enjoyed herself dressing Alice in frilled organdie. It had been a golden day in Alice's life. She had worn organdie, won a prize at hoop-la and caught a glimpse of royalty. She was a faithful child and, though she had not seen her lately, she had remained fond of Laurel. Like all the grandchildren, she knew about Laurel's room. She had often slept in it but never when Laurel was there.

In the bedroom she explained the situation to Maria.

'I'm not going to unpack. We'll just pretend. I expect we'll change with Laurel tomorrow. But don't say anything.'

Alice was tidying her own and Maria's hair for lunch when Laurel came into the bedroom. Banishment to a bed in the night nursery had made Laurel angry. There were two beds there, Nannie's and Tuesday's. It was true Tuesday's was a cot but there were plenty of beds in the house. It was deliberate nastiness on Gran's part. For some reason she didn't like her, or, more likely, she didn't want them living with her. That was probably it. She had managed to turn out Kim and Tuesday, and as she had to have herself and Tony she was making their lives as hateful as possible. Very well then, she would be hateful back. It was not her fault she was staying there. With flaming cheeks and stony eyes she slammed the bedroom door behind her and marched to her bookshelf.

'Sorry to bother you, but I'd rather like to have my own books if you don't object.'

Alice gave Maria's hair a final comb and led her to the door.

'Go down. I shan't be long.' She closed the door and leant against it. 'I've not unpacked. Maria and I would just as soon be in the nursery, we don't want your room.'

Laurel was piling her books on the floor.

'Gran's arranged it. You're her favourites.'

'It's just a muddle I think. She wouldn't mind our changing if we explained.'

'Thanks awfully but I'm not going to make a show of myself asking favours. I expect your mother said you'd got to have it.'

'Mummie doesn't care where we sleep.' Alice crossed to the bookshelf and knelt beside Laurel. 'Tell you what, let's change and not say anything.'

'We can't. Maria's too big for Tuesday's bed. Anyway they'd know when they called us in the mornings.'

Alice began putting the books back in the shelf.

'We can arrange something. I'd ask Mummie only she's too busy to listen.'

'What's she busy about?'

'Us. She wants to send me and Maria to a convent. She thinks we don't know but I do.'

'A convent!' Laurel forgot herself for a moment. 'But that's nuns. You aren't Roman Catholics.'

'No, but it's cheap and has an admirable educational standard. I heard Mummie say that on the telephone. She pretended she was talking about other children and I knew it was us.'

'Maria's very little for a boarding school, isn't she?'

Alice nodded.

'She doesn't know. You mustn't say anything.' She put the last book back. 'I tell you what. You unpack your things here, and I'll take Maria's and mine to the day nursery. Then it's your room except just for sleeping.'

Laurel considered the proposition. It was far better than nothing. She threw her arms round Alice.

'Sorry I was cross, it's not your fault.' Then her mouth tightened. 'But it's mean of Gran and I shall show her I know it's mean.'

Elsa, after her burst of energy, felt wretched. There was plenty to do and she drove herself to do it, but she had not got back her energy and her nerves were strained. It was, therefore, particularly unfortunate, she thought, that Laurel and Tony, who had been so charming last holidays, should be so difficult this. Laurel she could not understand. She seemed to go out of her way to be tiresome. She had always been such a gentle little thing but now, when asked to run a message, she slammed doors and made a fuss. Tony, always a sunny tempered child, was so morose that she had thought at first he must be ill, only his appetite was so good.

'I'm afraid, Dot dear, it's jealousy. We've had them since

the outbreak of war and I suppose they think it's their home and resent your three.'

Elsa was sitting in an armchair. Dot brought a stool and lifted her mother's feet on to it.

'Nonsense, darling. They're the best of friends. All children have moods. You've forgotten Lindsey at the same age.

'No I haven't. But Lindsey was born difficult. Laurel really is a dear little thing.'

'She's had an unsettling time. Lena and Alex have always spoilt their children. It's the best thing that could have happened that they've been forced to send Laurel to school. It'll be the making of her. As a matter of fact, I believe in wartime, with unsettled conditions at home, all children should be in boarding schools.' Dot paused to frame her words. 'As a matter of fact . . .'

Laurel and Tony had been too well brought up not to dislike the knowledge that they were noticeably badly behaved, and yet, when with the grown-ups, they could not be nice. Laurel only intended her disapproval to show to her Grandmother, but when her aunt raised her eyebrows, or her Grandfather said, 'That's not the way to speak to your Grandmother, Laurel,' she found herself being rude to them all and hating herself for it. Tony was not intending to behave badly, but, because he was rather silent, the grown-ups would probe to find out what was wrong. To defend his inner thoughts he scowled and answered quickly and rudely.

It was the cottage that made the holidays bearable. Alice and Laurel found it. It was on the edge of a long disused quarry and was tumbling to pieces. It was not on the Colonel's land so the children did not like to do anything to it without permission. Laurel went to her Grandfather about it. He said he would ring up the owner and he was sure it would be all right. It was the first time that Laurel had sought him out since she had come home. He took her hand and made her come to the telephone with him. He would not hurry and tried various hares of conversation. As they neared the house he said, with apparent casualness:

'As your father and mother won't be here for more than a couple of nights, if anything was upsetting you it might be worth telling me. I can put things right sometimes, you know.'

Laurel turned her face from him. It was true he could sometimes, like he had on the first day of the snow, but he could not do anything about Gran being deliberately unkind. He must know she was doing it because she did not want them here. She gave an angry jerk to her shoulders.

'Nothing's upsetting me. What on earth should?'

The Colonel said no more but, after he had telephoned and gained permission for the children to make what use they liked of the cottage, he took his dogs for a long walk. On his return he wrote to Alex.

'. . . We have muddled things this end I am afraid. Come when you can and straighten affairs out.'

Henry, who had just gone to Wellington, had been at rather a loose end. He considered himself too old to play with the girls and Tony but the cottage was different. It needed repairs and that was a man's job. Using Tony as his assistant

115

he re-tiled the roof, rebuilt the walls with bricks and mud, and bought glass and fixed it in the windows and re-hung the doors.

Alice and Laurel cleaned, made and hung some curtains, borrowed some simple furniture from the attics at the house, and cooked.

Maria, singing happily to herself, arranged little bunches of primroses on anything that would hold a makeshift vase, and put her dolls to sleep in the bedroom.

They were all busy and felt important. There was something to show for their efforts. While they were working, and still more when the door was closed and they were eating snacks they had cooked, they felt invulnerable. The adult world, where you were shifted round because of the war; where people whispered about how difficult you were, or whether you were to be sent to a convent, was a shadow; here was reality.

The Endens left the day before Lena and Alex arrived, and, because it was the easiest plan, Elsa arranged that they should sleep in Laurel's room. The kitchenmaid had left and another could not be found and the cook was tired and annoyed. An annoyed cook obviously meant a flustered housemaid and parlourmaid.

'Don't do anything much to the room,' Elsa said. 'Mr. and Mrs. Alex are only here for one night and the children are off in three days. We can have a grand tidy after they have all gone.'

Alex and Lena arrived in time for a late tea. They were greeted in the hall by Laurel, who was dancing with pleasure.

She flung herself first on one parent and then on the other. Tony clung to Lena as if he could not hug her close enough. There was, Alex noted, an aloofness in Tony's greeting to himself. Tea was waiting in the drawing-room. Elsa was smiling behind the silver tea tray but Alex, as he kissed her, was concerned to see how tired she looked.

'Sit down, Alex,' Elsa said, speaking as she always did, as if he could still be ordered about. 'How are you, Lena dear? I've given you Laurel's room, I hope you'll be comfortable.'

Alex took a sandwich and smiled at Laurel.

'Moved out for us? Don't you mind, old lady?'

Elsa passed him his tea cup.

'She hasn't been sleeping there, Alice and Maria . . .' she broke off, having caught a glance from Alex to Laurel and the look on Laurel's face. She spoke with a mixture of exasperation and dismay. 'My dear child, have you been behaving as you have all these holidays because you felt ill-used about your room?' Laurel muttered something inaudible. Elsa shook a teaspoon at her. 'You're a very silly little girl. If you felt hurt why not come and tell me so? Mind you, I don't say you could have had the room but at least we could have discussed it.' She turned to Alex. 'She's growing up as bad as Lindsey.'

Alex laughed.

'I won't have that. Laurel has her faults and Lindsey hers but there could not be two creatures with less in common.'

Elsa gave Laurel her tea cup.

'I'm not so sure. Your Aunt Lindsey used to harbour grievances, sometimes for months, and nobody could put them right because nobody knew what was wrong.'

Laurel was sitting on a stool by Lena. Lena put an arm round her.

'Silly goose, why didn't you tell Gran?'

Laurel was nearly crying. Had everything she had thought been wrong? Was Gran as loving as always? Was the black misery that had shut down on her as if it were a lid something she had invented?

Alex came to her rescue.

'It's growing pains.'

Elsa beckoned to Laurel who unwillingly came to her. She pulled her down beside her.

'Did you mind my giving your room to those evacuee children?'

Gran had hold of her hands, the truth was being dragged from her.

'Yes, but I know you couldn't help it.'

'But you thought I ought not to have given it to Alice and Maria?'

'Yes.'

'And then Alice and Maria would have felt slighted.'

'Oh no. Alice offered to change.'

Elsa gave Laurel's hands an annoyed shake.

'Really, you are too tiresome! One word from Alice or you and none of this fuss need have happened. Now, listen to this. I can't promise you that you will always have your own room, but I can promise you that I'll tell you why I'm putting someone else in it. Will you promise me in return that instead of behaving like a bad-tempered child, which you are not, you will say what's on your mind? Speak out. I'm not afraid of words.'

Laurel could not answer. There was a lump in her throat. It was lovely to have Gran back again, brisk and firm, but always kind and a friend. She nodded to show she agreed and stumbled back to her stool. Lena spread some butter and jam on a piece of toast for her. Alex gave one of her pigtails a friendly pull. The room was so full of warmth and kindness that it was unbearable to sit still. 'Oh God!' Laurel prayed. 'Let me remember this exact moment and then I'll never be a silly fool and make up things again.'

Alex got Lena alone after tea.

'Find out what's the matter with Tony. He's annoyed with me about something.'

'Tell them our news. They've been missing us, poor sweets. That's all that's wrong.'

'I'd rather clear the air with Tony first.' He held her by the shoulders. 'Happy?'

She nodded.

'Go and be nice to your mother. I'll talk to Tony.'

Lena took Tony up to help her unpack. He sat on the bed. She put a box of sweets beside him.

'Half are for Laurel. Have you had nice holidays?'

Tony told her about the house. Obviously his building operations with Henry had been memorable.

'Will you come and see it when you've unpacked?'

'If there's time. We must see what Dad's doing. He wants his share of you.'

Tony was bending over the chocolates.

'Does he?'

Lena was touched but amused. How alike full grown men

and little boys' reactions were. They kept things to themselves. Alex could worry for days about something and when she tried to find out what was wrong he muttered 'nothing' and attempted to push her aside in just the same aloof way. She kissed the top of Tony's head and changed the conversation. She was not going to let Tony out of her room until, at least with her, he was his gay chattering self. She was a brilliant listener when she liked, and Tony was given the full benefit of all her charm and attention. There was no better way of soothing a cross man than to let him talk down to you.

'Tell me, sweetheart, how you rebuilt the wall of the cottage. But don't talk too fast because it sounds difficult and I want to understand.'

The children took their parents to see the cottage. Lena, following instructions, fell behind with Laurel. Alex strode ahead with Tony. He wasted no time beating about the bush.

'What's up, old man?'

'Nothing.'

'Rubbish. Something's upset you. Let's have it.'

The dam broke and Tony's words fell over each other. What the housemaster had said. What the head had said. The gross unfairness.

'And when I said it was something special you never even answered.'

'You are a young idiot, you know. Didn't it strike you I never got the letter?'

'Letters always get to people.'

'This one didn't. If it had I should have written or rung you up. You know that.'

It was to Tony as if he had been walking in a fog and it was lifting. Dad had never got the letter. Love poured through him.

They discussed the desk situation.

'It doesn't really matter now because I'd have to share this term anyway.'

'You seem to have behaved like a pretty good ass. Throwing the poor kid's books about.'

'But they shouldn't have been there. It was Andrews who should have been picked.'

'Obviously that was a mistake, but throwing the poor new kid's books on the floor wasn't an answer. By the time you reached the head you were lucky to get off as lightly as you did.'

'He didn't let me explain. I didn't bully Perkins. I explained about the desk to him and I gave him three bars of chocolate to make up.'

'Can you see now that you went about things the wrong way?'

'There wasn't any other way. And it was dreadfully unfair. Everybody knew it was.'

Alex appreciated Tony's sense of injustice and his helplessness to gain his rights. It was sickening that particular letter had missed him, but even if he had received it the business would have been tricky to handle. He would have written to the head and asked him to see Tony and, if he could, tidy up the grievance. He would write now and explain his son was not a bully. Fundamentally, though, the difficulty still stood, Tony's trust in adult sense of fair play had been rocked, if not broken. He had taken, for lack of other redress, the law into his own hands.

'I shall put this right, Tony, with the head, though, of course, his ruling about the desk will stand; it's never any good trying to make wrong things right by doing wrong things. I quite see how you felt, it wasn't fair so you were jolly well going to show everybody you wouldn't take it lying down.'

'I certainly was.'

'But it didn't do any good.'

'Except that I was right and it wasn't fair.'

Alex knew that he must, perhaps tomorrow, go into the question of justice and taking the law into your own hands, but it needed thought. He must be sure that Tony understood. No one got justice always. There was the danger of harbouring a grievance so that it warped you; a danger to which evidently Tony had a tendency. Queer in so open and talkative a child. But these last months had been hard on him, no proper home and the school over full. Thank God they were making a better arrangement.

'We'll drop this for now but I can't have important letters going astray. I shall give you ten typed stamped envelopes addressed to me at the factory and my secretary will be instructed to get them to me at once.'

'For ordinary Sunday letters do you mean?'

'No, for an emergency. Like this desk business.'

'How'll your secretary know they're from me?'

'You write "special" on the left hand side. She's a very intelligent woman. She'll get them to me all right.'

In the cottage the children heard the news.

'It's Mum really,' Alex explained. 'I didn't see how we could rearrange things, but she said she was not going to live without you any longer. We've taken a house in Surrey. Mum will be there every night and I shall come down most nights.'

The children could not ask questions fast enough. In the end a picture grew. It was a modern house in a big garden. Most of the furniture from London was being moved. There was a dear little bedroom for Laurel, and a big room for Tony and Kim. There was a barn that could be converted into a play-room. There were some alterations to be done, but even if it meant picnicking they would be there for the summer holidays.

It was getting dark as they turned back to the house. There seemed, not only to the children but to Alex and Lena, a magic quality in the evening. The catkins and primroses glimmered through the greyness. Birds chirped. Automatically they all dropped their voices and slipped along as if a heavy footfall or overloud tone could smash something which could not be mended.

XXI

Tony sat on one side of Ruth, Laurel on the other. The hotel lounge was empty, for the stringency of the times made parents' week-end visits difficult.

Neither Lena nor Alex had been down and the summer term was more than half over. That things were wrong was, of course, known to the children, but their school worlds were so set apart that real world news seemed not to refer directly to themselves. They had heard that Belgium, Luxembourg and Holland had been invaded. They were told about troops landing by parachute. They knew of the Dunkirk evacuation. That France had surrendered. There was insecurity in the air. Children who had arrived at the beginning of the term expecting to spend a normal term were suddenly snatched away to be sent to Canada, America or Australia.

Ruth had seen neither child for more than six months. There were changes. Laurel had shot up. She was twelve now and had ceased to be a little thing. She was very much the school girl. It was hard to tell when you saw her only for a short time and that in an hotel lounge, but she seemed harder. It was probably a good thing, she had been too sensitive. The change in Tony was more difficult to define. He looked much the same and seemed the same. Yet Ruth could feel a difference. There was a faint air of truculence that was, to her, put on rather than indigenous to Tony.

Ruth explained why she had come to see them. Kim was old enough for school and Tuesday's lessons would not matter for a while yet. She felt she ought to be doing something more.

'I'm going to be what Kim calls a lady-soldier.' They stared at her with a stunned appearance. 'Don't look like that, darlings. I shall be seeing you, I shall get leave.'

'It won't be the same thing,' said Tony. 'Except for last holidays you've always been there.'

Ruth found a large sheet of paper and drew a map of Europe. She explained quietly but quite clearly what might be going to happen. How near the Germans were.

Tony banged his fist on the arm of the sofa beside her. 'Let them come. We'll murder them, there won't be one left alive.'

Alex and Lena arrived on a week-day in July. They brought food and there was a picnic in a wood. Before they came the children had realised that there was to be no house outside London that summer. Alex had broken it to them by degrees in letters. It had not been definite but more than a hint. On this visit he was perfectly clear.

'I wish you could come. You've no idea how exciting it is, dog-fights overhead all day long. Mum's got a crick in her neck from looking at the sky. But it's no place for children.'

Tony fought.

'Why not? People don't get killed, do they?'

Alex shook his head.

'No, but of course you never know. Can't have a whole lot of Spitfires having a battle over your head and none of them ever come down. The sirens go day and night.'

Tony continued to plead.

'We wouldn't mind. Honestly, we'd like it, wouldn't we, Laurel? And you did promise.'

Laurel did not answer. She could see from Alex's expression argument was hopeless.

Alex chose his words carefully.

'I know I promised but you've got to think of your mother and me. We wouldn't have a minute's peace. You understand, don't you, Laurel?'

Laurel picked up a fir needle and seemed to examine it.

'You've moved the furniture so we shall go there presently.'

Lena knew just how Laurel was feeling.

'Everything. Except just enough for Dad and me for an odd night or two. He can't always get down.'

Tony fixed his eyes trustingly on Alex.

'Then if we've beaten the Germans by Christmas can we come to the new house then?'

Alex's eyes did not leave Tony's.

'We shan't have, old man.'

They left the subject of the house after that. Alex told them a little of what was going on in the world outside their school grounds. The road blocks, the barbed wire and the sign posts coming down.

Laurel said:

'What happens to us if the Germans land?'

Alex spoke calmly.

'Mum and I have made plans. We plan to have you with us in the new house. But I can't promise anything. It depends if we're allowed to move about.'

The landing of the Germans was remote, the presence of Alex and Lena and the picnic was happening. Laurel gave Lena's hand a squeeze.

'One thing I'm awfully glad about and that is you haven't sent us to Mum's Mum in America.'

Alex avoided Lena's eyes.

'I don't believe in running away when the enemy's in sight.'

Lena went on eating. She appeared not to have heard what had been said. She thought, as she had her mother in America, it was lunacy not to send the children to her. She had been unable to shake Alex. It was as near a bad quarrel as they had ever had.

'Lots of our chaps have gone,' said Tony.

Alex realised he had, because he wanted to speak clearly, been tactless.

'And probably very sensible in their cases. It was our point of view I was talking about. Everybody has to do what they think right for their own children.'

Lena was in an overwrought state. She had attained happiness. It had been a delicate matter to so balance her life that it reached near perfection, but with skill she had managed it. The war had no use for delicate adjustments, it had torn most of her happiness to pieces. The home, with its full nurseries and schoolroom, its charm, its happy, well-trained staff, was gone. It had hurt pulling the London house to pieces to make the new country home, but it had been necessary. She needed to be the centre piece of a home and she had worked hard to put her stamp on the new place. The appalling war situation had swept over her and she had felt as if she were a piece of jetsam bashed by the tide. What had she now? A bedroom in London. An almost unlived-in home in the country. She never saw her children and Alex only very early in the morning or late at night. There was something gained in that Alex was, during the little she had of him, more the Alex who had fallen in love with her than Alex the father. Life was so precarious it made even Alex snatch at happiness and depend on her. Against that were the hours she was alone. She was terrified. She tried to fill her time working when in London in a canteen and when in the country, in the garden, but work could not numb her mind. In the country sirens screamed and battles went on overhead all day. In London there were sirens and guns and ever-growing expectance of something worse. What if the Germans landed? What if there were bombs? To love and be loved, to have a nice home and clothes, and a good time were her weapons against the ordinary dangers of life. She was defenceless now. She had lost the ability to relax. This picnic was making her jumpy. The children and Alex looked so contented and unconcerned. She got up.

'If everybody's finished let's put the stuff back in the car and go for a walk.'

Alex lit a cigarette.

'It's too hot. What d'you two say?'

Tony turned to stare at his mother.

'Do you know that's the very first time I remember hearing you want to walk. It's always been us that did and you who wanted to sit in the shade.'

Lena with difficulty held herself back from snapping at him.

'Well, I've changed. Come on everybody.'

Alex pointed at the food.

'Pack up, kids. If Mum says we're going to walk we're going to walk.'

They found a shady path through the wood. There were wild strawberries in a ditch. They found a honeysuckle with such giant flowers they picked some to send to Elsa, because it was even finer than the one that climbed on her summer-house. Dog roses sprayed over the hedges. Bees droned, everything was white with dust. They could not have chosen a quieter, more sleepy summer lane. It was, therefore, a shock to turn a corner and be met by a sentry with a fixed bayonet. He was not even a friendly sentry. He looked grim and told them to turn back, they were allowed no further.

'What was he guarding?' Tony asked in a whisper. Alex shrugged his shoulders.

'No knowing. Might be anything.'

To both Laurel and Tony that sentry was the most memorable part of the day. He left them excited and yet with a cold feeling in their stomachs. Anything might happen in a world where sentries turned you back in country lanes. Before, war at home was hearsay, now it was real. It was as surprising as if the ground under their feet had begun to shake, or cats had voices and could talk.

XXII

There was urgency and abnormality in the air. The Colonel was out all day training men to be Home Guards. In the early morning and late at night he and Sims worked in the loft cleaning bombs and rifles and making Molotov cocktails. The cook had left to cook for a factory and the parlourmaid had become cook. Elsa and the housemaid did all the housework. With Ruth away there was no one to interfere with the children, Laurel, Tony and Kim roved the countryside, getting wild and out of hand and nobody seemed to care. Every grown-up appeared to be listening, their ears so strained that they did not hear ordinary sounds like loud voices, shouts and slamming doors.

Suddenly Albert and Ernie were back. Mr. Parker had been

in the Army since April, the school the boys should have attended had been evacuated. Mrs. Parker, with the boys on the loose all day and no Mr. Parker to help her, had lost control of them. Albert was leader of a gang.

'Near on thirty of us there is. Smashin' time we 'ave. Get up when we like. Till the bombs came we'd stop up 'alf of the night.'

'What did you do?' Tony asked.

'Coo, you wouldn't believe the 'alf of it. Took thin's what was left about and swops'm. One day we collected more'n seventy lights out of shelters.'

Tony was impressed.

'Don't the police mind?'

'Coppers!' Albert gave Ernie a nudge. ''Ark at 'im! Scared stiff of us, they are. One of 'em come to Mum about me. She said, "You speak to 'im for 'e's tot'lly unmanageable."'

Laurel, Tony and Kim gazed at Albert with awe.

'But you can't be,' said Laurel. 'You're only just ten.'

Albert spat. A habit he had picked up.

'What's age? I calls out me gang and I tells 'em I'm expectin' the coppers, and they all get themselves a bit of glass or a stone. Did 'e come? Not 'im, 'e knew when 'e was well off.'

Laurel asked:

'Wasn't it dark in the shelters without any lights?'

Albert gave Ernie another nudge.

''Ark at 'er! Of course they 'ad lights. The wardens 'ad to put 'em back. People would create something shocking if there wasn't no lights.'

Ernie was proud of Albert.

'Show 'em 'ow a bomb sounds comin' down, Albert. Go on, show 'em.'

Albert and Ernie had pockets full of fragments of shell cases. They pooled this for Albert's display.

'Need some glass really to get the proper noise,' Albert pointed out. 'Now, you listen.'

He gave a remarkably realistic performance of the scream of an approaching bomb. At the finish he and Ernie threw the shell fragments on to the floor.

'O' course it's nothing like really,' Albert explained. 'You want to hear great chunks coming down. Ernie and me 'eard a 'ole polytechnic coming down, didn't we, Ernie? Went to look at it next mornin'. Coo!'

The three Wiltshires hung on every word.

'Go on.'

'Go on.'

'Go on.'

'It was early and there was smoke still curlin' up but there wasn't much to see. That was one of the places what they give up.'

Tony was fingering a shell fragment.

'How do you mean, give up?'

Albert tried to sound authoritative.

'Couldn't do nothing, see? Great 'uge place, size of Buckingham Palace fallen in on 'o's in the cellar.' He lowered his voice. 'In our shelter that night they said that you could 'ear tappin' and that they'd go on tappin' and tappin' until they was dead.'

Tony raised a startled face.

'Doesn't anyone dig for them? Couldn't you make a hole and pull them out?'

Albert, uncertain of his facts, was truculent.

'I'm tellin' you, aren't I? Not in a big building like the polytechnic. Of course they get 'em out when it's a little buildin'. They puts up a great piece of tarpaulin and you aren't supposed to see nothin', but Ernie and me 'ave seen, 'aven't we, Ernie?'

Albert and Ernie had disliked the country before. Now, after the glories of gangsterism in London, they were appalled at its dullness. It was the day they were taken to see the cottage that they broke out.

'Wot's the good of it?'

'I'll show you wot we'd do with it.'

Albert threw a stone. It cracked through the glass in the window. Ernie climbed on to the window ledge and pulled at a tile. Several slid off the roof. There was a second when the Wiltshire children were about to stop them, then suddenly they joined in. It was an orgy of smashing. All the pent-up excitement of the world around them came out. All the whispers and grown-up waiting for something to happen. All the disbelief in the ordinary world. Nothing was left. Everything that could be torn down or smashed was ruined.

'Now I'll show you 'ow we finish it off,' said Albert. 'We'll give it a nice wash down.'

He undid his fly buttons. The other boys followed suit. Laurel leant against the wall watching them, shrieking with laughter.

XXIII

'Don't let the children know.' 'Such a stupid woman to have them back.' 'Their poor father. I'm sure he would never have allowed it.' 'She may live but the boys were killed outright.'

There was snow. The children had got out the toboggans. There was ice. They skated better this year. It was rough on the ice for all the child evacuees of the neighbourhood were there. They had no skates but they made slides and knocked the skaters down. Sometimes Elsa and her friends came to watch. Elsa would call the children over to introduce them. Once or twice one of Elsa's friends would catch hold of her evacuee and introduce it. 'This is Violet. This is George.' Someone who did not know about Albert and Ernie would ask Elsa if she had children billeted on her. There would be a pause and exchanged looks. Laurel, Tony and Kim would get back on the ice, pushing each other, screaming with laughter. Anything to ward off the terror of what they knew had happened being put into words. Grown-up wallowing in things. Amongst themselves Albert and Ernie might never have existed, for none of them mentioned them.

'Queer children are, they never ask when the boys are coming back though they knew they only went home for Christmas.' 'Such a mercy they don't ask. It's splendid when you can shield children from suffering.'

XXIV

It was the first day of the holidays. Laurel and Tony were in the garden. Laurel asked:

'How did Kim get on?'

'He was nearly always in the san.'

'But he only had measles for five weeks.'

Tony kicked at a heap of sodden leaves.

'He kept going back.'

Neither knew the word malinger but its meaning hung between them. After thought Laurel said:

'Oh well, he's rather little and much too silly for school. I dare say he was better in the san.'

XXV

The Colonel and Alex stood on the steps getting a feel of the morning. Alex looked at the flower beds.

'Everything's a bit late, isn't it?'

'Nothing much been done. Sims has his hands full with the vegetables and all he does in the house, let alone the Home Guard. Lena looks thin.'

Alex leant down to pat one of the dogs. He knew his father had no intention of probing into their affairs. In saying Lena looked thin he was understating. Lena was skin and bones and her nerves were to pieces. The trouble was it was so hard to speak of Lena's health without lifting a corner of the veil which shrouded their intimate life. How explain Lena's terror of air-raids, which yet produced wild excitement which needed physical expression. He could hardly tell his father that if the air-raids had gone on being nightly affairs in the way they were last year he could not have kept up the pace. Lena's passion was a flame which ignited all right, but it left an aftermath of exhaustion and a kind of shame which dragged at energy and affected work.

'We're managing to be entirely in the country at the moment. I've been able to get down each night. She's taking an interest in the garden.'

'Good.'

'Mother tells us they want this house as an Officers' mess.'

The Colonel whistled to the dogs, and, tucking his *Times* more firmly under his arm, led the way down into the garden.

'Yes. Sorry she mentioned it in front of Lena. Don't want her upset. We'll be moving.'

Alex, walking behind his father, could not see his face, but his back was as straight as a flag-pole, and if he could see his face he knew there would be nothing in it to show the suffering which leaving the house meant to him. Since that day years ago when, having come into a bit of money and his time in India being up, he had retired from the Army and had found this house and decided to buy it, it had been all that he asked. He grudged spending even a night away from home.

'You must?'

'Apart from the Army wanting it, work's wearing your mother out.'

'Where will you go?'

'Into that new bungalow that they're using as a mess at the moment.'

'What, that place on the hill?'

'That's it.'

Alex saw the bungalow in his mind. A modern affair with

green tiles on the roof. Probably one big room downstairs and perhaps three bedrooms upstairs.

'What will you do with the furniture?'

'Leave quite a lot. They'll need the dining-room and so on. We'll shift what your mother needs. I've got them to hang on with the bungalow for a bit until you can make arrangements about the children. Still noisy round you?'

'Whenever there's a London raid.'

'Sylvia's got room, and whatever you paid would be a help there.'

'If you can't have them there's nobody I'd sooner trust them to than Sylvia. Trouble is the children have never cottoned on to Andrew.'

'No. Bit bleak in the vicarage. How about Selina?'

'My offspring have never hit it off with Bertie and Fiona. I have thought about Dot. Laurel and Alice like each other and Tony seemed to have a great opinion of Henry when they were all here last year.'

The Colonel bent down to have a look at the shoots of a bulb.

'Pity if they've got to shift you can't have them. Nice children, does them no good this shifting about.'

Alex looked across the quiet garden. For once an aeroplane was not passing and the chattering of birds full of housing plans, and the whistling of Sims in the kitchen garden, could be heard. He sighed.

'Can't risk it yet. They pass over both going and coming. Guns pick them up and more often than not you hear the engines clearly. Sometimes they seem to wander around.

Sometimes they drop a bomb. One chance in thousands but it's one I can't take. If it was death for certain, but it's the maiming I can't stand.'

The Colonel moved on.

'I see. Which of your sisters does Lena fancy?'

'She'd choose Lindsey.'

'Don't think Lindsey would agree. She's never been keen on children.'

Alex spoke more strongly than he knew.

'I'm not asking Lindsey.' They had reached the top of the lawn. From it they looked over the Colonel's fields. They were let now and had been ploughed up. Alex sniffed appreciatively the smell of spring. 'I rather think I shan't bother any of them. I might try that hotel in Devon again. It will do for Nurse and Tuesday. By the summer holidays things may be better and I can have them home. How soon would you be clearing out?'

'If possible, right away.'

Alex did not answer. Every fibre of the Colonel must be protesting. Odd how, in a world where such unnameable horrors were commonplace, a simple thing like taking his home from an old man could still wring your heart.

Lena was sitting over the dining-room fire. She looked cold and rather childish. Alex kissed the top of her head.

'It's a lovely morning. Shall we get the kids and go out?'

Lena looked out of the window and shivered.

'I bet it's cold.'

'Where are the children?'

'Laurel and Tony are making beds. I ought to be offering

to do something, but you never know quite what in other people's houses. I wish you'd talk to Nannie, she's gone peculiar.'

'Nannie! Never.'

'She has. She looks furtive. As if she might have hidden the family silver in her box. And she's too possessive over Tuesday. Of course, Tuesday will soon be outgrowing her and I dare say she feels it.'

Alex felt that Lena was annoyed and needed handling carefully.

'She's only just six.'

Lena tapped her foot against the fender.

'I went up to fetch her. After all, she's my child and I don't see much of her, goodness knows. Nannie said she would bring her down later.'

Alex tried to guess what was at the back of Lena's annoyance. Nannie had always been strong on nursery routine. She usually got on well with Lena.

'I'll fetch her for you.'

'It wasn't only Nannie. Tuesday looked so strange. It was as if she didn't want to come with me. If Nannie's turning Tuesday against me she'll go, whether we can get any one else or not.'

Tuesday was alone in the day nursery. She was sitting on the floor undressing a doll. Alex stood in the doorway.

'Good-morning, Tuesday.'

A flush crept over Tuesday's cheeks and mounted to her forehead. She did not raise her head but only her eyes.

''Morning.'

Alex was shocked. Where was the Tuesday who rushed at him and gripped his knees? He knelt by her.

'Where's my morning kiss?'

Tuesday raised her face. It was clearly an act of obedience. He had not seen her since January, but she was used to having her parents only for odd days and never before had it made her shy. He gave her a kiss and went in search of Nannie.

Nannie was in the bathroom doing some washing. She heard Alex's step and came out to meet him. She shut the bathroom door behind her. He saw at once what Lena meant. There was something furtive about her.

'Hallo, Nannie! Have you done with Tuesday? Her mother wants her.'

Nannie fidgeted with her apron.

'She can go now.' She was plainly looking for words, which in itself was noticeable, for whatever she said had always fallen from her as a reaction and not a thought. 'Children have their ways. It's best not to notice.'

Alex saw that he and Nannie must have a talk. He made a quick decision. He had not intended to explain his plans until he had discussed them with Lena, but now he needed a bridge to cross any awkwardness and bring him naturally to Nannie's confidence.

'I'll take Tuesday to her mother and then, if you can spare a few minutes, I want your advice.'

Nannie could not sit idle. She darned a sock while Alex talked.

'My feeling is that you and Tuesday might be better in an hotel than staying with one of my sisters. What do you feel?'

Nannie let her hands and the sock she was working on fall into her lap. 'Oh no, sir. Not a hotel.'

There was no thought behind that. It was almost a cry. A natural outburst from what he had said. He was feeling his way carefully. Something was very wrong.

'Then it must be one of my sisters.'

'There'd be plenty of room in the vicarage and Mrs. Smithson's a very understanding lady.'

Alex's voice was full of affection.

'I don't think great understanding is needed to get on with you and Tuesday.'

Nannie's needle paused half across the hole. She raised her head for the fraction of a second, and Alex saw her eyes were blurred with tears. He got up and sat on the table by her side. He laid a hand on her shoulder.

'What's up?'

There was silence in which the authoritative tick of the clock on the mantelpiece filled the room. Then Nannie got up. The sock dropped to the floor. She blundered round the room, blinded by tears. She had never known such a thing before. She had never had any trouble that way from Tuesday, not even as a baby. She had managed to keep the disgrace to herself. She washed everything so nobody would know. It seemed as if it wasn't naughtiness, for Tuesday was as ashamed as she was.

Alex tried to remember what he had heard and read. It was called enuresis. There had been a lot of talk about it at the time of the general evacuation. He had an idea it was a job for a doctor.

'When did this start?'

'I can tell you exactly. It was the very night after we heard Miss Glover was going. I remember thinking should I tell her and then thinking no I wouldn't as she was leaving us.'

Alex wandered round the room.

'I wouldn't fuss about this too much. The doctor will tell us what to do.'

'I shouldn't care to call him in. The whole house knowing.'

'Anyway, it wants a child specialist. When I write to Mrs. Smithson I'll ask her if there's any one good around her. I shall tell her. I can't have you worrying about this by yourself.'

'If any one has to know I should as soon it was Mrs. Smithson. Things have never been done, as you might say, in an establishment way in the vicarage.'

'They certainly have not.' He managed to sound happier than he felt. 'Don't worry too much. It's obviously something that has to be tackled but we'll tackle it.' He was by the door. 'Don't say anything to Mrs. Alex about this. She's not been too well lately. We don't want to give her any extra worries.'

'I won't, sir. There being children much her age at the vicarage may do good, it might shame the habit out of Tuesday.'

Lena had wooed Tuesday into a fair semblance of her usual self. She had bought a book in which there was a doll with all her wardrobe to be cut out. Kim had joined the party and for him there was a magic paint book needing only water to bring out the colours. Lena, fighting to re-create the natural relationship between herself and her children, shed her tiredness and forgot her jumpy nerves. She invented occasions for the paper doll, christened Petunia, to attend. She discussed the correct dress for each occasion as if it was all that mattered. She managed, with smiles and running a hand through his curls, to suggest that though she might be talking to Tuesday her mind was on Kim. She broke off her discussions with Tuesday to exclaim at the beauties appearing under Kim's brush.

Alex had collected Laurel and Tony on his way down. They closed the dining-room door and at once there was an atmosphere of home. Lena had brought Tony some stamps. He lay on the hearth-rug and stuck them in his book. For Laurel Lena had knitted a rabbit wool jumper, which she was wearing. She rubbed her sleeve against Lena's face.

'Feel it. I'm softer than a kitten that's quite new.'

Alex sat on a chair beside Lena. He pulled Laurel on to his knee.

'I do like my daughter out of uniform.'

Laurel stroked her chest.

'In the holidays yes. In term no.' She turned to her mother. 'That pink dress you made me take for dancing was all wrong. Matron says it needs ironing every time to look decent.'

'It's a dear little dress,' said Lena, 'and just your colour.'

Tony looked up from his stamps.

'I shouldn't have thought Laurel had a colour. She always looks the same to me whatever she wears.'

Kim felt he was being forgotten.

'Matron says blue is my colour.'

Tony and Laurel changed the subject. Dad might not know how often Kim had been in the san and Mum would fuss.

'Look, Dad, this stamp's Honduras unused. I got a swap. It's pretty rare.'

'Mum, can I have another frock for dancing class, awfully plain with nothing to get in a mess?'

Lena and Tuesday were sharing a chair. Tuesday was humming as she cut out her doll's dresses. Kim, splashing water on his book, was sure that he was making magic. He was too happy to mind if he was just one piece of the family. Now and again he called, 'Oh, do look!' but he was contented with mild response.

'There, darling,' Lena passed one of Tuesday's doll's dresses to Laurel. 'Like that only without those fearful sleeves.'

Tony leant against Alex asking about stamps, proud in the belief that he had a father who was never wrong.

The sun streamed in at the window. They ought to go out, Alex supposed. Make plans for spending the day. Instead he got up and threw another log on the fire.

XXVI

The train was late. 'Always late on a Monday' a man in the corner growled to his neighbour. A soldier leant across. 'Still clearing up after Saturday, shouldn't wonder, they say it was a shocker.' 'Nothing last night,' said the man in the corner. 'I telephoned before I started. Got a lot to do, no good trying to get about in a hurry when it's been bad. Ropes everywhere.' His neighbour looked wise. 'Underground, that's the only way. Even if it's not very direct it's quicker in the end.'

Tony went home by Underground. He felt confused. Since the head had sent for him last night and told him, he had been like that. Just one thing was clear to him. His pound note would take him home. In London he would see for himself. Their house was not very big, but rather big. Was it the sort of house that they gave up? Was the head wrong? Was Dad still alive, tapping?

The house was not quite flat. All of one wall was there. Tony could see a piece of the day nursery, the grey of the spare room, the half landing with a tag of curtains still hanging, the green of the drawing-room. The floor below was blocked with lumps of masonry. The rest of the house was just a heap. There were wardens about, one of them told Tony to run along. Tony knew the answer to that. You could get at the house from the back. Nobody ever did, you came through the front door or down the area steps, but you could. It meant climbing a wall but that would be easy.

The wall was down. At the back was an even greater pile of smashed wood, masonry and rubble. It had been thrown that way by the crane and the heavy rescue men. Tony stumbled over the wreckage, and, with his hands, tried to make a hole. The wind was blowing and somewhere something swung against a broken lead pipe. To his distorted imagination, listening for just that sound, it was tapping from below ground.

'Now then, young fellow me lad, what are you up to?'

Tony went on burrowing amongst the rubble.

'This stone's so heavy I can't move it. There's tapping.'

The heavy rescue man fetched the incident officer.

'Kid says there's tapping.'

The incident officer had been on duty the day before. He knew that there had been only one person in the house. They had rescued him after four hours, badly mutilated but alive. He had been able to say he had been alone in the house and to give his wife's address before he had died. From an incident officer's angle it had been a satisfactory incident, soon cleared up. There had never been an incident on which he had worked where they had stopped working until the last person concerned was accounted for. His professional pride was touched.

'I'll tap you. Run along now. Where d'you come from?' Tony did not answer. He struggled helplessly with the lump of masonry. The warden stooped and pulled him by the arm. 'You trot along home. This is no place for you.'

Tony fought.

'There is tapping. I heard it.'

They were out in the road. The warden, struck by the note in Tony's voice, stopped. He took hold of the child's chin and raised his face.

'Did you know the people that lived there?'

It was touch and go. The confusion was lifting. The warden sounded kind. Then the reticence of his age wrapped Tony like a cloak. A sullen mask covered his wretchedness.

'No.'

XXVII

Miss Brownlow put down the telephone. She went to her study window. The girls were out for their after breakfast breather but she did not see them. She saw one child's face as she had seen it at morning prayers. A hard little mask clamped down on grief as if it were the lid of a box. She came to a decision. She rang a bell and sent for Laurel's house mistress.

Across her desk Miss Brownlow faced her house mistress. She was usually crisp and decisive, now her doubts showed.

'I must do something. I can't leave her like that. I must try and break down her reserve and let her feel that we care for her and want to help. I liked the father so much. . . .'

The house mistress was young and softer. She could easily have cried.

'She's such a dear little thing.'

'Mr. Phillips of Wingsgate House has been on the telephone. He has the two little Wiltshire boys. He says the elder boy was missing all yesterday, did we think he came to see Laurel.'

'He didn't see her. I had my eye on her all day, of course. In the afternoon she played in the house team for the lacrosse cup. It was the children's own idea to include her. They arranged it.'

'She did her work as usual?'

'Except prep. I took her off that and sent her with some of her friends to tidy the studio. It had to be done sometime.'

'Obviously better doing something active.'

'That's all I could think of, she looks as if she ought to be in the sanatorium, but it's kinder to keep her running around. In the evening I told the girls to start a general game. They took me at my word, fox and geese and all that sort of thing. You never heard such a noise.'

'Has she slept at all?'

'She wouldn't like a special fuss made of her. We give all her room cocoa. Matron arranged with the doctor to put something in Laurel's. I went in on Sunday at ten, midnight, and, as I happened to be awake, just after two. She was asleep then. Last night I was in twice.'

'Mr. Phillips can't get out of the boy where he went. He came off the train from the junction but he had lost his ticket. I can't myself see that it matters where the poor child went as he's back safely, but Mr. Phillips thinks he might tell his sister. I rather think I'll take Laurel over, it will give me a chance to say something. I couldn't do more than break the news on Sunday.'

'She's very sensitive, as you know, about being made conspicuous in any way.'

'I thought she was getting over that.'

'A little. We trod very carefully. There hasn't been a soul in the school who hasn't tried to say or do something kind, but I notice it's all being done in that off-hand way children are so good at.'

'I think you've done all that anyone could, tiding her over the first shock, but now I must step in. She looks wretched. I'll have a word with the doctor. In the meantime tell her I'm taking her. You know how to do it so that it doesn't sound unusual or alarming.'

Tony had been sent to feed the school rabbits. Laurel found him. He looked surprised at seeing her and not pleased.

'What on earth are you doing here?'

'Miss Brownlow had to see your Mr. Phillips. She said I could come too if I liked. Where's Kim?'

'In the san.'

'Is he ill?'

'No.'

Laurel took a cabbage leaf and poked it through the bars of the nearest cage. She glanced sideways at Tony. He looked queer. He seemed miles away. She felt in her pocket and brought out a bar of chocolate.

'Here you are.' Tony broke the bar in half. She shook her head. 'I daren't. I felt sickish in the car. I can't think of anything worse than being sick in Miss Brownlow's car.'

Tony chewed the chocolate.

'I suppose she's jabber jabbering to Mr. Phillips.'

'Mr. Phillips asked if you had been to see me yesterday.'

'Sort of fool thing he would ask. Why should I go to see you?'

'Where did you go?'

'A place.'

'Is it a secret?'

'Yes.'

'Oh.' Laurel fidgeted a moment with another cabbage leaf, but Tony clearly did not want to talk. 'I'll go and see Kim.'

Kim was in a nervous state. He had not taken in that his father being killed meant that he would never see him again. He knew that was what happened when people were dead, but it was only words. He would not have been surprised if he was now told his father was coming down next Sunday. What he had known was that people were worried about him. When, on Sunday evening, he had been fetched from the junior playroom he had sensed drama. When Mr. Phillips, with the skill of practice, had told him and Tony what had happened he had screamed. There was something in the atmosphere which informed him that it was an occasion for screams. Mr. Phillips had been disappointing, he had paid more attention to Tony, who just stared and did nothing. Then matron had been fetched and in no time he was in bed having orange jelly for supper. Later that evening, again because of something in the atmosphere, he had started to cry. When he cried matron had told him to be brave. Until that moment Kim had not understood there was anything to be brave about. It was confusing and frightening. His sobs rose to howls. The doctor was sent for and gave him a sedative.

Kim was sitting up in bed doing a jig-saw when Laurel came in. She pulled off her coat, hat and gloves and sat down beside him. She picked up a bit of the puzzle. He snatched it from her.

'You can't do that part. It's a lady's dress, I'm doing it.'

'I'll do this then, it's sky.'

The matron hovered round. She brought them tea. Hot buttered toast and a special cake. About five o'clock she told Laurel Miss Brownlow was ready for her. Laurel kissed Kim and put on her things. 'Queer,' said the matron afterwards. 'Just played with a puzzle all the afternoon. Quite engrossed they were. Never spoke of anything else.'

Driving over, Miss Brownlow had laid herself out to amuse Laurel. She had told her of her childhood. She had been educated in France. She was an entertaining talker. Laurel had partially relaxed. It was soothing to think that a person as important as Miss Brownlow had been a child, it made the world seem more solid. She liked to hear of an upbringing so different from her own, and, since it was not English, presumably inferior. If it had not been that she felt slightly sick she would have liked the drive in as far as she was capable of liking anything. At intervals since Sunday she had been sick. Only one of her friends knew and she was sworn to secrecy. The thought of a long drive alone with Miss Brownlow had not distressed her as much as the thought of being upset inside and being forced to ask Miss Brownlow to stop the car. It was an appalling idea and she would have endured agonies of discomfort rather than frame the words. As it happened she had worried unnecessarily. Miss Brownlow stopped the car several times to get out and pick flowers. She also took it for granted that when in a car you sucked barley sugar. Barley sugar had been given to all the Wiltshires when they were small for car sickness. Could it be possible, Laurel wondered, that a person so remote and goddess-like as Miss Brownlow was sometimes car sick?

Laurel would have been amazed if, as they drove out of the gate of Wingsgate House, she could have seen into Miss Brownlow's mind. The humility that knew that her training and great knowledge of girls was not going to help her now. That she must feel her way and trust to inspiration for the right words. She drove slowly, herself sucking barley sugar, to encourage Laurel to do the same. She asked about Kim and Tony, but casually so that there should be no feeling of prying into family affairs. At the crown of a hill she pointed to a wood.

'That's full of bluebells later on.' She did not wait for Laurel's polite response. 'I think, if it's fine, we might have a picnic there for your birthday. It comes about the right time.'

Laurel was gratified that Miss Brownlow should know the date of her birthday. She made an effort to reply suitably.

'I'll be thirteen. Being thirteen will make me more responsible.'

Miss Brownlow laughed.

'Being any special age, even seventy, never made a person responsible. But as you get older we shall give you more responsibility.'

Laurel sighed.

'I know, prefects and all that.'

Miss Brownlow stopped the car. There was a wide, lovely view. It gave her calmness and strength.

'I shall see that you have your share of responsibilities. Your father wished it. From now on I consider you very specially in my care. You see, I liked your father so much and I know that's what he would like.'

There was silence. Laurel fought hard, but the words had been said. 'He would have liked.' The suffering kept to herself poured out.

'Dad. Oh, Dad!'

Miss Brownlow had Laurel in her arms. She did not know her crisp, sometimes biting, tongue knew such endearments. She had not realised that Laurel had accepted that she must bear her misery alone and what a blessed relief it was to the child to break down utterly, to go on crying without restraint. She hardly knew what words of comfort she was whispering and still less that Laurel heard them. That, in a capsized world, she was arising, not alone but with her school round as comfort and security.

Laurel was put to sleep in the matron's room. The doctor gave her sleeping tablets. Just as she was dropping off she recalled something dreadful had happened and shot up with a jump. It was Miss Brownlow who, with a kiss, laid her down.

'It's all right, my child. Hold my hand. Everything can be mastered, even dreadful unhappiness. We'll find a way together.'

XXVIII

The Colonel had aged. A general greyness covered him like a film. His back was as straight, and his manner as usual, but Alex's death had hit him hard and this could be read by anyone with eyes able to see below the surface.

Martin Phillips had eyes which seldom bothered with surfaces. He pulled forward an armchair, fetched a small table and placed on it cigarettes and an ash-tray. He sent for sherry. 'Good stuff. Not much left. I always like an excuse for a glass of sherry at midday.'

The Colonel came straight to the point.

'You've heard my daughter-in-law wants the children home for a bit.'

'Yes. I got her letter yesterday.'

The Colonel wondered about the letter, and covered up for it in case it should not have been what Alex would have wished.

'Still very upset. Doctor's kept her in bed these last three weeks.' Martin looked sympathetic and gave an understanding nod. The Colonel spoke with more vigour. 'My feeling is that it's better to leave the boys where they are. I believe it's what my son would have wished.'

Martin played with a ruler. In the pause the sherry was brought in. He poured out two glasses. He put one beside the Colonel.

'In the ordinary way I should agree with you.' He went back to his desk and sipped his sherry. 'We're doing no good with Tony.'

'What way?'

'That day he ran away, you know, the day after you telephoned me. Something knocked him sideways.'

'Might have been shock. Very close to his father.'

'We've all had a go at him and we've a feeling he saw something. We had to call in the help of the police when he was missing. We didn't check up once he was back but they think he went to London.'

'Had a look at his home? Shocking mess.'

'I doubt if a wrecked house means much to a child that age. He would normally take for granted another home would be provided. In Tony's case the insecurity angle was established by his father's death, but he still has his mother and you and so on. We don't feel that in itself is the root of the trouble. Was it possible he could have seen anything to upset him?'

'No. My son had intended going down to his home in Surrey. He was kept late at the factory and decided to stay the night in London. If there were a raid and he was kept he had given his word to his wife to sleep in the cellar. The bomb hit the place in the early hours of Sunday morning. They got at him by daylight. He could still speak. He died just as they got him into an ambulance.'

'There was nobody else in the house? No pet cat or dog?'

'No. Never had a dog because of living in London. If there was a cat they would have taken it to the country. What is it worries you about Tony?'

'He's brooding on something. He's bad-tempered and morose, and he has nightmares. Wakes screaming. There's a small room off matron's we've put him to sleep in. I agree with you entirely about shifting children about, but I showed his mother's letter to the doctor and he says running wild is probably the best thing for him, especially in new surroundings which he doesn't connect with his father. Time the autumn term begins he'll have had over three months on the loose.'

The Colonel sipped his sherry. It was impossible to discuss a daughter-in-law with an outsider. You could not say that she was all to pieces and was having the children home for her own sake. You could not describe her sitting up in bed saying emotionally, as if she was acting in a play, 'I want my babies.' You could not help pitying the poor little thing, but she was not showing the self-control and stiff upper lip that you would expect. Only his conviction that Alex would thoroughly disapprove of the boys being allowed to believe that private grief should upset your normal life had brought him to Wingsgate House. There were no raids at present, he could not urge them as an excuse, but if this fellow Phillips would back him he might make Lena see reason. At least he could have a try.

'What about Kim?'

Martin laughed.

'Three months' holiday won't hurt him. He's a clever little devil. He's got a temperament like a prima donna. He fits into no school pattern or ever will, but he'll always fall on his feet. Is the girl going home too?'

'Yes. Miss Brownlow's been written to too. Laurel was the beginning of the business really. Doctor thought my daughter-in-law needed companionship to take her out of herself. He suggested bringing her home.'

'What's Miss Brownlow feel?'

The Colonel finished his sherry.

'Haven't asked her. The question of Laurel was fixed before I went down this week-end to see my daughter-in-law.' He got up. 'I shall travel with the children. If it suits you I'll collect them on Wednesday.'

'I'll bring the boys in so that you can tell them. If you let me know the train plans I'll fix with Miss Brownlow about connecting with the girl. Nice to have some good news to tell them all. I suppose the kid isn't born who doesn't get a kick out of an unexpected holiday.'

XXIX

It was a modern house. It lay up a private road to the edge of the wood. It was big and had plenty of rooms. The garden had been made by clearing part of the wood. A fine lawn had been laid and there were herbaceous borders, but most of the garden was of the wooded type. First, masses of azaleas, rhododendrons and flowering trees, then spruce, larch and birch until it reverted to real woodland.

When the children first saw the garden the rhododendrons and azaleas were in flower. They had never lived in rhododendron country before and they were startled and intoxicated by the scent and blaze of the azaleas, and the piled mass of rhododendron flowers. The weather was fine and the garden and the surrounding country absorbed and hid the children. To Laurel and Tony the house was a place to avoid. As they approached the front door Laurel assumed an air of bumptiousness and truculence and Tony looked sour and ill-at-ease.

To Lena, Laurel and Tony's attitude was the last dreg of bitterness. She had been so prepared to sacrifice herself. So full of plans. 'I must pull myself together for their sakes.' 'I'll be gay.' 'I won't mind what happens to me, I'll think only of them.' Before the children arrived she took endless trouble. Flowers on Laurel's dressing-table. Tony's trains laid out and waiting for him in a spare room. The favourite books and ornaments of all three on the tables beside their beds. On the day when they arrived she was waiting in the doorway. For the first time since Alex had been killed she had been into the nearest town and had her hair done. Her face was nicely made up and she had discarded her black and put on a cheerful cherry-coloured wool dress.

The journey had been tiring. Laurel, crushed at being dragged from her school, had scarcely spoken, staring glumly out of the window. Tony, too, barely uttered a word and when he did it was rudely. Kim had saved the situation. He was enchanted to come home for a holiday. They were not alone in the railway carriage and almost at once he had the ear of the other passengers and amused himself by showing off. The Colonel had not reproved him, he disliked that trait in Kim as much as Alex had done, but on this occasion it had its uses. It covered the silences of the other two. He dreaded the arrival at the house. It would not have surprised him if Lena had made an emotional scene. He was touched at her gallantry, standing there with her painted face and cherry frock, smiling as if her world had not powdered under her feet. Because their arrival had been so much easier than the children had anticipated they were less difficult than they had been on the journey. Even Tony had flung himself on his mother, kissing her rapturously. The Colonel had to depart the next morning and he left considerably comforted. It looked as if this bringing the children home was a good idea. There was more stuff in little Lena than he had supposed. Perhaps she would make a good job of bringing her children up single-handed.

Lena had no real servants. Nannie was cook. Mrs. Oliver, a cockney evacuee, came in for three or four hours a day to do the housework, and there was an aged gardener-handyman known locally as 'Old Mustard'. On the first morning after the Colonel had left Lena explained the situation. She took a 'It'll be such fun' tone.

'Everybody's called up, darlings. You'll give Nannie and Mrs. Oliver a hand in the house and kitchen, won't you, Laurel? And, Tony, I'd like you to take on the cleaning of the shoes, and there're lots of jobs in the garden that both you little boys can do to help Mustard. We'll all work and then it will be like a game.'

Laurel and Mrs. Oliver made friends over the bed making.

'I left London with me daughter and her kids, ducks, to-day's the day for turning the mattress, but never on a Friday or a Sunday or you come into bad luck. My daughter had shockin' bad luck from turning a mattress on a Friday.'

Mrs. Oliver and her relations seemed to exist on the spin of a coin. Everything that happened to them was caused by passing under ladders, meeting black cats, tripping over dropped nails and the arrangement of tea-leaves in their tea-cups. Laurel was thrilled. She had a natural inclination for domestic things and any work done with Mrs. Oliver would have been a pleasure. The beds finished she followed her into the drawing-room and helped to dust.

'Go on, Mrs. Oliver, tell me what happened to your grand-son because he found the threepenny bit.'

Lena had been arranging flowers and cleaning the silver. She had been round the house, the beds were made and the rooms tidy. She came into the drawing-room to find Laurel still working. She was touched. Splendid of her, she thought. She's doing it on purpose to be helpful and kind. She gave her a light kiss.

'Dad would be so proud, darling.'

Laurel flushed and jerked herself away from Lena. She threw her duster to Mrs. Oliver.

'Catch. I've done enough slaving for today. I'm going out into the garden.'

Lena stared after her, hurt and puzzled. Mrs. Oliver glanced at her, wondering if she should say something, but her cockney dislike of being nosey stopped her. She went on with her work.

Mustard was a nimble old man. In his stolid way he got through an immense amount of work. He could do most things but he had clearly defined limits as to what he would do and, the limit reached, said ' 'Taint my job,' and, having said that, no person or situation could persuade him to do the work in question. Although his life seemed to be ruled by doing those tasks that fell under his eye, he had, in his own way, an exactly planned day and knew how to fit a boy into his scheme. In no time he had discovered that he was unlikely to get consecutive work out of Kim, but he took a fancy to Tony and put him to work, as he said, 'b'long side o' me'. Mustard had spent all his life working in gardens, as had his father and grandfather before him. He looked upon a garden as an enclosed place in a savage world. The weeds, rabbits and squirrels, which came in from outside, were the besieging army which nothing but relentless sentry work kept at bay. On that first morning he was repairing a gap in the fence and he let Tony share in the work.

'It's the same as they say in the Bible, "Watch and pray". If I take my eyes off a fence what's weak, one of they little grey varmints will be scoutin' round and back he goes to the others and before you can say knife he's said "quick march", and there they are inside and not a lettuce left.'

This view of the life outside the garden charmed Tony. He did not so much see himself as taking part in a siege, but more as St. George standing on the ramparts flashing a sword.

'We'll beat them, Mr. Mustard. You and me together, and I expect we could get Laurel to help, and even Kim.'

Tony and Mustard were repairing some nets to go over the raspberries when Lena joined them. She smiled at Mustard.

'Is he being useful?'

Mustard considered, and then said what had always been his seal of approval on a likely gardener's boy.

'He'll do.'

Lena ran her hand over Tony's hair.

'I know you'll give all the help you can, won't you, Tony? That's what Dad would have liked, wouldn't he?'

Tony froze, his face scowling and sullen.

'Where's Laurel?'

'I've come to look for her,' Lena explained. 'I saw her run down the garden.'

Tony gazed around, he saw a glimpse of Laurel's frock. He dashed off towards it.

When alone the children were exceptionally united. Each one had something to gain from a corporate life. Laurel was once more the protective elder sister. It was solace to be needed. She enjoyed fussing round the others, seeing that they did not get their feet wet and the walks were not too long for Tuesday, a hundred and one little motherly things that made her feel warm in her heart. She knew of Tony's nightmares. Quite often his screams woke her, but she knew too, by intuition, that they must never be mentioned, and that long days out of doors made him better. He looked less strained and difficult when he came in.

For Tony life was divided into two halves. There was the

dreadful indoors half when at any moment Mum might say things, or you had to go into her bedroom and there, though you tried not to look, was Dad's photograph, and at once it started. The tight feeling across his front, the beating of his heart, he would remember the tap tapping as though he could still hear it. The other half was filled with rather insecure happiness. There was Mustard. Impossible to exaggerate the comfort he brought. He talked, in what Tony called to himself, a safe way. To him there always had been gardens and there always would be gardens, and there always had been wild things to fight, and there always would be wild things to fight, and that was natural and nothing, as he said, 'to be upsettin' of ourselves for'. Wars, and all that were attached to them, were passing inconveniences, but they did not change the pulse of his world.

'Oh goodness, do look, Mr. Mustard,' Tony would say. 'There're simply hundreds of Spitfires going over.'

Mustard would obligingly cock an eye skywards, then he would be back at his seedlings, or whatever it was, merely remarking, 'Ay, there're a lot of they.'

From Laurel Tony got immense comfort, but this did not give him the same satisfaction as working with Mustard. He let Laurel fuss over him and he agreed to play what to him were rather girlish games, for he found her company soothing. Because of his bad nights he was often tired, and thankful to take the line of least resistance; but at the back of his mind he had the thought that he was being a bit sissy for somebody who would be twelve in November. He did not look at the thought clearly, because that would mean thinking of

Dad and he was not ready for that yet. Now and again, when the sky was blue, and the trees glittered, incredibly green, and the scent of young bracken filled his nostrils, he forgot everything except the glory of the day and the fun of being alive.

Kim got least out of the family life, but he needed the steadying effect of that summer. For him there was no fear in talking to Lena, for he did not mind his father being mentioned. He accepted him in the past tense. He could no longer see him clearly. He had, however, suffered from shock, and running about the countryside, mothered, and, because it made for peace, rather spoilt by Laurel, was just what his health needed. He was the ringleader in games, his was the imagination which saw that a glade was full of Red Indians, how an overhanging tree could be turned into a house, and it was he who filled a disused sandpit with brown bears. He found too another way of satisfying his ego. He was far and away the sharpest of the children, he loved to set problems. Who was the person who said . . . ? If you add this and this, what's the answer? Now and again Laurel and Tony would tell him, more often they did not bother to listen, and quite possibly would not have been able to answer if they had. Kim would bounce about bursting with eagerness. 'I'll tell you, I'll tell you. I'm younger than either of you, but I know.'

For Tuesday the arrival home of her brothers and sister brought undiluted happiness. From being with them day after day she got just that sense of continuity and security that she needed. Because the house was isolated, her family were always about, there were no visits to shops or cinemas, she was with them all day. She knew that Nannie went off on the bus to do the shopping but she did not see her go, and usually, by the time she went to look for her she was to be found in the kitchen saying, in her usual placid way, 'Well, my lamb?' By degrees the nervous habits of the last months left her. Within a week of her brothers and sister coming home she had no more trouble with enuresis. She stopped biting her nails and her movements, which had been jerky, became normal. If she was out of sight for a moment and the others should wonder where she was, they would say, 'Stop speaking everybody, and we'll hear her humming.'

Lena put up a fine struggle. At first she refused to notice Laurel's and Tony's off-hand ways and rudeness. Then, trying to think fairly as Alex would have done, she examined herself. Was it unkind to ask the children to help? Were they resentful? She knew what Alex would have said. With labour so short the children must help, and he would have told them what he thought of them if they had grumbled. Lena's policy with her children had always been that they should be charmed by her. A mother to admire, who was a little apart from the hum-drum side of life. It was entirely foreign to her but at last she screwed herself up to speak to Laurel and Tony. She gave great thought to what she should say, trying to use Alex's mind and not her own. She saw the two children together.

'Darlings, I know you don't mean it, but sometimes you answer rather rudely. I know it's hard to be asked to help but we're at war and everybody, even children, must do their bit.'

Laurel, conscious of happy mornings assisting Mrs. Oliver, and Tony, cherishing the hours spent with Mustard, stared blankly at their mother. They did not mind working and they supposed she knew they did not. What was she getting at? Tony looked sullen. Laurel prayed silently: 'Oh God, please don't let her talk about Dad, please don't.' Lena saw their strained, sullen faces, and suddenly it was more than she could bear. Was it not enough that she should have lost Alex? Was it not enough that she should struggle every hour of the day to appear gay and to look nice to please the children? Only she knew the agonies of tears she shed when they were safely in bed. She fought, but loneliness and self-pity engulfed her. She put her face in her hands, her shoulders shook with sobs. Laurel and Tony gazed at her with scarlet faces. This was worse than anything they had imagined. Pity and love rose in both children. Laurel would have liked to have flung her arms round Lena and said, 'We do love you, Mum, we do,' but horror kept her silent. Suddenly she rushed to the door and flung it open. Her voice rose to a scream.

'Nannie. Nannie, do come, Mum's ill or something.'

Then, not waiting to see what Nannie did, the two children raced out into the garden, pushing each other about and howling with laughter.

It was a losing fight for Lena. Her loneliness ate away her strength. Every day she gave way a little more to self-pity. For her children she found excuses. 'Tony doesn't sleep very well.' 'It's that horrible school that's changed Laurel. I shan't send her back there in the autumn.'

The children had been home about two months when, waking one morning after a few hours' jumpy sleep, Lena reached a crossroad. She spoke out loud.

'I can't face the day. I simply can't.'

It was as she heard her own voice that she thought of her brandy flask. She sat up in bed and drank a good three fingers of brandy neat. Wonderful! How much better she felt. For the first time since Alex had been killed she came down to breakfast. Clear headedly she tackled three problems which should have been dealt with weeks ago. She wrote to the Board of Trade. She had lost clothes when the London house was hit. Clothes rationing had now started and she must claim coupons. She wrote to Miss Brownlow and said that she would not be sending Laurel back next term, and, by the same post, wrote to her sister-in-law, Dot, to ask what she thought of the school to which she had sent Alice and Maria. She rang up the doctor and asked him to come and see Tony.

The doctor came that afternoon. The effect of the brandy had worn off and Lena was feeling flat and exhausted. The doctor had a look at Tony who, since he hated his nightmares discussed, was monosyllabic and off-hand. When he dismissed Tony, though he was busy, he stayed for a talk with Lena. While he chatted about Tony his experienced eye took her in. He saw unmistakable signs of the storms of tears which she was shedding. He saw that she was carrying on her existence with nothing but will-power. She had not called him in about herself and, in a case like hers, it was dangerous to say much. Take away her will-power and she would just fall in a heap as if she were a doll with the stuffing out of her.

'I'd like you to get this made up for the boy. I want him to have a tablespoonful the last thing at night, followed by a cup of milk or cocoa or whatever you can get. I don't think he's my case. I should say that we may have to send him to a psychologist. Let me know if there's any improvement and, if not, I'll come up and see him again.' He was rising to go. He spoke gently and with sympathy. 'What about yourself? You don't look as if you were sleeping very well. I'll give you a prescription for some tablets. How about a tonic?' He paused to smile at her. He knew that she must know that a tonic would not help. 'I dare say you could do with a bit of stimulant.'

The doctor drove away feeling dissatisfied. He had not done much for the poor woman. What the devil could you do? No such thing actually as a broken heart, but there was a state of being that was very like it, and all the drugs in the world would not help.

Lena, standing on her doorstep looking after the departing car, was more comforted than the doctor knew. He had shown her sympathy. Isolated from the outside world, sympathy was a quality which she had not been receiving. It cheered her. Then, too, he had mentioned a stimulant and said that it would do her good. Of course it would. Stupid to get in the habit of drinking, just as it was stupid to get into the habit of taking sleeping tablets, but just now she needed something. She looked down at the sleeping prescription in her hand, unconsciousness all night, and a good nip of brandy when she woke, perhaps with those aids she could face the coming days.

Dot wrote that Alice and Maria were immensely happy at their school. 'If I were you I should send Tuesday as well. It's time she started lessons and they're very good to the little ones.'

Elsa had over-persuaded Dot. Alice and Maria had not gone to a convent, but to a very large day school which took a limited number of boarders. Lena was pleased with herself for thinking of sending Laurel to school with Alice. The two girls were friends. It was bound to be nice for Laurel. However, she did not tell her immediately. Laurel was so difficult she waited until she had a good day. She now made all her efforts in the morning. It was wonderful what brandy on an empty inside did for you.

Laurel was making the beds with Mrs. Oliver. Lena called to her.

'Darling, come into my room a moment.'

Laurel started and flushed. Mrs. Oliver gave her a friendly push.

'Hop along. Your Mum's calling you. I'll get this one finished while you're gone.'

Laurel stood in her mother's doorway looking thoroughly disobliging.

'What is it?'

Lena, warmed by brandy, could pass over that expression and that tone.

'I've heard from Aunt Dot. You know she sent Alice and Maria to a school called Greenwood House. Well, I hear they're very happy there, and so I've decided that you shall go there next term.' She saw the startled look on Laurel's face and spoke almost pleadingly. 'You'd like to be with Alice, wouldn't you?'

Laurel stared at her mother, her world reeling. Not go back to the Abbey School! Not go back to Miss Brownlow!

When she had left so suddenly Miss Brownlow had said: 'It won't do you any harm, Laurel, to have a holiday. I know it seems long but next term will soon be here, and we shall be waiting for you, very glad to have you back.' Miss Brownlow had become the most important person in Laurel's life. Since that day in the car she had never spoken to her about Alex, yet Laurel knew Alex was the person she was thinking about. It had been a short time since that day in the car and Grandfather fetching her away, but even in that time Miss Brownlow had made plans. She had begun to make Laurel see that just being part of the school was not enough, that you had got to find your way to being a useful bit of it. Already she had fired her to make special efforts. It was one of these efforts that came to her mind now.

'I must go back to the Abbey School next term. I'm going to try for the junior jumping cup.'

To Lena all schools were a bore and the Abbey School a menace. It had made a gauche, bad-tempered child of her daughter.

'I hate you going to school at all, darling. Stupid places. I'd much rather keep you with me, but you must be educated, that's why I'm sending you to Greenwood House with Alice.'

It was only then that Laurel realised that Lena really intended to remove her from the Abbey School. Desperate, she raised her voice.

'I must go back. You shan't take me away. You shan't.'

Shouting and talking rudely were, to Lena, Abbey School legacies. Her gentle Laurel was not to blame. She refused to quarrel with her. She spoke quietly and firmly.

'Be quiet, darling. You are going to Greenwood House and there's an end of it.'

The scene that followed was so foreign to Laurel it felt as if it was tearing her to pieces. The basis of it was fear. There was little enough security in her world, and what there was was being wrenched from her. She screamed, she beat on the door with her fists and, finally, sank on the floor in a heap, crying.

Mrs. Oliver stood in the passage listening. Trouble about a school was natural enough. Children often got a fancy for one school or one teacher and there it was. She was in no way shocked or surprised at Laurel's behaviour. 'Do her good to let off a bit of steam, poor little thing,' was her reaction. What she was watching for was Lena. She alone, of all the household, knew that Lena had taken to brandy. 'If there's been spirits used, even as much as a cork passed through the room, my nose gives a twitch,' she was fond of saying, and it was true. Though it was many hours after the brandy flask had been opened, the moment she came into Lena's room, that first morning, she had smelt brandy, and she had smelt it ever since. 'Don't blame her, po'r thing,' thought Mrs. Oliver. 'You have to take your comfort where you can find it.' She stood in the passage as much for Lena's sake as for Laurel's. She did not mean to interfere, but you never knew what any one would do when they had a drop of drink in them.

Nannie, in the kitchen, raised her head. She listened to Laurel crying. Without putting her thoughts into words she accepted that the cries were genuine. Intuitively she knew fear and misery lay behind them. She hurried up the stairs. She put her arms round Laurel. She spoke as if she were once more her baby.

'You come along with Nannie, my lamb. Come along. Come along now. Nannie's here.'

XXX

Clothes rationing was not a system Lena grasped. In theory she knew that clothes were now unobtainable without coupons but some part of her rejected the idea. When she was near a shop she would remember that she wanted a dozen pairs of stockings, or she would see some crêpe-de-chine she fancied, and she would go in and order the goods and be really surprised when she was asked for her coupons. When she looked at the ration books the coupons seemed to stand between her family and semi-nakedness. 'We must be very careful of these and, when we have to use them, only buy the best of everything so the things will last.'

Lena had always considered school uniforms tiresome. They were ugly and did not show her children at their best. When, therefore, she got a list of clothes that Laurel required for Greenwood House she was quite indignant.

'Such nonsense, Nannie, they say she's to have brown tunics and a brown coat. Laurel's got all that nasty green uniform that she had at the Abbey School, she can wear that out. I shouldn't dream of spending her coupons on uniform.'

Greenwood House was a big school. There were over five hundred girls. Of that number about a hundred were boarded in a building called Greenwood House Over the Way. As

Laurel saw the school on her first day it seemed to her an ant-heap. Brown ants rushing here and there, tremendously busy knowing where they ought to be, where everything lived, with no time for strangers. It was bad luck that Alice was in quarantine for chicken-pox and was not at school at the beginning of the term. Laurel arrived the night before the term began. She was taken to the main school the next morning by a girl who was kind, but in a hurry to meet her friends. She dumped Laurel in the main big hall.

'You wait here for prayers and roll-call. Presently they'll call out your name and you'll know what class you're in.'

Laurel stood alone, painfully self-conscious, with girls eddying round her, agonisingly aware of her green uniform. If only she were dressed like everybody else! As she was a fragment of green in a sea of brown she could see everyone looking and staring. A bell clanged for prayers. She heard a whisper. 'Who's the frog?' She did not hear the answer, but she heard the word repeated and whispered amidst a rising chorus of giggles. 'Frog. Frog. Frog.'

Laurel, having fought her battle with Lena and lost, came to Greenwood House determined she would hate it. She arrived at an unlucky period. Before the war there had been about fifty boarders in the charge of an admirable house mistress. The house mistress had been offered a more important post and had been replaced, as a temporary measure, by an old house mistress who had retired. Miss Clegg had never been particularly brilliant in her handling of girls, but she had been kind and interested and much loved. She now had less strength and less patience, and was forced to squeeze over a hundred girls into a space intended for fifty. At the same time the call-up of women had reduced her domestic staff. She saw Laurel the night she arrived, and Laurel sensed she had not much time to spare for her.

'Oh, yes. You're Laurel Wiltshire.' She eyed Laurel disapprovingly. 'Your mother insisted you must wear out your old school uniform. Of course clothes coupons make a difference but it's not a very satisfactory arrangement. I do hope she'll soon manage to get you brown. We always have insisted on all the girls wearing brown.'

No one had told Miss Clegg about Laurel. She was just the Enden children's cousin. Lena had not mentioned in her letter that Alex had been killed, but only that she had removed Laurel from her previous school as she had not cared for its tone. There was nothing in the fair child with the rather sulky expression in front of her to lead Miss Clegg to the knowledge that Laurel was desperately in need of care and help. That after Miss Brownlow, who had taken such an infinity of trouble, she was causing a hurt just by being in a hurry and showing it. That the tone in which she spoke of the green uniform was salt in an already very sore wound.

Miss Clegg gave a quick glance at her watch and passed to the question she asked all new girls.

'Have you a special hobby, dear? What are you good at? Greenwood House Over the Way has always encouraged talent.'

Laurel looked sulkier than ever.

'I'm not good at anything. And I don't want to be.'

Miss Clegg dismissed Laurel. She wrote in her notebook

against Laurel's name, 'Seems badly brought up. Watch for sulkiness.'

Alice arrived at the school three weeks later. She and Laurel met in the passage outside the dormitory. They grinned at each other awkwardly.

'Do you like it?'

Laurel was so thankful to see Alice that she clutched her by the hand.

'Oh, Alice, I'm glad you've come! I think it's simply awful. Everybody hates me and I wish I was dead.' Greenwood House Over the Way did not allow the girls in the dormitories in the daytime. Laurel decided that Alice's arrival was an occasion to break the rule. She came in and sat on Alice's bed while Alice unpacked. The children spoke in whispers. 'It's partly not having the right uniform. It makes me so noticeable. If anybody else turns the wrong way in all that marching we have to do nobody notices who it is, but with me they can't help knowing because of my wearing green. It's the same with that awful dancing.'

Alice took a pile of blouses out of her box and laid them on the bed.

'That's called middle-European. It is pretty foul.'

'I don't know what it's called but I never know what we're doing and I do it all wrong, and that awful woman who teaches us shouts, "Girl in green, you're out of step."'

Alice looked at Laurel's tunic.

'I wonder if it would dye. You can get dyes to do at home. We had a cook who was always dyeing things.'

Laurel was past being hopeful.

'I shouldn't think so. It would be wonderful if we could. Alice, do you like it here? Your mother wrote that you were immensely happy at school. She made that up, didn't she?'

Alice put the blouses away in her chest-of-drawers.

'Honestly, I do rather like it.'

'Why were you so long having chicken-pox?'

'Maria had it. I had to look after her because she would scratch. Then, when she was well, I was in quarantine because I've never had it.'

'Why did you have to look after Maria? Where's Aunt Dot?'

'Working. She's awfully important. She wears uniform. Is Tuesday here?'

'No. She's supposed to come next term, but she won't if I can help it, poor little beast.'

Alice lifted the tray out of her box and burrowed for her shoes.

'I expect she'll like it, the little ones do. Maria simply adores it.'

'She can't. There's nothing anybody could adore.'

Alice knelt upright, a pair of shoes in each hand.

'There's such a lot of girls, you can't help liking some of them. Then I like games.'

Laurel suddenly understood.

'Of course! I forgot that. All your family are super at games.'

'Not super,' Alice objected, 'but I was runner-up for the junior tennis cup last term, and they think I might be in the second lacrosse team this term unless being late's made a difference.'

Laurel hugged her knees.

'And there are nearly five hundred girls and you're only thirteen! I suppose it's that sort of school. Of course, that's it. It is that sort of school.'

'What sort of school?'

'The sort of school where you ought to be good at something. Miss Clegg said that. Even my wearing green uniform when everybody else wears brown wouldn't matter if I were good at something.' Laurel's imagination carried her on.

'In fact it would be a good thing then. That awful dancing mistress would say, "Stand still all of you and watch the girl in green do it." And when I was marching, because I was good at it, my being green would be a help. Oh, Alice, all the girls here call me The Frog. But if I were good at something, I wouldn't mind, being called The Frog would be a kind of honour, wouldn't it? I mean, there's a lot of difference between being called The Frog to be laughed at and being called it to be admired.'

Alice thought that being dressed in the wrong uniform was one of the worst things that could happen to anybody. In her view it was a catastrophe that nothing could ameliorate.

'I wish we'd arrived at the same time, then I could have lent you some of my uniform. I've got a second tunic, only now, of course, they'd know I'd done it and there'd be a row. Still, we might try the dye.'

'No.' Laurel slid off the bed. 'I'd better nip down now before matron catches me. Even if we were to dye me they'd notice. I couldn't suddenly come down all brown one morning, could I? But you've given me an idea. Alice, I shall make myself good at something.'

'What?'

The blunt question brought Laurel back to earth.

'I don't know. It's not the term to swim.'

'Quite a lot of girls here do backward dives from the top of the spring-board.'

'I could act?'

Alice settled her spectacles more firmly on her nose.

'There's a girl here who's as lovely as Deanna Durbin and acts just as well. Besides, you have to have been at the school for years and years before you get a part in a play.'

'At the Abbey School I was fair at games. I once played in the second eleven of lacrosse, but I wouldn't be here. There must be something.'

Alice was incapable of following Laurel's dreams. What she considered mattered was the uniform. She clung to dyes.

'Things go to shops to be dyed. We could ask matron, she's awfully nice.'

Laurel opened the door and peered out. She looked back at Alice over her shoulder.

'No, Alice. I've started green and I shall go on being green. But one day all the five hundred girls here will be proud of me, and wish that somebody would call them The Frog.'

Alice was fond of Laurel but she knew her limitations. 'It would be better to get dyed. And much quicker.'

XXXI

Ruth had wanted to visit the children ever since Alex's death. It had been difficult. On her last leave they had been at home and she found it impossible to write to Lena and ask if she could come down. She had never been on those sort of terms with Lena. She could see her in her mind's eye reading her letter. 'Miss Glover. Oh yes, she went into the A.T.S. How tiresome! Why should she want to come down?'

Ruth had thought a lot about Lena. How was she existing alone? Take away Alex and had she anything to fall back on? Her life had been built like a game of spillikins with Alex as the bottom spillikin on which the whole structure stood. It was impossible that the structure would not collapse when you tore out the bottom spillikin.

Ruth wrote to Lena. She had seven days' leave which she was spending in the West country. She could so work it in that she could get to Wingsgate House to lunch with the boys on Saturday and break her journey back to where she was stationed and take Laurel out on Sunday. Would this be convenient? It was a carefully casual letter. She felt it would be a mistake to write as if she was desperately anxious to see the children.

Lena was touched by Ruth's letter. She thought it was extraordinarily nice of her to be prepared to spend so much of her precious leave looking up the children. She had received a most sincere and moving letter from her at the time of Alex's death, and she felt this wish to visit the children was an additional gesture of sympathy. She wrote back graciously. It would be very kind indeed if she really could be bothered to look the children up. She knew they would be thrilled. If ever Miss Glover should be near either school again and felt like seeing the children, she was to visit without asking. Lena said she was writing that day to Mr. Phillips and Miss Clegg to tell them about this present visit and she would add that if Miss

Glover ever visited again she was a friend of the children's and she was glad that they should see her at any time.

Ruth waited in the hall at Wingsgate House for the boys. Kim came down first. He flung himself on her.

'Oh, Miss Glover, I moved up last term, and I'm already top of my form and if I move up next term I'll be in the same form as Tony.'

She kissed him. He was as good-looking as ever. He had grown, of course. He seemed well and in the best of spirits.

Tony greeted her soberly. She was startled at the change in him. He would be twelve next week and, of course, was no longer a round little boy. It was not so much in appearance that he had changed as in his manner. He seemed reserved and aloof. He was pleased to see her, but there was none of the old talkative enthusiasm about him. She had a taxi waiting. Kim sat beside her and snuggled up against her, Tony chose one of the bucket seats facing them.

'There's a boy in my dormitory,' said Kim, 'who's a Roman Catholic, and Roman Catholics burn candles when they want to thank for things and when they want things. I gave him a pencil sharpener if he would burn a candle to ask his saints if you could come down in uniform. I'm absolutely the only boy in my form that nobody in uniform ever comes to see.'

Ruth hugged him to her.

'Don't your uncles ever come? You've three of them in uniform.'

She was answering Kim but her eyes were on Tony. He said:

'Uncle Paul has to go to Greenwood House when he gets leave to see Alice and Maria.'

Kim tugged at her arm to attract her attention.

'And he takes out Laurel too, lucky beast. Uncle John doesn't get much leave, sailors don't.'

Tony went on:

'And when he does he spends it with Aunt Lindsey, I expect. He hasn't time to come and see us. Why should he?'

Kim bounced up and down.

'I don't see why. Other people's uncles do. We've a chap in my form whose uncle's an Air Vice-Marshal and even he comes.'

Tony looked wearily at Kim.

'He only came once and that was to see the boxing.'

Ruth was still looking at Tony.

'And I suppose when Uncle Arthur gets leave he spends it at home with Fiona and Bertie and Aunt Selina.'

Kim got half off the seat.

'And this is Bertie.' He gave an imitation of exaggerated piano playing. 'And this is Fiona.' He stuck out one foot as if he were dancing.

'You sit down,' said Ruth, 'or you'll fall out of the door. And if I were you I should write to Uncle John. He might come as he hasn't any children of his own. Anyway there's no harm in asking him.'

Tony looked as if he were considering her words, but all he said was:

'I can't see why on earth he should.'

Ruth felt awkward with Tony. She did not feel as if she knew him. She was not sure that he wanted her to take him out. He had a quick snubbing way of talking that she found difficult to cope with. Inwardly she laughed at herself. Here are you looking after hundreds of girls, quite a lot of them really difficult, and you get shy and tongue-tied with a small boy.

'What's the news of Laurel? I'm going to see her tomorrow.'

Kim raised shocked eyes to hers.

'It's most terribly unfair. Somebody's always taking Laurel out. She gets her turn of Mum, Aunt Dot goes every three weeks to see Alice and Maria and she takes Laurel out too, and, as well, there's Uncle Paul when he gets leave.'

Tony fixed his eyes on Ruth's.

'Submarines sometimes go to the bottom and never come up again.'

'But not your Uncle John's fortunately. Does Laurel ever write to you?'

'Not often. Why should she?'

Kim looked at Tony with a shocked expression.

'That's an absolute lie, Tony. She writes almost every week because I see the letter.'

Ruth turned to Kim.

'I dare say Tuesday writes to you.'

Kim nodded.

'But she's very backward. You'd never think that she was going to be seven at Christmas. Nannie rules lines for her, and she says about one thing and all the rest is crosses for kisses.'

Ruth had heard at intervals from Laurel. The early letters, all written in term time, had been full of Abbey School doings, and she had obviously been happy. She had not answered Ruth's letter about Alex's death. Her next letter was heartbroken but about something else. She would die if she had to leave the Abbey School. There had not been a letter covering the holidays at home, then had come a distraught letter from Greenwood House. 'Oh Foxglove darling! Don't mind my calling you that but we always did and it seems more friendly somehow. This is the most awful place in the world and I ought to wear brown and instead I wear the Abbey School uniform which makes me terribly conspicuous. Some days I feel I shall go mad like Ophelia so if you hear I've been found floating on the water, don't be surprised.'

Ruth's question to Tony had been deliberate. Tony and Laurel had always been friends. Perhaps she was a subject on which he would expand. Tony was looking sullenly out of the window. Then he said abruptly:

'She doesn't like that school much. She says it's foul, but then all schools are.'

Kim bounced up and down with excitement.

'I simply love being at Wingsgate House. Last week, when it was wet, we had a mental arithmetic competition for everybody in the school except the very little boys, and do you know, I came out second of everybody, and I'm only just ten, and some of our chaps are nearly fourteen.'

Tony said:

'I was bottom but three.'

Ruth smiled at him.

'Mental arithmetic isn't everybody's subject. Unless you've altered, no form of arithmetic is yours. Is it still history?'

'History's worse than all the others.'

They had arrived at the hotel. Ruth paid the taxi.

'Pop along in you two and hang up your coats and wash.'

Her voice was cheerful but she felt heart-sick and as though she had not got the energy for the coming lunch. Nothing, she decided, could weigh one down like an unresponsive child. Tony of all people. She saw him in her mind's eye at Eastbourne. Brown as a berry with that noticeably open, honest air about him which was so endearing. His endless questions. 'I say, Dad. . . .' For a little boy his voice had been deep and rather serious in tone. She remembered the argument with Laurel as to where they should live. Tony had said: 'Everywhere is nice but London's different. I suppose that's because it's where we live.' There had been a stolid vein of good sense in Tony which Alex had fostered. Something had gone terribly wrong to change him into this 'don't care' boy. Kim had said that he was top of the form below Tony's and that he would be moving up next term. She had taught the boys. Kim was sharp and had the best brains but Tony was plodding and conscientious. He would normally keep up with his age. She had not liked the way Tony had capped Kim's bragging by 'I was bottom but three.' Alex had tried to train his children to face things. His death ought not to have messed up Tony like this.

Throughout lunch the talk went on as it had in the taxi. Kim, full of bounce and excitement, and she trying to draw Tony into the conversation and only getting monosyllabic replies. One thing she noticed with pleasure. Kim had improved. As usual his good looks made everybody in the dining-room stare. It was the kind of occasion which, in the old days, would have forced Kim to show off. Now he seemed unaware that he was being looked at and was only genuinely delighted to see her again and to talk to her. School life was evidently what Kim needed. He had clearly established some sort of position for himself.

'We're doing a play at Christmas. It's scenes from *A Midsummer Night's Dream* and I'm Puck. Do you know. . . .' He leant on the table and spoke earnestly, 'I start by jumping on the spring-board, and I come down in the middle of the stage exactly as if I flew.'

Ruth tried another tactic to get Tony to talk.

'Have you any special friends? Next time I come you might both like to bring a friend out with you.'

Kim shook his head.

'I'm friends with one person one minute and the next minute I find they're simply hateful really, and then I look proud and don't speak to them for weeks.'

'What about you, Tony?'

'There's nobody special.'

After lunch, as it was too cold to go out, Ruth borrowed a pack of cards and they played 'Old Maid' and 'Snap'. It was over tea that Ruth caught her first impression that there was something definite that was wrong with Tony. Kim was describing how he made the other boys laugh. It was at shelter practice.

'Once every week we have to march to the shelter. The warning goes when you aren't expecting it, when I'm lucky it goes in the middle of French.' Kim's voice burbled on. Ruth, apparently engaged in pouring out the tea, was looking at Tony. He had turned pale and he was breathing quickly.

'I was the last,' said Kim, 'and I slammed the door and I pretended for a minute it wouldn't open and, do you know, Tony fainted.'

Tony spoke quietly.

'It was nothing whatsoever to do with your fool joke. It was just that I'd eaten something bad. Matron said so when I got into the san.'

Kim refused to be squashed.

'I bet it was me shutting the door. I wasn't there but you fainted that time you went over to see the Abbey and were made to go into the script.'

Tony scowled.

'It's called a crypt. Anyway, heaps of people faint.'

Ruth walked the two boys back to the school. She hung about saying good-bye. Tony merely shook her hand and stalked off, but Kim clung to her, pleading for one last kiss. She had told them that Laurel had decided to call her Foxglove, and Kim had adopted it delightedly.

'Come on, Foxglove. One simply enormous hug.'

There were two small boys crossing the hall and Ruth saw them grin tolerantly. Evidently Kim was the school card. She had half hoped that Mr. Phillips would pass and she would have an opportunity to speak to him. She had no idea what she would say. She had no excuse to discuss Tony, but she hated to leave the school without saying anything.

She lit her torch because it was dark in the drive. Suddenly a voice spoke out of the shadows. It was Tony.

'I thought you might get lost. I'll walk with you as far as the gate.'

Ruth felt as if she were dealing with an opportunity made of spun glass. She dared not waste the time. She took Tony's arm.

'What's the matter, Tony?'

He was as surly as ever.

'Nothing. What should there be?'

'That's nonsense. There's something wrong. You've spent the whole day looking as if you'd eaten a sour lemon, and you don't sound to me as if you were doing much good at school.'

Tony changed the conversation.

'Do you know anything about submarines?'

'No.'

'Do you think Uncle John really would come down? There's something I've been wanting to ask him.' He broke off. 'About submarines, I mean.'

Ruth knew Uncle John and liked him. She had not known that Tony was especially fond of him or interested in submarines, but any interest was to be encouraged.

'I bet he would.'

Tony's voice came out of the greyness.

'I don't know his address, do you?'

'No. But I could get it. If you'd send a letter to him to me, I'll get it forwarded for you.'

At the gate she pulled Tony to her and gave him a kiss.

'Good-bye, darling. I know letter writing's a nuisance, but I should like to hear from you when you can spare time.'

Tony was running back up the drive. His voice sounded a shade less surly.

'I might. Good-bye.'

Waiting for her bus Ruth chewed on the subject of Tony and a letter to Uncle John. Uncle John and Aunt Lindsey had stayed quite often in London. Lindsey came up for literary gatherings and, though John hated being dragged from the country, she insisted that he accompany her. He had been secretary of a golf club. He became secretary of the golf club after he was axed from the Navy and seemed reasonably happy. Ruth had found Lindsey completely terrifying and marvelled that anyone could be happy with her. She was certainly fond of John in a possessive way and nicer to him than to any one else, which was not saying much. It was clear that Tony's letter to John ought to have a covering letter from somebody. He might spare a day of his leave to come over and see the boy. It seemed imperative somebody should see him. What a mess it all was. How could so nice a boy as Tony go to pieces like this? I suppose, in a way, they were too carefully brought up. They had too happy a home. Odd, I shouldn't have thought any one could have too much of that sort of happiness. She thought about her A.T.S. girls, coming as they did from all types of homes. Certainly the spoilt ones found life hard when they were thrown into the Army, but the Wiltshires had not really been spoilt. Alex had been quite ruthless in the code of behaviour he laid down for his children, taking special trouble with Tony. His father's death, shock though it must have been to the child, should not have had this effect on him. His training should have stood by him and he should have risen above it. What was all this about fainting in shelters and crypts? Tony, whose idea of the right way to spend a day was to prowl about the Tower of London imploring to be taken into dungeons, smacking his lips over ghastly descriptions of people's lingering deaths. Her visit had not been a success, unless it was good to have suggested a letter to Uncle John. It was a small thing to have done but you never knew where small things led, particularly with children. It was possible with a child that the right person saying the right thing at the right moment could change their whole outlook. Ruth climbed on to the bus and took a ticket to the railway station. 'And now Laurel tomorrow,' she thought. 'Let's hope she isn't in a mess. Queer that the child who seems to be doing nicely is Kim, who was always considered the family problem.'

Laurel was waiting at the gate of Greenwood House Over the Way. She flung her arms round Ruth.

'Oh darling, darling Foxglove, don't you look scrumptious in uniform. I've met you here because Aunt Dot's here for the day and she's gone out with Alice and Maria and she says will we be at The Royal Hotel at half-past four for tea. Do you think we could go on a bus to the next town for our lunch? Because then we needn't see any of our girls.'

In the bus Laurel poured out her troubles.

'And it's getting worse, Foxglove, because I'm becoming a woman and getting a chest, and you must agree it's worse to bulge in green than to be thin in green. Alice wants me to get it dyed, but I said no, I was going to bring it to fame, and that's where you come in. You know me better than any one else in the world. What could I shine at so that nobody could ever be better than me?'

Ruth knew for all its superlatives the question was asked seriously. She answered truthfully.

'You're what I should have called quite a good all-rounder.'

Laurel groaned.

'That's what Dad always said, and he said he liked me like that, but then he never knew about the green uniform and Greenwood House.'

Ruth was thankful to hear the easy mention of Alex. He had not been spoken of by Tony or Kim.

'That's quite true, but you can't be a star or a champion just by wanting to be one.'

'You can't make a silk purse out of a sow's ear.'

'I shouldn't exactly describe you as a sow's ear, but that's roughly what I mean.'

Laurel leant against Ruth and tucked an arm into hers.

'Well, I might be outstanding for goodness.'

'What have you been reading?'

Laurel nodded.

'You're quite right. It's called "Lives of Little Saints". If only I could see a vision like Bernadette of Lourdes. She wasn't much older than me when she saw a lady, and where she saw the lady water came up and cured people.'

'I never knew any one who saw visions, but my impression is that they didn't go about looking for the visions, but the visions sprang upon them unawares.'

'Then there was a child saint who found her dress full of roses at the wrong time of year. Just think, if I could come into the dining-room rather late with something in my tunic and Miss Clegg would say, "What's that, Laurel?" and

I would let my tunic drop and there would be roses in November. In "The Book of Little Saints", in the pictures, when the miracle happens there's always a light shining on the person's face.'

Ruth held Laurel's arm more closely to her.

'I think I should cut out miracles if I were you. They don't happen often.'

'It's queer the way some people are important. There's a girl at school whose mother's an actress, and in the holidays she goes behind the scenes in the theatres, just walking about, going where she likes. It doesn't matter what that girl does, it wouldn't matter even if she wore a green uniform, I think it would be rather distinguished really. And then there's another girl, she's fat and rather ugly, but she always makes everybody laugh, and there's one who's just distinguished by badness. You just take it for granted every week there's going to be an awful row for her about something.'

Ruth played with Laurel's fingers.

'I can't help thinking that being that sort of distinguished isn't a good idea, and I believe you'll think so presently. You're new now but in no time everybody'll have got used to your green uniform and, judging by the look of it, you'll soon have outgrown it and then I expect you'll have the brown one.'

'Oh no, I won't. Not ever. Mum says uniforms are a wicked waste of coupons.'

'Well, your mother won't be the only person to think that. Quite soon half the school will be wearing all kinds of clothes.'

Laurel spoke earnestly.

'But what you don't see is that it won't make any difference to me. I've started off by being called The Frog and it's not meant politely. Well, what I want to do is to make people think of The Frog as a name given in honour.'

'Tell me about the family. There's one thing at which I know you shine, and that's at being a good elder sister.'

Throughout the rest of the bus ride and throughout lunch and on the bus back to The Royal Hotel for tea, Ruth collected news of the family. She heard about the house in Surrey, and Mrs. Oliver and Old Mustard. She heard about the rhododendrons and the azaleas. In a shocked, worried voice Laurel confided to her the story of Tuesday's enuresis.

'Nannie thought I didn't know but of course I did. As a matter of fact, soon after we came home, it didn't happen any more.'

Ruth looked startled.

'Tuesday! She's going to be seven next month.'

Laurel nodded.

'Yes, it's a terrible disgrace. That's why Nannie never talks about it. Even Mum doesn't know. I made Tuesday tell me about it, but she wouldn't much. She just said it happened and trying didn't stop it.'

'Is she quite all right now?'

'I hope to goodness she is because she's coming to school next term. That really would be the worst thing that could happen if she did it at school. We'd simply have to leave, we'd never live down the shame.'

'Poor little Tuesday. She ought to go to a doctor. It's an illness, not a naughtiness. However, if it goes on, especially if it happens at school, they certainly will take her to a doctor.'

'There's a very nice doctor in Surrey. He came to look after Tony.'

'What's the matter with Tony?'

'Nightmares. He screamed and screamed.'

'What did the doctor do about him?'

'Gave him medicine and he had to have milk at night. He got all right again.'

'Well, he still doesn't look well.'

'Perhaps he had flu' when you saw him. Lots of our girls have had flu'.'

'Did you think he was well when he was at home?'

Laurel was evasive.

'I couldn't see anything wrong and he ate like a horse.'

Tony wasn't the only subject on which Laurel dodged Ruth. Each time she asked a question about her mother Laurel edged away.

'Mum's all right. Why shouldn't she be?'

Nothing that Laurel said gave Ruth an inkling into the life inside the house with their mother. Lena seemed to be grappling with her children. In hearing about Mrs. Oliver Ruth heard about the bed making. In hearing about Old Mustard she heard about Tony's work, but always Lena was left a shadow, there were no warm colourful touches to show that she was, as she must be, the mainspring of her children's lives. One thing came out clearly from Laurel's conversation, she had been intensely happy at the Abbey School and had cared so bitterly about being removed that she still could not talk about it. The only redeeming feature of Greenwood House seemed to be Alice.

'She's still exactly the same and she still has to wear those awful spectacles, but she's simply marvellous at games. She plays in the second lacrosse team, and she won't be fourteen until January, and nobody else in the team is younger than fifteen, and she was runner up for the junior tennis cup last term, and she's the junior champion at gym and none of that makes her the least bit proud. She's awfully keen to see you again. She's never forgotten you. She was simply sick that time she came to Gran's and Grandfather's and missed you because you were in Devonshire.'

'What does Alice think about your chances of becoming a champion at something?'

'I can't say that she really sees how desperately it matters, and, if you come to think of it, I can't think why she should. She's got uniform and in any case she does most of the things very well, even that awful middle-European dancing, and, of course, she's got games. She thinks they're just fun to play and it doesn't matter being good at them, but that's because she doesn't know what it's like when you're not good at anything at all.'

Just before they reached the hotel for tea Ruth told Laurel that Tony and Kim wanted to see Uncle John. She put the onus on to Kim.

'He says nobody in uniform ever comes to see him.'

Laurel's eyes shone.

'Uncle John! Next to Dad I always thought he was the nicest man I ever knew, though I can't say I've ever cared for Aunt Lindsey. If he comes I wish he'd come in the holidays. We've got a spare room, it would be super. If only he'd come next holidays, it would make something to look forward to.'

Ruth's heart contracted. She gave Laurel's hand that she was holding a squeeze.

'There's a lot to look forward to, darling, I'm certain of it.'

Dot and Ruth, having delivered the children at their school, travelled on the same bus back to the station. Dot eyed Ruth with friendliness.

'How d'you find the children?'

'They've changed a lot.'

'I suppose they have. Life's been rather tough for them, poor scraps.'

Ruth thought back to the days before the war, the regulated, graceful existence. Laurel's lessons, Laurel skipping along on her way to classes, Laurel flying down the stairs as Alex's car stopped at the front door. Alex's way of talking about his children. 'Tony'll have to go to his preparatory school next summer, though, mind you, that doesn't mean that you and I will stand easy. I don't mean to hand over Tony to anybody else to bring up. I shall co-operate with the school, of course, that's only right, but Tony, and later on Kim, have got to feel that at the back of everything there are their mother and myself, people you can talk anything out with – say what you like. . . .'

'They were an exceptionally united and happy family, weren't they?'

Dot clapped her hands together for the wind was cold.

'I never have believed in treating children as though they were climbing plants. Pruning and clipping and fixing down each shoot where you want it.'

Ruth stared up the road to the bend round which the bus would come. Most of the leaves were off the trees. An occasional dried-up leaf blew off a branch and was tossed up the road making a scratching sound. The clouds hung low and grey. She felt a sadness that was like lethargy after an illness.

'I suppose if Mr. Wiltshire could have seen into the future he might have brought them up differently, but, I don't know, they were happy and that's something to have by you.' She felt she could not pursue the subject. Dot's children had, from her point of view, practically brought themselves up, but it seemed to be working. Had too much trouble been taken with the Wiltshires? She decided that perhaps Dot could help her about Uncle John. 'Do you know their Uncle John's address? Tony asked me for it. Stupidly I forgot I was no longer part of the household and said "send the letter to me and I'll forward it," instead of saying "send it to your mother to forward."'

'I can give you Lindsey's address. She'll send it on.'

Ruth hesitated. The letter that Tony would send her to forward might be important. She looked at Dot's hard, clever but honest face, and decided to be open with her.

'I'm worried about Tony. Sometimes I think an outsider sees more than close relations. Of course I've had a great deal to do with the children. He's going through a difficult stage. If he writes to his uncle it's to ask him to come and see him. I thought perhaps I'd send a line explaining. I know it seems impertinent but I must do something. I know the Lieutenant-Commander. He was often in London.'

Dot looked up the road.

'Here's the bus.'

The bus ground its way to stop beside them. The two

women climbed on, there were no seats, they shared a strap. Dot laid a finger on the top button of Ruth's uniform.

'I should have thought that you had enough to do looking after all those young women under you, but if you like to take an interest in my nephews and nieces, I'm the last one to stop you. I was very fond of my brother. When there's room to get my hand into my bag for paper and a pencil I'll write down my brother-in-law's address.'

XXXII

Lena decided that on the whole the Christmas holidays had been a success. The children had been noisier than she cared for, and rather elusive, but they did seem to have enjoyed themselves. Even Christmas day, which she had so dreaded, had passed off nicely. Except for universal habits, such as hanging up stockings and Christmas dinner, she had meant to avoid those Christmas customs which were part of their family life and would, therefore, stress the absence of Alex. The children, however, would have none of that. They insisted on every smallest custom being remembered. It had made the day hideous for Lena but apparently in no way affected the children. Queer and insensitive of them, Lena thought, but she supposed children were like that. She racked her memory to try and recall how she had felt at their ages, but she had not a vivid memory and she had been a doted-on only child and had scarcely known momentary unhappiness, let alone tragedy. She had hoped during the holidays to get back her old relationship with the children. This she had not achieved.

She could not find the words to explain to herself what change there was. They used to come to me, she thought, as if a mother was something rather precious. She could not discover how they regarded her now. She was the planner and provider. She had arranged, as there was no enemy action at the moment, the day visits to London for a pantomime and a children's play. She had got to know those neighbours within reach and, no matter how difficult the rationing, she allowed the children to bring in friends to any meal. It worried her, and in fact she never quite admitted as a truth, that she was glad when the holidays were over. In retrospect it seemed as though the whole house had been put down somewhere like Waterloo station, and when the children left it settled back into its quiet woodland. Sometimes in the early morning, before she had taken any brandy, she had caught the frightening notion that she was behaving rather as if she were governing a savage tribe by the weak method of giving in to any demand to gain peace and some sort of order, but a nip of brandy dispelled such silly thoughts, and with a glow of pride she would get up, saying, 'They're having a good time and why shouldn't they, bless them.'

Laurel and Tuesday's holidays finished two days later than the boys. Seeing the children off made two exhausting days for Lena as they had to be taken to London, the boys to Paddington and the girls to Waterloo, where they were handed over to some member of their school's staffs. It was after the second trip that Lena, suffering from lowness of heart caused partly by a brandy hangover and partly by fatigue, felt the need for hearing somebody tell her that the holidays had been a success. She found Nannie in the kitchen.

'Well, Nannie, they went off happily. Tuesday was smiling.'

'Let's hope she keeps smiling, 'm.'

Nannie had offered no protest when she was told that Tuesday was to go to boarding school with Laurel, yet Lena had felt she disapproved. She wished that Nannie would speak her mind, it would give her a chance to explain that there was no school near, that at seven it was more than time she began being properly educated, and that it was bad for one child to be at home alone. She would also have liked to add that it was particularly bad for Tuesday, who was too much her nurse's child and not sufficiently her mother's. However, as Nannie had said nothing except to ask when the term began and to point out that Tuesday would need some new clothes, Lena had to keep her arguments to herself. This was an aggravation and made her wonder if she should try for a cook and get rid of Nannie, only she would not get a cook and if she did get one she certainly would not look after the children's clothes as well as Nannie.

'Little Maria's very happy at that school.'

Nannie opened her oven-door and had a look in.

'Maria's one thing and Tuesday's another.'

'I shall miss her. I enjoyed giving her lessons.' She waited for Nannie to shut the oven-door and attend to her. 'I thought they enjoyed the holidays, didn't you?'

Nannie stared in front of her, placidly stroking the overall that she now wore in place of her nursery apron. Her eyes appeared, as usual, unclouded by thought. She was registering rather than thinking. 'Very out of hand they were. Tuesday's going the same way as the rest. Mrs. Wiltshire doesn't mind. Queer, she was always one for nice manners.

Mustn't be upset, poor thing.' Her words fell out in the soothing tone which belonged to the nursery.

'Yes 'm. Very nice, 'm.'

Lena lingered. She would have liked to have forced a more definite statement. She recognized 'very nice, 'm' as that kind of approval which was always waiting on Nannie's tongue for a well-built brick house or sand castle, and had nothing to do with her opinion. Nannie, however, was busy with her cooking. She plodded around on her large flat black shoes. She was more than on the spread now. She was definitely fat. When she was walking about there seemed only room for herself. She was also very much captain of her ship when in the kitchen, and was able by merely glancing round to make a loiterer feel ashamed. Lena went to Mrs. Oliver.

'Good-morning, Mrs. Oliver. Rather less work today for you, I'm glad to say. We shall miss the children though, shan't we?'

Mrs. Oliver was dusting. She paused and leant against a piece of furniture.

'You've said it. I don't know 'ow you 'ave the 'eart to send them away. I never could have any of mine.'

Lena looked worried.

'I hate schools, but it's what my husband had arranged.'

'Well, I shouldn't wonder if we have some of them back soon.' Mrs. Oliver lowered her voice. 'In me teacup last night there was something funny coming to a house where I was but not where I live. My daughter read it. "Mum," she said, "look at this. There's a big surprise and it's to do with arrival by train." There was the train as clear as anything.'

'It needn't be the children. I had a letter from my mother in America, a son of an old friend of hers is coming over. He'll be coming down, I expect, and I've got a lot of sisters-in-law who might come and see me.'

'No. We reckoned it was the children, that's what my daughter said. "Mark my words, Mum," she said, "the children are coming back."'

'It's to be hoped they aren't. It would mean illness or something. I thought they enjoyed their Christmas holidays, didn't you?'

Mrs. Oliver shook her head and looked knowing.

'You can never tell with children. They laugh fit to split their sides, but there's things going on in their hearts that would surprise us.'

'But you saw a lot of Laurel. Didn't you think she seemed happy?'

'She enjoyed herself all right. Going to the pantomime and that, but she doesn't care for that school.'

'Children never like school, but they have to be educated.'

Mrs. Oliver went back to her dusting. In her opinion, if she had a daughter of rising fourteen who didn't like school, she would take her away from it on her fourteenth birthday and put her to work. People like Mrs. Wiltshire never did things like that, so it was no good talking.

Mustard was manuring a bed.

'How did you think the boys enjoyed their holidays?'

Mustard had not considered the point. He did not care for being interrupted in his work by foolish questions.

'Tony'll do.'

'Didn't you think he looked better?'

Mustard considered children as he would plants. If two plants of the same family, raised from the same batch of seedlings grew side by side and one flourished and one did not, he moved the one that did not flourish and tried it somewhere else. This was why the little world of his garden flourished and so cocked a snook, as it were, at the wild world outside, where one tree grew to cut the light and air from another and clambering things crawled over flowers and crushed the life out of them.

'Young Kim looks a sight better. It seems he sits more sweet in that school.'

Lena turned away. It was true Kim did look marvellous, and he was so amusing. It was nobody's fault, it did not mean there was anything the matter with Tony, it just was that Kim was unusual. Nobody had given her the answer that she wanted. She had tried so hard, she really did feel that she had succeeded. Of course it was silly to care what Nannie, Mrs. Oliver or Mustard said. She was the children's mother and she knew best. She went back indoors. There was a fire in the dining-room. She stood by it and warmed her hands. The children had changed. They had ceased to be her good-mannered little family. They had become noisy, rough and, now and again, unmanageable. She was often afraid to correct them. In order to keep on good terms with them she let things go by that she never would have in the old days and Alex would have certainly never allowed. But these holidays had been a lot better than last summer; then she had felt that Laurel and Tony almost avoided her, but this Christmas they had not done that, though their manner to her had changed. How tiresome of Nannie and Mrs. Oliver and Mustard to carp and put doubts into her mind. She had been so happy and now she felt awful. She looked at the clock. It was not twelve, a bit early for a drink, still, she needed cheering.

Walter Nissen came down to lunch on a Sunday. He was homesick for America. He was working under a completely tireless commanding officer whose job it was to arrange for suitable accommodation for the thousands of men and their vehicles who were on their way to the London area. Walter's family had a lot of money, he came from a lovely home, and landing in London in cold, grey weather, though his hotel was comfortable, his spirit had been bruised by the dinginess of the blitzed or evacuated houses which he had to inspect, and the damp cold ate into his bones. He knew the British had lived through shocking times, but he had spasms when he longed to give the entire nation a good shake. He felt they were complacent over their discomforts and that if this were America more would be done to put things right. He had also had something of a spiritual set-back. He had always been violently anti-fascist. He had wanted to fight what he saw in his mind as the powers of evil. It had been a blow to him when he had been shown that he could be made useful right away in a non-combatant job. On the other hand he had been glad to be a forerunner of the American Army. The British had been having one hell of a time, it was a pretty fine thing for them to know that an enormous army was on the way. He was far too well informed to think for a second that the war against Germany would finish quickly, but poor Britain, stretched out like an overstrained piece of elastic to cover the seas and the skies while attempting to get together the men and the weapons to finish the business, must see the coming of America just as Noah had once seen the dove with the leaf in its beak. He found that the British not only did not think that way but that their attitude was hurtful. They said Pearl Harbour had forced America into the war. Perhaps she would be able to help in beating Hitler, but she had nothing to show yet. The British were waiting with critical eyes to see what she would do. Saviour nothing – their saviour, if they had one, was Russia. Walter forgot that, by the nature of his work, he was not meeting necessarily good thinkers, he fell into the mistake of judging the thought of the whole by that section which crossed his path.

Walter had not been impressed by his introduction to Lena. He thought her mother the sort of tiresome woman surrounded by small dogs of which there were far too many in his own family. However, hers was one of the few near London introductory letters that he carried. The rest were to the owners of stately homes and his mother, who had been to Europe every year before the war, had impressed on her son that war or peace visits to these were better reserved for warm weather.

It was a spring day when Walter came to lunch. A day which, though in March, would not have disgraced June. There were primroses out in the garden, and prunus' caught the breath with their pink charm. There was a delicate green fuzz on the trees where the leaves were budding. Lena was looking lovely but pathetic in her black frock. He knew the outline of her story. That there were four children and her husband had been killed in an air-raid, but no more. He saw her only slightly distorted by his sympathy. She was about his own age. He liked an utterly feminine woman.

Lena saw the sympathy and admiration in his eyes, and that Walter was exceedingly good-looking. The pall of depression which dimmed her days lifted slightly. She greeted him with more natural gaiety than she had shown since Alex's death. They went in to have a cocktail, glad of each other.

After lunch they took a short walk, then they sat over the drawing-room fire and Walter talked. He talked out of himself much of his disillusionment. Lena said very little but she looked interested and full of admiration.

'It's wonderful to feel we aren't alone any more,' she said. 'Now you Americans are fighting with us this ghastly war will soon be over.'

He liked that, it was not a woman's job to understand wars, and it was their job to trust men to fight for them.

After a while he came off his own concerns and asked about the children. He loved children and felt sentimental about them. Nobody was better at drawing a sentimental picture of her children than Lena. In her gentle, soft voice she described them one by one. Tony, so like his father. My funny, loving little Laurel. Kim, so brilliant and amusing. My baby Tuesday.

'But oh, Walter!' They had become Walter and Lena before lunch. 'I feel so helpless bringing them up alone.'

Walter was so moved there was a lump in his throat. He lit a cigarette and, after a pause, began to tell her about his family. He had married rather young. He had three children. Wonderful kids but he didn't see much of them. His wife did not care for the East, she came from the South. It was a long story with a picture of his separated home, his wife and children living most of the year with her parents. He expanded, for Lena was a wonderful listener, she hardly said anything but she was clearly absorbed.

Lena heard scarcely a word of what Walter told her. Her eyes ran over him. Her thoughts made shivers run up and down her spine. Her cheeks burned.

Walter stayed to dinner. They drank a great deal of whisky. Afterwards, in the drawing-room, the closing of the door meant that they were in each other's arms.

'Can we go up to your room?'

Lena was gasping as if she had been running.

'Not until Nannie goes to bed and I can't wait that long.'

XXXIII

'Now, Tuesday, you mustn't mind not wearing a school uniform, heaps of the little ones don't. And you will come to me about everything, won't you? I'll spend every minute I can with you.'

Tuesday had heard Laurel say these things on the train. She had not been interested in the part about a uniform, but she got a lot from Laurel's tone. It was protective. Tuesday hummed contentedly. Ever since they had left London people had come and gone. First Dad and Mum and then Miss Glover. The world outside the nursery seemed a frightening place. Tuesday had subconsciously decided to remain a baby. Then came the move to the new home with Mum once more in the permanent background, and Laurel, Tony and Kim not on a short holiday but in the house for months. The nursery disappeared for Nannie was in the kitchen and Tuesday, for the first time, was left to the care of her brothers and sister. The string which tied her to her babyhood wore thin. She was now part of the family, with her own place in it, yet she was comfortingly the little one, and received from Laurel and Tony especial care. The autumn term had not been happy. Her lessons with Lena had been a moderate success. Lena was moody and petted Tuesday one day and was aloof the next. Tuesday turned back to Nannie; many of the subconscious habits formed to link her to her babyhood would have come back only she had influenza and was petted and cossetted to the extent of her need. Then came the Christmas holidays. The family returned, the niche, so very much her own in the summer, was waiting for her. She found the strain of the past months evaporating, she was again in the group. She did not in the least fear going to school. It was what the others did, besides, Laurel would be with her.

Laurel suffered for Tuesday. She was such a baby. It was so horrible at school, and Tuesday had not got a uniform. Of course heaps of the little ones did not have any, but Maria did. Then suddenly her breath was caught, as if in winter she had seen dog roses. Tuesday needed her. Foxglove had said that. She had said, 'There's one thing I know at which you shine, and that's at being a good eldest sister.' She had found the answer. Let the other girls be games champions, actresses and dancers, she was going to be a mother to Tuesday. That was how she would stand out. Let them call her The Frog, she would be above minding.

Tuesday had never been happier. There was a Mrs. Fellows, with a small daughter of her own, in charge of the little ones. She was really fond of children and made an especial pet of Tuesday, partly because Maria had told her that Alex had been killed, but more because Tuesday was an endearing little creature and charming to look at. That phrase, 'one happy family' was true in Mrs. Fellows' section of Greenwood House Over the Way. The regular hours, the unchanging days, the sense of having her own place in a large pattern was what Tuesday needed. The children were treated as the young part of the house and yet they were well away from babyhood. Even under Mrs. Fellows there were responsibilities, which, to the children picked to carry them out, seemed of enormous importance. Mrs. Fellows had noticed that Tuesday was inclined to shrink backwards rather than step forward into the world. In her first days she had clung to Maria and hung about waiting for Laurel. Mrs. Fellows would never interfere between sisters. She always had a smile for Laurel however often she appeared in her part of the house, and that was every moment of Laurel's free time; but she had to see that Tuesday stood squarely on her feet without support. After the first three weeks she made an announcement at the end of luncheon. It was a list of what she called 'officers'. It finished with Tuesday. She was put in charge of the sweet cupboard, a position, because of the temptations it offered, considered an honour. Tuesday heard her name called and her task. She had a moment's surprise which was so intense she felt as if the breath had been knocked out of her. She was a little one, people looked after her, they never expected her to look after things. School jokes flew round her head like bats. 'I bet Tuesday eats the lot.' 'I shall count every sweet from Sunday to Sunday.' 'I'll know if you've had even a suck of mine, Tuesday.' At that moment the chord tying Tuesday to her babyhood began to break. Later Laurel, her pigtails flying, rushed into the junior playroom.

'Sorry, Tuesday darling, I'm so late. Have you had a nice day? Shall I read to you?'

Tuesday wriggled free from Laurel's arm. She was busy at her own things and had not at the moment time for an elder sister.

'Don't bother me now, Laurel. I'm doing something important.'

It took several rebuffs before Laurel believed that Tuesday did not need her. As always with Laurel, her vision of what she intended had become to her a fact. She stood between Tuesday and a horrible world. Tuesday should be quite happy at school because of her. Tuesday should not be allowed to see how hateful a school Greenwood House was. Tuesday was depending on her for her happiness and she would never fail her. In the term, as well as in the holidays, Tuesday would be her baby, her especial charge.

Laurel blamed Greenwood House for the loss of Tuesday. She had to blame something or someone. For the three weeks when Tuesday's welfare had occupied her mind she had been almost happy. She had, too, practically achieved distinction. 'Is that your little sister, Frog?' 'I say, Frog, your little sister's sweet.' 'You ought to have dozens of children when you grow up, Frog, you'll be a super mother.'

Alice had showered common sense over Laurel.

'I wouldn't bother to hang around Tuesday all the time if I were you. I did a bit over Maria when she was new but they're all right on their own really.'

Laurel's eyes shone.

'Not Tuesday. She needs me.'

'She doesn't, and slopping over her all the time you've missed gardening twice and so you won't be picked to have a piece of allotment this term.'

Laurel loved Alice but she thought her regrettably mundane.

'What does a piece of an allotment matter beside Tuesday being happy?'

'Radishes for tea,' said Alice. 'You're good at growing things, you were a fool to miss your chance.'

The dawning of adolescence was no trouble to Alice. She accepted life and expected to enjoy it. She knew nothing of being tossed up to the skies and the corresponding drop into a well of despair. Laurel had been happy in her guardianship of Tuesday. She had in little felt the joy of motherhood. Her sensations were childish but there was sensual pleasure in being, as she conceived, so needed. There was satisfaction for her ego in her mental picture of herself. She broke away from Laurel, the unsuccessful schoolgirl, and became Laurel the mother. The pain, when it was forced on her that Tuesday did not need her, was very great. While she had established herself Tuesday's guardian, she had spent her days in a state of exaltation. When the exaltation was torn away, and the stark fact that Tuesday did not need her was thrust into her mind, she knew that life held nothing more for her. Her schooldays lay ahead, year after year, bleak and undistinguished. The holidays were no longer oases. If Tuesday did not want her, then neither did the others. She tried to make Alice understand her agony.

'I've nothing to live for, Alice. It's different for you. You're good at things. But here am I, fourteen, and not made a mark.'

Alice had been brought up on the *Just So Stories*.

'You ought to dig till you gently perspire.'

XXXIV

The bar was crowded. John, sitting at one of the small tables, eyed the swing doors anxiously. Would he recognise Ruth? He remembered her eyes, grey with everything that amused her stored up at the back of them, forbidden to reach the rest of her face. She had not been much in evidence when the Wiltshires lived in Regent's Park. Sometimes she appeared with Laurel and Tony, and, if they were allowed down for lunch, she was of course with them. He had a memory of her, silent, attentive to the children and always those amused eyes. It would be difficult to pick her out in uniform, uniform changed women so, the wildest hair became neat and their faces took on a sameness. It was difficult to recognise even women you knew well when they had got themselves up in a uniform.

Ruth had no difficulty in finding John. He always had been her idea of a sailor. Incredibly blue eyes with an appearance of permanently peering at the horizon. Not over tall, square with a balanced look as if to say 'pitch and roll to any degree you fancy, but I shall keep standing.' She had not before seen him in uniform. It suited him. She greeted him and sat down.

The war had changed her, he noticed. She was the equivalent rank of a captain and, whatever she did in the Army, it was obviously more of a job than being a governess. The uniform suited her. She was one of those square-shouldered, narrow-waisted, no behind, long-legged types. Her eyes had not changed. They were looking at him as if they were having a good laugh. Had she any idea that he felt a bit awkward about the meeting? Of course, if he had explained to Lindsey, she would have been the first to agree that he ought to have a talk to Miss Glover, only it had seemed easier not to tell Lindsey anything about it. Lindsey was funny about leave, grudged any minute when he was out of her sight.

He fetched the drinks and gave Ruth a cigarette.

'I'm hoping to pop down to see Lena and the children tomorrow. My wife's speaking somewhere for the Ministry of Information.'

'Have you told them?'

He could not explain to Ruth that it was a mistake to make plans. If Lindsey knew you planned to do something on your own, then she wanted you with her. She had always been like that, part of the artistic temperament, he supposed.

'No, thought I'd trust my luck. Don't want to make a song

and dance about it. I judged from your letter young Tony needs careful tackling.'

Ruth tapped her cigarette against the ash-tray, trying to find words to explain her letter and her anxiety.

'You may find nothing wrong – Tony's changed so. . . . He was so different when his father was alive.'

'It's little Laurel I remember. Does she still have tow-coloured plaits?'

'Yes, but she's not so little. She was fourteen last May.'

'No! Time does get a spurt on. When did you last see them?'

'Just before Easter. I had seven days.'

'Tony still worry you?'

She paused, seeing Tony in her mind. How explain the disquiet and discomfiture she felt in his presence? If she used the words 'mind' or 'mental' she would give a totally wrong impression. Yet, that he had some illness of the mind she was convinced.

'He doesn't work. Kim's in the form above him. Kim's eleven this month and Tony will be thirteen in November. He looks ill, pale, not a good colour. He cares about nothing. He suggests "what's it matter" about everything.'

'Perhaps he'll do better when he goes to his public school.'

'As he's going at the moment he'll not stay long there, he'll be superannuated.'

'Is his mother worried?'

'I don't know . . . I haven't seen her . . . I suppose so . . . she must be.'

'He definitely asked for me?'

'Yes. The first time was in the autumn. Then, in the Lent term, he showed me your letter. I haven't had leave to get down this term. Sometimes he writes. . . .' she broke off.

'What's he say?'

'Just that nothing happens, that it's being a foul term.'

'Wonder what he wants from me.'

Ruth leant forward.

'Quite likely if it was anything he won't say; but if you could make friends with him. . . .'

He looked at her eager face and thought that she ought to have children of her own, and that the man was lucky who married her. It must be very satisfying to have children and talk them over with your wife. Of course it was natural Lindsey had never wanted any. She had her work which had to come first, but he would have given a lot to have a parcel of kids. When they separated he asked Ruth if she could meet him again before his leave was up.

'I ought to give you a full report.'

Ruth said she could manage it. It was easy for her to get up and down to London. She gave him her telephone number. Travelling back on the train she thought about her meeting with John. She went over in her mind what they had said. It would be interesting to hear how he found Tony and what he thought of Lena. Then suddenly she pulled her thoughts up and scrutinized them. They were there just as they had drifted through her mind, but there was an additional thought, far more vigorous than the others, and that was pleasure because she was to see John again.

The children had accepted Walter with delight. He became Uncle Walter and was part of the household. He could not get down often but when he came he bulged with sweets, toys and chewing gum, and was prepared to spend his days at whatever occupation the children chose. For the sake of the children he almost quarrelled with Lena. He absolutely refused to come to the house while they were at home at Easter, as anything but the son of a friend of Mum's-Mum. He also, since he knew his own and Lena's weakness, refused to drink much during the holidays.

'The kids are swell,' he told Lena, 'and I'm not cutting in on their vacation.'

'But you won't be cutting in. There's no reason why you shouldn't stay to dinner and go back on the late train. They won't know anything about us.'

Walter could not bring himself to put exactly what he felt into words. It was awkward, and would sound as if he were a preacher, but he had strong feelings on the subject. There was something lewd in a mother pushing her children off to bed so that she might be made love to on the drawing-room sofa. Fired though he was by Lena he appreciated that she was a problem. If he did not come down to see her she came up to London. That was all right once or perhaps twice a week, but more than that was thieving the children's time. His coming down to see her was, though he got great pleasure from being with the children, an effort to keep Lena at home. He often felt as if she were a lovely but ferocious animal on a very frail lead. Physically he was immensely important to her, and with Lena that meant almost everything. She had soon learnt that she had been physically starved since Alex's death, and that being loved was a better anodyne for loneliness, sleeplessness and grief than brandy. Not that she gave up brandy but she had found what was more effective, and the two together were making life almost endurable. What she did not know, but Walter did, was that she was coarsening. It had not been possible with Alex to give way utterly, it was easy with him for rapture to become revulsion. Walter was different. A good time was a good time to Walter and, while it lasted, it did not matter how good. The good time over, he forgot it, shook it off and thought of other things until he saw Lena again. Then Walter liked to drink. It was part of having a good time. He did not drink much except on a party, but when there was a party he believed that every available bottle should be emptied. But parties of any kind were out as far as Walter was concerned when there were children about. He tried desperately hard to make Lena see this in relation to the summer holidays.

'Why, it's not so long and it would be just terrible if they cottoned on to anything.' 'Don't let's have a drink. One drink leads to another and I'd feel dirty if the children saw us lit.'

Even Walter, canny though he was, did not grasp that he was asking Lena for abstinence that she had weakened herself too much to achieve. Walter had given her something approximating to happiness; he could slide, once they had started on a slope, just as far as she could; she had never known that before. When he was not with her she was feverish with thoughts of next time. With Walter nothing was beyond imagination. By the end of July, when the children came home, she was as if addicted to a drug without which she could not live. When she found Walter really meant what he said she schemed to tempt him, and kept her spirits up with brandy. Only if she happened to wake in the night did she get a glimpse of the woman she was becoming. Then she saw herself with that ruthless perception of wakeful night hours, and shuddered. Her mouth would dry and she would whisper, 'Oh Alex, Alex, if you're anywhere come and help! I'm such a mess.'

Nannie, Mrs. Oliver and Mustard drew together to shield the children. Mrs. Oliver would have liked to have talked things out, and indeed, did at home and round the neighbourhood, but there was no talking to Nannie or Mustard. From the appearance of either it was impossible to say for certain that they grasped what was going on. What did Nannie think happened behind the closed drawing-room door? What did she suppose, when, after she was in bed, footsteps crept up to Lena's room? What did Mustard think of the empty bottles which, with a blank face, he buried? Only when the children came home an onlooker could have seen the watchfulness in the eyes of all three, and how each in her or his way tried to shield the children.

With Mrs. Oliver it was extra talkativeness and shut doors when the girls were helping her.

'Shut the door, Tuesday ducks, and while we're doin' the room I'll tell you what 'appened to my 'usband's sister, all from wearin' an opal which, not being her month stone, was a terrible unlucky thing to do.'

Nannie was nervous when the children were in the house.

'It's a lovely day. Run along out all of you,' or, if it rained, she liked them under her eye. 'I've got a bit of sugar and a half tin of treacle, you all come in the kitchen and make some toffee.'

Mustard's especial contribution was bonfires.

'Beautiful to see they wild things burn. You children watch it and when the heart glows come to me and I'll have some taters ready for cookin'.'

The children saw nothing wrong. The summer holiday was the nicest they had known since Alex had been killed and, in many ways, the best since they had left London. Their own rooms and their own things were waiting exactly where they had left them at Easter. There were Nannie, Mrs. Oliver and Mustard, all part of home and pleased to see them back. Mum was much more as they had always known her. She wore bright-coloured clothes, and laughed a lot, and never sat looking sad. Best of all, she never talked in that awful special voice about Dad. Then there was Uncle Walter. When he came to the house it was as if bright lights were turned on. He was full of ideas of gay things to do, he liked being with them and they knew it. He enjoyed the things they enjoyed. After a Sunday visit when the outstanding occupations had been an elaborate funeral of a dead bird, or a picnic tea, he would say and mean it, 'I've had just the best time.'

Kim and Tuesday expected to enjoy their holidays, but to Laurel and Tony the placid summer days, though they did not heal or comfort, had a sedative effect and both grew easier daily. Laurel, who had come home edgy and difficult, prepared to hunch her shoulders and say that nobody wanted her, smoothed out. The others did want her, she became once more the guarding elder sister; Tuesday relied on her, Mrs. Oliver was delighted to see her, Mum was pleased that she was back, Uncle Walter called her his sweetheart. In the world of home nobody found her plain or dull, and it did not seem to matter that she was not especially good at anything. Tony slept better at home. He was glad to sink into home life. Running about with the others, doing what they did and making no mental effort. His attacks of fear grew less frequent. At school he would wake knowing that he was about to have an attack of fright. He saw the attacks as if they had shape. Huge, black and soft, ready to fall on him. Sometimes, from the time he knew an attack was waiting, it was hours before it came. In the waiting time he was lethargic, dulled by fright. When the attacks came they might last an hour, or drag on for days. First he felt a tenseness in his diaphragm, which got steadily worse till he was hard in front, as if he were made of wood. Then he had a sinking sensation. The people round him were still there but on a different level, beyond reach. At some time he had to get away alone and let the attack reach its climax. Then everything swam before his eyes, his heart beat quicker and quicker, there was thumping in his ears and he believed he was buried with his father, dying inch by inch.

On the morning John came down Lena was alone in the house. Seeing nobody about he rang the door bell and, getting no answer, went round to the front and walked in at the open french windows of the drawing-room. The drawing-room was empty so he wandered into the hall. The door into the dining-room was wide open and at the sideboard he saw Lena having a drink. He greeted her.

'Hallo there!'

The passage was dark. She swung round, her face glowing.

'Walter! How on earth . . .'

John came into the drawing-room.

'Whoever Walter is I'm afraid I'm not he. It's John.'

The light went out of Lena's face. She became charmingly social.

'John! How nice. Did you ring?'

He held her hands.

'Yes. But nobody seemed to be about.'

'Nannie's gone in to do the shopping and I suppose my woman's out at the back somewhere. I ought to have heard you. I'd just come in here . . .' she glanced at her empty glass. 'I was taking my medicine.'

John's face expressed nothing. He smelt brandy. The hour was not yet eleven. Lena was lying. The facts lay in his brain untouched, ready for later consideration. He put his arm through hers. They went into the garden.

The children did not come in until lunch-time. By then Lena had given John a couple of pink gins and drunk two herself. It was after the second gin that he saw how much she had changed. As Alex's smart, sophisticated wife she had always been the dernier cri of the family circle. The women said of clothes or furnishings, 'Well, Lena likes it,' and that put a gloss on whatever was under discussion. The men had felt, without saying so, that Alex had done well for himself. Lena was smart, pretty, always had her house in perfect control. She was not clever like Lindsey and Dot, but she was a damn good wife and you did not really want women to be

218

clever. The whole set-up of the Wiltshire home was accepted as being the last word in sophisticated living, and Lena was admittedly the architect. She it was who arranged the meals, and organised the house so that it appeared to run itself. She chose clothes for her children that made them stand out noticeably as well dressed. There was criticism, of course. The children were pampered. Alex was dragged out to more parties than he cared for. On the whole though, admiration had been Lena's portion. Now, after her second cocktail, John saw a Lena that was new to him. She told a couple of stories which, when he had last seen her, he would not have supposed she would have understood. She asked him about his leave with a nudge and a wink in her voice. She hinted that a little of Lindsey went a long way and he was probably having a bit of fun somewhere else, and if not why not. Back in the Regent's Park days such a suggestion would have been unthinkable. It was taken for granted that everybody loved the people they were supposed to love. Alex had even pretended that he was fond of that ghastly mother-in-law of his, which, of course, he never could have been. Still, in a decently conducted world, you had to pretend those sort of things, and quite right too.

'What about just another tiny one?' said Lena. 'Splice the mainbrace, don't you call it?'

John shook his head. He took her glass from her and put it down with his own.

'Not at this time of the day, thanks old girl.' He lifted his head. He could not keep relief out of his voice. 'I hear the children.'

The children fell into the room all talking at once. For a

moment they did not see John. Laurel reached her mother first.

'Mum, the Jones' who've got that simply perfect dachshund puppy are going to live in Wales and we can have him.'

Kim had his arms round Lena's waist.

'Mum, he's got a face like this,' he gave one of his imitations, 'and his coat hangs loose as if it belonged to a much bigger dog.'

Tuesday was dancing with eagerness.

'We could fetch him this afternoon. We've never had a dog, only Pincher, who wasn't exactly ours.'

Even Tony added his plea.

'He's called Stroch. Can you guess why?'

Lena laughed.

'Look who's here.'

For a second the dachshund was eclipsed by John. He was welcomed with rapture by Laurel and Kim. Tuesday could not remember him and was gravely polite; Tony's greeting was off-hand. John turned to Lena.

'What's going to happen about this puppy?'

The children were again all talking at once. Kim lay on the floor and gave an imitation of a dog wriggling with friendliness.

'Mum. Darling Mum. Look. Just like this.'

Tuesday pulled at Lena's frock.

'And all the wriggle was for us.'

Laurel appealed to John.

'It would make all the difference to our lives. In the end we might have kennels and have thousands of dachshunds to sell. They cost pounds and pounds really only this one's a present.'

Tony looked at Lena questioningly.

'Stroch. Spelt S-T-R-O-C-H. Can't you guess?'

If Lena had not had two cocktails on top of brandy she might have taken longer to give way. The terms were long and the holidays short, dogs in time of war hard to feed, and she detested walking and it was not easy to see who would exercise a puppy while the children were away, but none of these things counted against the children's happiness. She had not been so much the centre of the picture since Alex had been killed. It was wonderful the children should have chosen to-day when John was here to see and report back to the family. Her eyes misted with tears. They were at this moment just the united group she wanted. The picture they were making was her ideal. The children clinging to her, their voices calling her. 'Mum.' 'Please, Mum.' 'Oh, darling Mum.' She shook her head to get rid of the tear mist and smiled at John.

'Obviously Stroch is ours.'

John took the children to fetch the puppy. He enjoyed his walk. He was especially taken with Laurel. He liked the anxious, serious way she looked at him. He was touched by her faith in his knowledge, and her motherly way with the others.

'We'll have to arrange who has Stroch on the lead coming home, or there'll be rows. Kim will want him all the time, and really Tuesday ought to come first as she's the youngest and has always been especially fond of dogs. Shall we make a plan?'

'Do dogs need special medicines? It would be simply awful if Stroch got ill just because we didn't know. Ought he to be inoculated against distemper?'

'Keeping dogs could be a profession, couldn't it? I mean, some dogs get famous. How do you start? Just by marrying two dogs?'

Laurel walked next to John and these questions came to him through the babel of noise created by the others. He remained calm and answered everybody in turn, always coming back to Laurel.

'You leave the routine of leading the puppy to me. I'll see fair do's.'

'I imagine you better have a talk with this Mrs. Jones. She'll tell you the little chap's medical history.'

'No, I believe it's a bit more elaborate than that. Have to get strong strains going and that sort of thing.' He looked down at Laurel's still childlike face and turned to botany. 'You know, like growing a champion rose.'

The children had been taught how they were made ever since they could remember. Alex had disapproved of what he called 'stork nonsense' and Ruth, remembering her own rummaging for knowledge amongst books and giggling girls, had taken immense trouble to see that the Wiltshire children knew their facts and did not find them a matter for giggles and whispers. John was amused at the discussion which followed.

'How would they know if Stroch was good stock?' 'Would the puppy's pedigree show it?' 'If he was a good strain how soon ought he to be married?' 'If he was married and the lady-dog wasn't theirs to whom did the puppies belong?'

When John hesitated for a reply to the last question Tony looked at Laurel.

'I know who'll tell us. Uncle Walter.'

The children then discussed Uncle Walter. A picture grew of him. Obviously he was considered a friend and a fount of knowledge.

'Americans,' Kim told John, 'know absolutely everything. Do you know, he even knows more about London than we do.'

'He reads books about it,' Laurel explained in an undertone.

Tuesday gave an excited skip.

'Just think how surprised he's going to be when he sees Stroch.'

Kim gave an imitation of Walter.

'Why say, that's the cutest dog. What's his name?'

Stroch's name was a great joke to the children. Tuesday clung to John's arm.

'We'll make him guess.'

'We'll have to tell him,' Laurel murmured. 'You never guessed, did you, Uncle John?'

Kim bounced on ahead.

'I shall say whose name begins S. T. and whose R. O. and whose C. H. I bet he guesses. He'll say Stalin, Roosevelt, Churchill, just as quick as a piece of snow coming out of the sky. You see if he doesn't.'

'When's he coming?' John asked.

'Quite likely tomorrow,' said Kim.

'Of course he won't,' Tony argued. 'He said he had a heavy week. I bet he doesn't come till Sunday.'

Tuesday pulled against John's arm.

'He will if he can. He doesn't mind how little time he comes for as long as he gets here.'

Laurel explained.

'He's stationed in London. He's down on all his days off, if they don't come often enough then sometimes Mum goes up to London to see him.'

Kim raised his voice.

'Sometimes! Twice every week at the very least, and she never takes us, which I call mean.'

John let them talk. He was not given to probing into the lives of others, but this Walter had been shoved under his nose. Lena had taken him for Walter when he had arrived. He spent all his leave in the house, and Lena went up to London at least two days in each week to see him. Lena had been having a drink when he arrived and had lied about it. He felt uncomfortable. Poor old Lena, she had every right to comfort herself, had a hard time, but he hoped she wasn't over-stepping it. These children seemed well informed. Judging from the way they talked they saw nothing unusual in the friendship. He hoped Lena would remember that kids were sharp. Old Alex would turn in his grave if he thought that there were funny goings on.

By skilful manœuvring John got Tony to himself on the way home. Kim was sent on ahead to call Stroch. Laurel would then let the puppy off his lead and they would see if he would obey. Where Stroch went Tuesday followed.

John was no beater of bushes. He went straight to Tony's letter.

'Sorry I couldn't get down during the term as you asked.'

Tony, in spite of the excitement about the puppy, had intended to ask his question.

'It was about submarines I wanted to ask.'

'Go ahead.'

'Sometimes, they get hit by depth-charges when they are under the sea.'

'Yes.'

'If that happens there wouldn't be any air after a bit, would there? I mean, everybody would die.'

John looked ahead at Laurel in her blue frock kneeling beside the minute orange red shape of the puppy. At Tuesday, also in blue, skipping with eagerness. Ahead lay the trees, dark with pine needles, and under them the light green of bracken. In the distance came Kim's excited cries. 'Come on, Stroch. Come on, good dog.' All this was home as it ought to be, as he dreamed of it when at sea. Children were happy. Little girls wore blue frocks and played in the sunlight with puppies. There was, of course, another side to that picture but there was no point in brooding on it. A man did his best. He, personally, had helped to send a lot of Huns to the bottom. That was the only payment he could exact for cruelties and suffering. Yet here, at this moment, was something more. His inclination was to laugh away serious talk and make up for any deficiency in understanding by a good tip when he left. He resisted the temptation. He drew his eyes from the girls and the puppy and gave Tony all his mind. Here was a boy, fatherless because of the war, brooding morbidly on a horrible form of death. Why?

'You mean a direct hit? No repairs possible?'

Tony felt an attack of fright looming ahead. He spoke in a strained voice.

'Yes. How long would it be before they died?'

John was not used to handling boys but he was accustomed to men, he knew the signs of strain and when a man was near breaking. He took hold of Tony's elbow and drew him off the main ride down a side track.

'What's worrying you?' Tony's attack was racing up on him. He always faced an attack alone. He tried to free his arm but John gripped him firmly. He saw the sweat beads on Tony's forehead and upper lip. The grey tinge under his skin. Then, inexplicably, he read Tony's trouble. 'This is to do with your father.'

John was thankful the other three were out of earshot. He had never seen an attack like Tony's. Because of the unexpectedness of his question Tony's defences broke. He had meant to discover how long his father had suffered by oblique questions. He had no intention of explaining himself. The attack was so sudden and complete it was like a fit. He stiffened and fell down. He saw John but on that other level where he was beyond reach. He was trapped, smothered. His fingers beat a tattoo on the moss, bracken and pine needles beneath him, but no one would hear, no one would answer.

John had no idea what treatment was right so he did what came to his mind. A stream ran in the dip below where Tony was lying. He meant to bring water in his hat but he found a rusty tin. He filled it and threw the water on Tony's face.

Tony's attacks were to a certain degree guided by himself.

He held them off until he was alone. Once one had started there were stages which automatically followed. It was as if he went down in a lift. There was his own floor, which he left behind, but eventually there was a basement from which he always rose back to normal level. There was a dread, which he avoided looking at, that one day he would reach the basement and stop there. So far, the crisis of his attacks past, there was his slow return to the blessed everyday world. The cold water changed this. One moment he was wallowing in the basement of despair, the next he was sitting up spluttering, with John's firm strong hands holding his, John's face close to his own, and, best of all, John's slow comforting voice, not speaking from a different level, which could not help, but from the ordinary solid world where it was August, the sun shining, and, just out of sight, the others and Stroch.

Lindsey was not a novelist for nothing. She was a good, graphic letter-writer. John had been at sea when Alex was killed. It was some months later that Lindsey's letter had reached him. Lena had been too upset to identify Alex's body. The Colonel had gone to the mortuary. Elsa had wanted to come with him, he would not hear of this so Elsa had telephoned to Lindsey to meet her father in London and see that he had something to eat. Lindsey had met the train and gone with the Colonel to the mortuary. She had described the room they had waited in, the shocked, grief-loaded people who had waited with them. The Colonel had been called at last. Lindsey seldom entered further than her pen carried her into the sufferings of other people, but she had been genuinely moved by her father's dignity and touched by his ability to carry himself straight and hide all he felt. The identification over she had taken him to his club, where they had lunch. Lindsey, in spite of being weighed down by depression at her brother's death, had clearly made one of her few efforts towards helping someone else. She had gossiped about the family, and talked of her new book. 'Father never heard a word,' she had written, 'but he would have thought silence over lunch ill-mannered and I spared him speaking himself.' It was in the taxi on the way back to the station that the Colonel had spoken of Alex. 'Your brother won't have suffered much. He had a bad head injury. Likely to have been unconscious most of the time they were digging for him. They were about four hours getting him. Air revived him, he lived until they got him into an ambulance. Talked sense too. Remarkable. You're good with your pen. Let the rest of the family know.' John had read and re-read this letter. He had liked his brother-in-law and his death at home shocked him. It was all wrong. To keep the homes safe was basically what most men were fighting for. Lena and Alex's home was just the sort of set-up he himself was fighting to keep. Beautiful, orderly, full of children. Sitting here in the wood beside Tony he could see Lindsey's typewritten sheets. He could see the exact position where the words lay on each page. As Tony had writhed on the ground he had panted out a few words. 'Tapping. Buried while he was still alive.'

John lit a cigarette before speaking.

'When the bomb hit your home you think your father was buried alive?'

'He was. I went. I heard him tapping to try and get out.'

'I don't know what you heard but it wasn't your father. The facts are these. He was buried for four hours. They got him out alive. He died in an ambulance.'

'But I heard him tap.'

'The person for you to see is your grandfather. You know what a mortuary is?' Tony shook his head. 'Place where they put the bodies of people who have died or been killed. Your grandfather identified your father. Had a look at the body and said it was his son's. Your grandfather wouldn't lie.'

Tony had hugged his knowledge for over a year. It could not be disproved in a second.

'It was real tapping. Somebody beating with their fingers.'

John got up.

'I'll make arrangements for you to see your grandfather. He'll tell you all about it. Dare say we could fix for you to have a word with the fellow who talked to your father before he died.'

'He spoke?'

'Yes. Said he was alone in the house and gave your mother's address.'

'When?'

John once more ran his mental eye over Lindsey's typed sheets.

'The Sunday. He was killed early on a Sunday morning. May the 10th it was.'

Tony stared at John.

'But it was Monday when I went. It was Monday when there was tapping.'

'Your father was not likely to have made a mistake. He said

he was alone in the house and he was brought out alive on the Sunday.'

The mist was rising. The nightmare was evaporating. Tony could not yet grasp that he was free. Too long he had lived with Alex suffocating under the ground, tapping for help which never came. Too long he had died slowly with him. John got up and held out a hand.

'Come on, old man. The others will think we're lost and it's your turn to train Stroch.' They walked towards the ride. 'I've told you the truth. You let it simmer. Next week you shall see your grandfather.'

Laurel, Kim and Tuesday were gathered round Stroch. They shouted at sight of John and Tony.

'Where on earth have you been? I let Stroch go and . . .'

'And I helped.'

Kim raced towards them.

'He couldn't see me or anything. I just called and he came as if he had been ours always.'

Laurel sat down and hugged the puppy.

'It's your turn, Tony. We thought you could go as far as the garden and then call. I believe he's so absolutely ours he'll squeeze under the gate.'

Tony ran up the ride. With every step happiness welled up in him. The sky was more blue. The pine and bracken smelt better. The ground had more spring. As he neared the garden gate he began to jump as well as run.

XXXV

The joining of Stroch to the family made the return to school hard for the children to bear. Even before the arrival of the puppy there was in them all a growing love for their home. Their possessions in the places where they themselves had placed them, waiting from holiday to holiday. Their discoveries, the spot where the Canadians were cutting down trees. The hollow tree big enough to hide the weapons of dead Home Guards if the Germans should land. The bank which must be visited next spring because last spring they had found lilies-of-the-valley growing wild. The hedge where this year there were fourteen birds'-nests. It was their second year for some things. This year they had been at school for the full glory of the rhododendrons and azaleas, but they had seen the buds forming in the Easter holidays and knew from the previous year what a show there would be. For two summers they had picked blackberries and bilberries and they had places named for them. 'The blackberry sand-pit.' 'The bilberry common.' There was a spot where in August gorse grew as nowhere else, a sheet of gold and scent that made you giddy.

As well there were the house things. Mustard, with string tied round his trouser legs, his face unchanging, wrinkled as a long-stored apple and the colour of the garden earth. Mrs. Oliver, with her cockney voice and her cockney ways, which years spent in the country would never eradicate and her superstitions which multiplied as she added country beliefs to her urban collection. There was above all Nannie. They had never had a home without Nannie. She was home. She might now be cook, but cut your finger, feel sick or be upset about something and the years rolled away and you were back in the nursery days, with Nannie's warm, calm voice saying, 'It will all be Sir Garnet Wolseley.'

Lena's place in her home was not the one she would have chosen, but it was a niche growing in solidity. She was rather unpredictable. Wildly gay one minute, aloof and morose another. But she looked nice and she never forgot welcoming things. There were flowers in their rooms when they reached home each holidays. There were new books, jig-saws and games for wet days. There were organised treats. Cinemas and theatres in the winter, and expeditions by bus in the summer. She had come off the pedestal on which she had lived when Alex was alive. She was anything but guarded and treasured. She was the provider, the planner, and it was she who ruled their lives. But she was valued now as she had never been in her treasured days. None of the children would have thought the holidays had started properly if she was not at the station to welcome them. They did not like the days which she spent in London, it was all wrong that she was not about to sit at the top of the table at meals and answer when they shouted. None of them would have dreamed of confiding an innermost thought to her, she was not that sort of person. She was Mum, rather unpredictable but as much part of home as the garden path and the front door.

Finally, there was Walter. The American tenet that childhood is a fleeting state and must, no matter what is sacrificed, be made as perfect as possible, was bone of his bone. He thought that Lena and Nannie were altogether too fussy. There was too much talk about what the children might and might not do and how they behaved. He seemed to hear nothing but 'don't do this' and 'don't do that,' and had no idea that by pre-war standards the children were running wild. When he was about there were no rules, what went to the making up of his idea of a good time prevailed. He provided sentiment. Laurel adored being called 'little sweetheart'. Kim was by turns everything Walter thought him. Little brother. Wonderful kid. Tuesday was Walter's pet. There was nothing he would not have done for her. She was not a child easily spoilt, for she gave in full measure for all affection received. Walter thought her too cute to be true. He loved the way she put her hand in his and asked questions, and confided in him. By British standards he sentimentalised over her, and spoilt her, but Tuesday blossomed under his treatment. Tony was the one member of the family with whom Walter was not entirely comfortable. He took a lot of trouble with him, sensing a deep sore, but sure he was not the right person to probe. He taught Tony things. Wood lore from his college camping days. Things to make. He let Tony come to him, he seldom made an overture. He was rewarded, though he had no idea of it, by Tony's liking. When Lena said at breakfast, 'Uncle Walter's coming down today,' Tony was the first to say 'Good'.

Before the children left for the autumn term each member of the household was instructed over and over again how to care for Stroch. This term the two schools tactfully returned on the same days. Even with the taxi at the door there were last words. Laurel flew down the garden.

'Oh, Mr. Mustard, if Stroch should make a little hole in your garden don't forget he's young. Next holidays I'll train him so that he knows weeds from vegetables and flowers.'

Tony pleaded with Nannie.

'Mum has said she'll take him for walks but you know how she hates walking. If she forgets, you will take him, won't you? He's such an outdoor dog.'

Tuesday cried at leaving the puppy. Mrs. Oliver consoled her.

'Don't you fret, ducks. Each of you 'as written out a piece so as I'll remember what to do if he's upset lookin'. Well, I'm puttin' them in me lookin' glass. Can't 'elp seein' them there, can I?'

Kim was already in the taxi. He snuggled against Lena.

'I absolutely like school but I must say leaving Stroch gives me a queer feeling here,' he held his stomach. 'Will you swear, Mum, that every single day you'll mind more what Stroch eats than what you do?'

Lena kissed him and called the others. The taxi drove off with the children's faces pressed to the windows. Nannie was holding Stroch and Mrs. Oliver was making him wave a paw. Laurel swallowed a lump in her throat.

'I feel as if we were his fathers and mothers being led away to concentration camps, and we shall never see him again.'

Kim drew himself up and looked grim and defiant.

'This is a father despising the Germans.'

Lena laughed.

'Silly darlings. We'll take great care of him and he'll be waiting to welcome you at Christmas, and not only you. I've written to Aunt Dot to ask if Maria and Alice can come to us for part of next holidays. Won't that be fun?'

XXXVI

Christmas day was over. Walter had leave. He had taken an infinity of trouble to make the children's Christmas happy and had succeeded past his imaginings. Kim, who was never afraid of the colourful phrase, told Mrs. Oliver, 'It was a day shimmering with happiness and joy.'

Walter had not an easy time. It was increasingly difficult to curb Lena. With him securely in her life, she relapsed more and more into the Lena who had refused to allow Alex to become the family man, the Lena who insisted that she was first a wife and, a long way second, a mother. The fonder Walter grew of the children the more tenacious became her hold as mistress. She dared put her feelings into words to Walter in a way she would never have done to Alex. Perpetually drinking far too much, she was not squeamish in her choice of words when it came to reminding Walter of what she meant to him, nor, when words were impossible, was she too nice in selection of messages by glance. She did not exactly grudge the time he spent with, or planning for, the children, but she had to be sure he grudged the time. She was able, with a whispered, 'Do you know what I wish?' to stir him into a fever. If Walter had not loved children, and felt that their innocence was a sacred trust, Lena, by words and looks, must have ruffled the children's curiosity. It would have had to be something fairly blatant for, to the children, mothers behaved simply as mothers. They knew, though they never thought about it, that they had been produced by Lena's union with their father, but he being dead they considered her physical life over. Walter knew that Lena could, if she had a drink or two, be blatant. He tried to safeguard the children by telling Lena before the Christmas holidays started that during the holidays there would not only be no love-making in the house, but, as far as he was concerned, very little drinking. As soon as the children arrived he doubled this safeguard by giving all his attention to them. He took them out to cut down their own Christmas tree. They went out with clippers and collected holly and, under Walter's guidance, spent all Christmas Eve on the most elaborate scheme of decoration. It was Walter who got the whole party out to church on Christmas morning. Lena had suggested that he and she should decorate the tree in the afternoon but he was not risking it. He insisted that the children helped. His idea of a good Christmas ran to fun rather than sentiment, and he accentuated his taste. When Lena thought carols round the tree would be pretty, he produced Stroch in a silver coat with silver paper wings as a fairy queen. When Lena said, 'Let's have the lights out. A tree is so much prettier in the dark,' he said, 'Let's have the lights on and see who gets the biggest parcel.' He also scotched Lena's ideas on games. When she said they would play Blind Man's Buff and wanted to make him the blind man, 'and you have to feel who you catch, you know, and say who it is,' he saw who would be the first to be caught and tied the handkerchief round Nannie's eyes. Even when the day was over and the children in bed he was firm with Lena. Whatever she said he parried with a joke, and succeeded in getting her up to bed sober and let her know he was locking his door.

Walter had to leave on Boxing Day. He had enjoyed his Christmas but he was relieved. He had known it was running a risk staying in the house while the children were home.

'When are you coming back?' the children queried.

He kissed the girls and dug a fist into the boys' ribs.

'I've got to go some place north for a day or two. Shan't be able to stay the night but I'll be down in a week's time.'

Laurel clung to his arm.

'You promise? Alice and Maria will be here and Alice is my great friend and I've absolutely sworn she'll meet you.'

Alice and Maria, on top of her own family, were too much for Lena. The weather was bad and the children indoors a good deal. The noise was deafening. As soon as Walter reached the house he knew he had picked on a day when Lena was going to be impossible. She had started the morning on brandy, her head ached, her nerves were to pieces, she wanted Walter's arms round her, she wanted to be loved. Walter took a quick decision. He told the children to get on their things. Yes, he knew it was raining, but he was fuller of grime than a railway engine, he had got to have a walk. He joined Lena in the drawing-room, shutting the door behind him. She was half crying.

'I'm so lonely and miserable and when you come down you go straight out with the children.'

He held her by the shoulders.

'Look here, beautiful, ring up the hire car place and book a table for dinner at that hotel with a comedy name.'

'What's the good of that? A beastly chauffeur with us the whole time.'

He gave her a gentle, affectionate shake.

'You must come to London one day soon. Meanwhile, unless that place has deteriorated, they've got good Scotch in their bar.'

Walter knew when at the railway station he said goodbye to Lena and sent her home in the car that she had drunk too much. He had done his best to prevent her but she had retaliated by ordering her own drinks and, since she overtipped the barman, she had no difficulty.

'They'll all be in bed,' he reminded her. 'You got your key?'

She clung to his hand.

'Yes. Come back with me. We can get you to London in time for your work tomorrow. Please, Walter. I do need you, I feel like Hell.'

Walter looked anxiously at the back of the chauffeur's head. He gave Lena's hand a quick squeeze and slammed the car door.

Lena lay back in the corner of the car. She was trembling all over. How was she to endure herself? Walter was cruel, it was better not to come down at all if he was going to leave her in this frustrated state. She felt in her bag for her handkerchief. She had taken to carrying a flask. Her fingers knocked against it. It was full of brandy, she tipped it up and swallowed it all.

Nannie heard Lena fall. She pulled on her dressing-gown. As she passed Laurel's door it opened and Laurel and Alice came out.

'What's happened?'

Alice was gaping over the banisters.

'It's Aunt Lena. She's sitting on the floor.'

Nannie, Alice and Laurel went down. They looked to Lena's hazy vision very funny. She began to laugh.

Laurel was scared.

'Get up, Mum. What's up?'

Nannie tried to pull Lena to her feet. Lena rocked with laughter.

'I can't get up. My legs feel as if they were made of wool. Nice, soft, fleecy wool.'

Alice took command.

'You take one of her arms, Laurel, and I'll take the other and Nannie push behind.'

In this way, after some labour, they got Lena up the stairs and into her room. Nannie shooed the two girls out.

'You run along now, I'll see to your mother, Laurel. It's a touch of flu' I shouldn't wonder.'

'Flu' nothing,' said Lena. 'I'm drunk. Oh, my God, I'm going to be sick.'

Alice and Laurel went back to their beds. Laurel's face was crimson.

'Was Mum drunk?'

Alice had thought the whole adventure rather exciting.

'I think so. I've seen drunk soldiers and they're like that.'

'But mothers don't get drunk.'

Alice looked at Laurel's stricken face.

'I shouldn't fuss. Yours doesn't usually. I expect it was just a mistake.'

'But it's hateful, she wasn't a bit like herself.'

'I know, but I still wouldn't fuss. It quite likely won't happen again. I'll tell you something I've never told anybody. Dad went to a British Legion dinner once and he got drunk. I heard Mum tell him so the next day. She said, "You must expect a headache if you get as drunk as you were last night."'

Laurel visualised her Uncle Paul and was comforted.

'Really! I wish I didn't have to grow up. Do you know, Alice, I'm beginning to wonder if we've not been told things wrong. I mean, we're told that children behave badly and grown-ups are always right. I wonder if we shan't find that grown-ups do worse things than children.'

'I've thought that a long time,' Alice yawned. 'Well, I'm going to sleep and so'll you unless you're an ass.'

Laurel lay down and for a few minutes there was silence. Then she called urgently:

'Alice. Alice.' Alice grunted. 'I'm sorry to wake you but this is important, you must listen. It was nice of you to tell me about Uncle Paul and, of course, I'll never tell anybody. You won't either, will you? About Mum, I mean.'

Alice sat up.

'You really are the limit, Laurel, to wake me up to ask a silly question like that. Of course I shan't tell anybody. Is it likely!'

XXXVII

Dot met her daughters in London. They were full of excited gossip. They had enjoyed themselves immensely. Stroch and Uncle Walter figured in a big way in their conversations. Dot was too busy to listen with more than half an ear. There was shopping to be done for next term, which was beginning in two days' time. If they were to get everything done, lunch, and catch their train, they must hurry. In Selfridges she sent Alice to choose herself a new school hat, while she took Maria to the shoe department.

Maria kept up a non-stop conversation. Dot answered now and again, 'Yes, darling,' 'No, darling,' and when some shoes were being tried on halted the flow for a moment or two. 'You are certain you like those? They don't touch anywhere, do they? You understand about coupons, darling? They are meant to be too big, they've got to last.'

The shoes purchased, Maria's dammed-up conversation flowed again.

'And one night me and Tuesday heard the most tremendous bang, and then we heard doors and voices, so we got out of bed, which we weren't allowed to do, and we peeped over the banisters and what do you think it was?'

Dot was examining Maria's ration book to be sure that the right number of coupons had been taken.

'What, darling?'

'It was Aunt Lena. She was sitting on the floor laughing and laughing.'

Maria had at last got her mother's attention.

'What?'

'And Alice was there and Nannie and Laurel. And do you know, Aunt Lena couldn't get up alone and Alice and Laurel had to pull and Nannie pushed,' Maria got off her chair, 'and she came upstairs like this.' Maria imitated Lena unable to walk without support. 'When she was halfway up Tuesday and me had to go back to bed or Nannie would have seen us and been angry.'

Maria was attracting the attention of other parents and guardians. Dot took her by the hand.

'Very funny, darling. Your Aunt Lena was playing I expect to make Alice and Laurel laugh. Now, tell me about the puppy. What did you say his name was?'

Before Alice left for school Dot tried to draw her on the subject of Lena. She had no success. Alice peered at her mother through her glasses and parried every question.

'Oh yes, Aunt Lena was very well.' 'No, Aunt Lena didn't seem to find it dull in the country.' 'No, Aunt Lena never went out to dinner except when she went to London for the day and then she came back late.' 'I don't know how late. We were in bed.' Over Walter she was more forthcoming. 'Uncle Walter's American. He's the nicest man, Mummy, I ever knew except Daddy.' 'Well, I suppose he started by being a friend of Aunt Lena's, but really now he comes more to see the cousins.' 'When Aunt Lena goes to London she sees Uncle Walter.'

Dot had her mind full. She had a big job in W.V.S. She was worried about Henry, who would be seventeen this year and was determined to fly. She had been warned that already the supply of trained pilots was exceeding the demand. Henry was the sort of boy who would want handling carefully if his ambitions were thwarted. Paul was being sent overseas and, judging by his outfit, it was somewhere hot. Now that she had not got him under her eye Dot worried about Paul, and she knew she would worry a lot more if he was fighting the

Japanese. A man who had thought he could make money out of hens and bees was obviously the sort to be fooled by the low tricks the Japanese were supposed to go in for. Apart from these major anxieties there was the daily round, which became steadily more complicated. Her only certain domestic help was a Miss Endwell, who insisted on the title 'lady help'. This meant that she would not do any scrubbing, and often, unless she was having a lucky patch with a daily woman, Dot had to scrub floors herself when she got back from her W.V.S. work. She had the usual network of wartime arrangements. Picking up the rations on the way to do this, fetching, or hoping to fetch, the laundry on the way back from that, spending a precious half-hour in a queue for fish because Miss Endwell liked fish, only to find it sold out before she reached the counter. Every third Sunday she went to Greenwood House and twice a term to Wellington to look up Henry. When the holidays were pending she had to pass a lot of her W.V.S. work to her deputy and take over the cooking from Miss Endwell. This had not so far worked, as the deputy had a mother with a weak heart whose heart attacks were apt to coincide with the holidays, and Miss Endwell took the opportunity when Dot was about to do nothing at all. Somehow, because Dot detested mess and disorder, she kept her house running reasonably while doing her job in W.V.S. brilliantly, but it meant early risings, late bedtimes, and endless thought and contriving. She was a strong woman but she knew that she was living an over-strained existence for which one day she must pay. The little more might mean that the day for payment came nearer.

Dot was not by nature a meddler, it went against her grain to probe into Lena's life. She also had some thinking to do on her own account. Suppose Lena was drinking, and possibly had taken a lover, and their home was unsuitable for Alex's children. What did she intend to do about it? As she drove about the country on her work she sifted her thoughts and came at last to a clear conviction. If Alex's children were happy at home, and saw nothing wrong even though there were quite a lot wrong going on, she would do nothing. Her own home was a muddle compared to peacetime standards, and Paul was away. The children adored their father and it was bad, especially for Henry, that they were being brought up without him; but the children were all right, absolutely normal, doing well at school, no complexes about any of them, thank God. Dot put down this state of affairs partly to the way they had been brought up, partly to the solidity they had inherited from her, but mostly to the fact that they had kept their home. No chopping and changing, children hated being messed about.

Dot, without excuse, could not visit the boys and question Martin Phillips. She had to get her information through Laurel and Tuesday. On her usual three-weekly visit she asked Alice for help.

'Could you arrange for me to have a word alone with Laurel?'

'I suppose so. What's up?'

Dot had known Alice would ask that.

'I'm writing to Gran. She wants to know if I think Laurel happy at school.'

'Well, I can tell you that. She simply hates it.'

'Why?'

'She liked the other school she was at. I don't think she'd mind it so much if she was allowed to wear uniform.'

Dot saw reckless generosity in Alice's eyes.

'We can't do anything about that. You're the same size so you can't pass down, and I haven't enough coupons to dress you properly.'

'As a matter of fact, I don't think Laurel minds school as much as she did. You see, having a puppy for the holidays makes all the difference. I wish we could have one.'

'I'm afraid we can't. Just imagine what Miss Endwell would say.' Dot gave Alice's shoulder a pat. 'You fix it that I get a word with Laurel without her knowing you've arranged it.'

After lunch Alice took Maria and Tuesday to feed the rabbits which lived in the Inn garden. Dot said:

'You stay and keep me company, Laurel.' She lit a cigarette. 'What sort of term are you having?'

They were sitting at a table in the lounge. Laurel leant on it and spoke earnestly.

'Not very nice. You see, I'll be fifteen in May and I'm good at nothing. Just a low, rather meanish average.'

'You and Alice are in the same form and I'm quite satisfied with her.'

'But Alice is marvellous at games.'

'I don't suppose your mother's disappointed in you, is she?'

'Mum! She doesn't care for schools. She'd like us to be at home always.'

'Would you like that?'

'Would I! With the Foxglove to teach us. You remember Miss Glover, who was our governess?'

'It's a charming house you have, Alice tells me.'

'Absolutely perfect. Did she tell you about Stroch?'

'Yes, and the American.'

'Uncle Walter. He's the most awfully nice man. I simply dread him being sent to fight somewhere.'

'How's your mother?'

'Very well indeed, thank you. She's spent her coupons on an absolutely lovely frock. They've taken four months making it. It came in the holidays. She's promised to wear it when she comes at half term.'

'Tell me about the house. I've never seen it, you know.'

Laurel burst into a eulogy on her home. The rooms and the garden. Mustard, Mrs. Oliver, Nannie, Walter, Lena and Stroch each had their own tone of voice which, as news of them was repeated, helped to build up a psalm of praise.

Dot, who was nothing if not thorough, had a talk with both Miss Clegg and Mrs. Fellows before she left. She got nothing from Miss Clegg, who supposed no mother wished to discuss any children but her own. Alice was just the sort of girl she liked, satisfactory in every way, it was a pleasure to talk to her mother and tell her so. She had not got over her idea that Laurel was inclined to sulkiness and badly brought up. She felt it was partly Laurel's fault that she had none of the school uniform, if she had pressed her mother she could surely have talked her round. She did not care for Lena, comparing her unfavourably with Dot. Lena was charming to Miss Clegg, but Miss Clegg distrusted charm, especially when it was allied to a frivolous attitude to education. So each of Dot's attempts to discuss Laurel she dismissed. 'Laurel? Yes, she's getting on all right, not at all outstanding, you know. . . . Now Alice . . .' 'Laurel happy? I'm sure she is, all my girls are happy. We're so proud that Alice . . .'

Mrs. Fellows was helpful. Her sitting-room was the room of a mother more than a house mistress. There was a shabby teddy bear waiting to have a leg repaired lying on a table, and her daughter's picture books in the shelves. On the mantle-piece was a large photograph of her prisoner of war husband. In a moment Mrs. Fellows grasped that it was the welfare of her nieces that Mrs. Enden had come to discuss. She picked up the teddy bear.

'Do you mind if I mend this? It's my daughter Viola's bed companion and I've promised to have him mended by tonight.'

Even to this nice Mrs. Fellows Dot could not ask point blank if Tuesday spoke happily of her home.

'My father and mother want news of the Wiltshire children. My brother was their only son. How is Tuesday really getting on?'

Mrs. Fellows dug her needle into the teddy bear's hip.

'Very well. She had been a bit babied before she came here, she's outgrown it. A most responsible little person. She needs care, she's a nervous little thing. She had a lot of jumpy tricks when she came to us.'

'You've got rid of them?'

'Not us. I put down the improvement to settled home conditions.' Dot made an interested querying sound. Mrs.

Fellows gave the bear's leg a pull to see if she was stitching it on straight. 'More than half the children in my care have either lost their father for good or they haven't seen him for months. It's been my experience that if the mother makes a decent home not much harm's done. This sitting-room and a bedroom upstairs are all the home my daughter has, but she's fine. It's a background and it's secure, she doesn't notice that it's only two rooms.'

'She's got all the rest of the school.'

'Yes, but these two rooms are home and certain times of each day and, of course, all the holidays, she can have me and my attention. It's not the children who have lost a parent, either temporarily or permanently, that worry us, it's the homeless ones. There are so many living in other people's houses. They need a lot of handling.'

'Evacuated, you mean?'

'Some of them. Worst of all, of course, children of broken marriages.'

'Have you any orphans?'

'Two. They've been adopted, they do at least know where they belong.'

'You are a great believer in a home?'

'Of course. Who isn't? A home and, if possible, both parents, but anyway one.'

'In my work I come across all sorts, sad stories sometimes. Parents who aren't fit for one reason or another to have charge of their children.'

Mrs. Fellows cut her thread. She exercised the bear's repaired leg.

'It would have to be a very bad parent before I agreed that
he or she wasn't fit to look after their own children. I'd rather
slave at educating a bad parent than take children away from
their ordinary background.'

Dot got up.

'Well, I must be going or I'll miss the station bus.'

Having seen Dot off Mrs. Fellows went upstairs to put the
bear in Viola's bed. 'I wonder,' she thought, 'what exactly that
pretty, silly Mrs. Wiltshire's been up to. This Uncle Walter we
hear about I suppose. Well, pray God I tipped her off from
meddling.'

Dot was still worried. The home was happy, the girls
were all right. What about the boys? Fatherless boys were a
problem. In the end she wrote to the Colonel. She said she
wanted to see him privately. When would he next be visiting
his club?

They met in London a week later. The Colonel detested
the bungalow, he was working too hard at a dozen war tasks,
and Elsa was working harder. There was no comfort for the
old these days, they got no privileges, if they were to survive
they must work. None of these things were mentioned. The
Colonel was as straight-backed and as groomed as ever. There
was nothing about him to show that he had started the day by
helping to get his own breakfast, that he had with difficulty
secured foot room on a crowded bus, and had then travelled
one of fourteen in a railway carriage, unable to unfold his
newspaper or fight his way up the corridor. Only he was
greyer, and thinner and had a tendency to accept little rebuffs
and discomforts almost with eagerness, as if to say, 'I don't

mind. Old people mustn't expect anything. Very fortunate really to be allowed the same comforts as more useful members of society.'

Dot knew her father detested gossip and malice, for he had brought them up to despise it. She told her story simply and finished with her findings at Greenwood House.

The Colonel listened in silence. There was a pause when Dot finished. He was wondering whether he would tell her about Tony. How John had brought him to him. He decided against it. Tony had been half-cured of his obsession before he saw him. There had been no need to say much, by now he should be himself again. He had, however, wondered if he would go and see Martin Phillips to find out how the boy was doing. He saw no reason why he and Dot should discuss Lena any further.

'I'll have a look at the boys. You'll keep this to yourself, of course. No need to upset your mother. Dare say there's nothing in this business, Maria's only a baby. Difficult time for Lena. I always liked the little thing.'

Martin Phillips was delighted to see the Colonel. He wanted to talk about Tony.

'You must have a look at him. He's a different boy. Afraid I can't offer you a drink, my little bit's late this month.'

'It was a pity we none of us cottoned on to the trouble earlier.'

Martin nodded.

'I've gone over every step. Perhaps we ought to have called in a psychiatrist, but it never struck me.'

'He's quite himself now?'

'Too late for him to make up the ground he's lost. But he's looking fine. Matter of fact, I'm giving him a bit of extra coaching myself. Want him to do all right at his entrance exam. Lucky really he's leaving us this year. I was wondering whether his mother would consider sending Kim to a different place when the time comes. Don't want poor old Tony dogged by a younger brother passing over his head. Not that it need happen. Tony ought to do all right now, nothing wrong with his brains. Sort of boy who comes on well when he gets to his public school.'

'Bad luck on the boys having no father.'

'Too much of it these days, but Mrs. Wiltshire seems to make a good job of them. Both Tony and Kim came back full of their holidays.'

The Colonel got permission to take the boys out to lunch. Tony was rather silent at first, self-conscious because of the last time he had seen his grandfather, but when it became clear that the Colonel considered the subject of Alex's death closed he relaxed. Going out to lunch in the middle of a week was an unexpected treat and their spirits soared. Kim gave an imitation of the reactions of the master who was teaching him and of all his class, when the news arrived.

'Mr. Jones, he speaks in a squeaky voice like this and he hasn't been called up because he's got flat feet, well, he said: "Indeed! Are you sure?" and then he looked at me as if I was something nasty he'd spat out and he said, "Wiltshire Minor, you are to wash and tidy, you will be lunching with your grandpapa."'

'I bet he never said grandpapa,' Tony broke in.

'Almost he did, you know what a wet he is. And this is the face all the other boys made.'

The Colonel led the conversation to their home. He at once heard about Stroch. Kim, in spite of being at the dining table, gave an imitation of the puppy.

'He looks as if he was a widow crying over a grave, like this, and really he's never known a minute's sorrow.'

'It's just the country for a dog,' Tony broke in. 'Wild wood everywhere, but we don't let him out of our sight much in case of traps.'

'How's your mother?'

Neither Tony nor Kim supposed this was a question requiring an answer. Tony, thinking of traps, had his mind on Mustard.

'He's a simply marvellous gardener. Do you know, we had more raspberries than we could eat. Knowing us you wouldn't think that possible, would you?'

Kim stuck out his chest.

'And I wish you could see Mrs. Oliver, she sticks out like this.'

'Got any friends round there?'

Tony nodded.

'Quite a lot. Our best friend is Uncle Walter, but he's stationed in London. He comes down when he can.'

'Who's he?'

Tony answered.

'You wouldn't think it seeing how nice he is, but he's a friend of a friend of Mum's-Mum. And do you know, Mum's-Mum has still got those awful yapping little dogs. If I was the American Government I wouldn't have let them land.'

'Nice for your mother to get news of her mother.'

'And nice to get all the presents she gets,' Kim added. 'Lipstick and nail-varnish and stockings and lots of tins of food.'

'Sent over from your grandmother in America?'

Kim spoke with a pseudo-American accent.

'I'll say not. I've gotten something right here in my pocket you might find a use for.'

Tony explained.

'Mum and Uncle Walter are great friends. He gets things she needs sent from New York. You can't buy the lipstick Mum likes over here now.'

The Colonel wrote to Dot that night. He said he had seen the boys, who looked splendid. They were clearly happy at home. He finished up: 'I feel this is an occasion for masterly inactivity.'

XXXVIII

Lindsey had been lecturing. She was a clear and amusing lecturer, and could produce any amount of charm. Never for a moment did she forget her position as a well-known novelist and so nobody else could forget it, which made those responsible for any meeting at which she spoke feel it was an occasion, and kept them on the fidget lest the audience was not large enough or the applause too feeble.

Everything had gone off nicely. The Women's Institute members had turned up splendidly. Lindsey had spoken admirably. Her subject, 'The next generation', had real appeal.

In a glow of satisfaction the President and the Secretary took Lindsey across to the hotel where she was spending the night. Over cigarettes and weak cocktails they relived the afternoon. The Secretary cooing with joy that in spite of bus troubles so many members of other Institutes had been able to turn up. The President, who in spite of the changing conditions of wartime had managed in her village to retain the right of the wife of an Earl to have unarguable knowledge on any subject, explained to Lindsey how absorbing her talk had been though she had not produced one idea which the President had not gone into thoroughly before. Lindsey was in a state of tiredness, mixed with a glow that came from knowing that she had found the words to say exactly what she wanted. She did not interrupt the President or Secretary more than to murmur occasionally, 'I'm so glad' and 'They did seem interested in that, didn't they?' She hoped that she was to be spared book talk. She refused private hospitality to avoid it. She knew from long experience that the President was the sort of woman who would ask if Lindsey had to pay her publisher much to get her books printed. Suddenly the Secretary leant forward and tapped her knee.

'There's somebody over there who ought to have heard you this afternoon. She has four children they tell me, and they say she lives with that American.'

The President was interested.

'Really! Who is she?'

The Secretary lowered her voice.

'Doesn't live here. They come in by hired car. Such a waste of petrol. It oughtn't to be allowed. I hear she's often the worse for drink.'

The President swung round and frankly stared.

'Really! I had no idea there was all that drink to be had in this place.'

Lindsey had shrunk back in her chair, her hand holding her cigarette across her face. How trying if Lena should see her. Why on earth could not she and her American drink in the bar, then she could get up to her room unnoticed.

Drink in the home was scarce. Lena was not able to get hold of a great deal. Walter brought some down but he helped finish any that he brought. Lena, with the long summer holidays ahead and bad days liable to crop up at any moment, never left herself without reserves. To achieve this she and Walter had to drink out. She hired a car and met him at the station, and they came home by their favourite hotel and drank all they could buy as a preliminary stoke up before touching the home supply. Usually Lena had a drink before she started for the station, or a nip from her flask on the way there. Today she had drunk two strong cocktails before she set out. It had been a tiresome day. She had woken up feeling ill. Nannie was silent and looked, as she increasingly did, disapproving without saying why. Mustard had asked for wire, and when she had said it was hard to get, had answered, 'You'm the only one with time 'm,' to which, when she had retorted, 'I haven't much, goodness knows,' he had replied, 'You've all there is, 'm.' Such impertinence! Lena had come indoors in a temper and for quite half an hour had considered giving Mustard, and perhaps Nannie too, notice. It was not until she had drunk some more brandy and taken two aspirins that she had calmed down. Walter hated hearing her complain of her staff. He liked all of them, and anyway they were part of the children's home and so not to be quarrelled with. It was to put herself in a good mood in which she would not grumble that she had taken two cocktails before she met his train.

Lena was waiting for Walter to fetch their third double whiskies when she saw Lindsey. She was not drunk but she was in that slightly gay stage when the conviction dawns that all the world loves you and would like to speak to you. She got up and came to Lindsey.

'My dear! What are you doing here? It was such fun seeing John when he was on leave last year.'

Up to that moment Lindsey had merely thought it would be an impossible situation after what had been said to be recognised by Lena. Now, at mention of John, she stiffened. John had not told her he had seen Lena. Why had he kept it a secret? Was this American the only man in Lena's life? Coldly she introduced Lena, saying firmly sister-in-law, with all the accent on the last word.

The Secretary glanced nervously round the lounge, not wishing to be seen talking to the scandal. The President, whose social training never failed her, drew forward a chair.

'How nice. It's so hard to see people these days, it was lucky you two ran into each other.'

Lindsey spoke as if her question had no importance.

'Where did you see John?'

'He came down to see me. He was sweet.' Lena turned to the President. 'She's got a perfectly enchanting husband.' She smiled amiably at Lindsey. 'Still writing?'

The question, accustomed though she was to it, never failed to enrage Lindsey.

'Yes. Though it's difficult with all my other wartime duties. What are you doing?'

Walter was hovering near with the drinks. Lena beckoned him over and introduced him. She patted the arm of her chair.

'Sit here. Lindsey was asking me what I'm doing. You tell her. I'm dreadfully overworked, aren't I?' She turned to the President. 'I've four babies.'

The President, who though pleased with the way the afternoon had gone had not taken to Lindsey, was beginning to enjoy herself.

'How nice, do tell us about them.'

Lena took a drink of whisky.

'I lost my husband in an air-raid and, though I try very hard, I think perhaps they need more than I can give them. I send them to boarding schools.'

Lindsey had been doing some calculating.

'Babies hardly describes them. Surely Laurel's fifteen.'

It was Walter who answered.

'Last month.'

Lindsey turned to him graciously.

'Are you fond of children?'

Walter saw the glasses on the table were empty.

'Let me get you ladies some drinks.'

The three refused. Lena felt Walter might think this ungracious.

'Lindsey doesn't need to drink, she's not like us, she's clever without. She writes books. I've told you about her, and, you remember, her husband was down last summer.'

Lena had never mentioned Lindsey to Walter and by some odd chance she had overlooked telling him that John had been down. Because he wanted to keep off her books, which he had never read, Walter gripped on to John as a subject for conversation.

'No, you never told me. When was that?'

Lindsey, though she smiled and kept the conversation rolling, longed to get away and think. Why had John not told her he was going down to see Lena? Why had Lena kept from this American, who was presumed to be her lover, that she had seen John?

In spite of the President's efforts the party soon broke up. The Secretary was twittering with anxiety lest she should be seen with Lena, and Lindsey wanted to be alone. Lena and Walter never quite took in what Lindsey was doing in the neighbourhood, and Lindsey managed to keep from them that she was staying in the hotel.

'It seems rather deceitful,' she confided to the President as she said her goodbyes, 'but she was always rather terrible I thought and now, without my brother to take care of her, she's quite impossible. If they know I'm staying here I'll have to ask them to dinner, and it's more than I could bear.'

When Lindsey came down to dinner Lena and Walter had gone, but the Secretary had come back.

'Forgive me, but I had to apologise. I feel so badly saying what I did about a relative of yours.'

'Only a relative by marriage.'

The Secretary was a plain woman, especially when, as now, her face was screwed up with nervousness.

'That's not the only reason I came back.'

Lindsey looked at her with distaste. She wanted her dinner, she had done her duty by the locals and wished to be left alone. Her inflection made her feelings clear.

'Oh?'

'It's my sister. We live together. She does evacuees. She sees a woman whose mother is a Mrs. Oliver. She works for your sister-in-law.'

Lindsey managed to express her fear that she was about to hear an impertinence.

'Is that so?'

'I would never have said anything only my sister heard you this afternoon, and she said, "Niggy," she's always called me that, "a woman who speaks as beautifully as that about children would want to know. They're her own flesh and blood."'

Lindsey was caught. Her reputation required that she should listen. She partially disguised her boredom.

'You must have dinner with me.'

The Secretary would have protested but Lindsey was masterful. She led the way into the dining-room and beckoned impressively to the head-waiter.

'A table for two. One in a corner would be nice. We want to talk.'

XXXIX

Lindsey hired a car the next morning and drove over to see Lena. Nannie was out shopping. It was Mrs. Oliver who opened the door. Lindsey said 'Good-morning. Can I see Mrs. Wiltshire?'

Mrs. Oliver's face remained unruffled while her mind shot up to Lena. Not in much shape she wasn't this morning. He'd only left on the early bus. Her daughter had seen him running for it. Mrs. Oliver had only one excuse, which tripped readily to her tongue, this was a disobliging 'I couldn't do anythin', not without askin' me 'usband,' but that would not be suitable in this case. What did you say when a lady wasn't up at eleven in the morning? She cleared her throat.

'She's got a nasty headache. . . .'

Lindsey nodded in an understanding manner.

'Yes, but I'm her sister-in-law, Mrs. Lawrence. Go up and tell her, would you please.'

Mrs. Oliver had not liked Lindsey's nod. 'Sauce box,' she thought, 'thinks she knows a lot,' but she took Lindsey into the drawing-room and went up to Lena. 'I might 'ave guessed she was a nosey relative,' she thought as she climbed the stairs, 'seein' one magpie the way I did yesterday.'

Lena was half asleep. It took her a moment or two to grasp what Mrs. Oliver was saying. Then she sat up.

'Mrs. Lawrence! Oh, bother!'

Mrs. Oliver was kind but firm.

'You'll have to see her. She puts me in mind of one of those foot-in-the-door chaps that come round sellin' things.'

'Tell her I won't be long.' Mrs. Oliver was at the door. Lena called her back. 'Don't say I was in bed.'

Mrs. Oliver's face expressed a wink.

'Not me. You put on that nice navy 'ousecoat. She'll never know you weren't washin' your stockin's or that.'

Lena, when she reached the drawing-room, looked very much her poised self. She was scared at this visit of Lindsey's, but she gave no sign. She greeted her sister-in-law graciously.

Lindsey never felt awkward, she was too sure of herself, but she did consider two or three different openings. It was annoying that Lena should look as lovely as she still did. She had gone off a lot but Lindsey, with her novelist's eye, could view the room and knew that however many lovers and however much Lena drank, the ten years, or whatever it was, between them made her look fresh compared with herself. It was because she knew this, and, though she valued brains and success beyond looks, felt jealous, that she started speaking on a sharp note.

'I shall come straight to the point. I learned last night that you are a by-word round here. There's talk about you and the man I saw with you, and they say you're often the worse for drink.'

Lena had taken some brandy before she came down but it did not help her much in the face of so direct an attack. The frail pretence of happiness that she had built over the grave of real happiness tottered. Her eyes widened. The colour faded from her cheeks leaving the rouge she had put on standing out, a pink smudge.

'It's – it's not your business.'

'Of course it is. You're the mother of my brother's children. Am I to hear these things and do nothing? From what I'm told you aren't fit to have charge of children.'

Lena swayed. That was a knock indeed. One of the more solid pieces of the scaffolding holding up her makeshift happiness began to give.

'They're happy.' She made an effort to gather her dignity together. 'What I do with my life is not your business. Anyway, nothing happens in this house that . . .' she fumbled for words, 'that Alex wouldn't approve of. In the holidays, I mean.'

Lindsey had not expected this quick breaking of Lena's confidence, a quality in her that had seemed unbreakable. Power excited Lindsey.

'Queer. I was told that one night at Christmas time you came home in such a state of drunkenness that the man who drove your car had to help you up the path and open your door for you.'

Only if her sleeping tablets failed to work and she was therefore awake in the night hours did Lena let herself remember that scene. She was confused about it but she knew both Laurel and Alice had been there. She felt her legs giving under her. She sat down.

Lindsey saw that Lena could not reply. She took a mental glance at the points she wished to make.

'Now listen, Lena. You must write to that American friend of yours and tell him that you won't be seeing him again. As for the drinking, if you have difficulty I believe there's a splendid place where you can go for a week or two and get rid of the taste for it. . . .' She broke off, frightened by the queer colour Lena had turned. 'Don't look like that, my dear. Nobody in the family knows about what's been going on except myself. You do as I say and it will be a secret between us.'

Lena was back where she had been before the days of

Walter, before her first sip of brandy, only she had weakened morally and physically. She put her face into her hands, her shoulders shook with sobs.

'I can't. I couldn't go on alone. Oh Alex. Alex.'

Lindsey got up and gave the heaving shoulders a squeeze to express consolation.

'Cheer up. Take a pull on yourself. It may seem difficult but you'll manage. It's a matter of courage.'

Lena raised her face. She looked frightful, tears streaming, her skin blotchy.

'You don't understand. I couldn't go on without Walter. I'm so lonely.'

'Nonsense. A woman with four children can't be lonely.'

'I can't go on.'

Lindsey was impatient.

'Rubbish. Now look, I don't want to threaten but I must do what I think right. You must write to that man today, and . . .'

'No.'

Lindsey raised her voice.

'Yes. And you must do something about this drunkenness or we shall have to make other arrangements about the children.'

Lena choked over a sob.

'They're mine. They had lovely Easter holidays. They all said so. You can't . . .'

'Oh dear me, yes we can. If necessary we could invoke the law. It's obvious that as things are at present a home like yours is unfit for children.' Lindsey gave Lena's shoulders a departing pat. 'Now I must be going. I'll be down to see you again in a day or two and by then I shall expect you to have everything tidied up.'

Lena heard the car drive off. She got up and, still crying, began to walk about the room. Broken sentences slipped out amongst her sobs. 'I can't write to Walter . . . I can't see Walter . . . She can't take the children . . . It's not true. They couldn't have been happier than they were at Easter . . . A drink now and again isn't being a drunkard . . . The children . . . ' She was facing the wall, beating it with her fists. 'Oh God! Oh God! I can't bear it. I can't bear it. Alex! Alex!'

It was some time later that she remembered the sleeping tablets. On the bottle it said it was dangerous to exceed the dose ordered by the physician. She filled a tumbler half full of brandy and with its aid swallowed the lot.

XL

Dot was waiting by the porter's desk in the entrance to Lindsey's club. Sylvia and Selina arrived together. She seized an arm of each and drew them into a corner.

'Thank goodness you've got here before Lindsey. I sent you both a card to tell you to be a little early because there's something we've got to get together about. Whatever plans we make for Alex's children, see that Lindsey takes her share.'

Selina looked less than her thirty-six years, and she accentuated her youthful air by buying clothes in 'junior miss' departments. Her straw hat was worn on the back of her head. She had quick, rather childlike movements and a light eager voice.

'Lindsey! Lindsey wouldn't look after children.'

Dot was eyeing the entrance anxiously.

'I can't explain, there isn't time, but please do as I say. It's for the children's good, I promise you.'

Sylvia was shabbily dressed. She had pulled off her gloves and showed hands not only work-worn, but scarred with burns, cuts and other pointers to inefficiency at housework. Almost all Sylvia's sentences, from a mixture of loyalty and pride, began or ended with 'Andrew says'. She knew her family were sorry for her and thought Andrew a muddler. They all managed their lives so well, and her own and Andrew's must appear a permanent mess. They did not see the Andrew she knew, the Andrew who lived only half in this world. They saw a thin, bony man, with a shabby cassock, too big for him, flapping round his legs. She was often too tired and too dispirited to see him quite in focus herself, but she knew there lived in her husband a rare spirit, he was of the clay from which come the saints and martyrs, through eyes such as his miracles were seen. She spoke fast, her words tripping over each other, a remnant of her childhood days where her more dominant sisters seldom let her finish a sentence.

'But, Dot, we must keep them together. Andrew says . . .'

Dot gripped both their arms.

'Ssh. Lindsey.'

They sat at a table in a corner of the reception room. Dot with her back to the wall, Lindsey facing her, Sylvia on her right, Selina on her left. Lindsey, because it was her club and because she had convened this family gathering, took as a matter of right the position of chairman.

'I wrote to you all fully about the distressing gossip I learned, and how I saw Lena. As I told you, she denied nothing. She became rather hysterical, but I hoped I had made her see things must change. I was going back in a day or two. . . .'

Dot leaned on the table.

'I really know more about the recent situation than you do.'

Lindsey took off her coat and hung it over the back of her chair. Dot was becoming more dominating as she grew older, she thought. Working in a big job was bad for her.

'Do you? I thought we all knew that Lena was ill.'

Dot looked at Lindsey, with her smart black hat, her good flowered silk dress and her pearls. She wondered, as she had wondered ever since she was of an age to think, why anyone had said that blood was thicker than water, and why what that implied was generally accepted. She had never liked Lindsey even as a child, and the grown-up Lindsey, glossy with success, she disliked. Dot had a good, quiet committee manner, she used it now.

'When you went to see Lena I understand you called her a drunkard.'

Lindsey had worried quite a bit over Lena's sudden illness. She had been able to tell herself that she had only done her duty, but her subconscious mind had been restive. She was, however, far too poised to appear disconcerted.

'I can't remember my exact words, but I should say I was more likely to have used the expression "drinking too much".'

Dot had her hands thrust deep into the pockets of her

uniform jacket, a custom with her when she wanted to hold herself in to say very little, and what she did say, say well.

'She thinks you called her a drunkard, and she thinks you told her that we should take her children from her and, if necessary, put the business in the hands of a lawyer, unless she gives up her friendship with an American. . . .'

Selina piped up tactfully with the exact question Dot wanted asked.

'Has what Lindsey said given Lena a nervous breakdown?'

Dot pressed her hands so hard into her pockets that she nearly burst the seams.

'After Lindsey left she tried to kill herself.'

There was appalled silence. Then Sylvia said:

'Poor Lena. Oh dear, it's dreadful. But, of course, something had to be done. I mean, children are so noticing and if there was immorality. . . . Andrew says . . .'

Lindsey spoke through the rest of Sylvia's words, her eyes on Dot.

'Who told you?'

'By a piece of luck I heard something was wrong and I went straight down to see her. As you know, Laurel and Tuesday go to the same school as Alice and Maria. The junior house is run by a Mrs. Fellows. There was some talk of Tuesday's tonsils being removed and she rang Lena up. The children's nurse, who is now cook, answered the phone. She sounded in such a state that Mrs. Fellows, who's awfully nice and very sensible, tracked me down at my office and told me it sounded worrying and did I know what it was all about. I got on first to the children's nurse, who said Lena had been taken suddenly ill, and when I asked what was the matter she said would I wait and she would see if she could get the doctor. I gathered from him that somebody better come down at once.'

Selina was gaping at Dot.

'How did she try to do it?'

'Sleeping tablets. There's an awfully nice doctor, somehow or other he avoided calling the police. He says it was a good thing she took them at midday as he was called in time. If she had taken them at night it would have been well on into the next day before anyone noticed anything wrong. Apparently she often sleeps late.'

Sylvia looked near tears.

'And then she would have died.'

Dot shrugged her shoulders.

'The doctor didn't say that, he said it was more difficult to kill yourself than most people thought, but he seemed to have had to be fairly drastic with Lena. I didn't see her until the next day, and even then she looked ghastly.'

Selina was gaping like a surprised school girl.

'Isn't it awful? Who's looking after her now?'

'Two nurses.' Dot turned her eyes back to Lindsey's. 'The doctor says she has been at breaking point ever since Alex died. Stupid handling and she was sure to go to pieces. Now she's collapsed with a very bad nervous breakdown.'

Lindsey lit a cigarette. Her hands were trembling, she almost dropped her lighter. When she spoke the other three could hear anger piling up behind her words.

'We know you, Dot, you've always ordered us about and tried to decide for the rest of us what's right and what's wrong, but now we're middle-aged,' she heard a gasp from Selina, 'yes, even you, and make our own decisions. Prophets never have any honour in their own countries, so it doesn't surprise me you don't appreciate that I'm considered something of an authority on child psychology.'

'Don't be silly,' said Dot, 'of course we know. We are all asked endlessly how you come to be so understanding about children.'

Sylvia laid a hand on Lindsey's arm.

'We're very proud of you. Andrew . . .'

Lindsey shook off Sylvia's arm.

'Imagine my feelings when a stranger told me what was going on. Alex's children! Psychologically the worst background they could have.'

Dot decided it was time recriminations ceased and they got down to business.

'Well, they won't have that background this summer. The doctor says Lena must have absolute quiet and rest for three months at least.'

Sylvia broke in.

'We'll . . .'

Under the table Dot pressed Sylvia's foot. She hurried on: 'He believes that with care by Christmas she'll be fit again.'

Lindsey said:

'But how will she be behaving?'

Dot went on as if there had been no interruption:

'He says that the idea that's she's not fit to bring up her children is a contributory cause of her breakdown. That knowing they are coming home for Christmas will help her to recover.' Dot took her hands from her pockets. Her voice pleaded. 'Do let's be careful. In lots of ways Lena's a good mother, and the children see no wrong and are fond of their home. If we let it break up what have we got to offer?'

Sylvia's words fell over each other.

'Of course Andrew and I haven't the sort of home they're used to. As a matter of fact, now it's not comfortable at all because we can't get any help and I do it all, and you know I was never any good at housework, but I expect Nannie would come with them. I'm awfully fond of their Nannie and so's Andrew and . . .'

Dot checked her.

'You can't take them all, Sylvia. You look dead tired as it is.'

Selina burst out:

'What a pity Mother and Father had to move.'

Dot tried to sound as acid as she felt.

'Yes, lovely for us if we could just park them on the parents. However, there's barely room for themselves in that ghastly bungalow, so the question of what happens to the children in the summer holidays is ours.'

Lindsey tapped some ash off her cigarette.

'I think the best plan would be for Sylvia to take the two boys and you, Dot, the girls. They're the same age as your two and go to the same school.'

It was the moment Dot had been listening for. She pressed her toe with added firmness on top of Sylvia's.

'I'm too busy myself to undertake more than one extra child. I think what would be fair is that we each take one.'

Selina ran a mental eye over the Wiltshire children.

Tuesday would need a good deal of supervision. Laurel and Tony had never been very kind to Bertie and Fiona, of course ordinary children could hardly be expected to understand unusual ones. She had always thought Kim a tiresome child, but he would fit in best with her family.

'I'll take Kim.'

Sylvia was cowed by the pressure of Dot's foot.

'I'm not tired really . . . I'd have liked . . . but if we're only to have one we'd love it to be Tony. A boy of that age Andrew says . . .'

Dot looked at Lindsey.

'Will you have Laurel or Tuesday? You can choose. Laurel is Alice's friend and Maria and Tuesday are the same age, so it's all one to me.'

Lindsey had various techniques for getting gracefully out of situations for which she did not care.

'I know, with you all being so splendid, I sound a meany, but I don't honestly think I ought to say I'll take a child. You see, my little house isn't suitable. I'm away a great deal and when I'm home I have to work, and that means shut up by myself. My secretary says there are days when she's ashamed to say good-morning because I really haven't time to answer her.'

Dot faked an air of surprised interest.

'What are you busy at?'

'Apart from lectures, my new book. Surely, Dot, as the two girls are friends of your two you could manage.'

'No. I'm too busy.'

'But surely the W.V.S. does without you in the holidays.'

'I can't throw it all up. I've a big job.'

'I'm sure you have, but you also have children, don't they come first?'

'My children are all right. The point is about you. What's it matter if your book isn't written?' Lindsey had not, during her writing career, heard such a suggestion. She was for a moment speechless. Dot took advantage of this. 'Anyway it's only one holiday that's under discussion, about two months.'

Selina wanted, as she was in London, time to do some shopping. She tried to hurry Lindsey.

'I should have Laurel. She's fifteen. A girl of that age can look after herself.'

Dot had taken her hands off the table and had laid one on Sylvia's knee. Lindsey saw that even Sylvia was failing her, tiresome though it might be, she must give in. Nobody could do that more charmingly than she. She smiled sweetly.

'Very well, I'll have Laurel. It will be rather fun really. I adore adolescents. I think they're absorbingly interesting.'

Dot knotted her scarf and pulled on her gloves. She looked at Lindsey.

'Right. I'll take Tuesday. Have you said anything to the parents about all this?' Lindsey shook her head. 'If you all agree I suggest we don't for the moment. Mother's looking dead anyhow.'

Selina got her mirror and powder box out of her bag.

'They'll have to know Lena's ill.'

Dot considered, and discarded telling them that the Colonel was already partially informed. Her upraised eyebrows questioned Lindsey.

'Just that she's ill I think, don't you? I'll be seeing them soon, will you leave it to me?'

Lindsey was thankful to hear that Dot considered it was better to keep the whole story from her parents. It was queer, but true, that it was almost impossible to grow away completely from family ties. It was still a cause of discomfort to be aware of parental displeasure. Much as she disliked Dot she trusted her. If Dot said she would keep the full story from the parents she would stick to it. She nodded acceptance. Selina sighed.

'How nice you look. I wish I was a successful novelist.'

Lindsey felt better.

'As you will be making arrangements about Tuesday, Dot, could you let me know where and when to meet Laurel?'

Dot asked Sylvia to lunch with her. Words burst from Sylvia the moment they were alone.

'It seems so awful to separate them. I may look tired but mostly it's because I've no time to do anything about my face and hair. Andrew and I would gladly have them all. . . .'

Dot took her sister's arm.

'Don't be a goose. Of course they ought not to be separated, but, what is even more important is that eventually Lena should get all right and they can go to their home. If we take the children Lindsey is quite likely to upset that.'

'Why should she?'

'She's a writer and not a mother. On paper her psychology is fine, but there's more in bringing up children than she sees. She lacks the nappy, school bills, sick in the train knowledge that we've got.'

'But ought the children to go back? If it's true Lena and that American are . . .'

'The children don't know a thing about it. He's a dear, I've met him. They never would have known, he'd see to that. He's devoted to children.'

'It all seems so queer. Andrew . . .'

'Fix your mind on one thing. We want to get Lena back in her right mind, it'll take time and care and we don't want Lindsey interfering. Believe me, when she's had a schoolgirl about the house for over two months, she will take endless trouble to see she doesn't have her again.'

'I'm not happy about it. You're much more clever than I am, but it seems hard on Laurel.'

Dot laid a restraining hand on Sylvia to prevent her stepping into the road under a bus.

'I'm afraid you're right there.'

XLI

Walter felt wretched. He was in something from which he did not seem able to get disentangled. The trouble lay in his decency and soft-heartedness. Nobody could wish to spend their free time travelling on a slow train to see a woman who either cried or talked in gushes and outpourings. Lena was often lying in a darkened room, for on her worst days she thought that people were spying on her, and only with the curtains drawn did she feel secure, and then, every minute or two, would ask to have the door opened as she was certain someone was listening at the keyhole. On her good days she was over-excited and full of plans. She must get new clothes, she must have a face massage, she was looking a perfect fright. She was sure the doctor was fussing unnecessarily, she would be quite strong enough by August to have the children home.

Every time Walter came down to see Lena he felt worse about the children. The country was looking beautiful. Stroch grew more engaging every day. In talks with the servants, he could feel he had them with him. Mustard shook his head.

'They wouldn't make no noise. It 'uld do her good,' he nodded towards Lena's bedroom, 'even if she never saw nor heard them to know they was safe where they did ought to be.'

Nannie found the nurses hard to bear with, and knew life would be far harder if the children came home, yet there dropped from her, rather than was said as a considered opinion, 'Children are best where they belong. They miss not having their rightful things.'

Mrs. Oliver, quite unaware that her tongue was the cause of the family crisis, was the most outspoken.

'Lot of nonsense, if you ask me. I don't believe there's much wrong that a good shake wouldn't cure. It's enough to make anybody feel rough havin' these two nurses 'angin' round. "Do this." "Don't do that." "I'd don't do that them, if I had my way." Can't have the children home! Unnatural I call it. I never let mine leave me. "You let the two eldest go away while baby's coming," the district nurse said to me, but I said, "Never." Seein' a woman 'ave a baby is 'ealthy and natural, pushin' them into places where they don't belong is un'ealthy and unnatural.'

Walter would have liked to have cut away from the whole business, and would have done so if Lena had not become so hysterical when he even hinted at the idea. He was fond of Lena, and she had certainly made his life exciting, but that was finished. He felt badly about the children, for he could not hold himself entirely blameless. He wished there was something he could do for them. One day, visiting Lena, it came to him what that thing was. He would temporarily adopt Stroch. Lena was writing no letters and was not well enough to take a decision. He approached Nannie.

Nannie had just come home with the shopping. Unable to get a seat she had to stand in the bus with her two heavy bags. She was still on the spread and standing in a bus made her feel self-conscious, for once the driver, when he took her fare, had made a joke about two tickets. Amongst her heavier parcels were some pounds of horseflesh. So it happened Walter chose a moment to speak when Stroch was particularly on Nannie's mind.

Nannie was not fond of cooking and cooking horseflesh for Stroch she disliked, but she had given her word to the children to take care of him and she would have gone without herself rather than he should go hungry. In the afternoon she faithfully took him for what she considered a good walk. It was a slow amble up the ride to the main road. Although Stroch, when Mustard was not looking, had dug hard for rabbits, he was not getting sufficient exercise, and was on the portly side.

Nannie had never allowed herself to think about Walter and Lena. She had tried so hard to keep ideas about them out of her mind that it often gave her the rather grim, disapproving look which had irritated Lena. Nannie had never admitted even to herself that Lena drank. The mothers of her children did not drink and that was that. In spite of the fact that he had brought trouble to the house she liked Walter. He was wonderfully good to the children, and always pleasant. He often asked her advice about gifts for the children in a way which reminded her of Alex.

Walter sat on the kitchen table and watched Nannie plod round putting away her purchases.

'Would you think it would please the children if I took on Stroch till their mother's well? He's getting a bit on the puffy side and I can fix to exercise him. He can feed well with us, shan't need to queue up for horse.'

Nannie was putting the fat ration in the refrigerator. She might not have heard what Walter said. Walter watched her, his eyes twinkling but affectionate. Presently, as he knew they would, sentences dropped from her.

'I do my best and so does Mr. Mustard, but things aren't as the children would wish.' 'We couldn't make a change, not without asking them.' 'Tuesday is the one to be most upset. Always been one for a dog, even that Pincher.' 'Tony and Kim would think it right.' 'Best to write to Laurel. She'll know how they'll feel.'

Walter took out a notebook and a pencil.

'Can anyone write to a school girl?'

Nannie unwrapped from newspaper her slices of horse, and put them on a tin plate.

'I write to one or other each week to say how their mother

is. You go along to the bureau in the drawing-room and write to Laurel. I'll put the letter in with mine.'

The letters at Greenwood House were laid out on a table in the hall. There was a vague rule that the girls only received letters from those people with whom their parents wished them to correspond. In actual fact Miss Clegg could rely on over three-quarters of the letters received coming from suitable sources. The last quarter were written to the sort of girls who needed watching. What Miss Clegg styled 'rather the silly type'. With these girls she now and again queried a letter, but in most cases the parents were of the same mentality as the girls, and thought what Miss Clegg styled 'silliness' fun.

Laurel had suffered more than the three others from the news of her mother's illness and the plans for the summer. She was terrified at the thought of being packed off alone to stay with Lindsey, but fear of that was partially overlaid by her dread about her mother. Was Aunt Dot telling all the truth? Was it just what they called a nervous breakdown, which Aunt Dot said meant being overtired, or was Mum ill? Was she terribly ill? Was she going to die? If Mum died what would happen to them? What happened to orphans?

Seeing Nannie's handwriting she opened her letter standing in the hall. Nannie had written to her twice since her mother had been ill and both letters, in their complete nannie-ishness had been wonderfully reassuring. She was surprised when four pieces of chewing gum fell out of the envelope. She saw there was an enclosure but she did not think of it, for her eyes were devouring Nannie's words.

'Picking up wonderfully. Fancied a nice piece of boiled chicken done that way she likes, with rice and a white sauce. Yesterday she sat up a bit and looked out of the window and noticed a tree and said would it do to cut down for your Christmas tree, fancy her thinking of that already. . . .'

'Frog, who's sending you chewing gum?'

'Frog, have you got a boy?'

Laurel had drifted home. She was standing in her mother's room. Her eyes were shining. Mum was getting better. She was already planning for Christmas. Oh, if only this holiday could never happen and it was the Christmas one which was coming.

'Look at The Frog. Look at the way her eyes are shining.'

'Come on, Frog, tell us about him.'

Laurel was back in the hall. She stared round her in surprise. The girls talking to her had scarcely spoken to her before. They were older than she was and were a set of themselves. Laurel had noticed them with some envy because, if their hair was straight, their mothers had it permanently waved. 'Lucky, lucky dogs,' she had thought. 'I wouldn't look pretty whatever anyone did to me, but I would look better curled.' A girl was holding the chewing gum.

'Come on, Frog, what's he say?'

Laurel remembered the other letter. She looked at the signature.

'It's from Uncle Walter.'

The girls were disgusted.

'An uncle!'

'Not really. He's an American. We call him Uncle.'

The girls drew nearer.

'Do you?'

'What's he call you?'

Laurel had her eyes on Walter's opening words. Never before she had thought of his way of addressing her as anything but a nickname. Now, with the whispering girls round her, she blushed; it would sound so sloppy.

'Look, she's blushing.'

'Come on, Frog, show us.'

One girl put an arm round Laurel's neck and peered over her shoulder.

'Oo-h! Who's a dark horse! He calls her sweetheart.'

Laurel's hands were damp, her cheeks crimson.

'It's . . . it's only a nickname . . . truly.'

'Have we heard that before?'

'Would you believe it! A kid her age.'

Laurel looked from one girl to the other. She was, for the first time since she came to Greenwood House, the focus of attention. Even queerer, she seemed to be being admired, and envied. It was extraordinary that getting a letter from Uncle Walter should cause such excitement, but it was, and though she was not clear what it was all about, it was gorgeous to be thought interesting. She tried to look as though she had something to conceal. She folded her letters and put them and the chewing gum back into the envelope. She wondered what to do with the envelope. She supposed really it ought to go down her chest, these sort of girls had things hanging round their necks which they showed each other and whispered about. Her frock, however, like all her other frocks, had a little collar close to her neck, and it would be impossible to push anything down unless she undid the back. Instead, since she had not a pocket, she pushed the envelope into her knicker leg.

The girls giggled.

'What a place to keep a love letter!'

'Are you thinking what I'm thinking?'

Laurel felt they would lose interest if she stayed any longer. She blurted a phrase she knew to be common amongst them. 'Aren't you awful!' and fled.

XLII

Ruth was stationed in Scotland. It was impossible on her short leaves to make time to visit both schools. She would have liked to, but she was increasingly aware that she was growing away from the civilian world, shut in by the invisible, but substantial walls of service life. She felt, if she were not to be out of touch when the war was over, she must keep up with her civilian friends. Stay in their houses, listen to what they said, try, in the few days she was free, to regain her knowledge of how it felt to be responsible for herself, to have no higher authority to see to her well-being and order her coming and goings.

Ruth, since her talk with Tony in November of forty-one, had paid two visits to Wingsgate House. She had seen John after he had tackled the boy. They had met in the same bar as on their first meeting, but not in the same atmosphere. John had told the full story of Tony's attack, and how he had brought the boy up to town to meet his grandfather and have the story of his father's death corroborated; but Ruth felt he was uneasy with her. She was not sure that he did not think her inquisitive. To her it seemed normal to ask what the house was like, and how Lena was, but John was reticent, and chilled her into silence. It was a sad, disappointing meeting. Only when she saw Tony did she lose the feeling. If in her life she had done nothing else worth while, she had done well when she had written to John. It had lifted up her heart to see Tony so much better.

Ruth's next visit to Wingsgate House was in the following spring. Then, with amusement, she began to understand John's reticence. Both Tony and Kim were delighted to see her. Kim, talking at the top of his voice, explained to her, with imitations, how all the household looked and behaved; the recital starred Stroch, but Uncle Walter came high on the list. 'Uncle Walter,' Ruth thought. 'Now why didn't I guess there'd be an Uncle Walter?' Tony, when he got a chance to get a word in, told her they were being pretty lucky this half as their grandfather had been down a week ago.

Kim burst out.

'And in the middle of the week. Absolutely nobody goes out in the middle of a week unless their father's been killed, and there were we, gorging ourselves at the hotel. And I missed French, and there was an awful lunch at school, one of our boys knew for certain the meat was horse.'

Ruth planned on her next leave she would look up Laurel and Tuesday. Tony was almost his old self and, anyway, was going on to his public school. She was not sure if he wanted visiting there. She told him she would let him know if she was moved, and would he send her a line if he would like to be taken out. She adored seeing Kim but she could not feel he needed visits. It was clear from his conversation that he had invitations to go out with some friend or other practically every Sunday. She could not imagine he would miss Tony. Tony was, on the whole, a curb, he corrected Kim's most violent inaccuracies. Kim seemed to have found a way of life which was better worked out alone. He was the card, the wit, as well as being brilliant at his work. Ruth could see he treated himself as if he were a Wurlitzer organ; if one stop failed to move his audience he tried another. This passion for being the centre of the picture was dangerous. What on earth would he grow up like? It seemed unnatural that before he was eleven he should have found a way to adapt his failings to feed his egoism. If all went well Kim might do anything, but what if things did not go well? He could never be poor. He would always have to throw his weight about, be surrounded with friends, even if he had to rob a bank or forge cheques to do it.

Even if Ruth had not planned to visit Laurel, a letter from her, breathing woe, would have made her try and manage it. It was the first she had heard of Lena's illness. 'Imagine, Foxglove, all that long, super summer holiday, when you can almost forget there is a ghastly hole like Greenwood House, I've got to stay with Aunt Lindsey, if it wasn't that Aunt Dot has almost promised Mum will be well by Christmas I should throw myself from a cliff. Not that there is a cliff in this hateful place, but I would walk until I found one.'

Ruth turned over the idea of writing to Dot for information, but she could still feel the discomfort of being held off by John. She had leave due in about three weeks, she wrote to Laurel and told her not to throw herself off anything at the moment, as she was coming to see her, and would prefer not to attend her funeral. She wrote to Nannie for news of Lena. Nannie's reply made Ruth aware that something was wrong. She worried as to what it could be. From the moment she had heard of Uncle Walter she had taken his relationship with Lena for granted. Knowing Lena, it was not to be supposed that she was leading a celibate existence. Equally, knowing the skilled elegance with which she ran her life, it was unlikely that Nannie would know anything about it. You could not think of gossip in connection with a poised mondaine like Lena. Yet Nannie wrote: 'You will be sorry to hear that Mrs. Wiltshire is far from well; she is not allowed to have any noise or to write, dear Miss Glover, and just lies in bed with two nurses looking after her. The poor children will be very disappointed not to come home this holidays,' and then underlined, 'but it is best they should not. I am glad, dear Miss Glover, you are going to the school to see Laurel and Tuesday, please do give them my love and make them see it is all for the best. . . .'

Nannie was no letter writer, this was a long letter for her. It was foreign to her to write and underline a clear statement of policy. '. . . it is best they should not . . .' It was even more unlike her to give advice, but there it was, 'make them see it is all for the best.'

Ruth spent Saturday night in an inn near Greenwood House. She took Tuesday out on the Saturday afternoon, and Laurel on Sunday morning.

Ruth had not seen Tuesday for almost three years. She had left a baby of five and she hardly knew the child of eight who greeted her. In spite of a missing front tooth Tuesday had kept her looks. She was almost as fair as when she was a baby, and her hair still curled deliciously. She had never been as much with Ruth as the other three, and it took time to break down a wall of shyness which stood between them. Ruth had brought a picnic tea, which included cherries, and unpacking this they made friends, and Tuesday was soon chattering as if Ruth had never left them. Ruth had remembered Tuesday's passion for a dog and asked about Stroch. Tuesday was sitting on the ground arranging the cherries on some leaves. She paused and raised her eyes to Ruth.

'I didn't think I could bear it when we weren't going home.' She lowered her voice. 'You know, if he's not watched, he is inclined to dig holes in Mr. Mustard's garden.'

'What does Mr. Mustard say?'

'You couldn't say he was pleased. Not when it's seeds. Do you know, once he dug up lettuces that Mr. Mustard had been simply weeks growing.'

'I expect Mr. Mustard understands.'

'He would try to. He's a very, very good man, but now he hasn't got to. Stroch has gone to live with Uncle Walter until Mum's well again.'

Ruth's head was bent over the basket. She succeeded in sounding disinterested.

'Who's Uncle Walter?'

Tuesday was amazed at such ignorance.

'You must know that, everybody who knows us knows

Uncle Walter. He's our greatest friend. He's an American officer. Laurel says he says that Stroch has been adopted by everybody where he works as a mascot.'

'I expect he'll bark with an American accent next time you see him.'

Tuesday thought that funny, she rocked with laughter.

'I'll tell Laurel and she'll write that to Uncle Walter.'

'Laurel's the letter writer, is she?'

'She does all the letters to Uncle Walter and then she tells me and writes to Tony, and he tells Kim.'

'Which of the aunts are you staying with in the summer?'

'Aunt Dot.'

'Will you like that?'

'Well, if I can't go home it will be next best. But you can't pretend it's nice when you expected to go home, can you?'

Ruth poured out a glass of lemonade and passed it to Tuesday.

'It's very bad luck but it's only for one holidays.'

Tuesday drank some lemonade and ate half a bun before she answered.

'If only the others could come too, and Nannie and Mrs. Oliver and Mr. Mustard and Stroch. I simply hate us being divided.'

'But you like Maria.'

'And Alice and Henry.' Tuesday raised her eyes earnestly to Ruth. 'You simply can't make me say I like it though. I simply hate, and always will, not going home.'

Ruth, watching Tuesday, saw that discussion of the holiday

distressed her. She had flushed and her face twitched. She changed the subject.

'Tell me how you like school.'

Laurel had been thirteen and a half when Ruth had last seen her, now she was fifteen. She had said then she was becoming a woman and getting a chest. There was still not much outward sign of womanhood. She had remained a slight little creature, rather plainer perhaps as her cheeks had rounded which did not suit her. Her hair was still tow-coloured and worn in two plaits. She was waiting for Ruth at the corner of the road by Greenwood House Over the Way. She wasted no time on greetings, but dragged Ruth back the way she had come.

'I'm not supposed to meet you here. I'm supposed to wait inside the school gates, but I didn't want the girls to see you.'

'Ashamed of me?'

'Of course not, darling Foxglove, but, you see, I said I was going out with somebody in khaki, and everybody thinks it's a man.'

This statement was so unlike the old Laurel that Ruth felt acutely the years of separation.

'Where do you want to go? Will you come to the Inn where I'm staying?'

'No. We'll meet the school there. Let's go a long way by bus.'

In the bus Laurel pulled Ruth's arm through hers, and leant against her. She sighed contentedly.

'Oh, Foxglove, it's simply gorgeous seeing you. I needed something nice to happen. The future looks very black.'

'Perhaps you'll like it with Aunt Lindsey.'

'Oh no, I won't. She makes me feel a worm under her feet. I know now how a camel feels when it's going to take weeks crossing a desert. That's exactly how the summer holidays feel to me.'

'It's only for the one holiday.'

'But much the longest and nicest holiday. If only we could all be together, even if it had to be with Aunt Sylvia and Uncle Andrew. Poor Tony's going there. Uncle Andrew will take him into his study for little talks, and he'll pray without it being any special time. I think praying out loud, except in church, is very bad manners. Neither Tony nor I have ever forgotten the shame of it.'

'Poor Tony.'

Laurel sighed.

'Poor all of us really. I don't like to think of Tuesday being on her own. In term time she's all right, but in the holidays she needs remembering or she misses her turn at things.'

'Couldn't you mention that to Alice?'

'I'm going to. Then Kim ought never to be going to Bertie and Fiona. Just imagine three show-offs like that in one house.'

Ruth pressed Laurel's arm to her side. In whatever other ways she had changed she was still the good elder sister.

'What's your ambition at the moment? Last time I saw you there was an idea of a halo.'

'Don't tease. I was a child then. I'm going to be confirmed in the spring, all our class is done then. Because of the war we don't have to have a white frock. I do hope Mum doesn't buy

me one. I don't think anybody of my age looks nice in white,
do you?'

'Not very. Tell me about your mother. What's the news
of her?'

'She's much better Aunt Dot says, but she mustn't write yet.
She's got something called a nervous breakdown. Did you
ever have it?'

'No. It comes from a shock. I expect your mother has been
needing a rest for some time.'

'A rest! She rests all the time. Half the days she has
breakfast in bed. The only tiring thing she does is sometimes
to go up to London for the day.'

'There're all kinds of rests.'

Laurel looked serious.

'Aunt Dot absolutely promises it's only a nervous breakdown. It couldn't be anything else, could it?'

'I shouldn't think so, anyway Tuesday tells me she's getting
better.'

'Yes, she is. She sits up, she looked out of the window and
chose a tree for our Christmas tree.'

'That's grand.'

Laurel was pleating her frock with her free hand.

'Of course she would get better in bed. It's when she gets up
I worry about. I mean, she could start again doing the things
that made her ill.'

Laurel's head was bent. Ruth could not see her face. She
felt she must go carefully.

'There is that risk. Most of us do things that aren't good for
us, I suppose.'

'Do most people? I mean, things they know for certain make them ill?'

'What sort of ill?'

'Well . . . of course Mum doesn't . . . but suppose it was strawberries . . . if a person knew for certain eating lots of them made them sick, do you suppose they'd still eat them?'

Ruth sensed this was not a casual conversation. Obviously strawberries were not the question, but something was. What could Lena . . . ? A thought came to her. Drugs. That would be a possibility.

'If somebody took anything beyond what was good for them, and had to go to bed because of it, the doctor would know. You can cure people of wanting things that are bad for them. Probably it would be because a person was ill that they wanted the thing that did them harm; when they were all right again they'd give up wanting it.'

Laurel raised her face. She looked radiant. For a moment Ruth thought she was to be confided in, but when Laurel spoke it was about where they should lunch.

They lunched in a tea shop in a back street. Laurel found it.

'I particularly want not to meet the school.'

'You wouldn't be allowed to go out with me if I were a man, unless I were one of your uncles.'

'Not really, but there're ways of doing things.'

Ruth gave Laurel a swift, anxious look. This sort of school-girl silliness was unlike her, or had been unlike the child she had known. There was, however, nothing silly about Laurel's expression, she was leaning back in her chair staring into the street, frowning with earnestness.

'Are there? Anyway you haven't anyone you want to see except the uncles, have you?'

Laurel's face lit up.

'Oh yes. I'd simply adore to see Uncle Walter. He's our greatest friend. He's looking after Stroch for us.'

'If he's ever this way perhaps he could get permission to see you and Tuesday.'

'He'll never be this way. He's stationed in London.'

'Does he write about Stroch?'

'Yes. He wrote to me and said he would have Stroch until Mum's well. I wrote to Tony and asked what he and Kim thought, and I asked Tuesday. We all thought it was much better for him. Of course he's a country dog, but he wouldn't get proper exercise at home. Nannie's rather fat and walks awfully slowly. Besides, Americans have marvellous food. I shouldn't wonder if Stroch sometimes has chicken. So I wrote to Uncle Walter and said yes. I asked him to write and tell me about Stroch as often as he could, but he's not a good correspondent. I do wish I could think of a way to make him write more often.'

'But you're not worried about Stroch?'

'No. Actually, Foxglove, it's the letters I want. I know you'll think this silly but you've no idea how esteemed I am because an American writes to me.'

'Esteemed by whom?'

'Not the sort of girls you'd like, but at least I'm being esteemed. I told you I'd bring the name Frog to honour. I'm beginning.'

'Do people like Alice esteem you?'

The waitress brought them their food. Laurel waited until she was out of earshot.

'You're quite right, she doesn't. All the same, with long years of being nobody behind me, and in front of me, I'm glad of any sort of esteem.'

Ruth turned over the idea of giving advice, then decided against it. She saw Laurel so seldom. The one thing she could do was to build up her friendship with her. If Laurel felt in her she had an uncritical friend to whom anything could be confided, perhaps, if she needed her, she would turn to her. She felt doubtful of her wisdom, but she was no longer Laurel's governess. It would be wretched if the girl went back to school feeling she had been stuffy with her and unsympathetic.

Only once more did Laurel mention Walter. It was after lunch, they were sitting in the tiny garden at the back of the tea-shop. Ruth was smoking. Laurel took a piece of chewing gum out of her pocket, she balanced it on one finger looking at it longingly.

'I'd adore to chew this but it's my last piece. It's simply heavenly. It tastes of peppermint.'

'What are you saving it for?'

'I make a point of always having one bit by me. I pretend Uncle Walter sends me some every week. Of course he doesn't, actually he's only written three times and only twice sent gum, so however big the temptation I have to keep my last piece to show, or my reputation would be ruined.'

Having deposited Laurel back at school Ruth returned to the inn where she was staying, to pack her bag. She was depressed. She was fond of the Wiltshire children, and she was not happy about them. She heard again Tuesday's earnest little voice, 'I simply hate, and always will, not going home.' Poor baby, she had been messed about. First her grandparents, and then the home in Surrey, and now she was to stay with the Enden cousins. One comfort, she did seem happy at school, but Ruth had not cared for the way she flushed and her face twitched. She wished she had heard her hum. Humming had been such a part of Tuesday. Laurel putting values on the wrong things. Except that she had Alice with her she was clearly not at the best school for her. She had never lost that vulnerableness to hurt that had touched the heart when she was little. She had lost so much else. There was now no sign of the carefully nurtured, rather sedate, air that had been hers as a little girl. Ruth could see her and Tony brushed, scrubbed and polished, sitting one on each side of her at family lunches at Regent's Park. Don't interrupt, never mention the food being served, eat nicely, don't speak with your mouth full. Oh yes, they had been carefully brought up. How Laurel had valued happiness, hugged it to her. How she had loved her home. How she had loved Alex. Now this schoolgirl, pretending she was carrying on a flirtatious correspondence with an American.

Ruth dragged the zip-fastener of her bag shut. It was no good worrying. What could she do tied to the A.T.S.? What could she do if she were not in the A.T.S.? She was no longer the children's governess, she had no right to interfere. Heaps of children grew up without much attention and turned out all right in the end. She picked up her bag and glanced round the room to see she had forgotten nothing, but her brain was not taking in what she saw. It was answering her own argument. Heaps did, but were they the Laurels, Tonys and Tuesdays? She herself had grown up all right with very little attention, and little of it wise. All right but bruised. The Wiltshires were having a harder upbringing than she had. If only bruising was all they got out of it. What if they grew mis-shapen?

Suddenly there were tears in Ruth's eyes. Angrily she brushed them away.

XLIII

Tuesday, glancing anxiously over her shoulder, crept behind some bushes. She paused a moment to see her absence had not been noticed. Obviously not, Alice was giving Maria some coaching at tennis. 'Keep your racquet straight.' 'You must take back handers. You can't run all round the ball to avoid them.' Tuesday tiptoed up the path that ran above the tennis court. It was hidden from the house by a laurustinus hedge. At the end of it was the danger, a piece of overgrown lawn to be crossed before she came to the gate into the kitchen garden. There were two ways of crossing that piece of lawn, one was to run very fast and hope you were not seen, the other was to walk slowly, as if you were going on a message. At the end of the path Tuesday stopped and listened. There were voices. Aunt Dot was talking to Miss Endwell.

'We'll have to keep that for this evening. Henry must have a decent meal as he has only had a picnic lunch.'

There was the sound of running water. Miss Endwell was washing up. Her voice, which was shrill, rose above the noise of the water.

'Very nourishing those spam sandwiches.'

'Yes, but harvesting is hungry work.'

Miss Endwell's reply was less clear, Tuesday guessed she had gone to the kitchen door to speak to Aunt Dot. She ran.

No voice pursued Tuesday. She was safe in the kitchen garden. She was still taking no risks. She put the peas and scarlet runners between herself and the gate before she slackened speed. In the far corner was the fig tree, and in front of it the mound on which grew vegetable marrows. Tuesday looked tense and worried, but as she approached the fig anxiety slid from her. She stood still and called softly.

'Are you there, Bobbie?' The wind rustled the August-dry leaves. Tuesday skipped forward, her face radiant. 'Hallo. I told you I'd come. How's Gipsy? Have you taught him to beg?' She listened, her eyes shining. 'You've missed me all that much? I came as quickly as ever I could. We had to help make beds and things, and then we went to the tennis court. Alice and Maria are playing.' She lowered her voice. 'They never saw me go. Aunt Dot and Miss Endwell are in the kitchen, it's quite safe for you both to come out. Shall we take Gipsy for a walk? You can go on telling me about where you live.'

'Tues–day. Tues–day.'

Tuesday started. Alice calling. It could not be lunch-time yet. She seemed only to have been playing with Bobbie and Gipsy a few minutes. She made a pushing gesture.

'Run, Bobbie. It's Alice.'

Alice, swinging her tennis racquet, came towards Tuesday.

'It's nearly lunch-time.'

Tuesday blinked and twitched.

'Is it? I thought it was quite early. Have you finished playing tennis?'

'Only about an hour ago. We knew you were here. We heard you talking.' She held out a hand. 'Come on. By the way, Mummy thinks you've been playing with us all the morning.'

They sat round the table. Tuesday was between Dot and Miss Endwell. Dot, having helped everybody to spam and salad, glanced round to see they were eating. Tuesday was gazing vacantly in front of her. Dot spoke firmly.

'Eat up, Tuesday. Don't daydream at meals.'

Miss Endwell had a way of laughing first and explaining the joke afterwards. She laughed now.

'I know a funny little girl who talks to herself. I heard you in the kitchen garden, Tuesday, when I went to get some parsley.'

Tuesday's face was crimson, her eyes blinked nervously. Alice came to her rescue.

'You probably heard me talking to her. Odd as it may seem, I do talk to her sometimes.'

Dot said mechanically:

'Don't speak rudely to Miss Endwell, Alice.'

Miss Endwell made clucking sounds.

'No, indeed. When I was a girl your age I was not allowed to speak until I was spoken to.'

Alice was sitting next to Maria. She gave her a nudge.

'I bet that was never.'

Dot frowned at her daughters for whispering, and led the conversation to safer ground.

'What are you three doing this afternoon?'

Alice had known the question was coming and had prepared for it.

'I'm playing tennis at the vicarage.'

'Then the little ones can play in the garden.'

Alice kicked Maria to remind her to keep her mouth shut.

'They were asked.'

Dot had a lot of telephoning to do and she wanted to combine visiting her office with the shopping. There was a basketful of household linen in need of mending. She was a poor needle-woman, Miss Endwell a good one.

'Splendid. You'll like that, dears.' Dot turned to Miss Endwell. 'No tea to get. If we put a chair in that shady place you are fond of, and Alice brings the mending out, perhaps. . . .'

Miss Endwell did not mind the prospect of an afternoon's sewing, but she never did anything without making it clear she was doing a favour.

'I'm not sure. . . . I know a housewife's work is never done but. . . .'

Tuesday was leaning towards Dot.

'Please could I stop here?'

Dot looked at Tuesday. She wished she had not acquired that nervous twitch. She must speak to Mrs. Fellows about it. She did not like this habit of the child's of creeping away alone, it was not healthy. She and Maria were much of the same age, they ought to play together.

'Of course, if there's to be tea to get,' said Miss Endwell, 'I can't do any mending. Needlework with me is not something to be picked up at odd minutes. It's work I like to sit right down to.'

'So you shall.' Dot saw that tears were not far from Tuesday's eyes. She patted the child's hand. 'You needn't have anything to do with the tennis. It's a lovely garden, you and Maria can play what you like.'

'What I like is tennis,' said Maria.

Alice kicked Maria and gave Tuesday a comforting smile.

'I said we'd bring some milk, they haven't enough if Maria and Tuesday drink it instead of tea.'

The children washed up the luncheon things. Alice washed, Tuesday dried and Maria put away.

'If only you wouldn't argue, Tuesday,' Alice said. 'You can trust me to get you out of things you don't want to do.'

Maria collected the knives Tuesday had dried.

'If you ask me you're a pretty rude guest. This is our summer holiday as much as it's yours, and you won't ever do the things we like.'

Alice jerked her head towards the door.

'Put the knives away and don't talk rot. Why should Tuesday play games if she doesn't want to? They don't in their family. Laurel doesn't really like them either.'

Maria felt argumentative.

'We liked other things when Daddy was home. Daddy let us help with his bees. We made smoke and wore things on our hats.'

Alice took her hands out of the water and gave Maria a push.

'Go on. Look at all Tuesday and I have finished and you haven't even put the knives away.' She waited until Maria was out of hearing. 'You'll have to come to the vicarage because Mrs. Adams will tell Mummy if you aren't there, but I'll see you do what you like, and you can sit next to me at tea, and you needn't speak to anyone else. Now smile.'

Tuesday forced a smile.

'It's just that it's nicer here.'

Alice groped on the bottom of the washing-up bowl for a missing spoon.

'Couldn't Bobbie come to the vicarage too?'

Tuesday gaped at her.

'Do you know Bobbie?'

'I hear you talking to him.'

Tuesday screwed up her face in an effort to explain.

'He's only partly real, you know, and so's Gipsy, his dog.'

'Of course I know. Even then I can't see why they need stop in our garden.'

Maria was back. Tuesday polished the last spoon and gave it to her. Alice looked round.

'You can go, Tuesday. There's only the tumblers and you mayn't dry those. I'll give you a shout when it's time to start.'

Tuesday ran down the kitchen garden humming as she ran. As she neared the fig tree she raised her voice.

'Bobbie. Bobbie. Alice says she doesn't see why you need stop in this garden. I'm going to take you and Gipsy to tea at the vicarage, and if you come there you can come anywhere. Church, even back to school with me. Would you like that, Bobbie?' She listened, her head on one side, her eyes shining. 'Just think, Bobbie, if you could come with me for always. I'll never, never, be all by myself again. We needn't know other people. Just us, Bobbie darling. Just the three of us.'

XLIV

The vicarage stood in a large, untended, tangled garden. The vicarage gate had a broken hinge, but it was of no importance for it was never intended to be shut. Andrew had no time to waste on gates, he generally went through it at a run, his cassock flapping. His parishioners had never known the gate shut. At all hours they passed through it, to sit on a bench inside the front door waiting to see Andrew. The oilcloth which covered the hall floor had a track worn between Andrew's study and the front door.

There were five Smithson sons and daughters, the eldest sixteen, the youngest eight. Andrew disapproved of birth control. 'It is for God to decide,' he said. Sylvia, when bowed by bills and housework, would find strength in thinking of God's clemency in this matter. It would have been so easy for Him to have decided not to stop at five.

Andrew loved his family but they were his pleasure, and he allowed himself little time for pleasures. His parishioners were his children. Only if one of his family erred were they allotted time. Then they were on the same footing as parishioners and took their turn in the study.

There were two distinct modes of life in the vicarage. There was Andrew's world of fasting, prayer, fervour, church going and good works. Outwardly all the family joined with Andrew in these things. In the dingy kitchen, where Sylvia spent half her days, there was the other mode of life.

None of his children criticised Andrew. Their mother considered she had married a saint, daily others testified to the same belief. Certainly their father might be a saint; if being quite unlike anybody else made a saint he was certainly one. As they grew older their view was tinged with pity and tolerance. 'Poor father.' Still, they had been suckled on Sylvia's faith. Besides, no one could live with Andrew and wholly disbelieve.

Sylvia, since the war, had become cook. She had great belief in the Ministry of Food, and, when not tying up cuts, burns and scalds which she daily inflicted on herself, was stirring strange concoctions. 'I heard it on the wireless, darlings, only I've added to it as there wasn't enough for us.' It was easy to be hungry in the vicarage, and poisoning was a likelihood rather than a possibility. Over the sink or stove Sylvia guided the other life of the house. The eldest girl would come to her about a dance. Sylvia would stir or wash-up furiously.

'Saturday night. Oh, darling! If you have to wait for them to bring you back it's certain to be after midnight and then it's Sunday.'

Mother and daughter would gaze at each other, both seeing with horrible clarity Andrew looking white and suffering. Andrew, at some time between services, holding out a hand and opening the study door. There would be protestations and penances. Andrew would suffer acutely because of the sin, his daughter merely from embarrassment.

Suddenly, as if a lamp were lit in a house, Sylvia's face would gleam.

'Darling! Old Mrs. Coppenshaw. She's always saying she can't get in to Holy Communion because of her eyes. I'll arrange you shall spend the night there. She'll let you have the door key. She'll never know what time you come in. You must take my alarm clock to be sure you get up in time for church. Poor old Mrs. Coppenshaw! It will please your father you had the kind thought.'

Or perhaps it was one of her sons.

'Oh, David. An all-day picnic on Good Friday! Oh dear!'

David would remain calm and trusting. Presently Mother would have an idea.

'If you were going to the Priory or some place like that it would be quite all right. Of course, that's why you're going. Lovely for you all to spend the three hours in so old a building. I'll tell Daddy, he'll be so pleased.'

'Tennis! Your school shorts! Oh, Agnes. Not through the village. Of course I know nobody thinks anything of them these days. Couldn't you wear a coat? No, of course you haven't a summer coat, only your blazer. . . .' Sylvia, frowning anxiously, would peer at the latest Ministry of Food recipe, but her eyes were not reading it. She was seeing Agnes, looking a darling, striding through the village in her school shorts and a blazer, swinging her tennis racquet. Then she saw Andrew standing in his study door looking pale and distressed. 'Sylvia, come in a minute. I want you.' This cleared her vision.

'If you cut through the churchyard, and cross the Park, you won't see anybody, and on your way you can drop the parish magazine at The Hall. Such a help to get those out-lying magazines left, and it's almost on your way. If anybody mentions seeing you to your father, you went in a hurry because of the magazines.'

Tony went to the vicarage prepared to loathe it. He had stayed there before and hated it. Martin Phillips had done his best. It was only for seven weeks, there was the interest of his public school in the autumn. 'It's out in the country, old man, why not offer to lend a hand with the harvest?' Tony had listened, and, because he was fond of his headmaster, tried to be reasonable, but he was thoroughly disgruntled. Why was he picked on to go to the vicarage? Anywhere would have been better. Why couldn't he have gone with Laurel? He knew very well he would not have liked staying with Aunt Lindsey, he knew he did not want to stay with Aunt Dot or Aunt Selina, but, because subconsciously he knew these things, the more surly he felt.

Tony was not a snob. He had been to a famous preparatory school, and was going to one of the best public schools, but he was not a boy who sniffed at the thought of a grammar school. What he did sniff at was being asked to live in discomfort. The vicarage was the epitome of discomfort. Tony was revolted. He despised the dingy bedroom he shared with David. He hated his iron bedstead with its sagging frame. He turned up his nose at the one grubby, old-fashioned bathroom and the shoddy lavatories, always short of toilet paper. The meals made him feel sick and he made no attempt to disguise it.

A family may think poorly of their home, they may admit to each other its discomforts, but throw in a critic from outside, especially a far more well-to-do critic, and there is a banding together to defend the home. The Smithson children, usually generous hearted, at the end of one day disliked Tony, and at the end of two had got together to make his life hell. They managed to keep up a semblance of cousinly feeling before Sylvia, but when she was not within earshot Tony was 'Little Lord Fauntleroy,' 'Miss Tony Pansy,' 'How's Fussy Drawers this morning?' They treated him with sarcastic politeness. 'Oh look, he's standing. Quick, get a chair and two cushions.' 'He's blown his nose. Get him a clean handkerchief, he can't use the same one twice.'

Tony responded, first by rudeness. 'Well, the house is dirty, absolutely filthy if you want to know.' Then by sloping off alone and sulking.

Sylvia, with sad eyes, watched and listened. Tony was Alex's boy and she and Alex had been very close to each other. She tried carefully to reason with her family.

'Be nice to Tony. He's still upset because Uncle Alex was killed.'

For once she got no response. Her children were not going to tell her that Tony's most hideous fault was that in criticising the house he criticised their mother. Sylvia let them know she knew all was not well.

'Of course it is rather rough compared to what he's used to. I'm not a good cook. It was bad luck you all got diarrhœa after that fish-pie. It was a Ministry of Food recipe, but I added that little bit of salmon, I expect I'd left it in the sun all day. I think it's put Tony off.'

It was no good, her children would not respond. She did not know what was going on, but she suspected, and she did see Tony, white and sullen, stalk off, always alone.

One of the things Tony hated most about life in the vicarage was his Uncle Andrew's calls to prayer. Andrew began the day with family prayers, he finished it with prayers, he ordered his household into church, not only on Sundays, but often for evensong or a Saint's day; and he took it for granted, and this was what riled Tony most, that they all wished to pray whenever he decreed that they should.

Tony, mooching round the fields and lanes, throwing aimless pebbles in the village pond, cutting himself switches from the hedges that he did not want and immediately threw away, brooded hour after hour on his uncle. 'The sauce of him!' 'Browned off with all his praying.' 'Anyone would think he had bought God.'

Andrew, as he hurried about his parish, gave thought to Tony. He did not notice anything wrong, he took it for granted the boy was happy in his house, but he was fatherless, and about to go to a public school, where dangers might await him.

It was a Sunday night and Andrew was tired. When he was tired he forced himself to action. He undertook some task much as an early monk might have put on a hair shirt.

'Come along to my study after supper, old man. I haven't seen much of you. We must have a talk.'

Tony quivered with horror.

'What on earth about?'

Andrew smiled gently.

'About nothing on earth.'

There was no doubt what was implied. The thought of a pi-jaw with his uncle about heaven was the final straw that was fated to fall. Tony turned crimson. His words fell over each other.

'Thank you very much, I don't want to talk about anything, and what's more, I won't.'

Sylvia whispered.

'Tony. Please, Tony.'

Tony raced on.

'If you want to know, I'm fed up with all this praying. I've been to church twice, and we had morning prayers and I'm going to bed.'

He got up and slammed the door.

Andrew looked after him, his face full of suffering.

'Come into my study after supper, Sylvia. I want a word with you.'

Sylvia kept David downstairs and went up to talk to Tony. She sat on the side of his bed. Tony looked mulish. Sylvia had her knitting, a scarf for the Navy. Because Sylvia felt she should knit, the local woman in charge of Navy comforts gave her wool, but she always implored her not to hurry. 'Don't slave at it, you've so many other things to do.' She was fond of Sylvia and did not even imply, 'And I've other things to do than unpick your work for re-knitting.' The present scarf was about eight inches long, and already was an inch wider than when Sylvia had cast on. Sylvia saw nothing wrong and knitted laboriously.

'We can't go on like this, Tony. You don't like staying here. I know everything is rather a mess and I'm not a good cook. They say taking infinite pains can achieve anything, and your Uncle Andrew says prayer can, but somehow nothing works when it's cooking. Would you like to go to one of your other aunts? I expect I could arrange it.'

Tony wished she would leave him alone.

'I never said I wasn't liking it here.'

'You don't need to. You're very like your father. There were four years difference in age between your father and your Aunt Lindsey, but only two between your father and myself. It threw us together, we were great friends. Of course your Aunt Selina is only two years younger than I am, but somehow she was always treated as much younger. She was the baby, you see. Your father used to look just like you do when he didn't like anything.'

The present faded, ushered out by Sylvia's placid voice and the click of knitting needles. Dad's Nan, who lived, in a cottage somewhere and whom Dad had taken them to see, was speaking. She had a thin, old voice and spoke in pauses, turning over her memories as she turned over the wools and silks in her work-bag. 'Very like you Master Tony's growing. . . . Your father took a while to shoot up. . . . Miss Sylvy was near as tall as he was. . . . Do you remember, Mr. Alex, that sailor suit with long trousers you had for a wedding, and how your mother bought a frock with a sailor collar for Miss Sylvia? People used to take you for twins.'

Sylvia spoke again.

'I shall ring up your Aunt Dot. I want to arrange with her to meet you in London to get the rest of your school things. She is doing your shopping when she does Henry's. Perhaps you could go back with them.'

Tony was at Eastbourne. He could almost smell the sea. He could hear the gentle plop of waves against rocks. What he could not hear was the tone of his father's voice, but he could remember the words. 'Your Aunt Sylvia's a darling.'

Tony's anger and self-pity ebbed. He felt ashamed.

'I don't want to go anywhere else . . . there's nothing wrong. . . .'

'It won't be easy to arrange for you to move. Your Aunt Dot's only got a lady-help, who isn't a lady and doesn't help much . . . if ever I have to go out to work I shall make it clear I'm not a lady.'

'It's all right. I've been a bit browned off but . . .'

'It isn't all right. You don't get on well with your cousins, do you?'

'It's mostly my fault.'

'And you don't understand your uncle.'

Alex's words floated back to Tony.

'He's a very good man. Dad told me so.'

'I've never found knowing people are good is a help. In a vicarage you meet a great many good people. Of course it's nice to meet them, but it doesn't make any difference to liking.' She held up her knitting. 'Do you think that looks the same size all the way?'

'It's a bit wider at the bottom.'

'Is it? I wonder if it matters. I expect not, the more there is of it the warmer it'll be. Would you like to work for one of the farms? They need help.'

'When?'

'As soon as I can arrange it. You can have one of the bicycles and go off after breakfast and you won't get back until about six. They are asking for help in the papers. I will arrange for you to have your midday meal at the farm. They have lovely food on farms. They are allowed things, you know, half a pig now and again, and, I expect, slices off their sheep and cows.'

Tony was hating himself.

'The food's all right here.'

'No, it's terrible. Would you like that?'

'I wouldn't mind. As a matter of fact, Mr. Phillips, he was my headmaster, he said I ought to help on the land.'

Sylvia got up.

'Good. I'll arrange it tomorrow. That'll mean no weekday services, and perhaps sometimes you'll work on Sundays. Your uncle will quite understand . . . it's a national emergency. He will want to talk to you sometime. He feels he must.' She wandered over to the window and peered out. 'Queer having it light almost all night. Your father used to have a game he played during a lecture from your grandmother. He filled his right hand pocket with dried peas and moved them, one by one, to the other pocket. It had to be done without any one noticing. The game was to get them all moved by the time the lecture was over. Of course now the peas would have to go back to the kitchen as they're food.' She came back to the bed and stooped and kissed Tony. 'Good-night.' She crossed to the door and opened it. 'Don't lie awake. We'll all manage better tomorrow.' She hesitated, torn by her loyalties. 'Your father did not really understand your uncle either.'

XLV

Bertie was practising. Kim leant on the top of the Bechstein grand. Bertie shook his head at him.

'You mustn't interrupt. I've got to play this at the rehearsal this afternoon. Selina's coming. I must play well.'

'But I want to know something. Do you honestly and truthfully like playing the piano?'

Bertie went on practising, but he considered his answer. He was a musical child. From babyhood he had liked sounds, the rhythm of wheels, wind in the trees; he had made up tunes to go with them. His father, with a Welshman's love of music, had encouraged him first to sing, and then, when he was four, to play the piano. It had been fun. It was Selina who conceived she had given birth to a prodigy. It was Selina who, almost tone deaf herself, saw that this rare little boy must be given a special education so that his wonderful talent could flourish. There was an understanding between Bertie and his father. They never put it into words but they each knew the other knew that Selina's dreams would come to nothing. That no matter how hard he worked Bertie would never be better than good second-rate. Arthur had a dislike of too much boarding school, he thought it was time enough for his son to be sent as a boarder when he was old enough for his public school, so it suited him that, with his musical education as an excuse, Bertie should attend a day school. If it were not for the boy's music he felt Selina's family would talk them into sending the child to a preparatory boarding school, they did not believe boys could be educated at home. As a small child, over-sensitive, spoilt and made to look foolish by fancy dressing and long hair, Bertie had been thoroughly disliked by all his cousins. They found him a weakling, apt to burst into tears and run to his mother at the first sign he was not to have his way. Kim, baby though he was when he had last seen his cousins, had subconsciously disliked both Fiona and Bertie, but for his own reason, which was, they took the limelight from himself. Meeting them again, he found he not only liked them but was interested. Fiona was now fourteen and Bertie twelve, but they were more like grown-up people. Talking together they had a mature outlook which astounded Kim. He was always struggling to understand them.

'Go on, tell, Bertie. You can't like it. Nobody could like spending hours and hours in their holidays doing that.'

Bertie stopped playing.

'I like playing the music I want to play, but I suppose I don't like exercises, they're necessary though to make my fingers supple and all that.'

Kim beat his fists on the top of the piano.

'Still I don't see. What's it for?'

Bertie tried to think of a way of expressing his feeling for music in some medium Kim could understand, but there was none. Everything Kim did he did without struggle. If struggle were necessary, presumably Kim would not bother. He played a bar or two from a concerto.

'I like that. I couldn't play it if I hadn't done a lot of these.' He played an exercise.

Kim flung himself about in his effort to understand.

'But you can get a gramophone record if you want to hear it.'

Bertie returned to his practise. He and Fiona had discussed Kim. He had brilliance and personality, they were fascinated by him. He had just had his eleventh birthday, they thought he was very young for his age in spite of the fact that, as far as lessons went, he was ahead in many subjects of either of them.

He took it for granted that if he wanted a thing sufficiently he could have it. He knew nothing of limitations to achievement. He seemed to suppose that he was not in games teams, or a champion boxer, merely because he was uninterested, that if he were interested he would be unbeatable.

Fiona came in. She had on her practise clothes of pink tights and a black tunic. Her practise bar, flanked by long mirrors, was at the far end of the playroom from Bertie's piano. She pushed Kim aside and gripped the piano for support while she limbered up. She raised her voice.

'Shut up a moment.' Bertie took his hands off the notes. 'I've broken the news.'

'How did she take it?'

'I eased her into it. I said that Madame thought I would do better as a ballet teacher. I'd dance sometimes.'

'Did she mind?'

'It went fairly well. I think we were right, she half knew.'

'Do you think she's guessed about me?'

Fiona lifted her left leg over her head.

'I'm not sure about that but I shouldn't wonder. As I'd promised you I'd find out I said that I might take a pupil on Saturdays after you'd gone to Sherborne. I might too. I'd like to find out if I can teach.'

'What did she say?'

'That it might be a good idea.'

Kim's eyes were racing to and fro. He could only see part of Fiona's face, but he could see all of Bertie's. He could contain himself no longer. He beat the top of the piano with his fists.

'Tell me. Don't leave me out. What are you talking about?'

Fiona answered.

'Selina has always wanted me to go on the stage. She was going to get an appointment for me to dance for Ninette de Valois. I had to stop her.'

'Who's Ninette de something?'

'Sadler's Wells. She wanted me to join that ballet.'

Kim gasped at her.

'Sadler's Wells! Well, isn't that what you want?'

Fiona went across to her bar and laid her left hand on it. She put her feet into the first position, and bent her knees. Then suddenly straightened and turned and leant against the bar facing Kim.

'I expect you'd better understand. Selina may say something to you about us.'

Kim had been instructed as soon as he reached the Llewellyns' home to call his aunt by her Christian name. 'The children used to call me Mummy, but it sounds silly now. I'm more like a sister to them than a mother. People often think I'm their elder sister.' Kim left the piano and slid across the playroom.

'Go on, I'm listening.'

'Selina has always thought that I was going to be a star. You know, like Margot Fonteyn. Well, I won't. I've quite good technique, but I'd never get anywhere.'

Bertie left his piano and joined them.

'Just the same here. She thought I was going to be a top-notch soloist.'

'Well, how d'you know you both aren't going to be?'

Fiona rose on to her points.

'Bertie's musical.'

Kim hated not to understand.

'Well, if he's musical, all the more reason.'

Fiona spoke slowly, as if she were forcing each word into Kim's head.

'That's why he knows. Arthur's musical. He's always known. It was only Selina who ever thought anything else.'

Bertie said:

'We thought she'd get hold of the idea gradually. Then suddenly, over these rehearsals, she met a woman who knows somebody to do with Sadler's Wells.'

Fiona came off her points.

'And that put the lid on it.'

Kim thought he saw what they meant.

'So now you've told her, and you needn't practise ever any more.'

Bertie looked at Fiona.

'It's no good. He can't understand.' He turned to go back to his practise. Then a thought struck him. 'We were telling you because of Selina. She's likely to be a bit disappointed, we'll have to ease her along. Arthur being away and all that.'

Kim bounced over to Fiona and shook the practise bar.

'But we're children. It's us that people have to bother about. Children don't have to bother about grown-up people.'

Fiona gave a slight, despairing shrug of her shoulders. She left her bar and came to the middle of the room.

'You might play "Sugar Plum" for me, Bertie, so we don't muck it this afternoon.' She grinned at him. 'It was the thought that Selina would shame me by making me do that in front of Ninette de Valois that made me have enough courage to speak.' She looked over her shoulder. 'You go down to the kitchen, Kim, and talk to Mrs. Biddle, you know she adores you and you've to see me do this at rehearsal this afternoon.'

Selina sat in the half-empty theatre with Kim beside her. She had on a simple, childish silk frock and, in place of a hat, had tied a ribbon round her hair. Her eyes were on the stage where a troupe of children were dancing, but she was not seeing them. She was incapable of facing any fact squarely, instead, half truths shot into her mind, to be as quickly as possible shot out again. She had been young for her age when she married, and Arthur had accepted the fact that she was a child. With the babies came responsibilities, Selina poutingly thought it all rather a bore, too big a load for such very childish shoulders. Then Robert, whom she insisted on calling Bertie, showed signs of talent. Selina, unable to make a niche for herself with her contemporaries, discovered a life she would like with her children. She was not contented with one swan, she searched for talent in Fiona and discovered she could dance. From that time life was fun again, she was the wonderful little mother of two wonderful children. For miles beyond their own town the children were known, Bertie playing first a solo and then accompanying his sister's dances. The children were a godsend to all who got up a show for charity. With the coming of the war the charity performances grew less frequent, Bertie and Fiona grew older. Arthur, who would have understood how Selina felt, went into the Air Force, and Selina who, when the war started had considered herself a still youngish mother, had become what Lindsey had so cruelly described as middle-aged. 'It was not true, of course,' Selina told herself. It was just Lindsey's hateful way of talking. Still, there was the fact, she was thirty-seven. Thirty-seven was the beginning of the middle years. As well, during the war years, she had begun to have doubts about the children. Not that she admitted to herself that she was doubting, but in weak and unguarded moments she was conscious of hovering doubts struggling for attention. Arthur, when he had leave, and in his letters, made it clear Bertie was going to Sherborne. Before the war he had his name down, but it was such a long way off that no decision had to be made, and Arthur did not contradict her when she said that perhaps the boy would always need a specialised education. It was not possible to sort out her mind in regard to Fiona. The child was musical, she was a good build for a dancer, and she had admirably shaped feet for the purpose, but temperament, that extra something, where were they? Because Selina was fluffy minded and defenceless, Fiona and Bertie with their father away, took charge. They had knowledge and technique, they knew where they were going. Selina was aware they were forming views of their own. She had put up a fight. She had slaved for the introduction to Ninette de Valois. Such fun a daughter in the ballet, travelling with her, stage doors, the envy of other mothers. It was bitter to have been told what she had learnt that morning. She had been so proud, other mothers had envied her. The dancing children dimmed and swam, for Selina's eyes were full of tears.

'Good-afternoon, Mrs. Llewellyn.' Selina blinked. Madame, the head of Fiona's dancing school, was speaking. 'My pianist has to leave early. May I ask your boy to play for the children after she's gone?' Selina had a lump in her throat. She managed a smile and a nod. 'And who's this?'

Kim beamed. The light from the stage lit up his face.

'I'm Kim Wiltshire, her nephew. My mother's ill and my father was killed in an air-raid. I'm watching the rehearsal and, if you don't mind my mentioning it, I'm bored.'

'What a pity we can't find a part for you. It is dull for you watching. I suppose you don't sing or anything?'

'No. I've acted a lot at school. I tell you what I could do if you like, I could announce everybody. There's awful pauses between everything.'

Madame held out her hand.

'It's not a bad idea. Let's see if you can do it. Your cousin is going to play his piano solo after these children have finished. You announce him.'

Selina watched Kim disappear through the pass door. She was too busy formulating thoughts and casting them out to consider him. Presently the curtains were dropped and, after a moment, he sauntered through them. He smiled at an imaginary vast audience.

'The next thing is my cousin Bertie. He's going to play the piano. If you don't like the noise, put your fingers in your ears, he won't mind.'

He smiled again and strolled off.

Madame sat down beside Selina.

'What a beautiful child, and how confident, and so amusing. He'll be the making of the matinée. I must say you're a remarkably talented family.'

A mother joined them.

'Who's that enchanting little boy?'

Selina was warmed and revived.

'My nephew. That sounds rather distant. He's more like a son really.'

XLVI

Laurel gently opened Miss Grigson's door. In the pre-war days Lindsey had a secretary whose life was spent wandering from author to author, and who was not only brilliantly efficient but could add a spice to life recounting the more lurid details of other authors' private lives. That secretary had been called up and put to work in a Ministry, and Lindsey, after struggling with various hopeless incompetents, had fixed herself up with Miss Grigson. She thought Miss Grigson stupid and ignorant, but she had two superb advantages. She was over fifty, and had lost her home through enemy action. 'Poor old thing,' Lindsey told her friends, 'a complete nit-wit, but imagine, she can type, she's outside the clutches of the Labour Exchange and everything she possessed destroyed. Nowhere else to go. Aren't I lucky?'

Miss Grigson turned as the door opened. She beckoned to Laurel. She spoke in a whisper.

'Just going.'

Laurel crept out again and walked softly down the stairs. She stood by the front door. Presently a door opened, she heard Lindsey's voice.

'You clipped my speech on to the papers about the meeting?' There was an inaudible murmur from Miss Grigson. 'Have that rough ready by this evening.'

Aunt Lindsey was coming down the stairs. Laurel straightened her frock. She stepped forward.

'Hallo.'

'Hallo, dear. Good-morning. Why aren't you outside this lovely day?'

Laurel flushed and swallowed. Dare she say, 'I was hanging about to say good-bye to you?'

She blurted, 'Good-bye, Aunt Lindsey. I hope you make no end of a good speech.'

Lindsey smiled.

'Thank you.' She gave Laurel a brisk, meaningless kiss. 'Have a nice day.'

Laurel stood in the porch. She watched Lindsey climb into the taxi and drive away. She heaved an admiring sigh. 'How simply marvellous to be Aunt Lindsey. Fancy, famous, with people asking for your autograph.'

Miss Grigson joined Laurel in the porch. When Lindsey was out of the house Miss Grigson relaxed so much, it was as if she slipped out of a heavily boned corset.

'Gone! I thought I might take a little walk round the garden before I begin work.'

Laurel, as always in this house, was torn by conflicting feelings. Aunt Lindsey was marvellous. It was gorgeous to think that she, Laurel, just a schoolgirl, plain and dull, was staying with a famous authoress, and Aunt Lindsey actually seemed to like having her. Against that it was a strain being a niece Aunt Lindsey would like. Never being seen or heard when she was working was part of it, and that was not easy on a wet day, for she did not want always to read, and there was nobody to talk to, and it was a temptation to turn on the wireless, hoping, if it was kept very low, Aunt Lindsey would not hear it. Then there was a high standard of tidiness expected, and, most important of all, to be a niece Aunt Lindsey liked, you must look after yourself. Aunt Lindsey detested what she called 'the physicals'. Laurel blushed to think she had asked Aunt Lindsey for a pill. It humiliated her still to remember the disgusted look on Aunt Lindsey's face, and the snubbing way she had said, 'I dare say you can find something in the bathroom cupboard.' In a way it was rather nice, though less exciting, when Aunt Lindsey was out of the house. If only Miss Grigson and Hannah did not look so pleased, and take it for granted Laurel was pleased too. Hannah was almost stone deaf and you would not think it made much difference to her who was in the house. For even when Aunt Lindsey was annoyed about something, the way a dish was cooked, or a piece of furniture polished, it was unlikely Hannah heard much of what she said. Still, there was no doubt it made a difference to Hannah when Aunt Lindsey was away. She would suddenly appear, beaming, with a cake hot from the oven or an apple. Usually, when Aunt Lindsey was away, Laurel helped Hannah do the housework. She would have liked to help her every day, it would have been something to do, but Aunt Lindsey had said, 'No nonsense now making your bed. Hannah can manage and I don't want her to get the idea she's overworked.'

Laurel and Miss Grigson walked round the garden. Miss Grigson sniffing the morning in a pleased way.

'Such a treat to get out for an early breather. I always have liked a lung-full before I start work. My little flat had a piece of roof I could climb out on. Such a joy. I could see the river.'

'Tell me about Aunt Lindsey's book. Has the man asked Jess to marry him yet?'

'The trouble is, dear, I never quite understand your aunt's books. It's all right when she gives me her rough in longhand, then I can go over it slowly. This last chapter she dictated. I find it very difficult to follow then. I'm afraid I lose interest. I like a sweet tale.'

'But you must know if he asked her to marry him.'

'I don't. He seemed, if I understood right, to be staying with a man friend. There was a lot about subjugation, whatever that might mean. I get so worried with difficult words. Oh well, I suppose I must go and type it.' Miss Grigson was held by an idea. 'As it's a lovely day why don't we eat our lunch in the garden? Just a little treat.'

There Miss Grigson went again. There was no reason why they should not have lunch in the garden, only it could never have happened if Aunt Lindsey were home. It would be fun, if only there was not the implication that anything nice could only happen when Aunt Lindsey was out.

Laurel spent the morning helping Hannah. Hannah sang and rubbed up the furniture. Laurel dusted. When Hannah worked round to the wireless, with a wink she turned it on to its fullest extent so that she could hear it. Then suddenly, she sat at Aunt Lindsey's desk and gave an imitation of Aunt Lindsey writing down the week's orders. The worst of it was Hannah was so funny and so like Aunt Lindsey, who wrote even a shopping list in a grand way, that Laurel rolled about laughing, but even while she laughed she felt disloyal. Somehow, without meaning to, she seemed to be joined with Miss Grigson and Hannah, not exactly against Aunt Lindsey, but rather like it, which was all wrong, for she admired her more than anybody she had ever met.

In the garden over lunch Laurel felt better because she talked about Aunt Lindsey. It was rather a one-sided conversation, but she did feel that she was making Miss Grigson see Aunt Lindsey more clearly.

'People who are awfully clever can't be expected to like the same things as ordinary people. She's exalted really, isn't she? Above us.' Miss Grigson munched and made a vague sound. 'You know, in the evenings when Aunt Lindsey and I are alone she treats me as if I was quite seventeen. She tells me all about her speeches. You know, she's marvellous on child psychology.'

'The woman who had the flat below me used to have her grandchildren to meals, their mother wasn't well. Seven of them. Splendid how she managed. I often wonder what happened to her. Never saw her after that morning we came out of the shelter. . . .'

'Should you suppose because you have an aunt who writes books you might be able to? I write simply foul essays, but, of course, books are different. I asked Aunt Lindsey if you had to write good essays at school if you were going to be a famous author, but she only said "Education in this country is fundamentally wrong." It's not exactly what I wanted to know, but she doesn't like being asked anything twice.'

Hannah came out with a dish of cherries. Miss Grigson looked greedy but cautious.

'Aren't they for dinner?'

Hannah heard her. She gave Laurel a nudge.

'Don't leave the stones about or you'll give me away. What time's she back?'

Miss Grigson saved herself from shouting by raising five fingers.

It was lovely in the sun feeling so easy and unstrained, eating cherries, it was unfair to Aunt Lindsey that Miss Grigson's five fingers should cast a cloud, but they did. Proud as she was of Aunt Lindsey and being Aunt Lindsey's niece whom Aunt Lindsey liked, Laurel's heart dropped.

The afternoon was glorious. Laurel lay on a rug reading a thriller. She opened the sitting-room window wide and had the Forces programme playing loud enough to be heard not only by herself but all over the house. Laurel adored thrillers but when Aunt Lindsey was about she did not read them. Aunt Lindsey said she was just the Austen age. Laurel was not caring for *Pride and Prejudice* but she was proud when Aunt Lindsey said, 'I was questioned on reading for adolescents today, and I told them I had a fifteen year old niece with me who was a Janeite.'

At four-thirty Laurel turned off the wireless, folded up the rug and put it back in the hall. She put away her thriller where it lived on the shelf in the empty spare bedroom. Then she went to her room to do her hair and wash. Aunt Lindsey would be tired and easily upset if she looked untidy. She decided her frock was crushed and she took out a clean one.

She would welcome Aunt Lindsey properly. Her head was in the frock when she heard the taxi stop at the gate. At the same moment the telephone bell rang. After a moment Miss Grigson padded down the stairs.

'It's Lady Rich, Mrs. Lawrence.'

Aunt Lindsey's clear, high voice.

'I'll take it on the hall phone.'

Laurel, buttoning her frock, hung over the banisters. She would walk down exactly as the call finished.

'Hallo, Lady Rich. Such ages since we met. I've been lecturing. I'm just in. I wonder, could you make it a week later? I've a niece landed on me for the holidays. Yes, frightful. Rather a moron. But one must do one's duty.'

Laurel tiptoed back into her room. Very softly she closed the door. Her legs seemed to crumple under her, so she sat on her bed. 'Rather a moron.' 'Rather a moron.' 'Rather a moron.'

XLVII

Walter, with Stroch at his heels, crept round the side of the house and peered in at the kitchen window. Mrs. Oliver was putting a kettle on the stove. She felt somebody was near and looked round.

'Funny, saw you in the cards Sunday. When did our front door fall off?'

Walter came into the kitchen.

'I came this way . . . I thought Nannie . . . I didn't want to disturb. . . .'

Mrs. Oliver looked at the parcels Walter was carrying and at Stroch. 'Walking out,' she decided. Aloud she said.

'Brought Stroch back?'

'Yes. I'm on the move.'

'Where you going?'

'Can't tell you that. Security.'

'We're never goin' to start that second front in the winter, are we?' His face told her nothing. 'Nannie's having a holiday. Those nurses. . . . Meadow ladies! We've only got one now and she goes when Nannie comes back next week.'

'How's Mrs. Wiltshire?'

'Still a bit rough, but she's up and about. Takes walks when it's fine. She's 'aving her nap now.'

Walter laid his parcels on the table.

'These are for Christmas. Those for the children, and that's candies. This for Nannie, and this for you.'

'Bit previous, aren't you? 'Tisn't November yet.'

'Probably my last visit.'

Mrs. Oliver looked at Stroch.

'Had his dinner?'

'Surely.'

'I'll give him something to keep him quiet.' She opened the scullery door. 'In there, and one sound out of you and you'll get such a wallop.' She poured out some milk and gave it to Stroch. 'Don't want him wakin' her.' She stood at the scullery door thinking. She was sleeping in while Nannie was away. She would have to put up with it if there was a scene. Mrs. Wiltshire was in no state for a scene, and she'd certainly create if he said good-bye. 'Tell you what, Cock. If I was you

I wouldn't tell I was movin', not for good. I'd leave a letter and slip off. You could write it so it didn't sound it was for long.'

Nothing could have suited Walter better. He was dreading seeing Lena.

He wrote his note and handed it with a small jewel box to Mrs. Oliver. He was turning to go when he remembered Laurel.

'When Nannie gets back, ask her when she's writing to Laurel to say good-bye from me. She might tell them all I've brought Stroch back and he's in good shape.'

XLVIII

Lena made a supreme effort at Christmas. She was still in a highly nervous condition, which was aggravated by fear and loneliness. 'I mustn't drink much. They'll take the children away.' She had heard nothing from Walter since he had left her a note and a little box of charms for her bracelet. He had said then he was moving but he did not suggest it was going to be for long, and still less that he would not be able to write. She had written, two or three times, and had rung up his office and his flat. She got no answer to her letters and no satisfaction from her telephone calls. She told herself it was just American fussiness about security, but it was borne in on her this was not true. Wherever Walter was and however secret his job, he could have written if he wanted to, if he could not put his address he could put one of those box numbers Americans went in for. Lena's weakness made her a prey to moods. One day she was full of confidence and hope. She would get perfectly well and strong. The children would have the most lovely holiday. They would be sweet to her. Walter would turn up again, and they would have a marvellous time. He just wasn't writing because he couldn't. Any day now there would be a letter. On days such as this she made plans. She would go to London. She really must order a frock, she would have the coupons by the time it was ready. She would have her coats remodelled. She would have her hair done a new way. On the following day she would be flattened under a blanket of despair. She would never get better. She was not improving a bit. How could she give the children a decent holiday while she was in this weak condition? Walter was never coming back. Nobody loved her now. The grey years stretched, hopeless, unlit by one gleam of light. On those days she would cry for hours, amidst her sobs she would murmur Walter's name, but it was Alex she was crying for. Strong, secure, somebody to lean against. If only this nightmare of fear would lift. She had never known fear when she had Alex.

The children came home on three different days. The doctor did not want to make an invalid of Lena, but she had to conserve her strength if she was to make a success of the holidays. Lena arranged to have the children escorted across London, and he had patients near the station and offered to meet the children.

The first to arrive was Tony. The last part of his summer holidays had not been so bad, he had liked working on a farm. He had enjoyed a couple of days in London with Dot and Henry. Even the most embarrassing talks with Andrew had been made less unbearable by Sylvia's tip about the peas. He was getting on all right at school, though, of course, he still felt a bit new. He had been looking forward to coming home. He hung out of the carriage window watching for Lena.

The doctor was overworked, looking after his own practice and that of another doctor who had been called up. He never could get through his round as quickly as he expected, he was always a little late, but that everybody understood. Tony had been standing by his luggage outside the station for close on half an hour when the doctor arrived.

'Hallo, young fellow my lad! I told your mother I'd meet you. Got held up over a broken arm.'

While they were getting his luggage on to the car Tony said:

'I was expecting my mother.'

'The taxi is dropping to bits, and it's better for your mother not to do more than she must.'

Tony fastened a strap round his trunk. He felt chilled by his welcome. Half an hour's wait, and then to hear Mum was still ill. He wanted he hardly knew what. A vague mixture of welcome, affection and being very much wanted. As he got into the car he said grumpily.

'Is she still ill? I thought she was all right again.'

The doctor caught the inflection in Tony's voice. He guessed something of what was behind it. Children were inclined to have pipe dreams of home. Cruelly easy to disappoint them. Tony especially. He had been in a queer way the first time he had seen him. Been in half a mind to put him in the hands of a psychologist. Boy must be fourteen now, or thereabouts. Lot of chivalry at that age. Might be good for the boy and good for his mother if he dropped a hint that as the man of the house he might be a bit firm with her. Take care of her. See she didn't overtax herself. Just as he started to speak there was a shout from a passing car. It was a fellow doctor. Through their car windows a case was discussed. When the doctor started his car again he was considering what he had been discussing, and had forgotten what he had meant to say to Tony.

Lena was nervous of meeting Tony. Had she changed? Would he be disappointed? She was over-eager. She drew him into the drawing room where tea was waiting. She kept up a steady flood of questions. It was all artificial, it was not what Tony needed. His answers grew shorter. He looked morose. Lena got frightened. She was changed. He was not as fond of her as he had been. To add to her fears she heard the old Tony out in the kitchen, teasing Nannie, asking Mrs. Oliver to read his teacup. 'It's just me,' Lena thought. 'I'm treating him all wrong somehow.' When Tony came back to the fire she said, with forced joviality:

'I thought you and I would go and cut down the Christmas tree tomorrow. We could plan it together. It would be rather fun, don't you think?'

Tony was playing with a wildly excited Stroch. He was making him bark, which Lena found a hideous noise.

'I don't see why you need bother. If you want a tree cut, I'll do it with Mr. Mustard.'

Kim arrived next, he was enchanting with Lena, and made Tony look and feel boorish in comparison. Kim had heard from Selina that she was going to ask Lena to spare him for the last two weeks of the holidays, as they were giving another show. Kim intended to take part in that show, but he knew it would take a bit of wangling to get away. Obviously the first step was to ingratiate himself with Lena. He had carefully planned his greeting. He had supposed it would take place before an audience on the railway station, but he was not put off by it taking place in the hall. He paused a moment, his arms flung wide, then he hurled himself at Lena.

'Mum. Most gorgeous, exquisite Mum. I've been simply miserable while you were ill, and it was dreadful in the summer not coming home.'

Lena hugged him, her eyes shining. This was wonderful. She was wanted. Darling Kim. Darling little Kim.

Kim was the only one who said how much he had missed Lena. Laurel and Tuesday, when they arrived, gave practically their whole attention to Stroch. There was nothing about Laurel to show that she had marked a calendar, scratching out the passing days to bring her home-coming nearer. Nothing to show the harm Lindsey had done her. Nothing to show the hurt she had in her heart because Walter had ceased to write. Nothing to show that the term had been almost unbearable, because the panache she had worn from receiving letters from an American had fallen from her. Nothing to show Lena how to tackle her, or to warn her that one of her first remarks should not be: 'I must try and get you some clothes, darling. You do look a funny in that little frill of a skirt.'

Tuesday was affectionate but aloof. Lena took her on her knee as she had always done, and the child sat there, quiet and apparently contented, but she was not the old Tuesday. Lena wanted words and hugs and she got acquiescence.

They spent an outwardly happy holiday. The children

were truly glad to be home, but they had grown away from each other. Tony drifted off and worked and gossiped with Mustard, and was out with boys of the neighbourhood. Laurel let herself be left out. 'He won't want to be bothered with me.' Even Tuesday went about alone and rather resented interruptions. In the house on wet days, and in the garden on fine, she played by herself. 'Look, Bobbie, Gipsy likes Stroch, I told you he would.'

Kim went to stay with the Llewellyns. Lena told him of the invitation.

'But, darling, I can't spare you. You don't want to go, do you?'

Kim looked as if he might cry.

'Of course I don't. I'd simply hate to leave my darling Mum, but as it's for the Red Cross I expect I ought to. They do need money dreadfully, don't they?'

Laurel and Tuesday's holidays finished two days later than Tony's. They left, as they had arrived, giving most of their attention to Stroch.

'Good-bye, most angel dog. You will see he gets walks, Mum. A dachshund so easily gets fat.'

Tuesday leant out of the taxi, kissing her hands, but Lena thought it unlikely the kisses were for her. Utterly exhausted and depressed she went up to her bedroom and cried.

XLIX

Uncle Charles was first heard of in Lena's letters. He did not start as Uncle Charles. He was to Tony, 'There is a friend of mine I so want you to meet in the holidays, Sir Charles Garden. He's so interested to hear about you.' To Laurel. 'I wore my new frock last week. I was lunching with a Sir Charles Garden. I told him you liked the frock, he said he must meet you, that you had a good taste.' To Kim. 'If enemy action stops I shall take you to London next holidays. I've a friend, Sir Charles Garden, that you'll like. Perhaps we'll go to a matinée.' To Tuesday. 'A friend of mine, Sir Charles Garden, was down on Sunday, and he thought Stroch one of the nicest dogs he had ever seen.'

It was when Lena went to see the children that he slipped into being Uncle Charles. Just a casual reference. 'That friend of mine, Sir Charles Garden, I think you better call him Uncle Charles, was asking if you cared for fishing.' 'Oh, darlings, we're going to have such fun at Easter if only this nasty bombing stops. That friend of mine, Sir Charles Garden, he says you can call him Uncle Charles, is full of lovely ideas. He thinks you ought to see some theatres, Laurel, and we thought you'd enjoy the ballet, Tuesday.' 'Uncle Charles is really excited about meeting you. He says he was keen on theatricals as a boy. Still, I don't expect he was as good as you.'

Lindsey ran into Lena lunching with Charles at the Ritz and spread the news. 'Rather a plain man and a bit common but obviously very nice. I had a feeling he was really fond of Lena. Would it not be splendid if he married her? A proper background for those children, which is just what they need.'

Charles was in love with Lena. He was fifty-two, still wealthy in spite of all taxation could do to his income. He was self-made, his father had been an elementary school-master, his mother a lady's maid. A mixture of brilliance and drive had got him where he was, owner of a vast chain of shops and chairman of a dozen subsidiary companies. His life had been all work and not much pleasure. He had a setback in his love affairs, he had fallen desperately in love when he was thirty, but the girl turned him down. Charles was so dominant, a woman he loved could have everything she wanted provided he chose the things, and dictated when they were to be used or worn. She could travel in the utmost luxury where she liked, provided it was where he liked, and at the moment he chose.

In the years since his broken love affairs, Charles had remained heart-whole. He took mistresses, but he despised them, they were an acquisitive lot and only stayed with him for what they could get. He met Lena at a lunch party soon after Christmas. She had been in need of distraction and had rung up friends and made a few engagements. Charles had been wondering since that lunch if fate had not been laying a restraining hand on his shoulders all the years, knowing that in his fifty-second year she had perfect happiness waiting for him. Little Lena, so lonely, so pathetic, needing a strong man to look after her, to spoil her, and order her about.

Charles intended to marry Lena. He never considered her as a mistress. Lena wanted to marry Charles but she found the waiting hard. It was lovely to be respected but she was not built for waiting. Charles decreed they must not announce the engagement until after the Easter holidays. 'The children must know me and look upon me as their father.'

Charles, amongst other possessions, had a mansion in Wales. He dismissed Lena's little house in a few words. 'I shall sell this house when the war's over and the military give up my place, and make a home for the children there. Meanwhile you and I will live in my suite at the Savoy, and get down in the holidays when we can.'

Nothing could change Charles. Even if Lena had tried to say anything it would have done no good. He was the plan-maker, it never crossed his mind that a girl of nearly sixteen, and a boy of fourteen, both of whom remembered their father perfectly, would resent an outsider dictating to them.

Charles came down the first Sunday after the children were home for Easter. He was a big man, and he seemed to fill the hall. Lena, nervously, for it was so important the children should like Charles, introduced them. Charles was tired and thirsty. He greeted the children pleasantly, but even as he was doing so he was planning his next move. He opened the kitchen door.

'Ice, and some of that lager I sent down last week. In the drawing-room.'

Mrs. Oliver did not come on Sundays, there was only Nannie in the kitchen. Laurel, flushing, looked at her mother.

'Do you want it? I'll get it if you do.'

Charles pulled one of Laurel's plaits.

'What I want your mother wants. Run along and get it, I like a girl to be helpful.'

Tony had never felt possessive about his home, but now a slow anger rose in him. He said nothing but followed Laurel into the kitchen. Nannie was in the larder getting the lager. Laurel and Tony stared at each other.

'What a simply ghastly man. What a nerve, saying he likes girls to be helpful. What business is it of his if I am or not?'

'It's as if this was his house, not ours. I never met such a cad.'

Even on that first Sunday the patch of darkness showed in Charles's happiness. As the days passed the patch spread. The air attacks on London, which had been renewed in February, had died down. Charles told Lena to bring the children to London.

'Splendid shelter under the Savoy. I'll take rooms for them all,' but the children refused the invitation. Laurel and Tony from a fierce jealous hatred, Tuesday because she preferred to stay at home with the others, Kim because Charles treated him as part of the family group and not as an individual. By the end of the holidays the children had banded together and were atrociously rude to Charles. They did not resent so bitterly his adoption of their mother, as the way he treated their home. It was the only home they had possessed since Regent's Park and was peculiarly theirs, to the last bush. Charles was always outraging their sense of possession. 'Tell Mustard I'll send down some creosote for that fence.' 'Tell Mustard I'm having some seedlings delivered. They are to be planted right away.' 'I'll get the roof overhauled, no harm in having it looked at.'

The tragedy was Charles had no idea why the children did not like him. This house was theirs and he intended to put it on the market at the right time and make a nice bit of profit for them. He wanted to adopt them and give them a fine home and everything he thought they should have. What could be making them so impossible except that they were spoilt, badly brought up children?

Charles, having made up his mind on a course of action, always took it. He had planned before the children returned to their schools to announce to them that he was marrying their mother. He saw no reason to change his plans. Lena, who could feel there would be a row, suggested writing, but Charles overruled her.

'Nonsense. Come down and tell them myself. The girls go back on the Monday, don't they? I'll be down on Sunday.'

Charles made his announcement as he made announcements of good news at Board meetings.

'I'm glad to say your mother is going to be my wife. We shall be married in June. I hope you will look upon me as your father.'

There was stunned silence.

Laurel's heart pumped. A father! This big, common, ordering-about man marrying Mum! Taking Dad's place! She gulped and raced out of the room, slamming the drawing-room door. She lay face downwards on her bed, sobbing. 'Oh Dad. Dad.'

Tony saw red. He began to shout.

'I can't stop you marrying Mum, but you'll never be our father. Never. We'd rather be dead.'

Tuesday was terrified. There was another change coming. Black specks flickered before her eyes and in her ears she heard bells ringing.

Kim alone saw the situation clearly. They had been the most important people in Mum's life, and in everybody else's whom Mum knew. Now Mum was getting married and they would come second. Kim was not accepting that. He spoke with drama.

'We'll manage for ourselves, thank you. We're not wanting a father.'

Lena would have been crushed and bowed by this avalanche of disapproval but Charles was not standing any nonsense.

'I shall announce our engagement right away. We'll be married quietly by special licence as soon as it comes through. You are not to worry yourself about the children. They are my worry from now on.'

L

Elsa, the Colonel, Dot, Lindsey, Sylvia and Selina attended the wedding, Andrew assisted at the Service. Charles gave a family luncheon before he and Lena left for a week's honeymoon in Scotland. When they had departed the family drew together. There was a general expression of thankfulness.

'Splendid man,' said Elsa. 'Can't imagine what he sees in Lena, but it could not be more satisfactory.'

The Colonel broke in.

'Always liked the little thing myself.'

'I know you did, but now she's not my son's wife I don't mind saying I have never cared for her. Lacks stamina. Inherits it from that unpleasant woman, her mother.'

'Thank goodness he's going to take on the children,' said

Lindsey. 'So sensible about them. Says they are being difficult but he won't stand any nonsense.'

Sylvia hesitated to say what was in her mind.

'They will be difficult at first, after all, he isn't Alex.'

Dot spoke briskly.

'We may as well be honest. Except for Lindsey we've children of our own, and we don't want to look after nieces and nephews, though we would have done, as we did when Lena was ill, if we had been obliged to.'

'Not again,' said Lindsey.

Dot was sorry her parents were there and she could not say, 'That's taught you not to interfere.' She went on.

'Charles says the children are being difficult. He also says he is not going to have Lena bothered, which means he will stand no nonsense. At the same time he's being good to them. He's arranging for riding lessons and buying them a pony.'

Andrew had been half listening.

'He's a good man. I spoke to him about Tony. He feels his duty there. The boy needs a father.'

Selina said nothing. She was depressed by Lena's marriage. Charles already talked as if Kim was his boy.

The Colonel looked round his family.

'They are still Alex's children, even though they have a stepfather. The long summer holiday will give them time to shake down. We can't interfere even though we would . . .'

'Nonsense,' said Elsa. 'My grandchildren are my grand-children. I shall certainly interfere if I think necessary.'

The Colonel went on as if she had not spoken.

'He seems, if rather a rough diamond, a good-hearted

man. He won't mind, if we felt there was anything about the children's upbringing of which Alex would not have approved, if we say so.'

It was the more annoying to Dot in the face of such family rejoicing to find Laurel unbearably difficult and Alice siding with her.

'Well, Mum, what d'you expect? Suppose Dad was killed, do you think Henry and Maria and I would slop over any man you married? Because you liked him it doesn't say we would.'

'You're being very silly, Alice. You ought to be trying to make Laurel behave. She's sixteen this month. In a couple of years she can get a job if she doesn't like being at home.'

Alice looked mulish.

'Well, I side with Laurel. She's says he's a foul man. He talks about their house as if it was his and he paid for everything. Actually, she says he doesn't pay for a thing.'

'He's going to give them riding lessons and buy them a pony.'

'Laurel can ride. She did before the war. Neither she nor Tony will take anything he buys, even a pony. They won't speak to him. Tony won't even speak to Aunt Lena.'

'Very silly and unkind, behaving like spoilt babies. A great girl of sixteen and a boy who'll be fifteen in November. I've no patience with it.'

'Well, it's no good cursing me. As a matter of fact, I told Laurel he probably wouldn't be such a hell-hound when she got used to him. I hope you aren't going to talk about him to Laurel, it will be just a waste of Sunday if you do.'

Mrs. Fellows was on the look-out for Dot.

'I wanted a word with you before you left. I don't see you so much now Maria's in the lower school. It's about Tuesday. I don't know what's the matter with that child.'

'Why?'

'When she first came to me she was rather a baby, she needed bringing out and she got on splendidly. She started to go backwards last autumn term. She moons about and day-dreams, and talks to herself. She should have moved into lower school this term, but I had to hold her back, the mere mention of it and she started walking in her sleep. I've had the doctor to her, he says she's in a nervous state. He's worried about her, says she's to be watched.'

'You know her mother's married again?'

'Yes. I told the doctor. He says that might have something to do with it, but, as a matter of fact, as I tell you, I was first worried about her in the autumn. All these nervous tricks, twitching and jumping.'

'He's not bad, the stepfather. In the end he may produce just what Tuesday needs. Her mother being ill probably upset the child and what she wants is an ordinary home-life. He means to give them that.'

Mrs. Fellows wondered if she should say more. Report how dissatisfied Miss Clegg was with Laurel. If her Viola looked as forlorn as either Laurel or Tuesday it would break her heart. She said nothing. After all, Mrs. Enden was only an aunt and a very busy woman, and she had her own children to worry about.

In two terms Tony had not made many friends amongst the boys. This third term they noticed him because of his bad temper. He flared up and argued about anything. He even did it in class; one master after another said wearily, 'Don't let's have an argument, Wiltshire.' The boys sometimes baited him to see him lose his hair, most of the time they left him to himself. They christened him 'Sour-puss Wiltshire'.

Selina visited Kim at school. She listened sympathetically to his grumbles about his stepfather. They made a plan that in the summer he would spend quite a lot of his holidays with her.

'I don't know how we're going to manage, darling. He's a man used to having his own way.'

Kim dismissed Charles with a grand gesture.

'Him! What about me? I always get what I want and I always will.'

LI

The flying bombs upset all plans. The house stood against an awe-inspiring network of balloons. The crash of bursting bombs went on night and day. Their home was no place for the children. All through June and into July Charles struggled and pulled wires to get a house, or rooms in an hotel, for Lena and her family. Even his wires were not strong enough. The hotels in safe areas barely bothered to refuse his request for four single and one double or three double rooms. Nobody knew of a house.

Long before Dot heard from Lena she had guessed what was coming. She took the blow lightly. The Wiltshires were almost off the family hands, and having some of them for the summer was nothing. The war in Europe was going well, it might be over before Christmas. She planned that once more they would parcel out the children between them. Selina, she knew, wanted Kim, Sylvia would love to have all or any of them, and Lindsey was damn well going to take Laurel.

Sylvia rang Dot the moment she got Lena's letter. She was stuttering and confused but her anxiety rang over the line.

'I love him but he doesn't like it with us. Could I have Tuesday, or Laurel, or both? I wish it could be Tony, but it wasn't . . . Andrew. . . .'

Dot intended to stick to Tuesday. Mrs. Fellows was not happy about her. She would have a talk with Maria and try and discover what was wrong. Lindsey was not to get out of having Laurel.

'I'll take Tony, I'll be glad to have him. Henry's been accepted for the Fleet Air Arm, but they are taking a long time sending for him to start his training. He is afraid the war will be over before he's trained. He blames all of us. Tony will be company for him. But if I take Tony you're not to tell Lindsey you'll have Laurel. She's too fond of getting out of things. Now, promise, or I won't take Tony.'

Lindsey rang up that night.

'I say, it's a bit thick. I had that lumping schoolgirl all last summer, now I really can't. Apart from anything else John's ill. Some sort of bug. He's home on sick leave.'

'Laurel will be a help. It's much easier for you than for me. You've got a cook.'

'It's the most awful bore.'

'You shouldn't find girls a bore. They should be copy. You can write a book about her.'

'Nothing interesting in her. Just an adolescent at the silly stage.'

'Anyway you've got to have her, so give in gracefully.'

To Tony, Kim and Tuesday the change of plans came almost as good news. Tony, in as far as he would like to do anything, was willing to spend his holiday with Henry. Kim was charmed to go to Selina. Tuesday had become scared of home, it was quite a relief to go with Maria. She knew the Endens, she liked the house and garden.

Laurel was the sufferer. She had never done well at Greenwood House, but after the Easter holidays she was really bitter and difficult. She already had a name for being tiresome, now she was classed as a black sheep. She was unreliable, took no responsibility, answered rudely, was noisy, on the slightest provocation shrieking with mirthless laughter. In the mistresses' common room, 'Rather like Laurel Wiltshire,' or 'The same type as Laurel Wiltshire' was an accepted description of a difficult girl. Even when she tried to behave she was suspect. Daily she heard, with a weary inflection, 'Yes, Laurel?' 'Well, what is it now, Laurel?' Miss Clegg was asked if some of her senior girls might give help at weekends to an understaffed evacuated nursery school. She asked for volunteers. 'I only want those of you who will stick to the work, are willing to do anything, and are really fond of small children.' Laurel offered. Her eyes shone. A whole house full of nothing but babies! What could be more lovely! Miss Clegg dismissed her offer with a half laugh, in which, by a glance, she invited the girls to join. 'No, Laurel, I hardly think you would be suitable. If you have time to give away over the weekends, you can do some extra homework. Your form mistress tells me your work is deplorable.'

Alice remained a friend. She was a prefect, games captain, and would one day be head of the school. Others would not have found it easy to stand staunchly by a scape-grace cousin. Alice did not find it difficult. Laurel was her friend, and nothing changed that. It was no good Miss Clegg saying, 'I wish you'd talk to Laurel.' Alice's face became a blank, her eyes, through her glasses, gazed out politely but without interest. No girl criticised Laurel in front of Alice. Alice was not afraid to say what she thought.

'You must feel pretty perfect if you think you're the right person to criticise other people.'

Alone with Laurel Alice was equally ruthless.

'I can't think why you make such an ass of yourself. No point in being rude to the mistresses, the poor old cows are paid to teach you. It's no good taking it out on them because you don't like your stepfather.'

'Why you fool around with girls like Shirley and her lot I can't think. They aren't your sort. Letting them think you got love letters, and all that rot.'

Ruth, through her letters, got some idea of Laurel's state of mind. Since the liberation of Europe had started she had been unable to get leave. She did what she could by writing. 'I'm sorry you have to go to Aunt Lindsey's again as you hate it so much, but perhaps, as it happens, it's better you should not go home until Christmas. You wait until I see you, I think you are getting things out of proportion about your step-father. After all, you are nearly grown up and can soon take up a career if you want to. Be sure to work hard and get your School Certificate with enough credits for matric exemption. You'll need it for a job and you'll shame me if you fail. I don't promise, but I might get leave this summer. If I do I'll meet you somewhere, perhaps I can find an hotel where I could invite you to stay with me. Send me Aunt Lindsey's telephone number. I have put mine on this notepaper. It's our Mess number. About nine o'clock at night is the safest time to ring. It's expensive ringing Scotland but if you can find a call box near Aunt Lindsey, and feel a talk will help, it will be worth the money.'

Laurel was still small and childish looking for her age, but her body was deceptive. It housed a creature floundering in the mud and flowers of adolescence. From Lena she inherited the need to worship someone, and she had no one on whom to expend her need. She needed to come first with someone, and there was no one whose first thought was ever for her. From Alex came purity. She felt no connection yet between her heart and body. The fastidious side of her disliked what Alice described as 'Shirley and her lot'. Yet she clung to them. They were an excitement, they lived in a continual surge of emotion. They revelled in each other, got pleasure in their own and each other's physical condition. They came back each term with news of boy friends, they whispered of, and magnified, slight adventures. As the term wore on they needed something more concrete than memories. It was then they had passions and crushes for a girl, or one of the mistresses. It worried Laurel that she knew none of the thrills they knew. She had been able to put over Walter at the time, but she had never fooled herself. She knew he was Lena's friend and thought of her as a child. She toyed with the idea of pretending she had a crush on one of the girls, but she was afraid of being snubbed. Shirley and her lot did not seem to mind being snubbed, but then they were not the butt of the school, called even by juniors The Frog. After Walter stopped writing she had ceased to be interesting to Shirley and her friends, and had been dropped. This term she had romantic interest. Her pallor, her moodiness and the fact that she was known to cry herself to sleep, brought her back into favour. 'Poor old Frog, you have got it badly.' Laurel played up, partly for the pleasure of being talked about and discussed. She could feel respect. She was the great lover. Still more, it was a relief to have an excuse for herself. She was behaving atrociously and knew it. Shirley and her lot spread the news. The Frog loved an American. 'Have you ever seen anyone so changed!' It was known that her mother had married again, but clearly that had not upset Laurel. All that was heard of Charles was a casual, 'He's all right.'

When the news came she was to spend the summer holiday with Lindsey, Laurel broke down. They thought she must be suffering from a chill, and put her in the sick-room.

There was only one other girl in with her. At night, when the lights were out and the girl was asleep, Laurel buried her face in her pillows and cried into the early hours of the morning.

'It isn't that I wanted to go home, not with him there. But

packed off to Aunt Lindsey, who despises me. They push me
about like a parcel. Nobody cares about me. Nobody at all.'

LII

Happiness was waiting for Laurel. She found it the moment
she reached Lindsey's house, and it grew with every hour.
John was home. He was feeling ill and wretched. Lindsey
liked having him under her eye, but she was impatient with
illness. He had picked up some infection which had lamed
him and stiffened one shoulder. He had spent two months in
hospital, and was temporarily out to see whether a period at
home would help. He needed encouragement and unending
care. What he got was, 'I think it would do you good to make
more effort.' 'You mustn't let yourself become a malade
imaginaire.'

Hannah and Miss Grigson had done what they could.
Hannah, running after John with glasses of milk, and sometimes a beaten egg. Miss Grigson by giving her spare time to
him. 'Is there anything you want? I've my bicycle in the hall. I
can get to the shops in no time.' 'How's the crossword going
today? I've brought the dictionaries down.'

John was what Laurel craved. He needed love, he needed
looking after. What they gave each other was as delicate as a
wood anemone. It was bruisable, intensely fragile. Laurel, at
one laugh, or even a wrong inflection, would have sunk back
into the self-conscious, angular, bristly girl who came to the
house. John had always wanted children, he had dreamt
sometimes of how they would be. Laurel told her troubles,

and even as she told them, because he did not find her plain or dull, the troubles began to evaporate. He laughed when she told him she was called Frog, and repeated it, pulling her plaits, and saying he had always liked frogs. She did not tell him about Walter, she would have liked to, but it might have worried him, as he would have thought her silly, and he was not well enough to be worried.

Laurel provided the encouragement John needed.

'Of course your foot's stiff this morning, it's raining. Mrs. Oliver, who isn't ill at all, says she feels her joints whenever it rains, or even if rain's coming.'

'Do you know, we've been so long a walk I'm tired and you aren't tired at all.'

'Of course you'll be well enough to go back to sea. I haven't been in the house long and you're miles better already.'

She had the faith of her age.

'You needn't be a golf secretary again if you don't like it. Think of something different. Such fun to start something new.'

With no word spoken John and Laurel hid their happiness in each other's company, from Lindsey. At meals and when she was about there were no confidences. Laurel tried not to run about anticipating John's every need. John hardly spoke to Laurel. They both said as little as possible. Nevertheless Lindsey sensed John was fond of Laurel, and was jealous. Bitter words spewed from her.

'Don't fuss over that girl, John, it isn't decent.'

'Really, you two! Can't you be a minute out of each other's sight?'

LIII

Ruth came south for a course. She telephoned to ask if Laurel might make the simple journey to meet her. Lindsey was out so Miss Grigson asked John to take the call. John was delighted to hear Ruth's voice again. Rather, of course. He'd bring Laurel over himself.

Ruth's course lasted three weeks. Whenever Lindsey was away lecturing John and Laurel went over to see her. They had picnic lunches, and sometimes, when Lindsey was away a night, picnic suppers. John and Ruth never let Laurel feel in the way, she was the reason for the meeting, all conversation was to her. They were glad to have her. The war had changed them both. Ruth, who had begun the war in her late twenties, had still considered herself a girl, and now recognised that Peace would find her beginning the middle years. That would need thought and adjustment, and taking happiness where you found it, came into account. John, through the years of separation, had given consideration to his marriage. It was a cold, fruitless, worthless thing. While Laurel chattered, John and Ruth stared at each other across her. They knew they were in love.

On the day before Ruth returned to the North there was a final picnic. John sent Laurel to buy some lemonade. Alone with Ruth, he said:

'Give me your address. I'll write.'

She said:

'Here it is. Where shall I answer?'

He had a card with his club address ready in his hand.

LIV

Laurel was packing. She did not cry, at sixteen you could not cry because you were returning to school. She was so depressed that she felt as if she were ill, her whole body ached. It was over. The lovely holiday. It was not as if there were another holiday to look forward to. By Christmas the flying bombs were sure to have stopped. She would go home to be ordered about and dictated to by Charles.

Her door was open. John looked in, he closed it softly behind him. He held out a flat leather box. Laurel did not take it.

'What is it?'

'Look and see.'

She took the case and opened it. Inside was a string of seed pearls. She raised startled eyes.

'Pearls! For me!'

'Only seed. Put them on.'

She fastened the clasp and went to her mirror, then turned and flung herself at him.

'They're heavenly. I shall wear them at school. No one will know, they'll be under my frock.'

'I wanted to give you something pretty. You've been a kind niece. I shall miss you more than I can say.'

Laurel fingered the pearls.

'Will you? It's awfully nice to hear somebody say that.' She raised her eyes. 'When I mind things at school, and when I funk my School Certificate exam, I shall touch these, and everything will be all right. Mum's given me lovely presents, of course, but this is the nicest I ever had. It's just a fondness present, isn't it? Not because you had to, because of birthday or Christmas, or anything?'

'Yes, it's just for fondness, and a little as a thank offering.'

'What for?'

He shook his head.

'I'll explain one day. Now put the pearls away. They're a secret, you know.'

LV

'The Frog wears pearls under her frock.'

'The Frog won't say who gave them to her, but she doesn't say no when you ask if it's her American.'

'The Frog looks quite different. You don't think . . .?'

'I say, have you heard the buzz about The Frog?'

Laurel was not to blame. She had been tempted to display her pearls and pretend there was a romance behind them, but she had refrained. Uncle John would think it silly and cheap, which it was. She was working hard. She intended to get that matric exemption when she took her School Certificate. Uncle John and the Foxglove had talked a lot about what she might do when she left school. She was for once without ambition herself. She had a dim idea that she would like to take a domestic economy course. If ever again somebody like Uncle John needed looking after, it would be nice to know how to do all the things, cooking, laundry, all of it.

A bad name in a school is hard to live down. None of the staff believed in Laurel's reformation. She seemed to be working better, but she would slide back. It was the games mistress who first heard the gossip. Her eyes bulging, she whispered it to a friend. The friend told Laurel's form mistress. Finally, the news reached Miss Clegg.

Laurel was quite unaware that anything was wrong. She received the summons to Miss Clegg's study without a quiver. So certain was she that for once she had done nothing to annoy anyone that she came in smiling. Her smile died at the sight of the look on Miss Clegg's face.

'I understand, Laurel, you are wearing a string of pearls.'

Laurel's hand flew to her throat.

'They don't show. Please let me wear them. They mean an awful lot. . . . '

'Who gave them to you?' There was silence. Miss Clegg repeated her question.

'I can't tell you. It's a secret.'

'I will tell you what I have heard. They're a present from an American soldier. There is a very silly story going round the school.' Laurel said nothing. It was pretty mean on Walter to let him be blamed, still, he would never know, and she was not going to tell old Clegg about Uncle John. Miss Clegg motioned her to a chair. 'Sit down, Laurel. You've always been unsatisfactory. It's hard work running a boarding-school these days, one depends on the co-operation of the elder girls, from you I've had none. You are a trouble maker, and now comes this unpleasant story. I've talked to the head and she is seeing you later. This incident, into which I shall not enquire further, happened in the holidays. It is, therefore, not a school concern; that a girl like yourself should be part of the school is our concern. We are writing to your mother asking her to remove you.'

Laurel gaped at Miss Clegg. What was she talking about? What silly story? Expelled! Mum was to be written to. She would have to take her back with her. It would be terrible, neither Mum nor Charles would want her. It was a secret about the necklace, but Uncle John would understand. She pulled out the pearls for Miss Clegg to see.

'I never said they were given me by an American. Actually they were given me by my Uncle John. Aunt Lindsey's husband. I was with them for the summer holidays.'

Laurel looked so earnest, and somehow, in spite of everything, so innocent, that Miss Clegg began to doubt. Could it be school gossip? She rang a bell.

'I shall investigate this. In the meantime you will work and eat alone. You are to speak to nobody.'

LVI

Lindsey knew something was wrong. John had changed. He whistled and sang about the house. He did not seem to mind as he used to when she criticised or complained. He had slipped from her. He was away for a day and refused to say where he had been, or whom he had seen. She grew angry. She insisted it was her right to know where he went. Before this sick leave he would have cared. He would have apologised. Now he laughed. Then, suddenly, without a word, he packed a suitcase and left a message he would not be back for two or three days.

John was to Lindsey a possession. Her background required a husband, just as it required a suitable setting of house and staff. She had always guarded him jealously. He was hers. Now, who was he seeing? He had been so faithful, she knew most of his friends. There had been a moment when she had suspected Lena. That was unlikely now with Charles about. She could not work. She could not sleep. She ramped up and down the house and made Miss Grigson's life hell.

The telephone call was for John. Lindsey took it.

'Well, you'll do just as well as a matter of fact. It's Miss Clegg speaking. I'm head of the boarding side of Greenwood House. I have your niece with me. Laurel is wearing pearls which have caused rather silly talk. She says they were a present to her from her Uncle John. Is this correct?'

LVII

It was gloomy by yourself with no one allowed to speak to you. They sent over her work from the school. The prefect who brought it, and the maid who served her food, used the least possible words. 'I feel like a prisoner in the Tower,' thought Laurel. But she was not too depressed. Miss Clegg would write to Uncle John and that would be the end. What on earth had old Clegg got hold of? Even if Walter had given her the pearls it seemed a queer thing to expel you for.

Lindsey arrived about tea-time. She asked to see Laurel alone. She waited while Miss Clegg closed the door. Her face frightened Laurel. She had risen to her feet when Miss Clegg and her aunt came in, now she moved back, putting as much distance between herself and Lindsey as possible. Lindsey's voice was controlled but harsh with anger.

'Give me the pearls.'

Laurel laid a hand over them, she felt them pressing into her throat. They comforted her.

'They're mine. Uncle John gave them to me.'

'You don't deny it?'

'No.'

'What did he give you them for?'

'Just a present.'

Lindsey's skin seemed to tighten, there were red patches on her cheeks.

'Aren't you ashamed? Or perhaps you're not as you're your mother's daughter. Don't you know right from wrong? These picnics! Pretending you were an innocent schoolgirl! What exactly did you allow?'

'I don't know what you're talking about.'

'Rubbish! You're sixteen and a half. Of course you know. You're still meeting, aren't you?'

'You know I'm not. I'm here.'

Lindsey brushed that aside.

'I must know how far this has gone.'

Laurel looked despairingly at Lindsey. What a flap she was in!

'I don't know what you mean.'

Lindsey's control broke. This was intolerable. These pert answers, this wide-eyed innocent look. She came round the table and shook Laurel so violently that stars danced in front of the girl's eyes and her ears sang.

'You filthy little beast. Messing about with men at your age. Your own uncle. Serve you right if you have a baby.'

LVIII

For quite a while Laurel did not move, she stared at the door which Lindsey had slammed. Her brain cleared. She covered her mouth with both hands, her cheeks flamed. She whispered meaningless expressions. 'Oh gosh!' 'Oh my goodness!' Suddenly she knew she must get away. Somewhere Aunt Lindsey was telling the things she thought to Miss Clegg and the head. They would send for her. She must not be here. But where? Not Mum. She wouldn't want her. Uncle John? That meant going to Aunt Lindsey's house. Home? No, they would look there first.

The door was not locked. Laurel ran to her dormitory.

She snatched a coat and a beret. Her mind was on a problem. Money was locked up at school. Yet she must have money. If only she could get hold of Alice. Alice would help, but Alice was over at the school. Money. On Matron's desk was a blue wooden collecting box. Matron's brother was in the Navy. It was for Navy war libraries. Matron's office was empty. Laurel found a piece of paper and a pencil. She wrote: 'I have taken your box. I will let you know how much was in it, and you can get it back from Miss Clegg. LAUREL WILTSHIRE.'

XLIX

Foxglove had said she would be in at nine. It had never occurred to Laurel she would not hear her voice. That a brisk voice would say, 'Any message?' Almost Laurel put down the receiver. She was half crying but she managed to gulp. 'Tell her it's Laurel. I'm at King's Cross. I haven't enough money to ring again. Could she come. I'm in the station.'

A police constable saw a young girl hanging about. He watched her for some time. Then he came over to her.

'Waiting for somebody?'

'Yes.'

'Who is it?'

'A friend. She was my governess.'

'Where's she coming from?'

'Scotland.'

'On what train?'

'I'm not sure.'

'How old are you?'

'Sixteen.'

A juvenile! Hanging about a station. The constable had daughters of his own, he spoke in an authoritative but fatherly way.

'You come along with me.'

The hostel shone with cheap linoleum. On the walls were texts. They gave Laurel supper but she was too exhausted to eat. Presently she was taken up to an office and questioned. A call from the matron had brought round a police woman, who, since Laurel was a juvenile, was in plain clothes. To Matron Laurel had only admitted that she was sixteen and her name was Laurel. The police woman got a little more. She heard of the money borrowed from the money-box.

'I left a note to explain. I've got enough to pay it back. It was an awful job to open the box. It was mostly pennies.

There was one pound twelve shillings and three-pence halfpenny.'

The policeman had reported to Matron that Laurel had been seen making a phone call. The police woman built on that. Who was the friend in Scotland?

It was kindness that wore Laurel down. They were not angry that she would not say from where she had run away. They did not press her when she said it would not be possible to get hold of her mother. There must be somebody she would like to see. She told them about Ruth, and gave them the telephone number.

Laurel was given a bath and lent a nightdress. She was in a small room with three other girls. It was a dreadful night. She could not sleep. Every time she dropped off she awoke with a start, shivering and crying. She would never be able to see Uncle John again. She was expelled from school. Would they keep her here for ever? In the dawn she lost faith even in Ruth. In the train she had seen her shining like a lamp in her darkness. She would hide her. She knew it was not true.

She was dozing when Matron shook her.

'Get up, dear, and come down. There's somebody to see you.' Laurel's first thought was Lindsey. Her eyes shone with terror.

'I don't want to see anybody.'

'Oh yes, you do. Come along, dear.'

Laurel put on her coat. Her teeth chattered from nervous exhaustion. She followed Matron down to the office. There was a text on the wall, 'Be not deceived. God is not mocked. Whatsoever a man soweth. That shall he reap.' Sitting under it, spruce in spite of a horrible journey, was the Colonel. He got up and kissed Laurel. He was just as ordinary as if he were greeting her in his own hall.

'Hallo, my dear. Go up and dress, will you. I have a car outside.'

'Where are you taking me?'

'To your home. I have telephoned nurse to have a good breakfast ready for us.'

LX

Laurel slept in the car, her head on the Colonel's shoulder. They did not say much. What Aunt Lindsey had said it was not possible to repeat.

It was so easy in the house. Nannie and Stroch were waiting, Nannie pleased, Stroch hysterical, neither inquisitive.

After breakfast the Colonel packed Laurel off to bed and himself went to the telephone. He rang Greenwood House, Dot, Lindsey, Ruth, and, finally, he located Lena. He was tired, he had travelled all night. It was warm for October. He sat in the sun. His thoughts were of Alex. Lindsey had not said much to Miss Clegg and the headmistress, but she had backed their opinion that Laurel was unsatisfactory. She was to be expelled. Dot sounded weary. 'That family! I had an awful time with Tony after Henry left. He's such a surly, unco-operative boy. Tuesday's a bundle of nerves.' Lindsey had been short. She had a guilty conscience. John had written he wanted a divorce. Whether he got it or not he was not coming back. He did not say who it was he loved, except that she was in one of the Services. She said she was glad that tiresome girl had been found. The rest of the call was complaints about John. Lena said they had spent the night with Selina. She had signed a contract for Kim. He had been offered a wonderful boy's part in a play. She would come down at once. It was all right. Charles would not be coming in any case, he was working. Ruth sent Laurel endless loving messages.

Mustard passed. The Colonel nodded.

''Mornin'.'

Mustard leant on his fork.

'You brought Laurel down?'

'Yes. She had a bad night. She's resting. She'll be about this afternoon.'

'She stayin'?'

'I hardly know. Her mother will be here soon.'

'Have 'em all four this Christmas. Flying bombs have cleared up nicely.'

'You bothered with the rockets?'

'No, never seen they. Laurel's a grown woman now. Nice if she could stop along. Make more of a home like for the others.'

Mustard was back at his work. The Colonel was almost dozing. Alex seemed close.

'Somehow we've messed it. Not a bad idea that. Motherly little thing. Might let her have a try. Might send her back to that other school whatever it was called. She liked it there. It's all this choppin' and changing.'

Mrs. Oliver looked out of the window.

'Aren't you cold?'

The Colonel got up.

'A little perhaps.'

'News is good, isn't it? Knew it would be. I read it would finish Christmas 1944 in my cards. Shockin', though, the state France and that are in. Turns you over, don't it, to think of the children? I was saying to my daughter only yesterday, "We got a lot to be thankful for in this country. Our kids 'aven't suffered 'o-ever else 'as."'

AFTERWORD

Noel Streatfeild is best known for her children's books, especially *Ballet Shoes*, which has been continuously in print since its publication in 1936. Her first love was the theatre, and it was only in her early thirties when her career as an actress threatened to decline into mediocrity that she started, tentatively, and with much misspelling to write. Her first book *The Whicharts* (named almost blasphemously by this parson's daughter from the Lord's Prayer: 'which art in heaven . . .') was at once hailed by the critics, including John Galsworthy, as a brilliant new talent. By the time *Saplings* was published she had already had ten adult novels under her belt, all out of print and forgotten today.

A consummate craftswoman, Noel Streatfeild knew better than to preach to her readers, which is one reason why she was so successful as a children's author. Yet *Saplings* is a novel with a powerful and deeply felt message, arriving, finally, in its last ironic lines, delivered in slightly stereotyped Dickensian cockney by the cleaning-lady, Mrs. Oliver: 'We got a lot to be thankful for in this country. Our kids 'aven't suffered 'o-ever else 'as.'

Saplings was first published in 1945. Streatfeild's purpose is ominously clear from the start: she sets out to prove Mrs. Oliver wrong. She takes a happy, successful, middle-class pre-war English family (and the Wiltshires, like their name, are *very* English – there is no hint of the Celtic fringe or the cosmopolitan exoticism which lurks in the background of *Ballet Shoes*), 'beautiful, orderly, full of children' (the four 'saplings'), with holidays at the seaside, a comfortable house in Regent's Park, a glamorous mother and successful indus-trialist for a father, nannies and nurses, prep schools and public schools – and then tracks in miserable detail the disintegration and devastation which war brought to tens of thousands of such families.

Streatfeild's supreme gift was her ability to see the world from a child's perspective. What makes *Saplings* special is her use of that skill to explore a very adult problem – the psychological impact of war and trauma on family life. Here she was and still is in tune with the zeitgeist. In the mid 1940s psychologists, psychoanalysts and child psychiatrists were just beginning to address the very same issues from a scientific perspective. Bowlby had just published his ground-breaking *44 Juvenile Thieves*, showing how adolescent delinquency arises out of loss and separation in childhood. *Maternal Care and Child Health*, his influential W.H.O.-commissioned study of the impact of war on child mental health appeared only a few years later; and at the same time he was also starting to pioneer psychotherapy with whole families. Winnicott wrote and broadcasted about the inner world of the infant, and Melanie Klein and Anna Freud were developing child psychoanalysis and psychotherapy, the latter, with Dorothy

Burlingham, running her nursery for orphans, most of whom were psychological casualties of war.

In the first half of the century children's well-being was mainly equated with their physical health. Novelists, among whom Dickens is the obvious example, had long been interested in the working of children's minds, and the impact of adult neglect and cruelty upon them, but science had lagged behind. Psychoanalysis – an area about which we have no evidence that Streatfeild took the slightest interest – had established two essential themes which nevertheless underlie the thrust of her book. First, that children's minds were as vulnerable as their bodies to disturbance and illness, and second, and as a consequence of the first, that children are autonomous beings with their own needs and projects, and are not merely objects to be controlled and manipulated by adults, however well-meaning.

Evacuation was an obvious response to the threat of a war which for the first time in history directly targeted civilians, but the psychological consequences of separating children from their parents was glossed over in the rush to ensure their physical survival. War posed a terrible Hobson's choice for families, and it was only afterwards that the toll it had taken in terms of depression and despair could begin to be recognised. *Saplings* is the literary equivalent of the psychological audit initiated by Bowlby and others. For Bowlby the Secure Base is the key to psychological survival, and the capacity of parents, families and nations as a whole to provide such a secure base is severely compromised at times of war. While psychological illness tends actually to decrease during active periods of conflict, the long-term effects on children are incalculable, a theme recently taken up by Pat Barker in relation to the First World War in her novel *Another World*.

It is fascinating to watch Streatfeild casually and intuitively anticipate many of the findings of developmental psychology over the past 50 years. *Saplings* starts with an apparently idyllic beach scene, where the youngest child, Tuesday, is filling her bucket as she

> hummed, a contented tuneless sound . . . Tuesday did not know that for a fortnight she had felt insecure because she was in one place and her father and mother in another . . . Because she was only four and people underrated her intelligence and spoke in front of her, she was the one of the children who was aware that Nan and Miss Glover [the attractive and perceptive Ruth, the governess, and Streatfeild's alter ego] and the servants at home were afraid of something. Because they were afraid Tuesday was afraid. She wanted everybody where she could see them.

Here we feel the faint whisperings of war, a tiny dark cloud in an otherwise blue sky, picked up by a sensitive child who is experiencing separation anxiety, and who feels that her secure base is under threat. Only once a safe haven is in place – her mother and father together – can she play and explore contentedly.

Lena, the Wiltshire children's mother, is perhaps the

pivotal character of the book. We see her painful decline from charming but wayward mother at the start, through her terror at the possibility of separation from her husband Alex during the blitz and inability to provide the necessary psychological security for the children, to her alcoholic, sex-obsessed and suicidal premature widowhood. The trauma of war, the death of Alex, and its diminishing and distorting impact on the lives of the children would all have been mitigated had Lena been different, more maternal and more psychologically robust. Psychological pain arises out of the combination of the personal and the political – external threat, and the internal responses it evokes.

The seeds of Lena's own insecure attachment, and thus her inability to provide real security in the face of threat for the children are clearly described:

> Her mother [the children's grandmother] had always been her ideal of all that was feminine and delicious. It had not hurt her as a child to be petted and exhibited one moment and to be shut away in her school-room or nursery the next . . . She had not got one unlovely memory of her parents when she had been a child . . . Mummie and Daddy were all charm, fun and happiness.

The idealisation, denial and inconsistency typical of insecure attachment are beautifully evoked here. Seen through the eyes of Ruth, Lena's narcissism and inability to take the child's point of view is highlighted:

Was Lena a good mother? There was no doubt that children were lucky who had parents, particularly a mother, whom they could show off... [But] on other counts Lena was not so good. She never even pretended the children came first... [that had to be Alex]. Was that not out-balanced by the perfect love always before the children's eyes? [But] was it perfect love the children saw? Certainly Lena loved Alex, but perfect love in her philosophy was an ill-balanced affair, almost all body, the merest whiff of soul.

And again she describes Lena's casual narcissistic approach to her care-giving relationships: 'She threw the group round the fire off as if they were a frock she had worn in the morning and changed out of for the afternoon.'

Perhaps Streatfeild *is* moralising a little here, albeit through the mind of Ruth. She herself was probably more than a little frightened of her own sexuality, having fallen passionately in love with the flamboyant socialite Daphne Ionides, at a time when sapphism would have been anathema to a well-brought-up bishop's daughter. *Saplings* is dedicated to Streatfeild's mother, Janet, whose late baby, born when Streatfeild was fifteen, had provoked this passage in the second volume of her autobiography, *Away from the Vicarage*:

Back in 1915 the girls' mother had given her two elder daughters a shock. She had told them she was having a baby. The girls had been horribly embarrassed by the news and had never discussed it. They knew – but how dimly – how babies were conceived and, of course, they must have been conceived themselves. But that was long ago and your father and mother didn't go on doing it – not when the rest of the family were nearly grown up.

Streatfeild's break from her sheltered vicarage upbringing had come, as it had for so many other girls, during the Great War when she had worked in a munitions factory in the East End of London. Here, and later though her 'Care Committee' social work she had encountered working class families. Albert and Ernie are the two East End little boys who accompany the Wiltshires on their evacuation to Yorkshire. Their mother, Mrs. Parker, is reluctant to let them go: 'She had heard of a child who had been taken to hospital to have its tonsils out, and, because it was separated from its mother, had died there of a broken heart.'

Here Streatfeild in 1945 is anticipating the revolution in parental hospital visiting patterns that Bowlby was to initiate ten years later. Ironically it is Mrs. Parker's insistence that the children return home that leads to their death from a direct hit on the family house. Mrs. Parker is as overprotective as Lena is neglectful; Lena is too dependent on her husband, while Mrs. Parker should not have been so easily able to overrule hers. The difference between them is that Mrs. Parker can imaginatively identify with her children and so see them as separate beings, whereas for Lena they are objects to be dealt with at her own convenience. Streatfeild's treatment of this theme points to the strain which such awareness creates for parents. Lena thoughtlessly packs her children off to their grandparents while Mrs. Parker succumbs to her knowledge of her children's distress, and thus indirectly causes their death. To insist on separation, while remaining aware of the pain it produces, requires a maturity of which neither woman was capable.

A key feature of secure attachment is the capacity of parents to be attuned and responsive to their children when distressed or threatened. The Wiltshire children are secure because despite their mother's narcissism, their father has the capacity to think about their needs and feelings. Boarding school is portrayed as an environment that amplifies the misattunement and unresponsiveness of insecure-making parents. That is why Tony's Hardyesque missing letter and Alex's consequent failure to respond to his distress-signal is so poignant, and the subsequent relief when all is explained so uplifting: 'It was to Tony as if he had been walking in a fog and it was lifting . . . Love poured through him.'

This episode prefigures the book's central tragedy: Alex's death in a bombing raid, Tony's conviction that his father is buried alive, that he has heard him tapping for help beneath the rubble, that he failed to rescue him, his inability to talk to anyone about this, and his subsequent descent into depression.

Once more Streatfeild's intuititons are uncannily accurate. Without the support of an attachment figure, Tony loses his capacity for reality-testing, and is tormented by his assumptions and fantasies about what happened. He blames himself for his father's death; at an unconscious level perhaps he may have wished that harm might befall him, partly because he is still angry about the letter incident, partly because, if unheard and untempered by a secure base adult, separation protest can turn into a perversity of rage and destructiveness. (In a separate incident we see the evacuees destroying the summer house, ending with a symbolic act of defiant urination – an orgy of destruction that is a metaphor for war and its attraction for the dispossessed and insecure.)

It is only when Tony's uncle finally tells him what really happened – that Alex died in the ambulance before reaching hospital and that the tapping, whatever it was, could not have been his father – that Tony is released from his nightmare:

> The mist [in Tony's mind] was rising. The nightmare was evaporating . . . Tony ran up the ride. With every step happiness welled up in him. The sky was more blue. The pine and bracken smelt better. The ground had more spring. As he neared the garden gate he began to jump as well as run.

Here Streatfeild, with a faint echo perhaps of Sassoon's 'everyone suddenly burst out singing . . .', beautifully captures an universal end-of-war feeling of release from depression and guilt through the mind of this adolescent boy.

The fate of Tony's elder sister Laurel forms the theme of the last part of the book. Laurel appears to be the antithesis of a *Ballet Shoes* girl. Generations of girl readers of *Ballet Shoes* were inspired by its implicit proto-feminist message that, as a woman, you are not condemned to a life of housework and subjugation to men and procreation, but that you can do and be whatever you want (even if it does mean taking the bohemian route via the performing arts, rather than becoming lawyers or doctors). Laurel is different from Pauline, Posy and Petrova because she feels she is not *good* at anything – and for Streatfeild it is important for children to shine – after all it was her talents as an actress and writer that helped her escape from the dreary constrictions of vicarage life once the Great War was over. We see Streatfeild struggle with this – she likes Laurel and wants her to be happy, but how can she find herself? Then Laurel discovers that she is good at understanding and helping younger children, we see how her honesty and capacity to talk about difficulties will stand her in good stead – but it is through her sexuality that she begins to find herself.

Indeed sex is a rather surprising central theme in the book as a whole, especially as Streatfeild is exploring the curiously neglected theme of married sex, and the pull between a couple's desire for each other, and the need not to threaten the Secure Base for the children. Lena is portrayed as driven by her sexual needs, while, in a reversal of the usual stereotype, Alex, and after his death Walter, have to restrain her voraciousness. Here are Lena and Alex on the beach at the start of the book:

> He would have gone into the tent to put on his things. When they were first married, or even a few years ago, she would have gone with him. She would not have

missed those seconds in the hot tent, the flash of passion that would have come from the closeness of his cool, naked body. But he had got so self-conscious, always worrying about what the children were thinking . . .

It is the men who are sensitive to the children's oedipal feelings, and see how important it is not to brandish adult sexuality under their noses.

With her father dead, and her mother embroiled with her new lover, Laurel gravitates to her aunt and uncle's unhappy marriage. After Alex's death, she forms a good relationship with her mother's American lover, Walter, but even more so with her uncle John:

> John was what Laurel craved. He needed love, he needed looking after. What they gave each other was as delicate as a wood anenome. It was bruisable, intensely fragile. Laurel, at one laugh, or even a wrong inflection, would have sunk back into the self-conscious, angular, bristly girl who came to the house. John had always wanted children, he had dreamt sometimes of how they would be. Laurel told her troubles, and even as she told them, because he did not find her plain or dull, the troubles began to evaporate.

John and Laurel are not lovers, but the unconsummated sexuality of her relationship with a man old enough to be her father helps Laurel to begin to find her self as a woman, symbolised by the string of pearls which he gives her and which she wears close to her bosom at school. She pretends they are from her American boyfriend, so raising her status with her peers – at last she has found something she *is* good at: boyfriends and sex. Of course it all goes wrong, she is threatened with expulsion, runs away, and is eventually saved by her kindly grandfather.

By today's neo-puritan standards Laurel and John's relationship might be considered 'abusive', but for Streatfeild John gives Laurel just the special feeling she needs to bring forth her burgeoning sexuality – just as a good father will make his daughters feel they are the most beautiful creatures in the world, within a context of absolute sexual security. With a dead father and a neglectful mother, Laurel would have been vulnerable to sexual abuse, but John's love is protective and encouraging.

There is a curious echo in *Saplings* of the extraordinary family constellation Streatfeild creates in *Ballet Shoes*. There it is almost as if the three girls are brought into the world by their father – three Athenes emerging fully-formed from their Zeus's brow. Their mothers, like Lena, are absent or neglectful, and the Professor collects them from different places around the globe and deposits them in the Gloucester Road – and then disappears himself. Without the constraints of a mother in whose footsteps they would dutifully follow, or a father to insist that they do so, they are able to discover themselves and their talents with the encouragement of various servants and tutors. Streatfeild had a difficult relationship with her own mother: as a child she felt misunderstood and undervalued, as an adolescent repelled by her sexuality, and in later life felt burdened by the responsibility of looking after her in her widowhood. In child fiction she can rewrite her own history as she chooses.

Lena, representing perhaps one aspect of Streatfeild's feelings about her mother, matures with suffering. As a widow she remains unpredictable, but she is more loving and focused on the children and:

> She had come off the pedestal on which she had lived while Alex was alive. She was anything but guarded and treasured. She was the provider, the planner . . . None of the children would have thought the holidays had started properly if she was not at the station to welcome them . . . She was Mum, rather unpredictable but as much part of home as the garden path and the front door.

The impact on Lena of the two aspects of war which run throughout the book are finely balanced. Streatfeild, for all her sensitivity to loss and separation in childhood, also sees the liberating aspect of conflict. If the Great War had not happened she herself might have remained for ever confined in her country parsonage. Without the pain of losing Alex, Lena would always have been a distant and idealised figure to her children. At least in her unhappiness they can begin to see her as she is, even when she descends into drunkenness and suicidality – here Streatfeild cleverly understands how destructiveness can so easily get out of hand and become addictive. Even the tapping and feeling of suffocation which Tony imagines comes from his trapped father can be seen, when the truth about Alex's death is finally revealed, as symbols of the social constrictions which war sweeps aside. Sexuality is liberated, social class barriers broken down (Albert and Ernie evacuated to the Wiltshire grandparents' middle class home), people are free to express feelings and are less bound by convention. There are winners and losers: Alex and the Parkers are dead, Lena only just survives, Tony and Laurel recover only after a huge amount of help from their grandfather, Tuesday becomes 'aloof', 'a bundle of nerves'; but the gifted and resilient Kim thrives, and Ruth gains in confidence and escapes from her subservient role as governess.

For all its contemporary relevance, when compared with her children's books *Saplings* is perhaps not quite a novel of the first rank. Its psychological insights are too fleeting, its exploration of adult character often superficial. It is almost as though Streatfeild lacks the courage to pursue the full implications of the scenario she has created: the contrast between Lena and Ruth's sexuality, the long-term implications of the trauma which the children have gone through. In 1945 it would have taken extraordinary powers of imagination to do so.

By the end of the book misery is forgotten, and we are reassured that the middle class values embodied in the Wiltshires will survive. *Saplings* has neither the full range of fantasy and make-believe which gives her children's books such an endearing quality, nor has it the psychological maturity and accurate reflection of reality which we expect in writing of the highest order. This criticism reflects perhaps Streatfeild's own dilemmas as a person. By nature rebellious, she became a pillar of the literary establishment, and in her life never really gave full reign to her waywardness or sexuality. The very success of her children's writing depends on her ability to keep these two aspects of her psyche separate. She could re-order the world at will and have an outlet for her fantasies, while remaining within the safety of a story with a happy ending, shielding its readers from the full impact of reality. For her adult writing to have achieved the same stature would have demanded a maturity and integration that she lacked. *Saplings* is perhaps the nearest she gets to bringing together her child-like and adult self. Ironically, had she fully succeeded in doing so her children's writing might well have suffered. We should be grateful; without *Ballet Shoes* – and it is surely Streatfeild's enduring qualities as a children's writer that draws us to *Saplings* – the world would be the poorer.

Dr Jeremy Holmes
Barnstaple, 2000